PRAISE FOR
EVERY MOMENT SINCE

"*Every Moment Since* will grip you with its compelling, 'just-one-more-page' mystery, then alter your heart with its beautifully drawn cast of characters. Full of real emotional insight and depth, it's a book to finish in the small hours, feeling utterly transformed."
—Hannah Richell, author of *The Search Party*

"*Every Moment Since* is an astonishing work that didn't let me go, even after the last line. This book has it all: rich characters who jump off the page, a present and past that feel so familiar, and a sense of urgency to see how it all unfolds. I miss this book already!"
—Ethan Joella, author of *The Same Bright Stars*

"*Every Moment Since* is unforgettable. Marybeth Whalen takes every family's worst nightmare and uses her amazing talent for exploring the aftermath to bring this story home. How do you go on when there are no answers? What does forgiveness really look like? In telling the story of Davy Malcor's disappearance, she's tapped into a whole new world of emotional family drama. Heartbreaking and suspenseful, this is Whalen's finest work to date."
—J.T. Ellison, *New York Times* bestselling
author of *It's One of Us*

"*Every Moment Since* is everything you want in a novel—a gripping story, nostalgia for lost childhood, exorbitant love, a deep sense of place, and page-turning tension. From the opening scene

where a child's jacket is found twenty-one years after he's gone missing to the heart-rending conclusion, this story is brought to vivid life with Marybeth Mayhew Whalen's pitch-perfect prose and signature ability to dive into the characters' deepest secrets and desires. As the lives of those left behind draw ever closer, we hold our breath to find out the truth. For those who love the work of Taylor Jenkins Reid and Jessica Knoll, you've just found your next book club read."

—Patti Callahan Henry, *New York Times* bestselling author of *The Secret Book of Flora Lea*

"*Every Moment Since* is a masterpiece, an important study of humanity, grief, and especially hope in the aftermath of unfathomable trauma. In her best work yet, Whalen expertly and delicately paints an unflinchingly real picture of what happens to a family and a town when weathered scars are opened anew. *Every Moment Since* will deeply resonate with all readers. I couldn't put it down!"

—Joy Callaway, international bestselling author of *What the Mountains Remember*

"Marybeth Mayhew Whalen is at her finest in this novel that dissects the harrowing toll on family and community when a child goes missing. This sophisticated and compelling novel establishes Whalen as an unflinching voice in fiction."

—Kimberly Brock, bestselling author of *The Lost Book of Eleanor Dare*

"Full of atmosphere and twists and turns, Marybeth Mayhew Whalen's *Every Moment Since* is a must-read!"

—Catherine McKenzie, *USA TODAY* bestselling author of *I'll Never Tell* and *Have You Seen Her*

EVERY MOMENT SINCE

EVERY MOMENT SINCE

Marybeth Mayhew Whalen

HARPER MUSE

Every Moment Since

Copyright © 2024 Marybeth Mayhew Whalen

Published by Harper Muse, an imprint of HarperCollins Focus LLC.

Scripture quotations marked CSB are taken from The Christian Standard Bible. Copyright © 2017 by Holman Bible Publishers. Used by permission. Christian Standard Bible®, and CSB® are federally registered trademarks of Holman Bible Publishers, all rights reserved.

This book is a work of fiction. The characters, incidents, and dialogue are drawn from the author's imagination and are not to be construed as real. Any resemblance to actual events or persons, living or dead, is entirely coincidental.

Any internet addresses (websites, blogs, etc.) in this book are offered as a resource. They are not intended in any way to be or imply an endorsement by HarperCollins Focus LLC, nor does HarperCollins Focus LLC vouch for the content of these sites for the life of this book.

Maple leaf art from Adobe Stock by elta11.

Joan Didion, "Why I Write," *The New York Times*, December 5, 1976, https://www.nytimes.com/1976/12/05/archives/why-i-write-why-i-write.html.

Library of Congress Cataloging-in-Publication Data
Names: Whalen, Marybeth, author.
Title: Every moment since / Marybeth Mayhew Whalen.
Description: [Nashville] : Harper Muse, 2024. | Summary: "A small Southern town. An ordinary Saturday night. A little boy disappears without a trace"—Provided by publisher.
Identifiers: LCCN 2024013632 (print) | LCCN 2024013633 (ebook) | ISBN 9781400345021 (paperback) | ISBN 9781400345038 (epub) | ISBN 9781400345045
Subjects: LCSH: Missing children—Fiction. | LCGFT: Thrillers (Fiction) | Novels.
Classification: LCC PS3623.H355 E94 2024 (print) | LCC PS3623.H355 (ebook) | DDC 813/.6—dc23/eng/20240329
LC record available at https://lccn.loc.gov/2024013632
LC ebook record available at https://lccn.loc.gov/2024013633

Printed in the United States of America

24 25 26 27 28 LBC 5 4 3 2 1

All I discovered is . . . there is no end to grief,
that's how we know there is no end to love.

—BONO

PART 1

Thursday–Friday
April 27–28, 2006

PROLOGUE

He was a boy back at summer camp, swinging on a rope out over the lake. He wasn't ready to let go yet, but he felt his grip slipping, gravity pulling him toward the water in spite of his efforts to cling. Then he heard a loud ringing sound. His eyes flew open, ending the dream. His head jerked up from where it had come to rest on his chest, his neck protesting the sudden movement. He scrambled for the phone before it could ring again.

"Yes?" He hoped the person on the other end couldn't hear the sleep still in his voice. It was midafternoon, not a time Pete Lancaster should be sleeping.

"Sheriff?" Jane Crutcher, the department's receptionist, asked. He thought he heard a note of judgment in her voice, but maybe he was projecting his own guilt for falling asleep on the job. He was supposed to be on baby duty while his exhausted wife got some rest. He looked around but saw no sign of his wife, no stirring from his infant son, asleep in the Moses basket next to him in the family room. He'd nodded off, yes. But he was still at his post.

"Yeah." He stifled a yawn and looked at the baby.

"A call came in that I don't think I should hand off to a deputy," Jane said. Pete sat up a little straighter, a little more awake.

"Ok," he said without taking his eyes off his son.

"A guy called—some business developer out of Arkansas."

"Uh-huh." So far this was not a reason to interrupt him on his day off.

"He bought the old Oxendine property. You know, out on Sims Church Road?"

"Yeah." He was growing annoyed with Jane. He wanted to say, *"Just spill it already,"* but refrained. Jane believed in setting the stage before starting the action.

"Wait a minute," she said. "If he's from Arkansas, you don't think they're planning to put a Walmart out there, do you?"

The sheriff couldn't tell if she was excited or dismayed at the prospect, but he didn't care. "Jane, why'd he call?" He tried his best to sound kind and gentle. Beside him, his son stirred, a single baby fist jabbing the air.

"Sorry. Got off track. He said he was out walking the property and came upon some old outbuilding. He went inside and, well, it sounds like he found something." She paused.

"What?"

"A jacket," she said on a breath. "He knew about the Malcor kid being from here—I mean, who doesn't?—so he figured he should ask us to come out and have a look at it. You know, just in case it's something."

Pete sat and absorbed what she'd said. As he processed, she hurried to add, "It's probably nothing. I mean, what are the odds that it has anything to do with Davy Malcor's case?"

Pete didn't have to think about the answer. "Likely nothing," he said. "Likely nothing at all." He took a deep breath and shook his head to dispel the cobwebs of sleep still hanging in his brain. He was exhausted all the time these days. He never should've let his young new wife talk him into a kid. His others were nearly grown and he was too old to be starting all this again. He looked down at his sleeping son and thought of Davy Malcor's parents as he stood.

"Still," he said, "I better head out there and take a look."

"I thought that's what you'd say." Jane sounded pleased with herself.

"Jane," he said, using his sternest sheriff voice, "let's keep this between us till I have a look-see."

"Ok, Pete. Mum's the word."

"I'll be in touch," he said and ended the call. He stood still for a moment, taking in what the call could mean, the implications of that jacket—though it was probably not *the* jacket—being found. If it hadn't been found by now, it was probably gone, same as Davy. That was the only thing that made good, rational sense. Still, Pete had been in the job long enough to know that a lot of things that happened did not make good, rational sense.

Beside him, his son gave a little squeak, a warning that he would be waking soon, no doubt hungry and angry. Pete stooped down until his eyes were level with the baby and peered at him over the rim of the Moses basket. He pressed his index and middle fingertips to his own lips, then pressed them to his son's forehead.

Perhaps it was just a goodbye kiss, or perhaps it was a blessing bestowed. Pete didn't stop long enough to ponder what it was as he turned away to wake his sleeping wife, to tell her he had to go.

Pete pulled up his truck behind another truck—another Ford F-150, this one newer and shinier than his own. A man wearing dress pants, a dress shirt, and a tie leaned against the other truck but stood straight as Pete got out.

"Sheriff," the man said, extending his hand. "Thanks for coming."

"Yeah, sure thing." Pete accepted the man's hand and pumped it a few times. He didn't bother asking his name; he'd find out later if he needed to.

"You found something?" Pete asked, intent on hurrying this along. He'd had strict instructions from his wife not to dillydally if it was nothing. The witching hour would arrive soon, the terrible time of day when the baby cried nonstop and nothing soothed him. If Pete wasn't there for that without a good excuse, she'd never let him hear the end of it. He had to do his time walking the floor, patting and singing and swaying—anything to stop the crying, if only for a minute.

The man waved toward the expanse of land behind him. "It's this way," he said and set off without waiting for Pete. Pete followed, half listening as the man explained that after closing the sale that morning, he'd felt compelled to go out and walk the property, every inch of it.

"I've never done that before with a property," he said. "And then I found that jacket and I thought of an episode of *Dateline* I watched with the wife a while back—she loves that show. Loves that Keith Morrison." He looked back at Pete, who nodded even though he didn't watch *Dateline* and didn't care about Keith Morrison.

The man resumed walking and talking. "The episode was about Davy Malcor, about how the case had never been solved, but those parents of his—especially his mother—have never given up. I mean, I'm a parent, too, and I can't imagine—I just don't know . . ." He stopped talking as a rusted-out equipment building came into view. Neither of them spoke as they drew closer to the building.

"Once I found it, I tried not to touch anything else. And I called you guys right away."

Pete studied the man as he spoke. The cop in him wondered about the guy, about his random discovery out in the middle of nowhere after all these years. His hand went to his service revolver, but he hadn't brought it along. He'd left in such a hurry that he'd forgotten all about it.

"I'd like to go in there alone," Pete said. He felt for his cell phone in his pocket. At least he had that. But he'd brought it along only because his wife had made him promise to answer if she called. Sometimes he thought his fearless bride was actually afraid of their ten-pound son.

"Oh yeah, of course," the man said. "I'll just wait out here."

Pete eyed him. "You got a business card on you?"

"Yeah, yeah, sure," he said. The man felt around in his pockets, then held up his hands, looking sheepish. "I've got one in the truck. Tell you what, I'll go get it while you're looking around in there. I think you'll see the jacket, no problem. I pulled it out about halfway but dropped it like a hot potato when I realized what it was."

Pete nodded but said nothing. In his mind he was already inside the little falling-down building coming eye to eye with either a castoff from one of the Oxendine boys from long ago or telltale evidence in one of the biggest missing child cases in America. He feared and welcomed this moment. It was the kind of thing that could make or break a career. It had darn near broken two of his predecessors', what with the outcry about a botched investigation for the first one, and the defamation lawsuit from the main suspect that cost the town money it hadn't had for the other one. He didn't want to think about what this discovery could mean for his own career. Was he prepared for this? No. Did he have a choice but to proceed? Also no. He took a step toward the building, but the man's voice stopped him.

"I saw that *Dateline* back then," he said. "And not long ago I saw a segment on one of those morning shows about that boy's brother writing a memoir."

Pete wanted to hurry the guy along, same as he'd had to hurry Jane along on the phone. But he held his tongue.

"I've seen that jacket is what I'm saying," the man continued, "in the photos of that boy wearing it." He pointed at the old building. "And that's the jacket that's in there. It's dirty, and it's been in the elements a long time. But I'd bet my life on it."

Pete nodded as his heart began to thump hard against his ribs.

"I'll be along directly," was all he said.

"Ok," the man replied. "I'll just be waiting up there by the trucks." Pete waited until the man was out of sight before he opened the door, the rusty hinges crying out in protest as he entered the building.

FROM *EVERY MOMENT SINCE: A MEMOIR* BY THADDEUS MALCOR

PUBLISHED SEPTEMBER 20, 2005

The farmer died the year before and his widow let the vast fields in front of their home go fallow. The land was left unplanted yet ready for whatever came next—perhaps another crop after the widow's period of grieving had passed, perhaps the sale of the family land, perhaps the site of a missing child case that would haunt the town of Wynotte, North Carolina, for years to come.

I often wonder what would've happened if the widow had planted a crop that year. The wide-open fields would not have beckoned to us if cornstalks had stood in our way. We would not have gathered there to play our night games. The stranger would not have seen the flashlight beams bouncing as we ran and hid, prey for a predator, moving shadows under a crescent moon. If the fields had been planted, none of it would have happened the way it did, and my brother, Davy Malcor, would still be here.

Don't get me wrong, I don't blame the widow. From what I've gathered, she was elderly and unwell. The farm had been a lot to keep up with before her husband died. And the land was worth more to one of the many developers sniffing around Wynotte in the mid-1980s as northerners migrated south, businesses moved headquarters to warmer climes, and their transplanted employees spilled over city borders and into our small town, looking for a place to settle. Letting the land go fallow was the first step in letting go.

The widow, like me, had no idea what one decision would set in motion, the many lives that would forever be changed because of it. She and I would both have to live the rest of our lives with the decisions we made. Decisions that, at the time, seemed inconsequential, yet proved to be anything but.

CHAPTER 1

Thaddeus Malcor

They had a good crowd. That was what the bookstore owner said. From the podium at the front of the room, Thaddeus surveyed the gathering of strangers, deciding for himself if it was a good crowd. What made a good crowd? The number of people who showed up? The level of enthusiasm? The number of pretty women in attendance? Some combination thereof? In all his travels promoting his bestselling memoir, he still wasn't sure.

Maybe a good crowd was one that made him forget his guilt for a while, kept his focus on what he'd written, not on what he'd left out. Thaddeus put his hand in the left pocket of his jeans, feeling for the object he always kept there. He rubbed his index finger across its solidness, then withdrew his hand.

"I'll take questions now," Thaddeus said, his stomach clenching with nerves as he segued from the reading to open the floor. The Q&A was always a crapshoot. He hoped the good crowd had some good questions, though he'd likely been posed all the questions possible at this point. He'd been touring so long the questions ran together like the faces and locations.

His initial book tour had been slated for a few weeks, but as sales escalated, so did requests for more dates. Months later, he was tired of being on the road, yet hesitant to come off it. Because, what then? What next? Until he could answer that question, he would keep saying yes to whatever his publicist sent his way. A rotary club in LaCrosse, Wisconsin? Yes. A ladies' luncheon at a country club in Savannah, Georgia? Yes. What about a short tour in the UK? Hell yes.

A few tentative hands went up.

"Yes?" he asked, pointing to an older woman three rows back. She wore a dark, pilling sweater and a concerned expression.

She glanced around before speaking, as if making sure it was indeed her he'd designated. He gave her an encouraging nod.

"I wondered," she said, "how your family feels about the book?"

This question was not unexpected, but a little early. Usually the crowd warmed up to asking about his family. But he did not falter; he had his answer, a reassuring half-truth at the ready.

"My family is supportive of the book and proud of its success—that so many people are interested in Davy's story. While what happened is a tragedy, they're glad I'm sharing the message"—he leaned forward as he always did and scanned the crowd, making eye contact with as many people as he could—"that you *can* move forward from tragedy. It's not easy, but it's possible." He eased back to his former stance, relaxing a little. "Though I'm the only one standing here, I speak for my family when I say hope is Davy's legacy."

He watched as heads nodded and found himself nodding along with them, caught up in his own rhetoric. Though what he said about his family's support wasn't completely true, he wanted it to be. And didn't that count for something? Never mind that his mother hadn't read beyond the first few chapters. Never mind that his sister had discouraged her book club from selecting it because it was "just too painful." Never mind that, while his father had read the whole thing, the note of praise he sent mentioned his disappointment in the chapter on the hotline.

"*It seemed you laid the blame for the divorce squarely on my shoulders,*" he'd written, effectively negating all the nice things he'd said prior. His mom, dad, and sister just didn't understand. It was his memoir, his memories. Or a version of them, the only version he dared to share with total strangers.

He slipped his hand back into his left pocket, this time pressing his index finger hard against the object's sharp edge, just enough to hurt.

"Next question," he said.

For the next twenty minutes he answered the usual questions: What led you to write this book? Did you always want to be a writer? What are you working on next? How did you get published? And one he'd never had: Did you listen to any music while writing?

"I did, actually." He smiled at the memory of being in that cabin in Wyoming with the fellowship he'd landed, music playing, words flowing, alone but not lonely. It was as if Davy had come back to him there, had given him his blessing. And wasn't that the only blessing he needed?

"I listened to hits from 1985," he told them. "The music really took me back to that time. And the *Back to the Future* soundtrack, of course." Anyone who'd read the book knew how much Davy loved that movie, which had come out the summer before he disappeared.

To his right Thaddeus caught the eye of a beautiful woman with long red hair. She smiled at him in that way some women smiled at him now. More than a smile, it was an invitation of sorts. He gave her a brief half smile in return. He was always a sucker for a redhead. She raised her hand.

"Someone asked about your family's response to the book," she said. "But I want to know, what about the girl next door? Has she reached out at all since the book was published?"

He rolled his eyes as he did anytime someone asked this question, and the crowd laughed as the crowd did anytime he answered this question. Larkin. He hadn't named her in the book. He was too much of a chicken to do that after all the years of silence between them. But she'd been part of the story, part of that night, part of the before, and the after. He did not name her, but he could not have left her out either. So he'd referred to her as "the girl next door," which she was. But of course, she was so much more than that—his first love (though he hadn't understood that until it was too late), an eyewitness to his family's pain, and the one who got away.

"No," he said, making his voice sound wistful, gathering sympathy from the onlookers. Was it manipulative to do so? Did he deserve their sympathy? He couldn't answer that; the show had to go on. "The girl next door has not reached out." He shrugged. "I have no idea if she's read the book or not. I kind of hope she hasn't." He gave a dramatic grimace that made everyone laugh again.

In the back the bookstore owner held up her arm and pointed at her watch, the signal that it was time to invite the crowd to form a queue at the signing table, where he would answer more questions, scrawl his name over and over, and make the joke about the signature adding another quarter to the value at a garage sale in the future. That joke always worked.

He thanked the people for coming, remarked on them being a good crowd, then made his way over to the table, where he sank into the chair the store had provided and picked up the black Sharpie pen laid out for him. His back ached from standing, and he felt the nagging weariness that crept in whenever he was still. He watched with a kind of detachment as the line formed, snaking all the way back into the store's shelves.

Off to the side the bookstore owner gave him a thumbs-up. Just behind her, he spotted the beautiful redhead who'd asked the last question of the night, standing with a friend. The redhead kept looking from him to the line that had formed and back again before finally tugging on her friend and pulling her to a spot at the very back of the line.

Thaddeus bit back a knowing smile as he asked the first woman in line how she spelled her name. There were just so many different ways to spell Cindy. And didn't she know it.

Thaddeus always attempted small talk in the mornings, offered breakfast, coffee, a shower, a ride. The one that particular morning said yes to the offer of coffee, wrapping herself in the sheet demurely as she accepted the cup and took a grateful sip. He'd forgotten her name and could not think of a polite way to discover it without asking directly. He could tell she felt bad; she never did this kind of thing, etcetera. He didn't want to make her feel worse.

When she excused herself to go to the bathroom, tugging the sheet free of the mattress and awkwardly clinging to it as she shuffled into the bathroom and closed the door behind her, he attempted to riffle through her small handbag to find her license. He was not above this sort of desperate act. He just hoped she didn't catch him at it.

Voilà! He filched the license from a handy little card slot right inside, squinting through the hangover headache that was as much a part of his morning routine as the coffee he'd offered her. (They went together actually, the coffee and the headache, always joined by their old buddy, ibuprofen. He usually swallowed four at a time. Thaddeus was not kind to his liver.) He heard the toilet flush as the name on the license swam into view: Elizabeth.

He frowned in confusion as he shoved the card back into its slot, then quickly took a seat at the little table in front of the large window in his hotel room. The bathroom door opened and he sipped his coffee as though he'd been there the whole time, staring out at the view of—what city was this? Oh yes, St. Louis—instead of trying to determine the name of the stranger he'd hooked up with after the signing last night.

Elizabeth didn't sound familiar. He tried to picture himself signing her book or talking to her later in the bar, tried to recall when her friend said goodbye (there was always a friend). Had the friend called her name? It was all a blank. The only thing he could recall about their time together was the way she'd listened to his stories with such interest and intrigue, which predictably turned to desire the longer they talked, the more they drank. That was the way it always was after his signings. No one had warned him this would happen. Sometimes Thaddeus wondered if that meant he was unique. But there was no one to ask.

He decided to go for broke. "Everything ok, Elizabeth?" he asked, trying out the name even though it didn't sound right.

She returned to the bed, took a seat in the space where she'd slept—if you could call it sleeping—and gave him a quizzical look.

"Elizabeth?" She used her free hand to smooth the sheet she was wearing.

Damn. Wrong name. He hadn't thought to look at the photo on the license. Maybe she'd grabbed the wrong purse and it was her friend's and not hers, which would mean it was her friend's name. And not hers. Internally, he chastised himself. Who did he think he was? He was not cool. He was not suave. He was not a ladies' man, no matter how often his book tour readings got him laid.

"We're being awfully formal this morning, aren't we?" She gave a little laugh that failed to cover up her nerves. "Last night it was all Lizzie this, Lizzie that, and this morning I'm *Elizabeth?*"

He managed to keep himself from exhaling his relief aloud. Instead he smiled at her.

"I was trying it out."

She wrinkled her adorable nose. Something else he recalled from last night: thinking as they talked that she had a very cute nose. The woman from the last reading had a rather large nose that he'd somehow managed to disregard until the morning after.

"Well, let's drop the *Elizabeth*, please," she said. "It's my given name, but I've never gone by it. It feels like a stranger's name."

Her words were Thaddeus's opening, the inevitable moment when he had to clarify what was happening between them. Which was, essentially, nothing. He had to help each woman realize that this was not the beginning of a great love affair. This was a fling in the truest sense of the word. He'd once looked up the meaning out of curiosity: *Fling (noun): a short period of enjoyment or wild behavior.*

Time to make sure Elizabeth/Lizzie knew she had just engaged in a short period of enjoyment (for both of them, he liked to think). Though some of his flings did involve wild behavior (he let the women lead; he never wanted to be accused of anything criminal—the press would have a field day if something of that nature got out), this one had not. But it didn't matter. Enjoyment was enjoyment. A pleasant evening was had by all concerned. Now it was time to decamp, so to speak. He felt bad saying what came next, but it had to be said.

"Well, isn't that what we are, Elizabeth? Strangers?"

The hand holding the sheet over her breasts tightened so much that he could see the white of her bones through her pale skin. When Elizabeth/Lizzie's hand had gone up last night to ask the question about Larkin, he'd been pretty sure she was the one he'd have this scene with. Though, of course, he hadn't pictured it happening exactly this way.

He had learned to spot the patterns: the woman's lingering position at the back of the book-signing line, her efforts to keep the conversation going to the point where he said he was hungry and could they continue talking at the bar/pub/restaurant nearby, the friend who had to be dismissed with assurances that a cab would be called later and everyone would be safe. The women were different, the questions were different (though not much), the food or drinks were different.

But one thing was consistently the same: the moment he understood that this particular woman wanted the same thing they all did. People came to his book events to get close to tragedy, to experience it as firsthand as they were comfortable with, to feel it in a way they could not merely by seeing photos and words in a book, newspaper, or magazine. They came because they wanted to see him in real life, to hear his voice, to watch as he held the pen that wrote their names.

There was always one who found that wasn't enough. One who discovered that the closer she got to him, the closer she wanted to get. She found herself wanting to taste him, to smell him, and then, with a kind of surrender, to take him in, convincing herself she was getting as close to his pain as anyone ever had, never knowing she was nowhere near the only one or that none of them had come close to the pain he carried, buried so deep that no one had reached it. Not one single time.

CHAPTER 2

Tabitha Malcor

On Fridays she made her regret list. It was nothing fancy; it didn't even have its own notebook. She certainly didn't want to save her regrets to reread later. Who wants to see that?

She simply pulled a sheet off a legal pad or her grocery list pad or a piece of copy paper from the printer. She grabbed a pen or a pencil or, when the kids were younger, a crayon. Whatever was handy, whatever was quick. The activity was not one she relished, and it was definitely not something she'd shared with anyone. It was just something she'd been doing since a particular Friday a long time ago, never intending to keep doing it, yet somehow doing it still.

Sometimes the regrets came to her immediately, as if they'd been waiting in line in her head all week. Other times she had to cast about to find some. Over the years she had formulated some rules for the list: regrets could come only from days that had elapsed since the last list—only the most current regrets were allowed. Some regrets showed up faithfully: impatience with a loved one, needless sarcasm when a gentler response would've been kinder, laziness in regard to exercise. If the regret list was meant to spur change, it hadn't worked.

And yet, for reasons she could not explain, she returned to the practice every Friday.

This morning she paused over her list, reviewing the past seven days in her mind. Over the years she'd been tempted to keep notes throughout the week in order to expedite the list-making process—a regret cheat sheet, if you will. But she decided that slowing down to recall the week, to replay the moments of regret in her mind, was part of her process. Her own kind of penance. She supposed it was akin to a Catholic confession. Marie, her best friend / next-door neighbor, was Catholic, but Tabitha wasn't sure she went to confession anymore. Tabitha wasn't sure she ever had.

Thinking of Marie brought to mind one regret from the past seven days. She wrote it down:

1. When Larkin arrived home, I did not take anything over there. I should have taken cookies or dinner or something for the little girl—a toy maybe or a coloring book. I regret that Marie's sadness has caused me to avoid her. I regret that I haven't been a good neighbor. Or friend.

Tabitha paused, thinking this over. (Sometimes the regret list took a long time to make because a lot of thinking was involved. For this reason she tried to start first thing in the morning so it didn't hang over her head all day.) Sadness still clung to Marie months after losing her husband, Jim. The real reason she had not gone over to welcome home Marie's daughter, Larkin, when she arrived was because Tabitha had been avoiding Marie.

She didn't want to see her friend's downturned mouth, her stooped shoulders. Though Marie was one of her dearest and oldest friends in the world, she struggled with being supportive and understanding about Marie's recent loss when she had lost her own husband long ago. Not to death, mind you, but to divorce. Tabitha had faced many losses, it seemed, while Marie had only the one.

At the thought of her ex-husband, other regrets, numerous ones, popped into her mind, erratic memories exploding like popcorn in her brain. She reminded herself of the rules: nothing beyond this one week. She banished thoughts of Daniel and continued her task.

When she was finished, her list was as follows:

2. I did not go for a walk except for twice, even though the weather was good every day this week. I regret not taking better care of my body.

3. I did not get on the scale this week because I was afraid. I regret that I've put myself in the position of being afraid of what the scale says. It looms in the corner of the bathroom like a beacon of my failures, flashing numbers I do not like. (See also #2.)

4. I was short with both of the kids on the phone this week. Thaddeus has just gotten so self-involved since his book became a bestseller. Talking to him has become insufferable. And Kristyn—well, it's not her fault, but one kid was singing loudly and one kid was crying as we tried to have a conversation. I know I've been there and should be more under-standing, but I just couldn't handle the noise. I don't think she could really hear me anyway, so I ended

the call more quickly than I should have. I regret not being the mother I should be to the children I have left.

Tabitha paused after she penned the last words. Was this venturing into past regret territory? Should she leave it? That was the problem when you made up the rules; you were always free to break them. But how to know when it was ok to do so?

She decided to leave it. Because Davy still counted. His lingering presence was current, not past. Davy was in every week, in every moment since the night he went missing.

Satisfied with her list, she nodded to herself and then she finished as she always did, writing the words *JE NE REGRETTE RIEN!!!* at the bottom of the page with a flourish. She let herself stare at the phrase for a long time, wishing this was the week that statement would become true—that she would truly regret nothing. That all her regrets—past and present—would release their hold on her and she would be free.

She relished tearing up the list into tiny bits as she always did, then dumped the bits into the bin, slamming the lid with a bit more emphasis than was necessary before she turned away to face the day.

CHAPTER 3

Gordon Swift

Sometimes when he was shopping or at a restaurant or at one of his parents' many doctor's appointments, he would get the sensation. That was what he'd come to call it: the sensation. And not in that old-York-Peppermint-Pattie-ad-campaign kind of way. This sensation was neither exhilarating nor refreshing. This was a prickly dread crawling across the expanse of his skin.

Sure enough, he would look up and find someone—man or woman, it didn't matter—looking at him but pretending not to. Their eyes, just before they averted them, asking the same old unspoken questions: Is it him? Could it be? Surely he's not still in Wynotte.

It happened that morning as he stood in line at Booker's Hardware to purchase a large sheet of steel wool to use in his latest sculpture. The cashier, an older gentleman, kept glancing at him over the top of his reader glasses, then returning his gaze to the register. When Gordon handed over his card for him to swipe, he watched as the man checked the name on the card, then looked at him one more time. In a blink his gaze had gone from curious to venomous. It was that fast.

Each time this happened, Gordon had to suppress the urge to speak up and affirm that yes, it was him, and no, he did not still live in that little house he'd lived in at the time of Davy Malcor's disappearance, but yes, he still lived in the small town he'd grown up in. He wanted to say he was still there because he had no reason to leave; he'd done nothing wrong. But he also wanted to explain that, while he'd love to have left long ago, he could not leave his parents, who needed his help. After all they'd gone through because of him, it was the least he could do. It was because of him that their health was failing, his fault they were now pariahs in a town his family had called home for generations.

He knew people stared at his parents, too, that they probably knew the sensation as well as he did. If anyone could understand, they would. But they didn't talk about any of it, ever. His parents were of the don't-ask-don't-tell mindset. No crying over spilt milk and all that. Better to move forward, do the best they could, and tell themselves all the while that it was enough.

But Gordon did not feel he could keep up that attitude for the rest of his life. Increasingly, he felt himself wanting to change things instead of merely accept them. He just couldn't figure out how.

He left the hardware store in a hurry, feeling eyes on his back. Would they talk about him after he left? Probably, he decided.

"*You know who that was, don't you?*" the cashier would say to the next person in line. And that was all it would take. They'd jaw about the missing kid, then speculate about Gordon's involvement in his disappearance. Davy Malcor would haunt him forever if he let him.

He went home, intending to work on his latest sculpture (this one was a commission so he actually had a deadline), but instead he went to the computer and turned it on. While he waited to log on, he made a cup of coffee, then took a seat. He'd returned three days ago from a gallery show in Franklin, Tennessee, and needed to write a thank-you note—a real, handwritten card, not a dashed-off email—to the gallery owners for their hospitality and their continued support of his work. He just needed to search online for the correct address.

While he was online, he figured he'd check his email. He told himself it was just business, not procrastination, as he watched his inbox appear on the screen. Near the top of the list was an email from her, the woman he'd met at the gallery, the one who'd openly flirted with him, who'd asked for his card and pressed her own into his hand. She wanted to "connect" later. That was how she'd phrased it. He'd said he was heading home to North Carolina, that a connection wasn't possible. Her email made it clear she wasn't giving up that easily. She had business that took her to Charlotte, she wrote, and wasn't that close to Wynotte? She'd love to see him next time she was in town.

With a sigh he deleted her email, then shut off the computer. No point in replying. Soon enough she would find out who he was, hear what he'd been accused of doing. Gordon had learned a long time ago there was no sense in starting something that would only, inevitably, end. He hadn't always known that, and it had caused him a lot of heartache. He was wiser now; he guarded his heart better.

He walked out to his studio in the backyard, opened the door, and threw himself into his work, the one thing that had never failed him.

CHAPTER 4

Anissa Weaver

After Seth left that morning, she cleaned her condo top to bottom, as if she could scour him—and her own bad decision—out of the house. She cleaned the toilets, scrubbed the kitchen sink, and mopped the floors with all the force she had in her, using the exertion to push away the pesky memories of the night before: Seth as he smiled at her in that knowing way; Seth's face over hers, their breaths mingling; Seth as he showered after. As if by showering he could wash away what they'd done. She'd said as much before he left, and they fought about it. He called her crazy, a favorite word of his.

"If you regret sleeping with me so much, why do you keep doing it?" he'd asked. She could hear the hurt in his voice. *"You initiated last night, not me."*

She'd shrugged, doing her best to appear nonchalant. *"I have needs, too, you know."*

"You don't always have to come to me *with your needs,"* he'd said. The hurt had turned to anger, tracing the outline of his words.

The problem was, she couldn't imagine doing anything but going to Seth. For a time, he'd been the love of her life, even though the marriage had failed. They'd called time of death over a year ago, and yet these interludes continued, no matter how many times she promised herself she'd put a stop to it. Back when they were still trying to be married, their therapist had said they were both afraid of transparency, of vulnerability, of exposure. So they fought instead of talked, joked instead of being honest, left instead of staying. And then, foolishly, went back for more.

"*I don't want to sleep with a stranger,*" she'd retorted, intentionally keeping her tone light, breezy. In lieu of a response, Seth had walked out the door. At least he hadn't slammed it.

She wished she had to work today, wished something big would happen so she'd get called in even though it was her day off. But that was the thing about being the Public Information Officer for the sleepy town of Wynotte's police department; there wasn't much to inform the public about. No one really needed to know that Myra Stockton had called the ambulance last night for the thirteenth time this year. The truth was, whatever the public needed to know in this town didn't require Anissa's input. The gossip mill worked faster and more efficiently, if a person wasn't fussy about facts.

She was grateful her job involved other responsibilities— victim advocacy, liaising with the mayor's office, and public relations for the department, putting on a good face for the press whenever possible. Anissa was happy to do whatever needed doing; she was one of those weirdos who truly loved her job. Once she'd told Seth it was her calling, and he'd teased her about it for days. But she'd meant it.

She went looking for the TV remote, moved out of her way in her cleaning frenzy, only to spy her phone where the remote usually sat. The screen said she had three missed calls from Pete Lancaster, the sheriff. She smiled as all thoughts of Seth retreated from her mind as surely as if she'd swept them out with the broom. If Pete was calling her on her day off it meant something had happened. Inside her a small voice said, *Finally.*

She called Pete back and waited for him to answer with that familiar *"This is Pete,"* in a slightly exasperated tone, like she'd just pulled him from something far more important. Right now the thing that was more important, she knew, was his newborn son.

Pete didn't answer, so she hung up and sank into the couch to wait for him to see her missed call. If she left a message, he wouldn't listen to it anyway. She got up and went to the window, scanned the minuscule patch of grass the condominium complex counted as a yard for a sign of the cat that had been hanging around lately, a skinny, skittish Siamese. It always darted away before she could try to help it.

Her phone's ring pulled her away from the window. She snatched it up and answered, her "Hello?" coming out far less poised and professional than she'd intended. *Rein it in*, she cautioned herself.

"Niss?" The female voice on the other end was not what she expected. Her sister Marissa chuckled. "You're awfully happy to hear from me."

Anissa rolled her eyes. "I thought you were Pete."

"Pete?" Marissa exclaimed. "A guy named Pete is calling you? This is news!" Marissa was clearly thrilled at the mention of a guy other than Seth.

"Pete Lancaster," Anissa said dully. "The sheriff."

"Oh." Marissa's voice went flat. "I didn't know his first name was Pete."

"Are you calling for a reason?" Anissa asked, barely concealing her impatience. She wanted to talk to Pete about whatever he'd been calling about, not get grilled about her love life by her nosy sister.

"Actually, I was probably calling about the same thing as Pete," Marissa said. A smug eagerness filled her voice.

"What?" Anissa breathed, her impatience with her sister quickly replaced by intrigue.

"They found that kid's jacket," Marissa said. She paused before adding, "Well, that's what they think it is, at least."

Anissa didn't have to ask what kid Marissa meant. She knew. Everyone in Wynotte knew. Or at least, everyone who'd been around for any time at all. Davy Malcor was a legend in this town, a cautionary tale, a ghost story whispered on the darkest nights.

Almost twenty-one years after eleven-year-old Davy Malcor had gone missing from a cornfield while playing games with his friends in the dark, everyone had theories on what had happened to him. His was the town's most famous case, one that still cropped up every so often—when some crackpot in prison confessed to abducting him, when supposed new evidence emerged, or when the press decided to run an anniversary story, reminding everyone about the cold case, lest Davy be forgotten. But of course, he was never forgotten. Davy Malcor was out of sight but never out of Wynotte's collective conscience.

Marissa continued. "I knew you especially would want to know. I mean—"

"Where'd you hear this?" Anissa cut her off. Her question was based on her graduate training and subsequent experience in managing public information: don't believe what you hear unless it's been verified by a reliable source. Her sister was not what the police department would deem a reliable source. And yet, Pete *had* called her three times while she was cleaning. He was probably pissed that she wasn't available when he needed her, day off or not.

Anissa began to change from her sweats into something more presentable as Marissa explained what she'd heard. The gossip was that the guy who'd bought the Oxendine land had found the jacket while walking the property—and not just a scrap of fabric but a whole, intact jacket, a very distinct jacket that anyone with access to media had seen at one point or another.

Anissa could picture the jacket, but not from the photos in the news. She'd seen it with her own eyes. Davy himself had shown it to her—on a warm autumn night, far too hot to be wearing a jacket, but Davy had showed it off even as sweat formed on his brow and dripped into his large brown eyes.

"My neighbor Sarah—you remember her?" Marissa continued, unaware that Anissa had all but stopped listening, lost in her own thoughts, her own private memories.

"Yeah," Anissa lied, tugging on jeans fresh from the dryer, glad she'd done laundry.

"Well, her husband works for the commercial real estate agency that sold the guy that property. He drove out there and said it's all taped off and cops are there." Marissa paused. "I'm stunned you haven't heard."

Her phone signaled an incoming call. "I gotta go! That's Pete on the other line." She hung up on Marissa in time to catch the call.

"Hello?" she asked, breathless and anxious.

"I assume you've heard the news." Pete wasted no time.

"Yep, already misinformation to start managing," she said. "The story's making its way through town."

"That's why I need you to get to the Malcor home," Pete said. "Be with them as much as they'll allow. Help them ward off the press as we figure out what's happening. I don't want them divulging anything until we're ready to make an official statement. See if you can help them understand the importance of that."

"I can do that," Anissa said, willing herself to sound confident. It seemed she had waited her whole life for this moment, but she wasn't sure she was ready now that it had come. She thought of the games they played as kids. *"Ready or not, here I come,"* they'd called.

"Good girl," Pete said. It should bother her that he'd called her a girl, but she was too thrilled by his praise to correct him.

"One more thing," Pete added, his voice dropping an octave as he spoke again. "And this isn't for public knowledge. But I think we're really close this time."

"Really?" Anissa breathed, incredulous. In the two decades since Davy disappeared, there'd been supposed sightings, false confessions, and continued efforts on the part of the family to keep the investigation open—all things that brought the press to town, sniffing around at the possibility of the case finally being solved. Anissa wanted to say she'd always believed it would happen one day. But was that really true? Had she lost hope along the way? She didn't want to think that way, even for a second.

"We're as close as we've ever been," the sheriff said.

"Wow," Anissa said. The word sounded inane and inadequate, but she couldn't take it back.

A moment of silence passed between them before Pete said, "Ok, well, you best get over there before the press starts camping out on their lawn. I'll send some uniforms over to help with that. Do you need the address? This case has been quiet for a few years. I'm not sure you've had cause to go over there since you started this job."

"No," Anissa said. "I know. Where they live." The sheriff didn't need to know why. She'd prefer he never did.

From outside the bathroom doorway, eleven-year-old Davy does his best to stay hidden as he observes his mother. She is applying makeup, unaware that she's being watched. She always opens her mouth as she lifts the mascara wand to her lashes. He's about to blow his cover to ask her why, but she spots him before he can.

"Davy Malcor, are you spying on me?" she asks and lifts one corner of her mouth without turning from the mirror. He grins and their eyes meet, two reflections smiling at each other.

"It's not spying," he says. "It's reconnaissance." He likes that word. He learned it from *The A-Team*. Or maybe it was *Magnum, P.I.* It was definitely not *Simon & Simon*. He isn't allowed to watch that one. It comes on too late. His parents make him go to bed too early. He's going to talk to them about that, and soon.

His mother screws the mascara cap back on and drops the tube into her cavernous makeup bag with a jumble of products Davy doesn't understand and is a little afraid of.

"Reconnaissance, huh?" she asks.

He nods in answer, but she isn't looking at him anymore. She is pulling other things from her bag, lining up products on the counter, lost in thought. She isn't thinking about him or his older brother or his little sister. She is thinking about going to a party with other grown-ups. He heard her talking about it on the phone with Mrs. Swain from next door. The Swains are going to the party too. They're all riding together. Which means the grown-ups next door will also be gone tonight.

Davy feels a little shiver of fear go up his spine. He doesn't like when his parents go out, doesn't like being home alone with only his older brother there for protection.

He watches his mother swipe red lipstick across her lips, then study herself in the mirror before grimacing and wiping it off with a tissue. Bored with the scene, he turns to go and plows into his older brother, TJ, who promptly shoves him as if he did it on purpose.

"Watch where you're going, twerp," TJ says. TJ rarely calls Davy by his actual name. He has a wide variety of not-so-nice nicknames he uses instead. His mother says they are terms of endearment, but Davy doesn't believe that.

Not one to take things lying down, Davy retorts, "You watch where you're going, you big jerk."

Their mother steps out of the bathroom hollering, "Boys! Don't start!" She is still wearing her robe. Once she has a full face of makeup, she will put a scarf over her head and then shimmy her dress on over the slip she is no doubt wearing under the robe. Then she'll pull the scarf off and presto! She'll be ready to go. Davy tries not to feel sad at the thought.

"Mom, I need to talk to you," TJ says.

Their mother holds up a hand and shakes her head. "I'm getting ready to go out. Go talk to your father. He's already ready."

"Ready ready," Davy says and laughs.

TJ smirks at him. "You're so lame."

"Am not," Davy says.

"Are too."

Their mother points at her bedroom door. "Boys, out," she commands. Then she begins mumbling to herself but still loud enough for Davy to hear what she's saying.

"Can't I have a few moments to myself? Is that too much to ask?"

"Mom, seriously," TJ continues, ignoring her command. "I need to talk to you. It's, like, urgent."

Ever since he saw *Fast Times at Ridgemont High*, TJ has been inserting the word *like* into his sentences here, there, and everywhere. He sounds stupid if you ask Davy. But of course, TJ doesn't ask Davy for his opinion about, well, anything.

"Danny!" their mother hollers down to their father. "A little help up here!"

From somewhere in the house a deep voice answers, the words unintelligible.

"What?" she yells. When there is no reply, she sighs deeply and returns to the bathroom. TJ follows her. Davy sits on his parents' bed, curious what TJ's important question is.

Their father enters the room carrying four-year-old Kristy, who is holding a fish stick in each hand, her face smeared with ketchup.

"Tabby," their father says. He is nearly out of breath from carrying Kristy up the stairs. "You told me to feed her, so I'm feeding her. Then you call me up here. So which is it?"

"TJ has some important question he has to ask," their mother says. "I'd like him to ask you, for once, and let me get ready in peace. Why is this so hard to understand?"

Kristy waves at her mother with a fish stick, then crams half of it in her mouth, smacking loudly as she begins to chew.

Their mother wrinkles her nose at the sight. "You need your face wiped," she tells her daughter. Kristy laughs and tries to reach for her mother, who ducks out of the way with a look of genuine fear.

"Everyone out!" Tabby says to the whole lot of them, making shooing motions with her hands. "You're going to make us late."

"Oh, Tabby, we won't be late," his father says, shifting Kristy to his other side.

In response Kristy runs her ketchup-laden hands down her father's shirt as Tabby looks on in horror.

"Well, I thought you were already dressed, but I'm glad you weren't," she says.

Unruffled, Davy's father winks at Davy's mother. "You say that like I'm a rookie at this." He turns to apprise the messy child he holds, now biting into the second half of her fish stick. "Let's go clean you up, kiddo," he says and leaves the room. Davy follows him out.

Tabby turns back to the mirror, picks up a compact, and pulls an applicator from it. She is about to apply eyeshadow when TJ speaks up.

"Mom, I really need to talk to you," he says again. Tabby, not realizing he is still standing there, jumps at the sound of his voice, causing her to drop the applicator, leaving a smear of smoky-blue eyeshadow on the counter. Tabby curses under her breath as she reaches for a tissue to wipe away the mess.

"I told you to talk to your father," she says to her oldest child. She uses her most patient voice, though she feels anything but patient.

"He can't, Mom. He's taking care of Kristy. You're the only one not doing anything."

"Not doing anything? Not doing anything?" Tabby exhales loudly, lifting the eyeshadow wand in the air as proof that she is, in fact, doing something. Or does it not count in her family's eyes if the thing she is doing is solely for herself? She closes her eyes, inhales and exhales, centering herself. Soon she will be at a party with other adults, talking about things adults talk about, a cold glass of crisp white wine in her hand. She just has to get there first.

"What do you need?" she asks.

TJ has come to the bathroom doorway, standing in the same spot where Davy stood moments ago. Tabby has no idea where Davy has gotten off to, but he is worried about tonight. She can tell. He's afraid to be left at home with TJ in charge. She knows this, knows what he'd been thinking as he watched her.

But she hadn't said anything, hadn't wanted to open that can of worms. Because to do so would possibly throw off their plans for the night. And just for one night, she doesn't want to know her son's fears, doesn't want to ponder the depths of his psyche. Ignorance, Tabby knows, can be bliss. Complete and utter bliss.

TJ pauses before answering, which means he is working up to something. "So Phillip and some other kids want to go play night games and—"

"What are night games?" The term sounds nefarious to her.

TJ huffs and Tabby knows he is thinking that his mother is slow, that she requires his patience. "It's just kids playing normal games—like freeze tag or capture the flag. But, like, at night."

Tabby raises her eyebrows at him. "Where are these *night games* going to happen?"

TJ brightens at the question. The fact that she is asking means there is hope of gaining the permission he seeks. He points in a vague southeast direction.

"Those fields over by the fork in the road. You know, where that old farm was?"

"Is," Tabby corrects. "The old farm is. It's still a farm."

"Well, there aren't any crops anymore," TJ argues. Around the time he entered his teens, TJ became an excellent arguer. Neither she nor Danny saw it coming, this transformation from child to miniature lawyer, always pleading some case. At fifteen, he is a master at it. They both find it exhausting. Exhibit A: Danny has opted to clean a ketchup-stained child over hearing TJ out.

"Still," she says. "I don't think you kids should be traipsing around on property you don't own."

"Phillip says people do it all the time and nothing ever happens. He says they're gonna sell that place anyway and build another neighborhood."

"Uh-huh," Tabby says, turning back to the mirror and applying the eyeshadow. "And how is Phillip so knowledgeable about local construction plans?"

"His uncle told him," TJ says.

Tabby sighs into the mirror, her breath fogging it. "I don't like that uncle of his. He seems . . . I don't know"—she casts about for the right words—"out of it."

"Aw, Mom," TJ says. "It's just because he's an uncle and not a real parent."

Tabby rolls her eyes. "That's comforting, TJ."

"No," TJ persists, "I mean he didn't, like, choose to be Phillip's dad. He just, you know, had to. Because his parents died. Or whatever."

"Well, that is certainly sad for all concerned," Tabby says, thinking she really should take time to learn more about TJ's friends. If only there weren't so many distractions. She puts down the eyeshadow wand and steers the conversation back to where they'd started.

"I'd love to say yes, but I need you here." She turns the faucet on, then off again. "We're going out tonight. Remember?"

"I know, I know. But I had an idea," TJ says, holding up a finger. TJ's ideas are legendary. He is uncannily good at figuring out an angle that will benefit him best yet still placate others. She and Danny often muse over whether this means their oldest child will be a success or a swindler.

"*He could just be a politician,*" Danny likes to say. "*Then he'd be both.*"

"What's your idea?" Tabby sighs, beaten. She squints at her makeup job in the mirror. She isn't very good at applying eyeshadow. As a stay-at-home mom of three, she doesn't have much reason to perfect the skill.

"Davy can stay here with Kristy and watch a movie. I'll just be, like, down the street and Larkin will be right next door if there's an emergency. I'll stay for one hour, then I'll come right home." He holds up the Scout's honor sign, even though he'd quit Cub Scouts at age eight after only three months of meetings, claiming earning the badges had been "too stressful."

Tabby's head is already shaking, even as he holds out his arm and points at his watch to imply he can be trusted to use it.

"Come on, Mom. One hour. That's all," he pleads. But even as he does, she recalls Davy watching her in the mirror from the same spot where TJ now stands, the barely contained anxiety welling behind her younger son's eyes.

"Davy's not ready for that yet," she says. "I'm sorry." She can feel the situation devolving, can feel Davy's unspoken fear, TJ's mounting anger, and Kristy's small sticky hands reaching, reaching, reaching. All she wants to do is go to one party. Why, she thinks, is this too much to ask?

"That's not fair," TJ wails, sounding like the child he still is, even as his body morphs into something that increasingly resembles a man.

Tabby opens her mouth to speak, but before she can offer her normal retort, TJ rolls his eyes. "I know what you're gonna say. Life's not fair. Well, it really isn't in this house!" he exclaims, then storms out of the room.

Tabby stands motionless, alone for the first time all evening, and grips the edge of the bathroom counter. She studies the mirror and wonders briefly if she recognizes the reflection.

Danny's face appears beside her own. This time he is not carrying Kristy, but he is still wearing the ketchup-smeared shirt.

"Do I even want to know?" he asks, already sounding worn out even though the night is young.

"He wants to go play so-called night games down the street with some friends," she says. "Wants us to leave Davy and Kristy alone here for an hour so he can go. Says he'll watch the time and Larkin will be right next door if the kids need anything."

Danny, always the more lenient parent, shrugs. "It's not a terrible plan."

"If Davy weren't so nervous about being here alone, then TJ's plan would be fine."

"Well, maybe we force Davy to toughen up, face his fears. I mean, Larkin *is* right next door."

Tabby is shaking her head again, disagreeing before he can finish speaking. "I get the feeling he might really be afraid of something."

Danny raises his eyebrows. "Maybe we should talk to him about it."

Tabby closes her eyes and shakes her head, this time more emphatically. "I am not getting into that tonight. We can talk to him later." She waves her hand in the air. "Tomorrow. Or something." She turns to Danny, puts her hands on his shoulders, and kisses him full on the mouth.

He smiles and pulls her closer. "To what do I owe this honor?" he asks, his grin going from playful to lascivious in a second.

"To a night out. Just us. As grown-ups. Not as Mom and Dad but as Tabby and Danny, the people we were before the kids came. The people I hope we still are, if we could just get the chance for a couple of hours."

Danny pulls back and studies her for a moment. "You really need this, huh?"

She nods and buries her head in his shoulder. "You have no idea," she says into his stained T-shirt.

She wants him to change out of that shirt. She wants to see him in the golf shirt he'd laid out earlier, the new jeans she picked up at the mall for him. She wants to see him out of the house, away from the kids, shed of the personas they wear within these walls. She wants him to wink at her from across the room like he used to when they went to parties in college, back before they knew what the other was thinking with just a look.

He claps his hands together. "I think I've got a solution. TJ!" he bellows.

"What are you up to?" she asks, feeling hope bubble up. The situation can be fixed. The night can be saved. They can all get what they want.

TJ appears in the doorway, looking mournful. "What?" he asks.

"Let's make a compromise," Danny says, rubbing his hands together.

At the word *compromise*, TJ's mouth droops even more. "Just forget it." He starts to walk away, but Danny reaches out and catches him.

"You haven't even heard my offer."

TJ stares at the ground. "What is it?"

Danny looks over at Tabby. "You sure Larkin is home?"

Tabby nods. "Marie said she was going to be."

"Well, we can ask Larkin over to babysit Kristy for a couple of hours so you can go play your games."

At this TJ lifts his head and looks at his father. "Really?"

Danny is usually of the mind that there is no reason to pay a babysitter when you have one who will work for free already in the house. He is making a magnanimous decision in the name of keeping both his wife and his son happy. This is worth the fifteen bucks it will cost him.

"But"—Danny says, and TJ's shoulders drop; he is a balloon deflated with a single prick—"we let Davy choose whether he stays here with the girls or goes with you."

"That's not—"

"Don't say *fair*," Tabby interjects. "If you say *fair*, we'll cancel this whole offer and you'll stay home as planned."

TJ's eyes move from his mother to his father and back again, gauging the strength of their union. Deciding it is stronger than he is, he sighs deeply.

"Ok," he says quietly.

Danny claps his son on the back. "Good man." He says this often, even though TJ is far from a man.

Not yet, a little voice inside Tabby says. *Not just yet.*

"So I can tell Phillip I'll be there?" TJ asks. Tabby hears the excitement creeping back into his voice.

"You can," Danny says, "after we talk to Davy and find out what he wants to do." TJ's face falters, but he recovers quickly, not wanting to lose his parents' goodwill.

"I'll go get him," he says and races off in search of his little brother.

Danny turns back to Tabby and kisses her again. "See? Everybody wins." He waggles his eyebrows in a way that suggests he expects to be the big winner later that night.

And Tabby laughs because she believes it is just that easy.

CHAPTER 5

Thaddeus

The email had been sitting unopened in his inbox for two days. This one from her personal account, not her business one. He stared at the little box for a few minutes before he succumbed to curiosity and clicked to open it, feeling slightly ill as her words filled the screen. What did they call it? A vulnerability hangover? Well, that was exactly what it felt like. A hangover.

He read what she had written:

> *We work together, so we can't avoid each other for-*
> *ever. If you want to pretend it never happened, then*
> *fine. We will pretend it never happened. I know you*
> *might have regrets, but I don't.*

No wonder she'd sent it from her personal account. If someone else saw that email, they might think they'd slept together. In actuality what they'd done had been far worse. The words *bared his soul* floated through his brain, the nausea intensifying at the thought. Stupid. He'd been so stupid and now he couldn't take it back, nor could he figure out a way to fix it. And, as Nicole had just pointed out, avoidance wasn't a long-term solution.

Thaddeus clicked the little *X* to close his email inbox just as his cell phone rang. He looked at his BlackBerry, a device his family teased him about mercilessly—how important he thought himself now with his fancy phone, Mr. In-Demand Author. He needed the phone to communicate with author escorts in cities all over the country, navigate his constant travels, and connect with producers of the various morning and news-magazine shows he'd appeared on since the book's rise up the bestseller lists. (Even his mother had seemed impressed that he'd been on *Good Morning America*.) But it wasn't true that he thought himself important. No matter what his family thought.

A familiar number filled the screen, the word above it stating that *Home* was calling, even though it had not been his home in many, many years. Funny that he named it that in his contacts, perhaps in a fit of nostalgia. Was home always home? Did it ever get replaced, another house coming to mind at the mention of the word? He supposed if he was married with children and a mortgage, then a new house would become home, more by default than choice. It was the proper order of things. If one's life was going in the proper order, that is.

He silenced the call. He wasn't in the mood to hear from home.

He pushed away from the hotel room desk, turning his thoughts to the piece he was supposed to be writing for *The Pacific* magazine about how the reception of the book had changed his life. He wondered how much he could expound on the theme "I get laid a lot more than I ever did before." He grinned, letting himself forget the email from Nicole for a moment.

The phone rang again, making his grin turn to a grimace. He picked up the phone to see who was calling this time. Home again. Gripping the phone, he said aloud to no one, "Can't you people see I'm working?" He closed his eyes, thinking of his parents, who, after all, weren't getting any younger.

He answered, bracing himself as he did.

"Thaddeus?" his mother asked. He was grateful for the effort she made to use the name he preferred. No more TJ, as he had once been known. TJ was a child's name. He was a man now. Or at least he pretended to be one.

"Yes?" he asked, knowing she could hear the alarm in his voice. Before she could speak again, he asked, "Is it Dad?"

"What?" She gave a panicky little laugh. "No, no. It's not Dad. And I wouldn't be calling about him anyway. I've heard he's got a girlfriend now. So I guess she'd be calling you. If there was a reason." She paused and swallowed. Then, "It's Davy."

Thaddeus had felt this moment coming for such a long time, an out-of-control 18-wheeler barreling toward them all, building speed and momentum with every day that passed. Two shameful thoughts occurred at once: (1) he hoped Davy wasn't alive, a damaged stranger returned to them, and (2) now he could write that second memoir his editor had been clamoring for.

A third thought followed the other two, this one even worse: If there was news about Davy, did his book make it happen somehow? Was he responsible for dredging up answers that had eluded them for two decades? If so, would that make him a hero?

It took his mother less than a minute to dispel that fantasy. A property owner walking his newly acquired land had found

Davy's jacket. The discovery was not due to a tip from a reader; there was no confession from the perpetrator because he'd read Thaddeus's memoir. Instead, it was happenstance. Now the authorities were searching the property extensively, looking for more evidence and possibly, finally, Davy.

Thaddeus reached into his pocket but felt nothing there. He scanned the room and found what he was looking for on the dresser, where he'd left it the night before.

"So they haven't actually found *him*?" Thaddeus clarified.

"The sheriff says they're closer than they've ever been. He thinks . . ." She didn't continue, unable or unwilling to utter what came next.

"He thinks they're going to find him," Thaddeus said.

"Yes," his mother said, and he heard the tears threatening at the edges of her voice. If she started to cry, he knew she might not stop. She would be stalwart through this, just as she always had. She would get through this discovery and all that came with it and fall apart later, alone. It was the family way.

"I'd like you to come home," she said. "I think you should be here when . . ."

The *if* they'd lived with for so long had become a *when*?

"Mom, I can't. Not now. I'm in St. Louis, and I leave tomorrow morning for Seattle. Then I have to go to New York for some pretty important meetings. But I could come after that?" The question was a placation, even though by then he'd have thought up another excuse, and they both knew it.

"Thaddeus, your family needs you. And I doubt they'll be able to handle your book events once this news breaks. It won't be safe for you to make any public appearances. You know this kind of thing brings out the crazies." She'd slipped into her mom voice, one he was very familiar with, yet had almost forgotten. Even now he felt himself tense, the reaction Pavlovian. Or Freudian. He didn't know which.

"That's a discussion for me to have with my publisher. Not my mom," he said, sounding—and feeling—like a sullen teenager as he said it.

She wasn't having a debate. That was what she used to say when he was a kid and tried to argue with her.

"You need to come home, Thaddeus. Start checking flights and let me know what you arrange. Or have your fancy publicist do it for you. I don't care." She went silent, waiting, he supposed, for him to respond.

When he didn't, she added one more thing. "You've spent the last year profiting off your brother. Now it's time to come home for him." He heard a click and she was gone.

Thaddeus sat still for a moment, listening to the hum of the air conditioner, processing what he'd just learned. Already he wished to go back to ten minutes ago, when his biggest problem was oversharing with a woman he both worked with and had a crush on. That was nothing compared to this.

They'd found Davy's jacket after all these years. How was that possible?

He sat alone in his hotel room and wished for someone to talk to, someone he could call. But he could think of no one. Then it dawned on him: what he really wanted in that moment was a brother. He wanted a brother who knew their mother, who knew their history, someone he could truly share this with, who didn't have to pretend to understand.

What Thaddeus wanted most was to call Davy, to tell him his jacket had just been found.

FROM *EVERY MOMENT SINCE: A MEMOIR* BY THADDEUS MALCOR

PUBLISHED SEPTEMBER 20, 2005

If you've ever watched a news report about my brother, you've no doubt seen the clip of him juggling. That clip was filmed one week before he disappeared. Because it was the most recent image of him—and because they were desperate to find him—my parents eagerly shared that video with the police and the press. They figured the live action of him talking and moving around would make him more recognizable when someone, surely, found him.

My parents didn't stop to process the ramifications of sharing something so private, so personal, with the world. They could not have known how that video would haunt us all for a very long time. I've seen that video play across multiple televisions in the electronics section of a Walmart, muted on a tiny television mounted over a bar, and broadcast on a jumbotron at a sporting event during the half-time show. It's weird to be in a public place and see a piece of your own family history, to watch it and remember it at the same time.

If you're not familiar, the video was filmed at my little sister Kristy's birthday party. Davy had volunteered to be the entertainment by doing a few magic tricks and then—the grand finale—his juggling act. The clip was cut to just a few seconds and shows Davy juggling four yellow balls, little moons orbiting the sun that is Davy's round, smiling face. At the end of it he's so pleased with himself, he exclaims, *"Mom, did you see? I juggled four balls! I kept them all up! All at the very same time!"*

In the clip he makes the juggling look easy. But getting to that point was not easy. Davy could juggle three balls, but he didn't want to do the easy trick. A true feat, he decided, would be to add one more ball. He practiced and practiced in the weeks leading up to the party, often begging me to be his audience. At first I was willing, but I grew tired of it and began dodging him. So he conned the girl next door into being his audience. I'd see them out in the backyard and feel a prickle of jealousy that Davy was getting her attention.

More than once I thought of going out to join them but talked myself out of it because I had to play it cool. If I could go back to those days before he went missing, I'd go outside and sit with the girl next door to watch my brother. We'd watch him juggle all day long. And we'd clap every time he kept all four balls in the air. All at the very same time.

CHAPTER 6

Tabitha

Tabitha crossed the yard between the two houses that had stood side by side for decades, as had the two families who lived in the houses. She had to warn Marie about what was happening. She spotted someone sitting on the screened porch that stretched along the back of the house. With the news about Davy, she'd almost forgotten that Marie's daughter, Larkin, and granddaughter had arrived just days ago.

She tugged the porch door open, startling Larkin, who was sitting at the table with a computer open in front of her. Larkin turned, hand on chest, her large blue eyes blinking rapidly.

"Sorry to scare you," Tabitha said. "I just came over to talk to your mother." She moved closer and squinted at the computer in front of Larkin. A handsome man's face filled the screen, his expression a mixture of confusion and concern.

"Is this your husband? On the computer?" Technological advances never failed to mystify—and slightly concern—her. "In . . . real life?"

"Yes," Larkin said with a little laugh that sounded more sad than happy. "The army set it up so we could talk to each other while he's deployed." She sighed. "It's not the same, of course. But it's better than nothing."

Tabitha bent closer and waved at the man on the screen. "Hi, Tyler." She touched her chest with her hand. "You probably don't remember me, but I'm Tabitha Malcor, Marie's next-door neighbor. I was at your wedding."

"Oh, sure," Larkin's husband said, though Tabitha doubted he actually remembered her from the single handshake in the receiving line.

Tabitha had always hoped Larkin and Thaddeus would grow up and get married, but that was not to be. There was a brief spark between the two when they were teens, filling both her and Marie with the crazy hope of shared grandchildren someday. They would daydream about imaginary youngsters traipsing back and forth between their grandmothers' homes, each already declaring herself to be the favorite grandma who baked the best cookies. But after Davy disappeared, Thaddeus seemed to lose interest in Larkin, in a lot of things.

The thought of Thaddeus made her heart rate increase all over again. The nerve of him, saying he didn't have time to come home when a family crisis was happening. He was needed! But Thaddeus wasn't good at being needed.

"I'll just let you guys get on with your conversation," she said to Larkin and Tyler. They'd gotten the news of his deployment right around the time they called in hospice for her father, Jim. The timing wasn't fair, two losses in swift succession. A lot of things in life weren't fair. If Tabitha knew anything, she knew that.

"Is your mother inside?" she asked, even though she knew the answer already.

"Yes," Larkin said. "But Audrey's sleeping, if you could try to be quiet." She winced a little as she said it. Audrey was Larkin's four-year-old daughter, a spitfire if ever there was one, and part of the reason Larkin was staying with Marie—to have help since she was newly pregnant and dealing with morning sickness.

Tabitha gave a quick nod of understanding and stepped inside the cool dimness of the house, its scent distinct. She would know this smell anywhere. She could be blindfolded and instantly know that this odd combination of cloves and lemon Pledge and Jim's lingering cologne (Polo—a gift from Larkin in the '80s that she kept giving him right up until his last Christmas) was the exact scent of her next-door neighbor's house. It felt to Tabitha like coming home, or next to home, as it was.

She paused to take a moment before she went to tell Marie what had happened. To warn her? Prepare her? Tabitha didn't know. Already the press was gathering at her house, knocking on the door, then when turned away, forming their little encampments, if not in her yard, then near it. That sweet girl from the police department was over there now trying to tell her how to handle things, as if Tabitha didn't already know the drill.

Marie came bustling into the kitchen and jumped at the sight of Tabitha standing by the door. "Good gracious, you startled me! I expected you to be Larkin!" she exclaimed, clutching at her chest.

"Just me," Tabitha said. She took a step toward Marie, furrowing her brow as a warning that what she'd come to speak about was serious. So much of what they spoke about was serious these days. She missed when they used to have fun, when they used to laugh. She missed being lighthearted. She could no longer remember a time when her heart didn't weigh a thousand pounds.

"What's happened?" Marie asked, her brow now furrowed as well.

Tabitha looked over her shoulder, her eyes scanning the kitchen window, which looked out at the Malcor house. Sometimes after Davy had gone missing, she would look out her window and watch Marie wash dishes in her own kitchen. She would wish she was Marie with her one placid daughter, her humdrum life, untouched by tragedy. Now she turned back to Marie.

"The circus is back in town."

That was what they'd called it back then, when Davy went missing, when the media descended on them with their prying eyes and invasive equipment and feet trampling the grass with no regard for whose property was whose. Marie and Jim had gotten as good as Daniel and Tabitha at running them off, shouting at them from their open front doors to please go away, to leave them in peace. As if peace would come if the press left, as if that was all it would take.

Every few years when there was news of Davy, it happened again. People, it seemed, would always be interested in her missing son. She remembered something suddenly: Thaddeus, back when he was still called TJ, charging at a reporter like an angry bull, screaming as he ran, *"Leave us alone!"* She wondered if he had put that episode in his book. Tabitha wouldn't know. She'd never read past the first few chapters. She often wondered if that made her a bad mother. (For the record, she had included it on her regret list the week she'd closed the book and put it away.)

"They found his jacket," she said. "There's a police spokesperson already at the house to handle the vultures." She gave a bitter laugh. "Or try to."

"*The* jacket?" Marie asked.

Tabitha nodded. Marie had gone with her to the fabric store to help her look for a paisley that would be a close match to the paisley on Marty McFly's *Back to the Future* denim jacket cuff. They'd been so overjoyed to find something that worked, they'd done a little dance in the aisle, the two of them in on the birthday surprise they knew would delight a certain little boy. Davy, the sweeter of her two sons, the one who was easiest to love.

"Where?" Marie's voice had nearly left her from the shock.

"The old Oxendine place. Some developer finally bought it. Decided to walk the property after he closed on it, and . . . there it was."

"Just lying out in the open?" Marie's voice was barely more than a squeak.

"No. In some old outbuilding that I guess was never searched. One of the many places they neglected to look." Tabitha felt heat in her cheeks. Old anger rose within her at the thought of the botched investigation into Davy's disappearance, the cops' lack of follow-through, their insistence that he'd run away or gotten lost, that they had nothing to worry about and he'd turn up, all while precious time was lost.

"Never searched . . ." Marie echoed. And Tabitha knew what she was thinking because she had already had the same thought. If Davy's jacket was there, was he also?

"They've started a search," she said. "A proper one this time." Marie crossed herself, a reflex that seemed fitting.

"Have you spoken to Daniel?" Marie asked.

Tabitha nodded. "He's coming over." She shrugged as if it was nothing. "The police would like us to be together, just to keep us informed of what's going on as efficiently as possible."

Marie raised her eyebrows. "Well, that won't be awkward at all," she said, then smiled.

Tabitha couldn't help but smile in response. It *would* be awkward having Daniel back in the house they once shared, a house he hadn't lived in for over fifteen years. They'd limped along for five painful years after Davy went missing, their determination to stay together ebbing with each passing year. By the time they threw in the towel, it was a mere formality. He started traveling extensively for work, any excuse to stay away. And when he was home, she often slept in Davy's bed.

They'd handled the grief so differently that it had rendered them different people. People neither of them knew anymore. She thought of his voice on the phone earlier, tight and guarded, as if she was a stranger, which, she supposed, she was. That they would be stuck together waiting for news of the child they both lost only added to the stress of an immensely stressful situation. But what choice did they have? She only hoped he didn't bring his girlfriend; she was thankful he didn't have a wife.

"Well, you can hide out here anytime you need a break. I'll be right here," Marie said. Her voice shook and Tabitha saw that her eyes shone with unshed tears. Marie wasn't just her neighbor; she was her best friend, the one person other than Daniel who'd walked through all of this since the beginning. Marie had been by her side when they got the call that Davy was missing. And there she had stayed.

Tabitha pointed a finger at her old friend. "Don't start," she admonished. Even as she said it, she could feel the prick of her own tears trying to collect. She blinked them away.

The back door opened and Larkin entered the kitchen, which made it as good a time as any for Tabitha to take her leave.

"Well, I better get back over there. I left that girl Pete Lancaster sent over all alone in the house."

Tabitha didn't really want the girl there—didn't want to feel the constant need to entertain her—but there hadn't been a choice. The girl's job, as Pete had explained it, was to update them on new information and serve as a buffer between them and the media. They'd never sent someone over to sit with them, which told Tabitha this time was different from the others. The other times had never lasted more than a day—a sighting quickly proven to be mistaken identity, a confession from a prisoner revealed to be a hoax in a matter of hours, a de rigueur story on the anniversary of the disappearance. Usually the press showed up, then left just as quickly as they'd come.

"It's not like I haven't done this before," she tossed over her shoulder as she headed for the door.

Tabitha had been elected the family spokesperson from the beginning. She'd done the talking on TV and radio and on panels and once in front of Congress. Until Thaddeus wrote that book, she'd been the only one of them to speak publicly about Davy. Daniel had refused, claiming stage fright. But someone had to tell Davy's story. And now she would do it again. She could feel the heavy mantle of responsibility settling back on her shoulders, weighing her down as she said her goodbyes, exited Marie's house, and made her way back across their yards.

At some point she crossed the line that delineated where one yard ended and the other began. But damned if she knew where it was.

TJ stands in the driveway and waves goodbye to his parents and Larkin, balancing his bike against his hip as he waits for Davy to come out of the house so they can ride the short distance to the field where Phillip and the other guys are waiting. TJ just has to ignore the creeping guilt he feels for not being completely honest with his parents about their plans for tonight.

Their plans aren't *that* bad, he reassures himself. They're just going to try beer. It's no worse than Phillip looking at the *Playboy* magazines he hides under his bed. It's just one of those things teenagers do. And TJ is a teenager. He has been for two years, and this is the first time he's done anything that would qualify as teen rebellion.

He is not, he justifies to himself as the birds start to sing their goodbyes to the sun, a bad person. And if you get right down to it, he hasn't actually lied. Still, he hears his mother's voice as if she is standing right beside him and not on her way to a party: *"A lie of omission is still a lie, Thaddeus James."*

He looks back over his shoulder at the house and wonders what's keeping Davy. A trickle of sweat snakes down his back, landing in the waistband of his shorts. Though it's October, it's still hot outside. His mother has complained about the heat, saying she wants to make soups and casseroles, fall comfort foods, like she used to do back in Ohio at this time of year. But since they live in the South, that has to wait till much later when it finally does get cold. His mother rarely seems to miss Ohio, but she does miss having a real fall. TJ knows this because she says it all the time.

The door opens and TJ huffs his displeasure at being kept waiting. "Finally," he says, turning to see that it's not Davy but Larkin emerging from the house with Kristy by her side. His heart's rhythm goes from a whole note to an eighth note just at the sight of her. When he kissed her last week, the beat went to a sixteenth note. He hadn't known a heart could go that fast without passing out or dying. TJ learned about music stuff from his grandpa, who died a year ago, and who he misses but doesn't like to talk about.

Seeing TJ standing there, Larkin stops short, shifting awkwardly as she points to Kristy. "She wanted to come look for lightning bugs," she says, answering a question TJ didn't ask. TJ wonders if Larkin's heart is also racing. He wishes he could ask her but instead he just nods, blushing a little at the mention of the lightning bugs.

Larkin and Kristy had spent hours catching lightning bugs together in the evenings this past summer. They'd made a little house to keep them in—a mason jar with holes Larkin poked into the lid with an ice pick. She'd wielded the ice pick like she was Michael Myers or Jason Voorhees, and TJ had laughed. He'd never realized Larkin was funny. He'd never paid her much attention till then. Then it was like she was everywhere and on his mind constantly.

The first night they'd caught lightning bugs, he'd stayed outside talking with Larkin long after Kristy and the lightning bugs had gone to bed. Before that night, his conversations with Larkin had been limited to the kind that required one-word responses. But that night TJ discovered that Larkin was more interesting to talk to than he'd expected, different from his friends and, in some ways, better.

He'd wanted to keep talking until the sun came up and would have, if not for her father calling her inside, leaving him sitting in the dewy grass alone, looking up at the stars, until he also went inside. But not before throwing a backward glance at Larkin's house and wondering if she was also thinking about their conversation, if she, too, felt that something between them had changed, the path forward suddenly veering in a whole new direction.

That next morning the lightning bugs, trapped in their prison, had all died. He'd had to make up a story for a bawling Kristy about how they'd all fallen into a deep sleep like Sleeping Beauty but would come back to life when it got dark. He pretended to go outside and "free" them with the promise that they would return and she could catch them again.

That night as the little lights had begun to appear, Kristy had crowed that TJ was right, telling Larkin the whole invented tale. When his sister had scampered away to find more victims in the recesses of their yard, Larkin had turned to him, fixing him with her blue gaze.

"*You're a good big brother,*" she'd said.

He'd shrugged off the earnestness of her words, the compliment in them. "*I just made up something,*" he'd said.

She shook her head and smiled with one side of her mouth. "*We both know that's not true.*"

And though he knew less about the ways of male/female relationships than he did about the magic of lightning bugs, at that moment TJ had sensed that there was something under her words, something deeper that, for a brief moment, had breached the surface.

Perhaps, he thinks as he stands there waiting for Davy, dealing with girls is like dealing with those lightning bugs—you just make it up as you go along. He looks up at Larkin, standing on his front porch, looking as uncomfortable as he feels.

"I told her the lightning bugs are gone till next summer, but she won't believe me," Larkin adds. There is a note of defensiveness in her voice, but he doesn't know why. He's the last person who would challenge her story. The lightning bugs are something he likes to think they share.

TJ grips his bike tighter, pulling it close to himself as he shrugs a response, trying his best to play it cool. Phillip has coached him on this: he can't let on that he's gone around the bend for this girl. If he comes on too strong, Phillip has told him, she'll get scared and shut him out. *"One kiss is all you'll ever get,"* Phillip had intoned, shaking his head.

One week ago, after Kristy's fourth birthday party, when he and Larkin were supposed to be cleaning up while the adults drank gin and tonics inside Larkin's house, he'd kissed her. Since then, though he's replayed that kiss in his mind countless times, he's been at a loss for what comes next.

To his relief, the door behind her opens and Davy bolts out—dressed from head to toe like Marty McFly from *Back to the Future*. TJ is wearing board shorts and a Panama Jack T-shirt, still sweating even as the light drains from the sky. Davy is going to look like an idiot wearing jeans and a jacket. At the very least, TJ notes, he has not added the red puffy vest to complete the look.

Still. His brother is a colossal embarrassment. This summer, all of TJ's friends started calling Davy "McFly" and the dummy preened like it was a compliment. Because to him, it was. To him, Marty McFly is the coolest. But TJ knows better; it's clearly Indiana Jones.

When his parents made their compromise, he'd hoped Davy would choose to stay home with Kristy and Larkin, that for once the kid would get that TJ doesn't want him tagging along. But tonight is no different from the time Davy sat between TJ and Larkin while they were talking, or when he tried to play Marco Polo with TJ's friends at the pool, or when he sat in the dugout with TJ's teammates during baseball games. His friends like to include Davy just to razz TJ. They don't realize how saddled with his brother he feels. Tonight is just another example.

"Hell no," TJ announces as Davy lopes off the front porch past Kristy and Larkin, his face open and eager. "I'm not taking you anywhere in that ridiculous outfit." He points back at their house. "Leave that stupid ass jacket here. And do it quick or I'm leaving. You've already kept me waiting long enough."

Davy extends his arms and looks down at himself as if unaware he is wearing a jacket. "I like my jacket," he says, still looking at it. "It was my birthday present."

"Well, your birthday was weeks ago. Time to give the jacket a rest. At least for tonight." TJ tries to soften his voice, hoping kindness will help.

But no. Davy frowns and crosses his arms. "Mom said I can wear this jacket anytime I want. And I want to wear it tonight. It's cool." On the porch Larkin takes Kristy's hand.

"It's not cool. It's the opposite of cool. It's hot out and you're wearing a damn jacket. You look stupid." TJ glances nervously in Larkin's direction, fearing he sounds like a jerk, yet he's committed to the battle now.

"I'm telling Mom you said I was stupid," Davy says. Making derogatory comments about someone's intelligence is a cardinal sin in their household. Punishment would be swift and harsh.

"I didn't say *you* were stupid. I said you *look* stupid wearing the jacket when it's this hot out."

"Well, I'm still wearing it. I don't care what you think, TJ."

TJ smirks at him. "Yeah, right." Standing there arguing is only keeping him away from the fun happening in the fields, so TJ changes his approach. "Whatever. Just stay away from me tonight, Davy. I'm sick of you embarrassing me."

He jumps on his bike and, without waiting for Davy to mount his own bike, pedals away, dreaming of a coming day when he'll have his driver's license and never have to ride a bike again. He does not turn to see if Davy is following him, but he does keep an ear out for the sound of Davy's tires coming up behind him, his legs pumping, his lungs burning from the exertion it takes to catch up to his big brother. At the thought of Davy catching up to him, TJ pedals even faster, keen to put as much distance between them as possible.

Only later, after he gets to the field, does he realize he never said goodbye to Larkin. He tries not to think about her standing there on the porch with nothing to do but watch him go.

CHAPTER 7

Gordon

On Friday afternoons he taught art at an adult continuing education program in Charlotte, a forty-five-minute drive from his home, but one he gladly made. It wasn't about the money—the sales and commissions for his sculptures provided a nice living. He genuinely liked encouraging students. Some were there pursuing a long-deferred dream, some just discovering a latent talent. Every once in a while someone came through his class who had real promise. That made him work harder, smile more.

As he exited the classroom he waved goodbye to his students and wished them a good weekend. He didn't give much thought to what his students got up to on the weekends. He assumed that whatever they did was far more exciting than what he typically did. As he walked to the parking lot, he thought about the pretty new student in the third row, imagined asking her to have drinks on the weekend. Then he imagined her saying yes. He went a step further and let himself envision the two of them at a bar, in public, living without reproach. This, he knew, was a step too far.

When he reached the parking lot, he spotted a woman loitering near his car. He recognized her from a distance, and his reaction was immediate. His heart raced, his breath grew shallow, his blood heated. He didn't want her to see that she had affected him, but it was too late. She was looking right at him from her position at the hood of his car, crouched and waiting to spring, those familiar yellow-brown eyes fixed on him.

He'd shifted under that gaze more than once since she started as a reporter years ago, looking for a Big Story, intent on that Big Story being him. She was a piranha, just waiting to pick his bones clean. The closer he got to her, the more he thought she did, in fact, resemble a piranha: that underbite, those oddly set eyes. She seemed like one of those people whose career was all she had, which made her desperate and therefore dangerous.

"Gordon," Monica Allagash said as he walked within earshot.

He despised her use of his first name, as if they were familiar, friendly. He was betting she thought it would disarm him, open him up. So she could go for the kill. But this wasn't a new game he was playing; it was a game he'd been forced to play for half of his life.

Game. Just the word took him back to that night. The kids were playing games, their shouts echoing across the dark fields.

Fresh out of college, he hadn't been that much older than them, at times still feeling like a kid himself. He'd heard them through his open windows. It had been a mild night, the air cooling after the sun went down. Not cold but no longer hot. Perfect, really. There'd been no indication that it was anything but a normal night. He'd had no warning, no sense at all that his life was about to change forever.

He walked past Monica Allagash as if she were invisible. He bent to unlock his car, but his fingers betrayed him and he fumbled with his keys. He wished he had one of those little fobs that unlocked the door from a distance. Then he could click a button and gain access to the sanctuary of his vehicle, slam the door in her face, and race away.

She sidled up to him and stood so close that he could smell her cloying floral perfume. Flustered, he lost his grip on the keys and watched helplessly as they fell to the asphalt. He and Monica stared at the keys for a beat, then in unison raised their heads to regard each other. He could see that his recall was accurate: her eyes were indeed a golden-yellow color with brown flecks.

He wondered why her parents hadn't sprung for orthodontia. Why she hadn't as an adult. He found himself wanting to render her likeness, to sculpt his version of her. He would put ink—and blood—on her grasping hands. He would take away her underbite, remove the brown flecks from her eyes and make them simply yellow. He would make her all that she could be, yet exactly who she was. That was what he did best. Or at least, that's what the critics said.

She reached down and retrieved the keys before he could, then dangled them in front of him. He started to take them, but she moved them out of reach, clutching them to her chest. Now her awful perfume would permeate his leather keychain.

"I need my keys," he said flatly. He was a child in the schoolyard and she was the bully who'd snatched his lunch.

"One thing first." She arched a single eyebrow over a yellow-brown eye.

He sighed. "What?"

"Give me a comment on today's discovery."

He'd been in class all afternoon. He'd seen no news, received no calls. He'd thought of nothing but his students. He'd been, he thought now, happy that way. He stared past her shoulder at the building, wished he could go back inside, back to a place where whatever discovery she was alluding to didn't exist. *Here we go again.*

"I'm not aware of any discovery."

She smirked in response and crossed her arms, his keys disappearing into her bosom.

He held up his hands like a man surrendering. "I swear. I've been teaching. I have no idea what you're talking about."

The smirk morphed into a smile as she realized that meant she got to be the bearer of bad news. At least, he assumed it was bad news since she was there.

"They found Davy Malcor's jacket," she said. "Over at the old Oxendine place." She paused, studying his face for a reaction he hoped he was keeping at bay. When he didn't respond, she continued. "They've started a formal search. Dogs, police, backhoes. You name it, they're bringing it in."

Her eyes scanned his face as if she were reading a book. He could tell from the look on her face that she was finding nothing. He tried thinking of something else: the sculpture he was in the middle of, the thank-you note for the gallery owners he still needed to write, what he would eat for dinner. Anything but what she'd just told him.

"You familiar with that property?" she asked, another attempt.

He said nothing. It was too late and he was too tired to grill himself a burger as he'd planned. He would swing by the Chinese place for takeout instead.

"What are they going to find there?" she asked.

"Please give me my keys," he said.

"Are they going to find Davy there?" she responded.

"I have no idea," he said. "Please just give me my keys or I'll call your editor." This time he didn't bother to keep the irritation from his voice. "You might consider yourself a professional reporter, but this is far from professional behavior."

She thrust the keys at him with a huff. "I'm just the first, you know. There'll be more. I thought I'd give you the chance to talk to someone local, not some stranger. But suit yourself. This is just the beginning. You'll see."

As Gordon watched her stalk away, he saw it all unfolding, a movie playing just for him right where he stood in the parking lot of a school that would surely fire him as soon as the press amped up its coverage. They would flash his photo on television and print it in the newspapers, exactly as she'd promised they would. His name would be mud again, the little bit of freedom he'd grappled for destroyed once more.

They hadn't just dug up Davy Malcor's jacket. They'd dug up a past that, try as he might to bury it, never stayed that way.

Aloud he said, "I didn't do it." But Monica was too far away to hear him.

CHAPTER 8

Thaddeus

He was sitting at the little desk in his hotel room, trying not to think about his mother's call, her command that he come to Wynotte and wait for news about Davy. He could think of nothing he wanted to do less, and he had a valid excuse for not complying. People were expecting him elsewhere tomorrow, counting on him even. If there was real, actual news in Davy's case—which was doubtful—then he would go home. Of course he would. Because that would make sense.

He used his fingers to drum out a rhythm on the desk's surface and exhaled loudly into the room. He wished he didn't have this dead day in the middle of the tour. It wasn't good for him to be alone with his thoughts. He turned his attention back to *The Pacific* article he'd been sitting in front of for hours, typing nothing more than gibberish he hoped would magically morph into actual prose.

He was staring at the blinking cursor when his phone rang. Thaddeus picked it up and blinked at the number as he processed the identification displayed on the tiny screen. He answered immediately.

"Philly!" A smile filled his face as he said the name. "To what do I owe this honor?"

He heard that unmistakable laugh on the other end. His old buddy Phillip Laney calling him out of the blue. Man, how he'd worshiped the guy when they were kids. Wanted to be him. *And what did that cost you?* the voice inside his head asked. He ignored it, listening to Phillip's laugh instead.

"Oh, I've been meaning to call ever since you became a famous author," Phillip said. "Give you a hard time."

"I'd expect nothing less," Thaddeus said, still smiling.

"But then I had to call when I heard the news," Phillip said, "about Davy."

"Oh," Thaddeus said, the smile instantly gone. Dread crept up the back of his neck, hot and cold at the same time.

He was going to have to go back and face all of this. If even Phillip knew about the discovery, it wasn't just another incidental concern in the long, drawn-out story of the Famous Missing Boy, Davy Malcor. It must, Thaddeus accepted, be real.

"In the news they said they found a jacket. They described it." A weighted pause filled the air. "It was the one he was wearing," Phillip said, his voice strained, "that night."

As unbidden images from that night—Phillip raising his beer can in a sloppy, slurred toast; the back of Davy's head as he walked away; running through the dark field calling Davy's name—raced through his mind, Thaddeus tried to find his voice. Not finding it, he grunted an affirmation and closed his eyes to will the images away.

"I can still picture him. You know, wearing it. He was hanging around, and you said—"

Thaddeus held the phone away from him so he couldn't hear whatever Phillip was saying. He didn't want to rehash that night. Didn't anyone understand? Didn't they grasp the theme of his memoir? He wanted to move on. He had written a "brave exposé of a family proceeding after crisis" (source: *Library Journal*). The key word was *proceeding*.

The point wasn't that the Malcor family lost a child. It was that the family went on with their lives after that child went missing. This message, this hope Thaddeus peddled, was what gained him the bestseller status, the hotel suites with welcome baskets waiting, the women in his bed after his readings. It wasn't because he sat around and cried over his poor lost brother; it was that he'd moved past the tragedy.

But did you really? the voice inside his head asked.

Thaddeus put the phone back to his ear. "You're there right now?" he asked, interrupting Phillip. "In Wynotte?"

"Man, I've been back here for years," Phillip said. "I came back after my uncle died." He laughed. "I guess you and I need to catch up more often."

"I'm sorry," Thaddeus offered. "About your uncle."

Phillip snorted. "Don't be. The guy was a son of a bitch."

"But he got us beer," Thaddeus argued, sounding every bit of fifteen years old again. He'd been so jealous of Phillip back then with his cool uncle as the only authority in his life.

"Getting underage kids beer is not the sign of a stand-up guy," Phillip responded. "Just take my word for it."

"Oh. Man. I guess I should've—"

"Water under the bridge, my friend. Water under the bridge. I've moved on, built a life for myself apart from all that." Phillip chuckled. "I sell insurance now."

Thaddeus's eyes widened at the image of Phillip wearing a suit, sitting behind a desk, pushing a pencil, and schmoozing clients. It was a far cry from how he remembered his old buddy, sporting a cocky smile, a mullet, and the Wayfarer sunglasses he bought because of the Don Henley song.

"Wow. Phillip Laney, insurance guy. Never thought I'd see that day."

"Neither did I, buddy. Neither did I. But I'm married now. Kids. The whole nine. Gotta be responsible. Ya know?"

Thaddeus didn't know. He'd tried and quit several jobs before he committed to writing the memoir and getting it published, managing to avoid marriage, kids, and responsibility along the way.

"Sure," he said.

"So you're headed home." Phillip posed what should've been a question as a foregone conclusion.

His mom, he was realizing, wasn't the only one who expected his return. He'd dismissed her suggestion as an emotional reaction from a woman who wanted company in her misery. If—and that was a big *if* based on the past—this thing proved to be something real? Well, that was a different story. But he wasn't running home just because they found an old jacket.

In his mind Davy sprang to life, defiantly defending that jacket as they faced off in the driveway. Thaddeus blinked the memory away.

"Earth to TJ," Phillip said. Thaddeus flinched at the use of his old nickname. He stared at the computer screen in front of him, at the inanity he'd been typing just before Phillip's call. He put his finger on the Delete button and watched the words disappear one by one.

"Man, I can't," he said. "It's just my schedule right now. I've got some events that would be hard to reschedule. Obligations. You know." (*Yes*, he thought as he said it, *that sounded reasonable. Didn't Phillip just speak of responsibility, of growing up? As a father and a businessman now, surely he understood obligations.*)

He quickly added, "But if things escalate back home, you can bet I'll be on the first plane." (This, too, he thought, sounded good. This was a temporary no, not a hard-and-fast one. He was reasonable.)

"I think you should be on the first flight you can find," Phillip said, shooting down his intentions in one sentence.

Thaddeus gave a defeated sigh. Thirty long seconds of silence passed before he said simply, "I can't."

"You should come home," Phillip said, his voice softer, more coaxing than demanding. "I feel like . . ." He went silent. Thaddeus waited for him to finish the sentence, but he didn't.

"What?" Thaddeus's voice was barely above a whisper.

Phillip exhaled. "I think . . ." He stopped, rephrased. "I feel like your family is gonna need you. Or maybe you're gonna need them. Either way."

Thaddeus started to argue, to offer more excuses and explanations. He could feel himself digging in his emotional heels. And yet, there was something in Phillip's voice, something prescient, even though Phillip was the least intuitive person he knew. Maybe he'd matured. Maybe he, too, had changed in the years since that fateful night.

"Let me see what I can do." Thaddeus exhaled into the phone.

He heard Phillip's relieved smile through the phone. "Text me when you get home. I'll buy you a beer."

"I'm probably gonna need more than one," Thaddeus said, and in spite of himself he smiled too.

"I'm counting on it," Phillip said. And then with a click he was gone.

Thaddeus held the phone for a moment. In his mind a memory reel played—baseball in the yard with Davy. Larkin was there, watching from the picnic table in her yard. Kristy picked dandelions nearby, blowing on them, watching the seeds take flight.

"You can't go home again," he whispered. And yet, it seemed he had to. People would think badly of him if this did turn out to be something big and he wasn't there for it.

Thanks to the book he'd written, people would expect him to show up now more than ever. That damn book. In some ways it had been a dream come true to see his name on the cover, to revel in the praise for his writing, his "courage to tell a tragic tale of navigating unspeakable loss" (source: *Booklist*). But he had underestimated how hard it would be to keep talking about his missing brother, about that night. Writing the book had been an attempt to exorcise his demons. But instead it had riled them.

With a sigh he pressed a few buttons on his BlackBerry and watched as the screen told him it was connecting him to his publicist.

"Hi," Nicole said, answering on the first ring.

"I got your email," he said. First, the apology he owed her for avoiding her calls and emails, then the real reason for his call. "And I'm sorry. For going AWOL."

"It's ok," she said, even though it wasn't. But there wasn't time to get into that just now.

"I'm actually calling about something else, though," he added quickly. "About Davy, about his case."

"Yes," she said, and he felt with that one word her agreement to put the other stuff to the side, at least for now. She had a good heart, an inherent kindness he admired. She was far too good for him. He'd known it even before the night he'd let alcohol loosen his lips, accidentally letting her in. As much as his recent silence had been about his own embarrassment, it was also an effort to save her from him, much the same as he'd tried and succeeded in saving Larkin all those years ago.

His answer came in a rush. "Something's happened. They, um, found evidence. So, um, it looks like I'm going to have to reschedule some of the tour and—"

"Go home," she finished for him.

He'd told her so much that night. Very nearly all of it, his words like toothpaste squeezed from the tube, impossible to stuff back in.

"Yes," he said, his hand resting on his pocket, feeling the lump under the fabric. "So, um, I need a plane ticket, I guess. I guess I have to go home."

CHAPTER 9

Anissa

She positioned herself in a spot in the Malcor family room that allowed her to monitor the situation. One glance to the left and she could keep an eye on the press in the front yard. One glance to the right and she could monitor how Davy's parents were doing. She looked both left and right, taking in the whole scene as she reminded herself to do her job well, remember her training, and not get rattled. *You got this*, she told herself, using positive affirmations like her sister was always going on about.

So far the parents, Daniel and Tabitha Malcor, were the only family gathered. They were cordial to each other, but Anissa could feel the tension between them. She knew they'd divorced, a casualty for many parents of missing children.

As for the press, the local affiliates were the only ones gathered so far, loitering as close to the house as they dared. The larger outlets were no doubt on their way, but for now the situation felt manageable. A few cars had slowed as they drove by, but no creepy lookie-loos, no crazies prophesying about Davy's fate. Not yet. One neighbor had stopped by to deliver brownies and lasagna, the token meal of bereavement if ever there was one.

The smell of the food reminded Anissa she'd forgotten to eat that day. She watched with longing as Tabitha carried the dishes into the kitchen and deposited them on the table. Tabitha looked up to see Anissa watching her.

"This is only the beginning,"Tabitha said, pointing at the foil-covered dishes. "Soon there'll be casseroles on every available surface in this kitchen and stacked in the fridge. More food than we can possibly eat. And I just got rid of the chest freezer last year." She sighed and ran a hand through her short dark hair, shot through with silver threads.

Anissa thought Tabitha, with her hair cut short, looked a lot like Davy. She wondered if that had been Tabitha's intent, to remind people of Davy every time they looked at her. Or, at least, the Davy Anissa remembered. The one in the photos on the evening news tonight, the same old shots recycled for this latest news cycle. She wondered if Davy would look like Tabitha still, now, as a grown man.

Had Davy grown into a man? Anissa did not think it was likely. She wondered if that disqualified her to do her job. Didn't she need to believe in the best outcome for the people she helped? To truly speak on behalf of the family, shouldn't she feel the way they did? She supposed it didn't matter. She was there now. For better or for worse, she was the woman for the job.

The Malcors' doorbell rang and she startled, caught off guard.

Tabitha exited the kitchen and strode toward the front door. "I've got it."

Anissa rose to cut off her pathway to the door. "No, I should get it. If it's a reporter, then—"

Tabitha gave her a bemused, sarcastic half grin, a habit Anissa had noticed.

"Then I'll tell 'em to get the hell off my lawn," she said. "You forget, this ain't my first rodeo." She sidestepped Anissa and reached the door. On the couch her ex-husband made no motion to intervene. Anissa stood by as Tabitha tugged it open.

She was meant to protect the family; she was not supposed to let the victims answer their own door. The confusing part was that Davy's parents didn't act like victims.

The door opened to reveal a reporter, just as Anissa had feared. And not just any reporter. The most annoying, the most tenacious, the slipperiest of the slippery: Monica Allagash. Blonde and calculating, she was a reporter for the Charlotte CBS affiliate gunning hard for an anchor position. She was not conventionally pretty, yet oddly attractive. Her smile was less a smile and more an animal baring its fangs. Monica was, Anissa had long ago decided, as much a predator as the ones she reported on. They'd had a few run-ins in the past, Monica pressing her on camera, making her look ruffled and down-right foolish on the evening news.

Seth used to tease her about it. *"You let her get to you. You can't let her get to you."* Now as Anissa moved to step between Tabitha and Monica, she thought of Seth that morning standing in her shower, water dripping off that Roman nose of his, daring her to get in with him. *I let you get to me too*, she thought. Then she put Seth out of her mind and moved between Tabitha and Monica.

She looked directly into Monica's golden-brown eyes as she spoke. "We are asking members of the press to respect the family's need for privacy as they wait for more information regarding their loved one." She spouted off the party line a bit more tersely than she might have with someone else.

Undeterred, Monica cocked her head and bared her teeth. "Oh, I don't need to speak to the family," she said, giving

Tabitha the side-eye before turning back to face Anissa. "I can speak to you."

Beside her, Anissa felt Tabitha stiffen. In the yard at the base of the entry steps, Monica's cameraman recorded the three of them in the doorway. Self-centered as it was, Anissa's thoughts went to how she looked. She'd dressed in such a hurry, thrown her unruly curls into a messy bun, smeared a streak of color across her lips, and dashed out the door. From the angle he was shooting, she vainly and unprofessionally wondered if she'd have a double chin in the shot.

She lifted her chin, willing her neck to look long and slender as she spoke. "I have no further comments at this time. There'll be a press conference when there's a new development."

Her voice sounded unemotional and robotic, which was the intent. Sometimes her job was so rote and mechanical that she wondered why the position even existed. But someone had to be the gatekeeper. Someone had to speak for those who couldn't or shouldn't be expected to. She reminded herself she was doing exactly what she'd dreamed of—helping Davy's family. She straightened her back and visualized her spine morphing into steel like some sort of superhero, battling evil reporters at every turn.

But instead of backing away, Monica Allagash leaned toward Anissa and Tabitha and smiled conspiratorially.

"Just tell me." Her voice was nearly a whisper, as if the conversation was meant only for the three of them. "Is there a warrant yet to search Gordon Swift's residence?"

Tabitha inhaled at the mention of Gordon Swift's name and Anissa rushed to speak before she could.

"Gordon Swift is not a suspect in the disappearance of Davy Malcor," Anissa parroted yet another oft-repeated line when it came to this case. After Gordon sued the department, they were instructed to make it clear to the press that they would not under any circumstances smear his name any more than it already had been. For her part, and with good reason, Anissa believed in Gordon Swift's innocence, no matter how unpopular that opinion was in Wynotte.

"Ok, he might not be a suspect. But he remains a person of interest, right?" Monica Allagash countered. Her voice took on a fake saccharine tone. "He seemed super flustered about today's discovery when I spoke with him earlier."

In her head, Seth's warning repeated, *"You can't let her get to you."* Working hard not to appear angry or even rattled, Anissa calmly replied, "We have no further comments about the case at this time." Then she looked away from Monica and directly at the cameraman still filming. "Except that we expect the public to keep in mind the difficult time this family is facing, and to give them the privacy and respect they deserve."

"Oh, for sure," Monica said, nodding sympathetically. Then she looked past Anissa, directly at Tabitha. "But when you *are* ready to talk, I hope you'll come to me. I'd like you to consider me a trustworthy repository."

"Suppository?" Tabitha retorted, an unmistakable leer in her voice.

Monica's shiny veneer slipped away. A panicked look replaced the smug confidence as she sputtered, "No, I-I didn't say— I said re-pository. Not sup-pository. A repository is a—"

"I think that's enough, Monica," Anissa said and closed the door in the reporter's face, then turned to find Tabitha bent over laughing.

"Hoo! That was too good," Tabitha said, her body quaking with laughter. "I couldn't resist." She straightened and put her hands on her hips, her brown eyes fixing on Anissa. "I can't stand her. She's been relentless ever since she first came here, convinced herself she's going to break this case somehow, ride it all the way to a network news position." Her smile disappeared and she was all business again. "But my son isn't her career maker."

Anissa nodded her agreement and gave Tabitha a little smile that she hoped conveyed not just her gratefulness to Tabitha for leveling Monica with the perfect put-down, but for the privilege of letting her ride out this wait with them when no one else was granted admission.

One day not long after Davy disappeared, she'd walked to this very house. She'd picked some wildflowers growing along the way, clutching them in one sweaty palm, determined to present them to Davy's mother and tell her about that night. But a police officer had refused to let her in and sent her away. She'd thrown the flowers in a ditch as she walked back home, her head hung low, tears wetting her face and blurring her vision. She couldn't help then, but she could now.

Daniel entered the room carrying a plate heaped with lasagna. "Y'all want some dinner? It's getting about that time."

Tabitha raised her eyebrows at Anissa, an unspoken invitation. Anissa's stomach growled in response, but she forced herself to ignore it.

"Oh, you guys go ahead," she said. "I'm here to work, not eat."

Tabitha shook her head. "If you're in my house, you're eating with us." She waved in the direction of the kitchen. "I'm not kidding when I say there will be more than we can eat." She cocked her head. "I might even send you home with leftovers."

Anissa smiled reflexively. She did not belong there—that was what the policeman who'd shooed her away that day had said. But here was Davy's mother offering her dinner and a seat at the Malcor family table.

"I guess I could eat something," she said.

Tabitha headed toward the kitchen as Daniel asked, "What were y'all laughing at just now?"

"Suppositories," Tabitha said and smiled.

Anissa, in spite of her better judgment, couldn't help but smile too.

Marie's husband, Jim, drives them to the party. Tabby and Danny sit in the back seat holding hands like teenagers. Her thoughts stray to their own teenager, and Tabby wonders if TJ told the truth about his plans for the night. Is he still young enough to want to play night games with friends, or was that a cover for something else? She's heard the other mothers talk about teenage schemes—lying, sneaking out, trying cigarettes, alcohol, drugs.

These are the years they are entering—and will stay in— for quite some time. She'd once thought parenting would get easier when her children were out of diapers, but that doesn't seem true anymore. Though there are moments when Tabitha feels the rewards she thought came with parenting—an unexpected hug, a thank-you she didn't have to ask for, something funny one of the kids says—those moments are fleeting. She finds herself looking forward to a time in the future where the rewards will become more evident. It is a time she can't envision but has to believe is out there, somewhere. Sometimes she feels duped, that having kids is a trick she has fallen for, a trick that must be perpetuated for the human race to survive.

Danny leans in, pressing his lips to her ear as he whispers, "Penny for your thoughts." His warm breath on her ear makes her shiver and she laughs away her worries about TJ. Tonight is a kid-free zone. They agreed before they left the house.

"Just wondering who'll be there. Running through my small talk options," she lies. "I'm out of practice at parties. Not sure I'll know how to behave."

He squeezes her hand. "You're Tabby Malcor. It'll come back to you."

She rolls her eyes. "Lately all I feel like I am is *Mom*."

In the dark car Daniel waggles his eyebrows and leans in again. "Tonight you'll remember you're so much more than that."

She bats her eyes at him. "I take it you're gonna help with that?"

"You bet your sweet ass I am."

Tabby laughs. When Marie asks from the front seat what's so funny, they both answer, "Nothing!" at the same time, which makes them laugh harder. Jim parks in the Myerses' driveway and they all tumble out of the car, the laughter subsiding as they walk inside.

CHAPTER 10

Tabitha

They were in the middle of dinner when the sheriff showed up, his knock at the door more certain and insistent than that of a neighbor or reporter. Their knocks said, *"I don't know if this is ok,"* while his said, *"I'm here because I'm in charge so let me in."* Daniel rose to get the door, and Tabitha watched as Anissa all but dropped her fork onto her plate, a look of guilt and panic replacing what, moments ago, had been a relaxed expression. For a moment they'd just been people gathered around a table. For a moment they'd let themselves forget.

Tabitha had learned to take the moments of peace and happiness where she could find them, even in the midst of crisis. She'd learned to find ways to laugh, even if it sometimes required the darkest of humor. She'd had a lot of practice at coping in the midst of tragedy.

Anissa, however, was uninitiated and Tabitha found herself wanting to protect the girl. Though she was not a girl, Tabitha knew, she was young. She was, Tabitha guessed, around Davy's age. Sometimes it caught her off guard, how old Davy would be now. In her mind he was forever eleven.

The sheriff walked into the room, and a look passed between him and Anissa. The sheriff's eyes asked, *"What the hell is going on here?"* Anissa's eyes replied, *"I'm sorry."*

Tabitha spoke up, running interference. "Would you like some supper, Sheriff? We coerced Anissa here to eat with us. I'd be glad to make you a plate too." She waved at the containers on the counter. "We always end up with more than we can eat when this happens." She also wanted to remind the sheriff that for them this was just another episode in a long-running series. What was to him a high-profile case was their life. And they had to live it as best they could.

"No, thank you," the sheriff said. He stood shifting his weight from one leg to the other, clearly uncomfortable. Anissa ducked her head and stared at her plate. She'd wolfed down the lasagna. All that was left was a tributary of red sauce and a lone string of cheese. She looked like she wanted to crawl under the table. But she had done nothing wrong.

A few beats of silence passed before Tabitha tried again. "Anissa sure has been a big help today. She's kept us informed and tried to make us feel comfortable."

Truth be told, she knew why the sheriff had sent the girl. On the surface it was to protect the family, but it was also an effort to monitor what they said and didn't say to the press. He wanted to control the narrative. Tabitha didn't like the intrusion, didn't want a stranger sitting in her den day after day as they waited for another search to be over, another lead to not pan out. Still, none of that was the girl's fault.

"Good to hear she's doing her job," the sheriff said, though Tabitha could tell he was merely paying lip service. "I've got two guys who'll be doing drive-bys at regular intervals this evening, monitoring things. I suspect there will be more press arriving, but we'll do our best to see that they don't breach the perimeter." He made it sound like they were in the midst of some kind of a siege. Which, she supposed, they were.

He glanced at Anissa, then back at Daniel and Tabitha. "I heard one of 'em already did that today, and for that I apologize."

Anissa looked up as he spoke, her eyes wide. That was what the sheriff was here for, a passive-aggressive redressing.

"I apologize for that too," Anissa's words came out in a rush.

Tabitha laughed it off. "Oh, *that*"—she fixed her eyes on the sheriff—"was my fault. I opened the door even though she"—she pointed at Anissa—"tried to stop me. And don't you worry about that reporter. I know better than anyone that she's trouble."

The sheriff nodded once, then looked at Anissa, all business. "It's gotten too dark, so I called off the search of the property for the night. We'll start again at first light, and we'll be better outfitted tomorrow." He glanced over at Tabitha and Daniel, then back at Anissa. "I think with the drive-bys I've got arranged, it's fine for you to go home and let these people have some privacy."

Anissa sprang to her feet and grabbed her plate. "I'll just rinse this and be on my way." She darted off with the plate before Tabitha could tell her she would clear the table. It would give her something to do besides make stilted conversation with Daniel.

The sheriff followed Anissa into the kitchen. Thinking fast, Tabitha gathered her plate and Daniel's and, though Daniel reached out and attempted to stop her, she dodged his grip and race-walked to get close enough to hear what the sheriff was going to say to Anissa. If he berated her for what happened with that bitchy reporter, Tabitha would intervene.

But first, she stood just out of sight and listened. For once, she was grateful she lived in a house built before the open kitchen concept so she could lurk around the corner and eavesdrop. Though he spoke in low tones, she heard the sheriff say something about Anissa following him to the station.

Tabitha's eyebrows crunched together. Why would he need Anissa to go back to the station if there was no news to report and none expected tonight? Maybe just to debrief about the day, or maybe so he could chastise Anissa more thoroughly for the situation with the reporter. Whatever it was, she hoped they weren't purposefully keeping something from her and Daniel. She took a deep breath and bustled into the kitchen pretending to be oblivious. The sheriff and Anissa stopped talking and took a step away from each other like guilty lovers.

"Just wanted to start cleaning up," she said, her tone apologetic. Yes, she heard herself apologizing to strangers for entering her own kitchen.

"Of course," the sheriff said. "I need to get going anyway. Got things to wrap up at the station before I go home myself."

He bid them goodbye, gave Anissa a solemn look, and left. Following in his wake and avoiding Tabitha's eyes, Anissa scurried to the dining room to gather her things—her phone in one spot, her purse in another, her shoes still under the table where she'd relaxed enough to slip them off as they ate. That done, she returned to the kitchen, where Tabitha and Daniel were wordlessly divvying up the tasks involved with closing down for the night.

"I just wanted to apologize again," she said, looking miserable, the light that had entered her eyes during dinner now extinguished. "I was unprofessional today." She cleared her throat nervously. "It won't happen again." She thought about it. "You guys are just so nice, and I—" she broke off, waved her hand. "It doesn't matter. All that matters is that I will do better tomorrow." She nodded once, agreeing with herself.

Tabitha reached for a towel to dry her hands before she responded. Daniel busied himself with packaging the leftovers and putting them away. He would, she knew, say nothing, leaving the talking to her as he always had. Anger started to rise in her chest, surprising her at how quickly the old feelings could come back, as if no time had passed at all.

That was the crux of the situation their family was in. Time was both fluid and congealed; they were swept away by it and mired in it. *All at the very same time.* She heard Davy's voice in her head and smiled to herself at the memory. But the smile quickly died on her face as it occurred to her that today's news meant they would start playing that video clip of him over and over on the news.

She turned her attention back to Anissa. "You did just fine today. Don't let the sheriff get to you."

Daniel put the last container in the fridge, walked over, and patted Anissa on the shoulder. "We all just have to do our best over the next few days. And somehow we'll get through this." He glanced at Tabitha and she dipped her chin in affirmation and thought, but didn't say, *Just like we always have.*

Later, as she readied for bed, Tabitha stood in front of the mirror. For a moment she imagined Davy there like he used to be, half hidden by the door, thinking she was unaware of him. She looked over her shoulder, even as she scolded herself for doing so. Of course Davy wasn't there. Wasn't that what today had been about?

She turned back to the mirror and bared her teeth, squinting at her front tooth. She ground her teeth at night, her body working out the stress she'd suppressed during the day. At her last appointment her dentist remarked that he was concerned about a miniscule crack in the tooth. He'd chastised her for not wearing the night guard he had prescribed. There was always something, it seemed, that she was neglecting, something she could or should be doing better.

She put on her reading glasses and leaned closer to the mirror, struggling to see the crack, wondering if it was silently growing. The dentist had told her enamel was the hardest substance in the body. And yet it could still crack under pressure.

Behind her she felt a presence, this time a very real one. She pivoted to see who it was, even though she knew. Daniel, who had decided to stay the night in Kristyn's old bedroom, just in case. That was how he'd put it. *In case of what?* she'd thought. Pete Lancaster said they'd suspended the search for the night. But she hadn't had the energy to put up a fight about it. Deep down, she knew he just wanted to be here, in the only place in the world where Davy still, in some ways, lingered. It was why she'd never moved.

"What were you looking at?" Daniel asked.

She bit back the urge to snap, *"None of your business."* Instead, as civilly as possible, she replied. "My tooth. Dr. Birch said there's a crack in it. He wants to watch it."

"Better stay on top of that," he said.

She looked heavenward and sighed deeply. "Thank you for the advice," she deadpanned as she pushed past him from the bathroom into what had been their bedroom but was now solely hers. She had not yet changed into her nightgown and was grateful for that. It was strange enough being fully dressed in this space with him.

"Did you need something?" she asked. He still stood in the bathroom doorway.

"Actually, I was wondering if you had a toothbrush handy. You used to keep extras for the kids' friends when they spent the night. I was hoping maybe you still had some lying around."

Tabitha nodded. "They're in the hall closet." She did not say, *"Where they always were."* Because maybe he had truly forgotten that part. Maybe he'd allowed himself to forget the things she could not. Maybe it was time for her to do the same. She just had to figure out how.

"Thanks," Daniel said and began walking toward the bedroom door. "Oh!" He stopped short at the foot of the bed they once shared. "I totally forgot to tell you that Kristyn called when you were outside talking to Marie."

Tabitha gave him a guilty look. "I was going to wait to call her till we knew more."

He shook his head. "You know it doesn't work that way." Was that a scolding tone in his voice? Probably, but she chose to ignore it.

"I'm sure some helpful old friend was only too kind to call and ask how she was in light of the news." She rolled her eyes even as she internally chastised herself for not calling Kristyn. She should've been the one to tell her about the discovery and not let her hear it from someone else. She would add the oversight to her regret list next Friday. She had a feeling the coming week's list would be a long one. She might need to break her own rule and work on it ahead of time.

"She mainly wanted us to know that she plans to come, but she can't get away for a couple of days. She's got some . . . stuff going on." He waved his hands vaguely. "She told me the whole story, but I kind of—"

"Didn't listen," she finished.

He ignored the dig. "Anyway, she wants to be here. She's working on it."

Now a married mother of two living in California clear across the country, Kristyn had only been four years old when Davy disappeared. Though she claimed to remember him, she didn't really, couldn't possibly. Kristyn remembered the Davy they'd described to her, a child who, in memory, had eclipsed the child he was in reality. For her other two children, Tabitha knew that Davy—the invented one—had been hard to live up to. They struggled with resenting their perfect, absent brother—though they tried not to and probably felt guilty for it. But they never talked about that.

"She didn't seem angry?" Tabitha asked. "That I hadn't called to let her know?"

"No—not at all. It seemed like she was apologizing to us because she wasn't already en route."

"Well, that's silly. I never would've expected her to hop on a plane just because they found his jacket. She's got a lot on her as it is."

With a pang Tabitha thought of her earlier phone call with Thaddeus. She'd demanded his presence, accepted nothing less, heaping guilt on him. Her expectations of Thaddeus and Kristyn were completely different. And not just because of their different lives. She suspected it was because Thaddeus was there that night, while Kristyn had been too little to understand. She still saw them that way: the one who was aware, and the one who wasn't; the one who should be there, and the one who got a pass.

"I wish she wasn't so far away," she said, for lack of something else to say. Daniel nodded his agreement.

"Well, good night."

"Sleep well," she said. She took a step back, leaving him a wide berth to exit the room, then shut the door behind him and, ever so quietly, pushed the little button that locked the door. She laughed at herself for doing so but left the lock engaged all the same.

She changed into her nightgown quickly, then crawled into bed. Upon lying down she could feel her body surrendering to the exhaustion that had been simmering since late afternoon, since that bitchy reporter breached the perimeter. She just needed sleep, the ignorance unconsciousness allowed her. In sleep she could forget what this day had brought and stop thinking about what tomorrow would bring. She had a nagging feeling it wouldn't be good.

Tomorrow, more press would show up. Tomorrow, the images of Davy would play on the news on an endless loop, unavoidable and as painful as ever. They would run the video clip of him at Kristyn's birthday party the weekend before he disappeared, juggling for the little kids. She would have to see him on TV, forever eleven years old, saying, *"Mom, did you see? I juggled four balls! I kept them all up! All at the very same time!"*

The media loved that clip, not caring how it tore at her heart to be faced with Davy, to see him alive and as animated as ever, to hear that little voice call her Mom just one more time.

FROM *EVERY MOMENT SINCE: A MEMOIR* BY THADDEUS MALCOR

PUBLISHED SEPTEMBER 20, 2005

The last time I ever saw my brother was when we left to go play night games. He was wearing his *Back to the Future* jacket our mother had made for him, and—to be honest—I was mad about it. I thought the jacket was stupid and got tired of seeing him wearing it day in and day out. Plus, it wasn't cold enough for a jacket. I fussed at him but he wouldn't relent and leave it behind. So we set off on our bikes, the girl next door standing on our porch with our sister, watching us go. I'd been so focused on that jacket that I forgot to tell her goodbye.

We rode our bikes down the driveway and through our neighborhood, until the street took us to the main road. I was faster than Davy, but I could hear the whir of his pedals just behind me. He was humming the *Back to the Future* theme song, "The Power of Love." To this day if that song comes on the radio, I quickly change the station. I can't bear to hear it because it takes me back to that moment.

It was under a mile from our neighborhood to the field, so we made it there quickly. The sun was beginning its slide from the sky as we arrived. We parked our bikes where other kids had left theirs at the seam where the road met the field. We hadn't said anything directly to each other since we left the house, so I felt I should say something before we separated. Something an older brother would say. So I said, "Be careful tonight." And Davy, still mad at me, grumbled an "Ok" before scampering off to find his friends.

I am ashamed to admit it now, but I didn't watch him go. I quickly turned to find my own friends, eager for fun, for an adventure. It was just an ordinary moment in time: two brothers riding their bikes to meet their friends to play games in the dark. On any given night we could've gone to that field, then come right back home again, dirty, tired, and happy. But that's not what happened that night.

And I've lived with it every moment since.

CHAPTER 11

Gordon

He stopped at the Chinese restaurant on the way home, partly because he did not feel like cooking anything after his run-in with the reporter and partly because at the Chinese restaurant he never got the sensation. The workers there didn't care who he was, interacting with him the same as they interacted with anyone else. They didn't stare at him just a little too long, and though he didn't understand Chinese, when they spoke to each other it didn't seem that he was the subject matter.

He tended to frequent the Chinese place whenever a new story about Davy Malcor surfaced, opting to go there rather than the grocery store or other restaurants, keeping a low profile until things died down again. For that reason Chinese food always made him think of Davy, of that night. Of mistakes that were made. To him Chinese food tasted like regret.

Once home, he poured a rum and Coke and fired up his computer. While he waited for it to connect with the internet, he plated his food and sat down with his feast. He'd treated himself to an egg roll, splurged on the fried rice instead of the white rice they automatically included, anything to make himself feel better, to think about something other than the accusing look of that reporter in the parking lot. Unbidden, unexpected, it was all happening again and he would have to ride it out this time just like all the others.

After he'd eaten, he picked up the phone and dialed a number he hadn't had cause to use in a long time yet kept on speed dial. Harvey didn't answer with a hello. Instead he said, "I'm already on it."

"I was teaching this afternoon. Didn't see the news, didn't know until I left the school. I got to my car and that Allagash woman was waiting for me wanting a statement."

"I hope you told her to go pound sand," Harvey said. This was a favorite phrase of Harvey's, though Gordon didn't totally understand what it meant. As a sculptor, he sort of did pound sand, shaping and molding and, yes, even pounding, until the medium yielded to his vision, until it stopped being clay or cement or metal and became what it was meant to be all along.

"I did," he said.

"Good. Not that you need reminding, but no speaking to the press. I've already sent a friendly reminder to the sheriff, told him I'm ready to take action the first time I don't feel good about how you're being portrayed. He said he's going to talk to the Public Information Officer, remind her about the rules. I can't restrict the press, but I can sure as hell scare the police into running interference with them as much as possible. With any luck we'll keep 'em at bay and it'll die down quickly. If they don't find anything else in that field, then that jacket'll join the other evidence they've got and that'll be the end of it."

"That would be nice," Gordon said. "Maybe I could keep my job."

Harvey scoffed. "I don't know why you took that teaching gig in the first place. It's not like you need the money, buddy."

"They asked," he said, remembering how touched he'd been to be wanted, to be trusted. "And now I just hate to desert the students. I'm actually helping some of them." He shrugged, though Harvey couldn't see it. "At least it feels like I am."

"Well, if they tried to let you go over this, I'd be the first to remind them it'd be foolish to let go of a popular, qualified teacher who has never been charged with any crime, much less convicted."

Gordon couldn't help but smile at Harvey's bravado. Talking to his lawyer always made him feel better, even if it cost him roughly five dollars a minute to receive his particular brand of comfort. He should have hired a lawyer the moment they questioned him back in 1985. He might've saved himself from some of what he still dealt with.

"I'll let you know if it comes to that," Gordon said.

"Ok." Gordon heard the sound of Harvey taking a drag from his ever-present cigar. He could almost smell the pungent aroma that hung around Harvey like a fog.

"Hang in there, buddy," Harvey said. "I'm gonna go see what Eileen made us for supper."

"Hope it's something good," Gordon said, for lack of anything else to say.

"One can always dream," Harvey said and then was gone.

Gordon turned to hang up the phone and thought he saw movement in his backyard. He moved closer to the window, squinting in the direction of the outbuilding he used as his studio in the far-right corner of his property. He blinked and wondered if he could trust his own eyes. It was probably just his imagination, his senses on high alert over the news, the paranoia showing up right on schedule.

Over the years he'd been yelled at in public, verbally threatened with bodily harm, and, once, punched in the stomach by a woman who claimed he'd looked at her kid funny. Anything, he'd come to understand, was possible.

He watched as a figure in the gathering dusk walked the perimeter of the studio, then walked around it a second time. Gordon's pulse raced as whoever it was came to a stop in front of the studio door, then reached out to tug on it. Luckily Gordon had locked it this time, though he often forgot.

Undeterred, the person tugged on the door again. Gordon reached for the phone, keeping his eyes on the figure. He wondered if it would serve him better to call 911 directly or to call Harvey and let him call 911 for him. Based on past experience, the Wynotte police didn't really count Gordon as someone worth protecting or defending.

Before he could decide, the figure looked toward the house and Gordon saw that it wasn't a short adult. It was just a boy. He laughed at himself, getting all worked up over a kid. This case sure did set him on edge. Emboldened and a little embarrassed about his fear, he strode to the back door and opened it, calling out, "Hey, get away from there."

The kid stood frozen in place, blinking at him from behind glasses too large for his face. In spite of the nip in the early spring air, he wore shorts that revealed scabbed knees, and his hair looked like it was overdue for a cut by several weeks.

"I-I," the kid stammered, "I was just exploring."

Gordon took a step toward the boy yet maintained a distance. He knew better than to approach a child.

"Yeah, well, this is private property. You're not allowed to explore here."

The kid took a step toward Gordon. If he'd been in this situation as a child, he would've already turned tail and run. But this kid seemed unfazed. He pointed at the studio behind him.

"What's that place?"

Gordon frowned, recalling another kid, another time. He wanted to tell the kid it was none of his business and to scram, but better to be cordial and exit the situation gracefully. Somewhere, this kid had parents. Parents who could stir things up with the slightest provocation, which was the last thing Gordon needed, especially on the heels of today's news.

"It's my studio."

"What's a studio?" the kid asked.

"It's a place where I make things."

"What kind of things?" the kid pressed.

Gordon sighed. Inside his stomach, he could feel the rice he'd eaten expanding. "Art things."

The kid's eyes widened almost comically. "You're an artist?"

The way he said it, he might as well have asked if Gordon was an astronaut or a race car driver or something equally amazing to kids. He couldn't help but feel a bit of pride as he answered, "Yes."

"Wow!" the kid said. "I'm an artist too. My mom says I'm really good."

Gordon gave him a small smile. "I'm sure you are."

"Can I see your . . ." the kid looked down at the ground, then back up. "What's it called again?"

"Studio," Gordon said.

The kid nodded like Gordon had gotten the right answer. "Yeah, studio," he agreed. "Can I see inside your studio sometime?"

Gordon was not one to shoot down the dreams of youth, but he also wasn't about to let a male child of a certain age inside his private residence.

"Well, now's not a good time." He pointed at his house. "I was about to eat dinner." A small lie, but a good excuse to end the conversation.

"Oh," the kid said, looking dejected. "Ok." His glasses slid down his nose and he pushed them back up. "Maybe some other time?"

"Yeah," Gordon said. "Maybe." Even as he spoke he was thinking, *Not in this lifetime.*

"Ok, great!" the boy said. He pointed at the wooded land that separated Gordon's house from the house next door. He'd bought the place because of the privacy it afforded him, the chance to live away from prying eyes.

"I live next door, just through those woods. My mom and I moved in last week."

Gordon nodded, even as a sinking feeling filled him. He'd seen the moving truck but had never considered a child's things might be inside it. The kid pointed at himself.

"My name's Stuart. Like Stuart Little, except I hate when people say that. What's yours?"

"Gordon," Gordon said. Then an idea came to him, a surefire way to make sure the kid never came around again. "Gordon Swift," he said, accentuating his last name. "Go home and tell your mom you met me, ok? Tell her you met your new next-door neighbor, Gordon Swift, the artist. Make sure you tell her my whole name."

"Ok!" Stuart said. "I'll tell her you have a studio in your backyard!" He waved furiously before taking off toward the woods.

"And what's my name?" Gordon called after him.

"Gordon Swift! I'll remember!" Stuart hollered just before he disappeared into the woods.

"I'm counting on it," Gordon said to himself. He returned inside and began gathering the detritus from his dinner. He almost threw away the takeout bag but remembered to retrieve his fortune cookie.

When he was that kid's age, he'd thought fortunes were fated, godlike in their ability to dictate a person's life. He'd been ceremonial in selecting just the right cookie, the one bearing the fortune meant just for him. His parents teased him about it, his father reading his fortune aloud in his deepest announcer voice as his mother giggled. He liked thinking about those times, not just because it was nice to recall happier times, but also because he liked remembering that version of himself, the one who believed a simple piece of paper could affect his destiny.

He opened the plastic and broke the cookie, fishing out the slip of white paper tucked inside. He held the paper under the overhead light in his kitchen and read, *An acquaintance of the past will affect you in the near future.* He groaned aloud, reminded of Monica Allagash and her efforts to smear him at every opportunity. With the discovery of Davy Malcor's jacket, there was no doubt more people from his past would resurface, would affect him in the near future. As in, tomorrow.

He tossed the slip of paper into the takeout bag, then crushed the whole thing with both hands before burying it deep in the bin, so far down he couldn't see it anymore.

October 12, 1985
6:30 p.m.

As soon as he reaches the field, TJ ditches his bike and, without waiting for his brother, takes off toward the woods that border the farm, veering away from the kids who've gathered, already forming teams and calling out the games they want to play—Mother may I and red rover, king of the hill and freeze tag.

Davy stops his bike and watches his brother run away from him without so much as a backward glance. He is uncertain what to do now. He thought they were both going to play the games—together. But that was stupid. Sometimes he forgets that TJ is different now. They might still be brothers, but they don't know each other anymore.

Above him, the sky changes from blue to navy as darkness overtakes the light. Soon, Davy knows, the navy will change to black. Once that happens, the kids will turn to shadows without faces; it will be hard to know who is who. In spite of his jacket, Davy shivers a little and goes in search of TJ to see if he thought to bring a flashlight.

Davy wishes he hadn't come. He wishes TJ had never brought up this stupid idea. He wishes his parents hadn't gone to the party. He wants to be back at home as a family, the way it used to be.

As he walks, his shoe kicks up something sticking out of the dirt and he stops to see what it is. In the waning light, he sees a round object on the ground. For a moment he thinks he sees a glimmer of something. It might be gold. His heart speeds up at the hope of it. There's not enough light to be sure, but he thinks he may have just found a piece of fool's gold.

A long time ago, he and TJ used to hunt for the stuff, believing it was real gold that would make them rich. They would scheme about what to buy with their wealth: their own amusement park, a trip around the world, a Ferrari like the one in *Magnum, P.I.* Davy doesn't believe in that stuff anymore. He knows fool's gold is just fool's gold.

Still, he bends over and picks up the rock, rubbing it against his jeans to clean off the bits of dirt clinging to it, and continues his search for TJ. He will ask TJ for a flashlight so he can see if what he's found really is fool's gold. Maybe, he thinks, TJ will help him. Maybe for a minute they will be the brothers they once were. The thought propels his steps.

He finds TJ with a group of boys his age behind a copse of trees just a few steps into the woods that border the field, tucked away from where the younger kids are beginning the games. TJ and his friends are all hunkered over a garbage bag, peering into it. Davy can't tell what they're looking at, but as soon as one of them spots him, he calls out, "Hey, kid, you're not supposed to be over here!"

The group of boys freezes, all heads turning in his direction like they share one neck. Spotting him, TJ jumps up.

"Davy, get out of here!" He turns to the boy next to him, who, Davy sees, is TJ's best friend, Phillip. "Fucking pest," TJ says to Phillip, who laughs.

Davy decides to ignore Phillip, who is sort of a pest himself. He holds up the rock like a ticket that will gain him admission.

"Do you have a flashlight?" he asks no one in particular. He waves the rock a little. "I want to see if this is fool's gold." He tries to catch TJ's eye, to see if he remembers. But TJ avoids the attempt, focusing instead on his friends and the black, lumpy trash bag on the ground.

Another boy, taller and stronger, grabs the bag, closing it with his fist as he eyes Davy.

"You should go play with your little friends now," he says.

Davy feels the multiple pairs of eyes boring into him. He takes a step backward, knowing he should leave, yet desperately wishing TJ would defend him. He glances over his shoulder, back in the direction of where the kids are playing.

He says one word—"But"—then quickly closes his mouth, understanding it is useless. TJ is here to do something he isn't supposed to do, something he doesn't want Davy to see. This is why he wanted to come so badly, why he hadn't wanted Davy to come too, why he was so angry at Davy before they left, yelling at him about the jacket.

Davy looks down at the jacket, at the pattern on the cuffs. It's not the exact same as Marty McFly's but it's close enough. It is the best present he's ever gotten. Just the sight of it makes him feel better, makes him think about how clever and brave Marty is, gives him hope that tonight maybe he can be brave and clever too. Just like Marty.

He clenches the rock in his palm, feels a sharp edge pressing back. Tears blur his eyes and he blinks them away. He will not let TJ see him get upset.

Instead he hurls the rock toward the cluster of TJ and his friends, feeling his anger soar along with it, a brief, furious flight. The rock lands with a thud in front of TJ, and for a moment, the two brothers look at each other but say nothing.

"Scram, McFly," one of the boys says, and they all laugh as Davy turns and walks away, the laughter fading a little more with each step he takes away from them.

CHAPTER 12

Anissa

She shifted her Ford Escape into Park and cut the engine. It was 7:00 p.m. yet still light outside, a fact that filled her with childish joy. Daylight saving time was a welcome reprieve after the short days of winter, though she found it hard to accept the extra daylight for weeks after it arrived, not quite trusting that the darkness wouldn't return somehow.

She sat in the car for a moment, eyeing the squat, beige building that housed the Wynotte, North Carolina, police department. The structure had the same facade as the addition they built on the elementary school back in the '80s, as if the town had gotten some sort of bulk deal on building supplies. The city had grown as people relocated from Ohio, Pennsylvania, New Jersey, and the like. People "not from around here," seeking better weather, new opportunities, and the chance to leave behind the places they came from.

Anissa's mother had been one of those people. Hearing about a job in Wynotte from a friend who'd heard about it from her sister who had a cousin, etcetera, etcetera, she'd packed them up and left Bloomington, Illinois, a town Anissa barely remembered and had never returned to. Her mother had spoken of the South as if it were a mecca, a promised land. She was in

Florida now. She'd continued her Southern pilgrimage after several years in Wynotte, never quite reaching the destination she seemed to be searching for, merely stopping when she got as far south as she could go without leaving the country.

Anissa breathed in and out, exhaling the memories of her childhood, inhaling the fortitude she needed to go inside and face Pete. She knew he'd not yet said his piece about her gaffe with the reporter at the Malcor house. He'd say more when Davy's parents weren't standing there watching. She thought of Davy's mom, Tabitha, as she insisted on being called, defending her. It had been a sweet effort, but Anissa needed to promise the sheriff personally that she'd do better next time. Hopefully that would be enough. She'd done her job well in the past, even garnered a few commendations along the way, but never with a case of this magnitude.

She got out of the car. Though it was officially spring, winter lurked in the cold edges of the evening breeze licking at her heels as she trudged toward the door. *"You think this is cold?"* her mother used to exclaim. *"You don't know cold. Where we came from—that was cold!"* But Anissa could only know what she knew.

She scurried inside, waved at Jane, the receptionist, and headed straight for the sheriff's office, rounding the corner to find him in a tête-à-tête with none other than Monica Allagash right there in the hallway. They stood close, their heads inclined toward each other.

Pete Lancaster towered over the reporter's tiny frame; she had to crane her neck to meet his gaze. They hadn't noticed Anissa approaching, which gave her time to gauge whether Pete was chastising Monica or allowing her an interview. The thought of Monica and Pete in some sort of alliance was unacceptable.

Anissa stopped short of where they stood, waiting from a respectful distance. She heard Pete say, "Never again."

She hedged over what to do next and decided to wait for him to notice her. He'd told her to come; it wasn't her fault he was wrapped up in a private conversation with the world's most annoying reporter when she arrived.

Pete stepped away from Monica and waved Anissa over. Monica blushed and Anissa wondered what was going on.

Pete gestured at Monica. "Monica here isn't going to breach the perimeter of the Malcor home again. Right, Ms. Allagash?" he asked, his voice firm.

"Never again," Monica said, but her voice had a teasing quality to it.

"We've also discussed the situation with Gordon Swift." Pete pointed at Anissa. "Which is what I need to talk to you about."

He turned back to Monica and his voice sounded even sterner. "Mind your manners." He reached up and adjusted the police-issue ball cap he usually wore. Monica, for her part, gave him a little mock salute and strode off without even looking at Anissa.

When she was out of earshot, Anissa said, "I really can't stand her."

Pete waved his hand. "Eh, she's just doing her job." He gave Anissa the same look he'd just given Monica. "We've all got a job to do here. And if we do it *right*, we can hopefully keep this thing from going off the rails." He raised his eyebrows. "Capisce?"

Anissa nodded as she relaxed. Pete wasn't angry at her. He was just stressed, which was expected.

He clapped his hands together, his way of initiating a subject change. "So." He widened his eyes. "Gordon Swift."

She nodded again. She knew about Gordon Swift, of course, both from that night and all that came after. There'd been no more night games in the fields by his house after Davy's disappearance. As a kid, she'd heard the tales of the man who captured and cooked little children, how the sculptures he made contained the bones of those children. But the kids who told those tales hadn't seen what she had that night.

"Got a friendly reminder from Swift's attorney a bit ago. With the case back in the news, we aren't to entertain any on-camera mentions of him. He's not a suspect and should not be portrayed as such." Pete sounded like he was reciting a script. Which he probably was.

"But he is still a person of interest, right?" she ventured.

The sheriff narrowed his eyes. "*Everyone* is a person of interest until this case is solved." He lifted his index finger in the air as if he was testing which way the wind was blowing. "But I don't want to hear the words 'person of interest' anywhere near his name." He gave her a hard look. "Got it?"

She nodded, hoping she looked appropriately penitent.

Pete softened. "Look, I've got to tread lightly here. This guy's gunning for us. He blames us for his life being ruined. Blames us for his parents' bad health. Says we made him out to be a homicidal homosexual pedophile." He allowed himself a small smile. "I guess it really hurt him with the ladies."

Anissa forced herself to smile along with him, even though she did not find his joke funny. Gordon was a good-looking guy and a talented artist, yet he'd never married, never seemed to move on from that night. In her own way, Anissa understood him.

"But that's why I wanted you to come by," Pete continued. "I think you should pay him a visit, try to create a dialogue with him, make sure he feels respected. I've gotta keep him calm and happy." He sighed. "The mayor will have my ass if he sues again. The town can't afford it. Literally."

Anissa wanted to ask him the amount Gordon had settled for but knew Pete wouldn't divulge that. Not that it mattered. The settlement might've stopped the police from publicly speculating about his involvement, but it didn't stop citizens from talking among themselves. No amount of doing her job could stop that either. And she knew for a fact that Monica Allagash believed him guilty and was ruthless about "pursuing justice," her term for all but stalking the guy.

"So you'll pay him a visit tomorrow?" Pete asked. His look told her the question was actually a command.

"Sure," she said, though her heart beat harder at the thought of actually talking to Gordon Swift.

"I'll get his address for you," Pete said and turned as if to walk away.

"I already know where he lives." Then she quickly added, "I mean, everyone does."

Pete turned back around and shook his head at her, his eyes closed.

She held up her hands. "Everyone believes he's the town monster," she explained and lowered her hands. "People want to know where the monsters live. So they can avoid them."

Pete shook his head again, this time adding an eye roll. "And that's why we've got our work cut out for us."

In the parking lot as she was going back to her car, she spotted Seth getting out of his cruiser to talk to a fellow officer, yukking it up with his buddy at the end of his shift. She stood in the shadows and watched longer than she should have. She wasn't watching him because he was doing anything especially interesting. It was less about watching than about waiting for him to notice her there, to feel her eyes on him and turn toward the sensation of her nearness like he once would have. But he never did.

She rolled her eyes at herself, turned, and got into her car. She drove away, the lasagna from her dinner with the Malcors sitting heavily in her stomach. She reached for the radio dial to find a song to distract her from thoughts of Seth, of Pete's lecture, of the surreal experience of having spent the day inside Davy Malcor's house with Davy Malcor's parents. Before she could settle on a song, her phone rang, and though she knew she shouldn't answer it while driving, she did.

"Ok," her sister said, skipping any sort of greeting and diving right in. "I know you're probably going to say you can't talk about the case, but I'm dying to know what's going on. Were you with the family today?"

The eagerness in Marissa's voice stirred a protective feeling in Anissa. Her sister didn't have a right to know what happened inside the Malcor home, but like many others, she thought she did. Anissa felt a sense of pride that she was a gatekeeper for the family, keeping nosy Nellies like her sister away from Davy's family.

"Yes, I was there today. But you are correct, I can't discuss what's going on," she said, her voice curt. She wished she hadn't answered the phone. "Is there any other reason you called?"

"Hey now," Marissa protested. "I get that this is your job, but don't forget, I'm not just anyone. And I know more about this case than your average joe. You weren't the only one there that night."

Anissa sighed loudly into the phone. "Marissa, you were only there at the very end."

"Yeah, but I'm the one who called 911. Don't forget that."

"How could I? You only bring it up every chance you get."

Marissa harrumphed. "What happened to you, Anissa? You used to be fun. You used to be adventurous. You had gumption."

Anissa rounded the curve and watched as her condominium complex came into view, thinking about what her sense of adventure, her gumption had led to. Better to play by the rules, she'd decided long ago. Better to plant both feet on the side of caution.

"Anissa?" Marissa asked. "You better not have hung up on me."

Anissa arrived at her condo, parked in her designated spot, and turned off the engine. "I'm still here," she said. "I just don't know what to say in response. I can't help how I am."

Marissa was quiet, thinking of her own response. When she spoke again, her voice was softer and a little sad.

"You let it change you too much."

"Maybe I did." Anissa sighed. "I don't know how I could've avoided being changed by it."

"Well, sometimes I miss the girl you were before."

"Sometimes I do too," Anissa agreed instead of arguing further. She said goodbye and put her phone back in her purse, taking a moment before she got out of the car. Her sister was right, but she was also wrong. She had changed that night, but not as much as Marissa thought. Deep down she was still, in so many ways, the same little girl who once ran through a field looking for a boy named Davy in the dark.

She got out of the car and headed up the sidewalk, spotting movement in the bushes as she approached her door. She felt the faintest flicker of fear, but quickly realized it was not a wild animal or an attacker hiding in the bushes. It was the stray Siamese cat.

Anissa spied two blue eyes peeking out from the darkness and stooped down, her purse thudding on the cement. She and the cat studied each other for a fraction of a second.

"Hi," she whispered. "Are you—" Before she could say "hungry," the cat darted away, running off into the night, away from someone who only wanted to help.

FROM *EVERY MOMENT SINCE: A MEMOIR*
BY THADDEUS MALCOR

PUBLISHED SEPTEMBER 20, 2005

There were no Amber Alerts in 1985. In some places you still had to wait twenty-four hours to report a child missing. Then they were treated the same as adult cases. Most police departments had no special training for cases of missing children; they were usually dismissed as lost or a runaway who would turn up given time.

In Davy's case no ransom was demanded after he disappeared, and though local businesses took up a collection and offered a sizable reward, no credible leads surfaced, no answers to the questions we walked around with day and night. After public interest waned and normal life (for everyone else) resumed, my parents did what they could to raise awareness about Davy's case, to ensure people wouldn't forget him.

Some boys remember playing golf, or hunting, or fishing with their dad. Some remember accompanying their father to his alma mater for Saturday college football games, decked out in the school colors, learning the fight song. Some boys recall shooting hoops in the driveway as father-son bonding moments. For me, the special times I remember with my dad revolved around looking for my brother, traipsing in lockstep through woods and farmlands, faithfully replenishing the "Missing" posters that hung around Wynotte and neighboring towns.

There was a poster of Davy on a light pole by the entrance to my school. It remained there all through my high school years, my brother's eyes watching me as I entered and exited. I tried not to look at it as I passed each day, but I knew it was there. I could feel Davy watching me have the life he was denied, growing taller and leaner while he stayed the same, at least in our minds. All I knew was that the poster faded a little more every year. By the time I graduated, his face had mostly disappeared.

I began noticing that shopkeepers would avoid eye contact when we came in carrying our printed sheets bearing Davy's photo. One finally told me that, in all honesty, Davy's "Missing" poster turned people off, made them forget all about spending money in his establishment. The missing kid was bad for business, bad for morale. Wynotte used to be a happy little town, idyllic and insular. Davy had disturbed all that, disrupted the peace the townspeople had taken for granted.

But my father didn't understand that. I don't think it registered with him for a long time—much longer than it took my mother—that people no longer thought Davy could be found. They'd given up. And so, whenever he looked at me and said, "I'm going searching; do you want to come?" I would always say yes because I couldn't bear for him to go it alone, to believe by himself. We would put on cool clothes in the summer and warm clothes in the winter, and out we would go: looking and looking and looking with dogged determination.

On the best days, we would stop afterward and get a McDonald's hot fudge sundae. Dad liked his with nuts; I liked mine plain. We would sit in the car and eat our sundaes and he would say, "Don't tell Mom. She'll say I spoiled your dinner." And I would promise not to tell. And he would say, "One of these days, we're going to find your brother."

And I would promise him that, too, even though I knew one of those promises was impossible to keep.

PART 2

Saturday, April 29, 2006

CHAPTER 13

Thaddeus

The car Nicole had arranged to take him to the airport pulled up to the hotel curb on time. Thaddeus pocketed his phone in response and felt an empty space there. He looked up, his eyes locking on the driver, who'd emerged from the car's interior just as panic took over.

"C-can you wait just a m-minute?" he stammered at the man, who stopped midstride. "I-I forgot something."

To his credit, the man did not grimace or even looked surprised as he nodded. Thaddeus turned to sprint back into the hotel, his heart hammering in spite of his attempts to calm his anxious thoughts. At the front desk he managed to convey that he needed another key to his room, that he'd forgotten something important. Key card in hand, he went to the elevator landing, pressed the button to summon one, then stood waiting.

It'll be where you left it, he consoled himself as the panel showed the cab's descent, each floor number lighting in a slow, methodical pattern. *It'll be there; it'll be ok.*

When the door dinged open, he rushed inside and smashed his thumb into the button to close it again, then drummed his thumb against his thigh as the elevator ascended to the fourteenth floor. Before the door was fully open, he squeezed through and ran to the room, fumbling with the key card as he tried, failed, then tried again to let himself into the room where he'd spent the past two nights.

He charged over to the dresser, but the surface was clear. His panic surged as his eyes swept the room until he found it, there, on the desk where he'd left it.

He exhaled and strode over to pick it up. He held it for a brief moment before putting it back into his pocket, where it belonged. Because he never knew, did he? When he'd need it again. When he'd keep the promise he'd made that night.

Mission accomplished, he turned to leave, then looked back at the room one more time, thinking of the woman he'd bedded there. Instead of recalling the scene with a kind of triumph, he felt a wash of pity overcome him. But this pity wasn't for her; it was for himself. He felt like a joke.

Shoulders slumped, his pocket heavier, he left the room.

Outside, he saw that the driver had stowed the luggage he'd left on the curb, leaving him nothing to do but get in the car. As the car pulled away, Thaddeus rested his head on the cool glass window and looked out at the still-dark morning, watching the lights of St. Louis slip away.

His heart rate returned to normal as he patted his pocket and closed his eyes. Before he knew it, the car was pulling up to the departures gate. The ride was over.

It seemed just as fast that the captain's voice came over the loudspeaker on the plane, alerting the passengers that they were landing in Charlotte, North Carolina, and the temperature was fifty-four degrees with an expected high of seventy-one today. He wouldn't need the sweater he had needed in St. Louis. He followed his fellow passengers' lead and pulled his phone from his pocket, switched it on, and waited for it to load whatever messages he had missed during the two hours he was in the air.

For a panicky moment, he wondered if they'd found his brother while he'd been above the clouds, if his parents were already mourning news he had yet to hear.

He exhaled in relief when the phone showed only one missed text, from Nicole. She'd written simply:

Hope your flight was good.
Please don't worry about anything while you're with your family.
I'll field everything from here for however long you need.

He pocketed his phone with a smile. The text was kind of her. She *was* kind. Which was what had gotten him in trouble the night she attended one of his readings. The night she was the woman waiting for him at the end. And though he had a crush on her, he knew better than to think the evening would proceed the way his others had. Nicole was a professional. Nicole was also not someone he could put in a taxi and send on her way the next morning.

So he'd done something much worse than sleep with her.

They'd gone to dinner, they'd had some wine, and she'd started asking him questions. The more they drank, the more she probed. Not out of nosiness, just out of interest. Warmed by her gaze, emboldened by her concern, he'd let himself go. He'd said too much, told her things he'd never told anyone. Embarrassing things. Vulnerable things. He'd told her things he'd left out of the memoir, unsafe things he usually kept under lock and key.

The next morning, though he'd woken up alone, he'd still stumbled to the toilet and vomited as if he'd drunk too much. The truth was worse. He'd said too much. He could get over a hangover. He couldn't get over exposure.

He waited for his baggage, then walked out of the arrivals doors to look for his father's car, a Toyota Camry that had once been new with all the bells and whistles of its time, but was now old and outdated. And yet it kept going.

Thaddeus scanned the line of cars and sniffed the air, wondering if it would smell like home. But it smelled only of car exhaust and jet fuel. He spotted the familiar dark green vehicle moving toward him and stepped closer to the curb, lifting his hand in a little wave, letting his father know he was there.

Beyond a few cursory pleasantries, both Thaddeus and his father were quiet on the drive home. It seemed as though both knew small talk was too small for the occasion, but anything else was too big for the confines of the Camry. So neither spoke, each lost in his own private thoughts. Thaddeus wondered what his father was thinking but did not ask.

As the miles went by, Thaddeus watched the place he used to call home swim into view. He noted signs of growth and development: new neighborhoods and shopping centers, a much larger fire station to replace the little one that used to be sufficient for the town of Wynotte, another elementary school to educate the spate of children born to the town's ever-growing population.

When his family came to Wynotte, it had been considered rural, but it wasn't anymore. His mother had demanded that he come home, but it was impossible to truly return to the place he'd left. It kept changing and growing, becoming less recognizable and thus unfamiliar. Like seeing someone who once mattered to you but who, thanks to time and distance, had become a stranger.

He turned his gaze from the passenger window and focused on the windshield in front of him. A fly buzzed and bounced along the glass, frenetic in its efforts to find an exit. Thaddeus wondered where they'd picked up the little stowaway. Had it flown in with him as he got into the car? He wondered if it mattered to the fly where it ended up, if home was even a concept in the insect world. When they opened the doors and the fly found its freedom, would it emerge confused, or just carry on?

Thaddeus concentrated on the fly as they passed the entrance to his neighborhood, as they made their way along the familiar street that led home. When his father parked the car and opened his door, Thaddeus watched as the fly saw the opening and flew out of the car, disappearing into the sky. Then he got out of the car himself.

His mother's eyes filled when he walked in, but she managed to keep the tears at bay. Instead, she gave him a quick hug and asked if he was hungry, then began whisking eggs without waiting for his answer. She pointed at a bowl of cut fruit and a basket of muffins already sitting on the counter.

"Mrs. Shea," she explained. So the food brigade had begun right on schedule.

His stomach rumbled in response, and he realized he was actually hungry. He and his father stood and watched his mother make the eggs until she shooed them to the table. They took their seats, the same ones they'd always occupied, as though nothing had changed, their seats assigned for all time, Davy's chair forever empty.

Thaddeus stole a glance at it, pictured Davy sitting there, that face etched forever in his mind, those wide brown eyes—their mother's eyes—looking at him expectantly. Davy, right there in front of him, wearing that jacket that had just been found. If Davy had not gone missing, would he still be called Davy, or would he, like Thaddeus, have changed his name to something that sounded more grown-up? Would a guy who called himself David be sitting across from him right now, regaling the family with stories of his exciting globe-trotting career or showing off photos of his gorgeous wife and kids? Or would he be just an average Dave with the same kind of humdrum life most people had? There was no way to know who Davy might have been.

Thaddeus blinked Davy away, then scooped out eggs from the bowl his mother placed on the table, steam dancing up from the dish. His mother had made too much, just like she always did. The bowl appeared to be new. But everything else was the same as it always was, the family home preserved like a time capsule meant to be broken open the moment Davy walked back through the door.

His mother broke the silence on his second bite. "So," she said. "The girl called while you two were on your way here and said she'd be a little late getting here today. She had some business to attend to first thing this morning."

"What girl?" he asked, feeling a little zing of alarm at the thought of some strange girl coming around.

"The Public Information Officer," his mother said. "We've never had one before. I guess it's a new thing." She took a bite of eggs and chewed thoughtfully before swallowing and continuing. "She's here to keep the press at bay, keep us informed of news about the search, and any other kinds of help we might need from law enforcement."

Thaddeus nodded, relieved that the girl in question was just some cop sent to monitor his parents so they wouldn't say or do the wrong thing during the investigation. The police were getting smarter. He had to hand it to them: they'd convinced his mother that having a babysitter was a good idea.

"She's going to take us out to the search site today, just so we can see what's happening. She's a really sweet girl," his mother said. She cocked her head, thinking. "She's around your age." She scooped another bite of eggs into her mouth.

"Mom." He dropped his head and looked down at the crocheted pattern of the tablecloth his great-grandmother had made for his parents when they got married. The thing had lasted longer than their marriage had.

"What?" Her tone was defensive.

"Are you actually trying to matchmake me with the police officer who's here because of Davy?"

He watched her flinch like she always did when he said Davy's name. She shrugged. "I was just making an observation. She's cute." She looked to his father for affirmation. "Don't you think so, Daniel?"

His father scrunched up his face. "I don't know. She's a kid." He picked up his plate, stood, and carried it into the kitchen as Thaddeus wondered if that made him a kid too. Sitting at that table with his parents certainly made him feel like one again.

His mother, undeterred, continued. "A little more . . . curvy than you might normally like, T— I mean, Thaddeus. But her personality really makes up for it. She has a very calming presence." She raised her voice so his dad could still hear her. "You find yourself trusting her. Don't you think, Daniel?"

His dad, who had begun to wash the dishes, pretended not to hear her over the running water. His mother harrumphed as she picked up her own plate, then reached for Thaddeus's plate as well. The two plates clattered loudly as she dumped one on top of the other.

"She's got a pretty face. You'll see."

As she walked away with the plates, he called after her, "I could've done that, you know."

"I know," she called back. "But you're a guest."

"A guest?" he shouted, surprised at her choice of words. "I grew up in this house! How can I be a guest?"

There was a knock at the door. "She's here," his mother said instead of answering his question. He heard the clatter as she dropped the dishes into the sink, then doubled back and headed toward the door. As she passed the table, she stopped to give him one of her mom looks. "You be nice to her, Thaddeus."

Before she could get to the front door, he stood up and walked out the back door, escaping just as his father had. He didn't want to meet the babysitter cop. He didn't want to be fixed up with her. He didn't want to be there at all.

He stood in the backyard, his eyes scanning the familiar, yet unfamiliar, landscape until his gaze landed on the house next door. He quickly looked away and removed his phone from his pocket. He scrolled through his recent calls until he found Phillip Laney's number and pressed Dial.

"Philly," he said when his friend answered. "I've been here less than an hour and I already need a drink."

Phillip laughed. "Sounds about right."

"Things are . . . tense in this house."

"Well." Phillip cleared his throat. "That's to be expected. Right?"

"Yeah, well, is that offer for a beer still good? Like tonight?"

"Um, I think I can swing that." There was a pause, presumably while Phillip checked his calendar. "I mean, my daughter has a T-ball game that'll go into the evening, but I can scoot out early and my wife can take her home. She'll understand. I mean, it's not every day that your old pal needs you like this. Right?"

"Right," Thaddeus agreed, then added, "thank goodness."

They both gave a nervous laugh before forming a plan for the evening. Then Thaddeus went back inside to ask his dad to borrow the car for the night, like he was sixteen all over again.

CHAPTER 14

Gordon

On Saturday mornings he still had breakfast with his parents, a family tradition they'd continued far longer than any of them had expected. He supposed if he'd been able to leave town as he'd originally planned, moved somewhere more art-infused than Wynotte, North Carolina, or if he'd gotten married like his mother wanted, the weekly breakfasts would've come to a natural end.

Instead they persisted. Only now, rather than his mother rising early and cooking a full spread, Gordon swung through the Hardee's drive-through and bought them all biscuits. His mother just couldn't do it anymore, much as she wanted to. He was always sure to say that Hardee's biscuits couldn't hold a candle to hers.

The three of them were sitting around the table talking about the weather, observing how spring would give way to full-blown summer too quickly as it always did, when there was a knock at the door. His father, still head of the house in spite of his frailty, began to rise, but Gordon held up his hand.

"No, Daddy," he said, his voice stern. He looked from his father to his mother, taking in one rheumy gaze, then another, before asking, "Did y'all hear about the jacket they found out on the old Oxendine property?"

He'd known he'd have to bring this up. He just hadn't known when to bring it up: Before or after they ate? Get it over with early or wait until he was walking out the door? He had to go over the rules with them again, provide a refresher on what to do to minimize the inevitable attack on his character that came whenever news of Davy Malcor broke. He felt like every time this happened, it took a year off his parents' lives.

His mother and father nodded in unison, eyes wide like children's. The loose flesh of his mother's neck jiggled rather grotesquely with the movement. Sometimes he didn't recognize the woman in front of him. It was easy to forget she'd once been beautiful.

"We have to be careful," he said, keeping his voice level yet firm. "We don't know how far it'll go this time." The knock sounded a second time, more insistent than the first.

"What about Harvey?" his father asked, and Gordon felt the happiness he felt anytime his father remembered something like a name or a place or an event from long ago. His father didn't have dementia or Alzheimer's, but he was forgetful. He was far from the certain, decisive man he'd been when Gordon was young. They'd recently stood in a Belk's department store for a half hour as his father anguished over choosing a simple tie. In the end Gordon had chosen for him.

"I've talked to Harvey," he said. "He's taking care of things." He fixed them with his gaze. "It won't be like the other times," he promised, but even as he spoke, he knew it was futile to make such a promise.

They nodded again and Gordon rose from the table to see who was knocking at the door so early on a Saturday morning. He peeked through the window in the front room that gave the best vantage point and saw, unsurprisingly but disappointingly, Monica Allagash with her cameraman, the pair a poised, sleek version of Tweedledee and Tweedledum.

He walked to the door and opened it a crack, not enough for the cameraman to get a full shot of his face. The guy had started filming as soon as he heard the locks being turned. When Monica saw that it was Gordon opening the door rather than one of his parents, her face fell. She'd clearly been hoping to get to the weaker links, to trick his parents into saying something she could twist and edit into a salacious sound bite. She called herself a journalist, but she was just an entertainer.

"No comment," he said and started to shut the door, but she stuck her foot into the tiny crack he'd created.

"Wait!" she said. The cameraman was still filming. Gordon closed his eyes and tried to move out of the camera's view. He thought about shutting the door hard on her foot, hearing her cry out in pain and shock. It would serve her right.

"I've been in touch with my attorney, and if there needs to be a statement, he will arrange that later. As of now, we are private citizens on private property. So please leave. Now."

"Mr. Swift," she blurted, desperate. "You have nothing to say about the discovery yesterday?"

Was it really just yesterday? It seemed like a week had gone by since he'd found her standing by his car.

He turned back to her, his face still barely visible through the crack in the door, the cameraman still recording.

"Our thoughts and prayers are, as always, with the Malcor family during this time."

He looked pointedly at her foot until she removed it. Then Gordon closed the door and leaned back on it, thinking of how he wholeheartedly meant what he'd said. His thoughts and prayers were with the Malcor family. No matter how much they questioned his innocence or held him responsible for what happened to Davy, he could not feel anything but sorrow for their loss and a twinge of responsibility for his contribution to it. He waited a moment for his heart to slow before returning to the table to reassure his parents that it was all right. That everything would be ok, even though he didn't believe his own words, and he doubted his folks did either.

It's such a nice night that, once the sun goes down and the heat lets up, Gordon opens the windows to get some fresh air. Then he switches on the television.

He still can't believe the little house in the boonies came with cable. When he'd gone to check it out, he'd been impressed that the place had electricity and running water. The cable had been a bonus, and, while not the reason he'd said yes to the arrangement, it was a definite check in the "pros" column.

When his parents proposed that he live there and help out the farmer's widow, a woman from their church, he'd scoffed at the idea. But eventually he'd caved. It was his own place, his parents had pointed out, and he could live there rent free in exchange for driving the old lady to and from church, fixing things around the main house where she lived, and just generally being a human nearby so she wasn't all alone on that big old farm.

Just that evening he'd changed a light bulb for the widow, and she'd given him some homemade biscuits as a thank-you. He'd eaten them for supper with butter and preserves she'd insisted he take to go with them. *Made 'em myself,"* she'd said.

He'd thanked her, patting her elderly hand, frail and spotted, the opposite of his own. He carried that contrasting image of their hands across the small yard between the two houses. Her house is large and imposing; his is tiny, a dollhouse version of hers. But he doesn't mind; he has all he needs for now.

This is just a jumping-off place, a story he will tell later at dinner with friends after a gallery opening, perhaps, an amusing anecdote about his humble beginnings. That's what he will call the piece he plans to start tonight: *Humble Beginnings*. In his mind he sees the image he aims to create. He will sculpt the widow's hands, extended.

If he does his job, those hands will tell her story about once being busy, useful, needed. But now empty. What if, he thinks, his mind whizzing, he creates a pair of outstretched hands—one young and smooth, holding a bounty of fruit, and one wizened and spotted, holding shriveled, empty stems? He needs to start sketching while it's all coming to him. This is his favorite part—the inspiration at the beginning, when the concept is there in all its perfection and reality has not intercepted it yet.

He rotates through the many channels available till he finds the baseball playoffs. The St. Louis Cardinals are playing the Los Angeles Dodgers. He doesn't care who wins. Though not a huge sports fan, he likes the sound of a baseball game on low in the background as he works, likes the dull roar of the crowd, the steady murmur of the commentators' voices calling plays, the general hum that serves as a soundtrack to his creative process. It reminds him of being a kid, drawing in his room with the sound of baseball emanating from his father's TV in the den. It's funny, the things that stay with you, he thinks, the things you don't anticipate will form you.

He sits on the couch in the living area that he's turned into a kind of makeshift studio, since it's the largest space available to him. He has a table for all of his tools, stacks of sketchbooks, watercolors, acrylics, pencils, and pens. It isn't perfect—nowhere near the studio provided in college—but he's turned it into a decent enough place to make his art, a space where he can be creative.

And he does feel creative as the breeze from the open window ruffles the blank page he turns to in his sketchbook where he will start sketching out this new idea. He marks through his poor first attempts, then quickly turns to a new page, the baseball murmurings providing just the right amount of noise to keep his mind humming along.

When he hears the sounds of children playing, he thinks at first he is imagining things. But no, there the noises are again, coming through the open windows: thundering feet, a screech, belly laughter. There are definitely kids out there on the widow's property.

He stands and wanders over to the door of the cabin, tugging it open so he can squint out into the darkness, blinking as he tries to make sense of the dark shapes in the distance. But the sounds, which had come close, have moved away. Now they are off in the distance, up toward the main road.

He leaves his front door open and goes to the phone, his hand poised over the receiver as he debates calling over to see if the widow, too, has heard the children. He knows that by now she will be in her nightgown, climbing into the huge four-poster bed she shared with her husband for fifty-three years. To call her now would upset her nightly routine.

No sense in worrying her needlessly, he reasons. It's probably nothing. He moves back over to the door to take one last look, deciding as he does to leave the door open but keep the screen door in place. That way he can listen for anyone approaching the widow's place, anything that may harm or frighten her. That is, after all, what he's there for.

CHAPTER 15

Anissa

Gordon Swift did not answer his door when she knocked that morning. She'd tried to arrive at his house as early as possible, yet not too early for a Saturday morning. Still, she'd missed him.

She debated what to do. She'd promised Pete she'd stop by to make nice with Gordon, but she'd also promised Pete she'd run interference at the Malcor home. Davy's parents had received permission to go to the search site for a bit, and it was her job to escort them. The fear of what could happen while they were there made her stomach hurt. She said a quick prayer that nothing would.

She took a few steps away from Gordon's house and paused, debating whether or not to leave a note for him. She turned to look at the little building that stood behind his house, wondering if perhaps he was in there, when a flash of movement caught her attention. She squinted against the bright morning sunlight as she registered what she was seeing.

A child had been hanging around the building, but he'd hidden when he saw her. She could see him there still, the glare from his glasses giving him away as he tried to peek at her. Sorry to have frightened him, she waved a greeting and he disappeared entirely.

"Hey," she called out. "It's ok. I'm—"

But all she heard was the sound of footsteps beating a path through the woods beside Gordon's house, twigs snapping and pine needles shifting under the child's feet. She wondered why a young boy would be there, and what had scared him off. Was it being caught, or did it have something to do with Gordon? She'd always been sure the scary tales about Gordon were myths and legends because of Davy's disappearance. In the absence of information, people would always make up stories. Still, she didn't think it was a good idea for Gordon to be seen in the company of any child, much less a boy of a certain age.

She heard a noise behind her and turned to see a car pulling into the driveway. She walked quickly back over to her car and reached inside for her purse, fishing out a business card like some sort of badge. She stood, awkwardly holding the business card, and watched as Gordon Swift parked his car in the space next to hers and turned off the engine. He turned to look at her, wincing as if preparing to be struck.

This close to him she confirmed that he looked nothing like a monster. He was attractive—a handsome face and longish hair, thin build, with a gentle demeanor—nothing like most of the cops she worked with, with their broad chests, thick necks, and buzz cuts. He looked like what an artist, a sensitive soul, should look like, she decided. Inexplicably, she felt the urge to reach out and touch his face, to smooth away his pained expression.

He opened his car door and she hurried over to intercept him before he could hustle inside his house and close the door behind him.

He strode quickly away from her, calling over his shoulder, "No comment."

"No!" she cried. "I'm not with the press!" She waved her business card in the air as proof.

He stopped and turned to look at her. "Then who are you?" His voice was weary.

She lowered her hands and pointed at herself. "My name is Anissa Weaver. I'm the Public Information Officer assigned to the Davy Malcor case. Sheriff Lancaster asked me to stop by and check on you."

She approached him slowly and handed him the business card, then gave him what she hoped passed for a warm smile. He seemed not to notice. Instead he took a few steps away from her, then blinked a few times, saying nothing. He kept his gaze just over her head, staring at the tree line that separated his house from the house next door, never bothering to glance at her card.

She continued. "Pete—I mean, Sheriff Lancaster—just wanted me to make contact with you, to let you know I'm here if you need anything—help with the press, questions about the investigation, or even police assistance in case . . ." In case things got ugly. In case people decide to mete out their own version of justice as they had before. She'd seen his files.

Looking at him, at his shoulders hunched in a permanent protective posture, she again felt the urge to comfort him. At that moment it didn't occur to her to think about him as a possible murderer, the bogeyman in the field the night Davy went missing. Sure, he could've left that little house where he'd lived. He could've come after them. She knew that was possible. And yet, she'd always felt that was not what happened that night.

"Tell the sheriff I appreciate his effort."

"We want to be here for you," she said. She spread her arms wide and wondered if she looked magnanimous or just ridiculous to Gordon Swift.

He cocked his head, an ironic grin crossing his face, then disappearing. "What a nice sentiment," he said. He began walking away again, seeking the shelter of his home. "Too bad it's twenty years too late."

She left Tabitha and Daniel Malcor behind the yellow caution tape meant to keep the public at bay and walked over to where Seth was standing, closer to where the search was taking place. She stood beside him saying nothing, feeling a sense of reverence come over her as she took in the scene.

The dog handlers milled about, their charges kenneled or leashed, all panting in unison. The forensics team members sifted, transferred, and dug in marked-off areas. Hot and tired, some sat in the shade and guzzled water.

Would they find Davy? Would this be the end of his mystery? Or would this just be another false alarm?

"I don't think it's ever gone this far before," she whispered to Seth.

"No," Seth replied, his demeanor stalwart, his mouth a grim line. He was there to monitor the crowd, but the crowd didn't seem to need monitoring. They, too, stood silently by, many of them stealing glances at Daniel and Tabitha. A few patted their shoulders or spoke briefly to them, their faces sympathetic and kind. So far, so good.

"I wonder," she mused, again in a whisper, "why this place was never searched before."

Seth leaned over. "Come on, you know why," he whispered, his mouth so close to her ear that it tickled. But she did not smile. Seth pulled at her elbow and indicated for her to follow him away from the scene so they could talk. She glanced back, checking on the Malcors.

"They'll be fine," he assured her. So she followed him over to his car.

He opened the driver's side door and pulled out a water bottle from the center console, tipping it in her direction to offer it to her first, but she shook her head. He shrugged, then took a long pull from the bottle before speaking.

"They didn't search here for the same reason they never followed up with you or the other kids after that night. The same reason they didn't cordon off the farm to keep the public out until later the next day. The same reason they delayed analyzing the tire tracks till numerous delivery vehicles and plain ole nosy Nellies had already driven up and down that drive. So if there had been a car like you claimed—"

"There was!" she protested, her voice too loud. She looked around to make sure no one had heard her outburst, then, softer, said, "There was a car. I saw it. It's been a long time, but I remember that clearly."

Seth looked at her with something akin to fondness. "I know that. I'm just saying, it was a small-town police force and it was a long time ago. They were out of their element and not prone to thinking the worst. They decided Davy was lost or had run away, and he'd turn up by morning." He laughed, a scoffing sound. "I heard they sent up a helicopter to make a loop over the area just to appease the parents. But they weren't really looking." He shrugged. "They didn't make it the priority it should've been because things like that didn't happen here."

"But they did," Anissa said, looking back to check on her charges again. Daniel and Tabitha were both stone-faced as they observed the search. Tabitha had asked to see the jacket they found, but Anissa had to tell her no. It was evidence now.

Seth saw her looking at them, then asked, "Have you told them the truth yet? About that night?"

Still watching the Malcors over her shoulder, Anissa shook her head.

"Don't you think you should?" Seth pressed. "I mean, if it comes out some other way, it might . . ."

Anissa jerked her head in his direction. "You better not breathe a word. I mean it, Seth."

Seth huffed his exasperation. "I didn't mean it that way. I won't say anything, but it could still come out . . ."

"There is no other way," she said. "The only people around here who know that I'm the little girl from that night are you and my sister. And both of you"—she fixed him with a stern gaze—"have promised never to mention it." She went back to whispering, though it was doubtful anyone could hear them from where they stood. "I could lose my job."

"Ok," Seth said. "Sorry." He glanced over to where the action was, to make sure the small crowd that had gathered was staying within the boundaries. He lowered his voice to a whisper. "Maybe later I could . . . come over?"

Anissa looked up at him, then over at the Malcors, then back at him.

"No," she said. "I'm pretty tired. I think I better sleep *alone.*"

Seth shook his head, his cheeks reddening out of anger or embarrassment. She didn't know which. It occurred to her that she didn't care.

"Fine," he said. He kicked at a loose rock, dislodging it from the dirt. "Seems like whenever I start to wonder why we split up, you come along and give me a reminder."

"Funny," she said, crossing her arms and turning on her heel to stride away from him. "I was just going to say the same thing."

As she rejoined the Malcors, she thought of a fight she and Seth had gotten into just before they separated. She was still pretty new in her role as Public Information Officer and a man in prison had confessed to Davy's abduction. Pete Lancaster had told her to be ready to get over to the Malcors if the claim panned out. She'd been anxious, nervous to the point of feeling ill, at the thought of facing Davy's parents, pacing around with her hands in her hair, her fingers knotting her curls.

"They're no different from any other victims you help," Seth had said, trying to be a comfort. But she'd lashed out at him, yelling that he didn't understand, that he could never—would never—understand what that night had rendered.

Seth had ducked and mumbled something, a wounded look on his face. She'd known she should ask him what he'd said, but she hadn't bothered. The truth was, she hadn't cared. Not when Davy felt so close, so present.

In truth, some part of him always had been.

CHAPTER 16

Tabitha

Tabitha knew that to anyone standing near them, she appeared to be intently focused on the search taking place. In reality, while she wanted to keep her mind on what was happening, her thoughts kept returning to Thaddeus.

He had outright refused to go with them to the site, claiming he had a call with someone or other about the book. Tabitha knew that was just an excuse. She'd said as much to him, her decibel level rising in tandem with her frustration, then stomped off to shelter in her room until it was time to go.

When Anissa had arrived to transport them to the site, Daniel had said goodbye to Thaddeus, but she, nursing her anger, had not. She made a mental note to add that to her regret list. She knew better than to leave someone she loved without a proper goodbye. But Thaddeus could get under her skin like no one else.

Watching as strangers searched for her lost son, she wondered why she could not make peace with the one who was still there. Something stood in the way, but she could not seem to name it. It seemed that she and Thaddeus would forever stand on opposite sides of whatever *it* was.

Someone tapped her on the shoulder and she turned, thinking it was Anissa, but Anissa was still behind the tape where they weren't allowed. Instead Tabitha saw a face that seemed familiar but she couldn't quite place it.

"Yes?" she asked the young man.

"Mrs. Malcor," he said. "It's me, Phillip Laney."

She blinked as two Phillip Laneys merged in her mind. One was Thaddeus's childhood friend who always seemed to be in her kitchen eating her food, and this other one, the grown-up version. She could see how the one had become the other. Still handsome, but he'd gone a little bit soft. All that eating must've caught up to him.

"Daniel," she said. "Look who it is." Daniel turned to greet Phillip, then turned back to the search, watching it like he watched football. As if someone was going to score or fumble, win or lose.

She wanted to ask Phillip why he was there. For that matter, she wanted to ask all the onlookers why they were there. She knew why she was there. She was Davy's mother, and they were looking for Davy. Strangers' fascination with her son's disappearance never failed to surprise her.

Phillip glanced around. "Did Thaddeus come?"

"No," Tabitha said. "He had an important call he had to be on."

Phillip looked disappointed. "Oh, well, I'm glad I saw you guys." He shrugged. "I'm seeing Thaddeus tonight anyway."

"Yes," Tabitha said. "He mentioned that." They both stood silently for a moment as Tabitha wondered how to extricate herself from the conversation.

"It was nice of you to come," she said.

"I felt like I should. I mean, I don't know if you remember or not, but I was there." He shifted his weight from one foot to the other, then added, "I mean, that night."

Tabitha nodded. Of course she remembered.

Phillip continued, "I guess there are things that happen to you as a kid that, you know, stay with you. Like no matter how old you get and how many other things happen, there are some things you just don't, or can't, forget." His eyes flickered over to the team of people searching, then back to her. "That night was like that for me."

"I understand," Tabitha said.

Phillip nodded grimly. He looked toward the makeshift parking lot that had been created on a bare patch of land.

"Well, I better get back to work."

Tabitha nodded. He turned back to face her.

"It was good to see you," he said.

"You too," she said, meaning it. She gave him a little wave and turned back to watch the search, thinking of all that had been altered that night, to whatever degree. It was easy to make Davy's loss her own, to forget how the ripples of that night spread out and out and out. She looked around her at the people gathered, wondering if any of them were there because, like Phillip, that night meant something to them.

Beside her Daniel hummed softly, a tic that showed up whenever he was uncomfortable. The noise was almost inaudible, barely more than the sound of someone inhaling and exhaling. Tabitha doubted anyone else could hear it. But she knew to listen for it. She'd asked him about it long ago and he'd looked at her blankly. *"I was humming?"*

She'd smiled and nodded. That had been long before Davy went missing. They'd been at one of her pregnancy appointments for Kristyn, back when men were first getting involved with the birth process, and Daniel wasn't sure that was a good idea.

"What was I humming?" he'd asked.

She'd laughed. *"It's so faint, I can't tell."*

He'd grinned and started to hum for real, picking a tune at random, one that had played in the car as they'd driven to the doctor, "Keep on Loving You." But he hadn't. Or she hadn't. They hadn't.

After Davy, it was just too hard. In her experience, once a heart had broken, it never loved quite the same again. They'd given what love they could to their remaining children with little to nothing left over for each other. It happened all the time in cases like theirs. In the end it was easier to succumb to the statistics.

There'd been no big blowup. The end had come like a fire dying. The coals just grew colder and colder.

She glanced over at Daniel, wanting to tell him he was humming. She wondered if he would remember that scene from the doctor's office so long ago. She doubted it. Still, she quietly hummed a few bars of "Keep on Loving You" to herself, her voice soft, so soft she doubted anyone could hear.

After Anissa had gone home for the night, Thaddeus left to meet Phillip Laney, and Daniel went next door to help Marie fetch her granddaughter's tiny plastic doll from a sink drain. Tabitha sat in her house alone, appreciating the silence and stillness. She peered through the front window and watched the last of the press pack up to go home for the night.

There had been no new news since the jacket was found. If something else wasn't found soon, they'd pack up and leave for good. One could only hope. A police car drove by patrolling, as it would every half hour, twenty-four hours a day, until this blew over.

As the cruiser's taillights faded, her mind went to her regret list for the coming week. Though she would no doubt have many, she wondered if they would be worth writing down. Doing so never seemed to change anything. Was it time to stop the weekly ritual? The regret list, after all, had not put a stop to—or even ebbed, for that matter—her regretting. It never touched the biggest regrets, the ones that lingered no matter how many times she wrote *"Je ne regrette rien!"*

Through the window, in the failing light, she could make out Daniel emerging from Marie's house and trekking back over to the home they once shared. He gripped a toolbox he'd left behind when he moved out and never bothered to come back for. Despite the gathering darkness, she could see that he wore a satisfied smile, which meant he'd been able to fix Marie's problem. Daniel took great satisfaction in fixing other people's problems, especially when he couldn't fix his own.

She studied his expression and wondered the same thing she'd wondered for so much of their marriage: *What are you thinking?* The question made her think of the awful year after they'd started a hotline for people to call in with leads after the police had moved on to other solvable cases. Many nights she awoke to the sound of Daniel's muffled voice on the other side of the house as he talked to strangers, one in particular. He shared what he was thinking then. Just not with Tabitha.

The woman had phoned initially to say she was a psychic with information about Davy. He was safe, she claimed, abducted by a woman who'd lost her own son. He was living on a farm, doing the chores of the dead boy. He wanted to come home, but he was being fed, his basic needs met. So, while Davy wasn't happy, he was alive. They should hold on to hope, she said, that Davy would be found, that in short order he would return to them.

Every few weeks, the psychic would call with some new image that had come to her: Davy beside a tractor with dirt smeared on his cheeks; Davy with a cut on his hand, rinsing it with a hand pump at an old-fashioned well; Davy washing dishes at a large farmhouse sink, gruel-like oatmeal slipping out of a bowl and into a drain. Daniel had relayed all of this to the police, who promised to investigate. But the psychic's claims never led anywhere, and Tabitha wrote her off as a crackpot.

Daniel, however, needed the hope, needed the psychic's visions of his son rather than the more likely ending the police had tried to prepare them for. He preferred her version of Davy's fate, and he went out in search of it, traveling to farms and land farther and farther out, traipsing all over the countryside. He would turn down long, winding dirt driveways and knock on farmhouse doors, sometimes being chased away by big angry dogs, sometimes being met with a gun, but other times being given a seat at the table and served a piece of pie.

By day he searched and by night he told the psychic what he'd seen. The psychic encouraged him to keep looking. She assured him Davy was out there, while Tabitha, with all her practical stoicism, worked on accepting that Davy was likely never coming home.

Had Daniel had an affair? Not physically, no. But emotionally, yes. At least as far as Tabitha had been concerned. Daniel had opted to reach out to the woman who shared his views instead of the one who shared his bed. Funny how that could hurt her even now, all these years later, long after the incident was over. In the end, to Daniel, the psychic had been a fraud, but to Tabitha she'd been a thief.

Daniel entered the house and she arranged her face to disguise what she'd just been thinking.

"I guess you were able to fix it," she said to the man who had once been her husband, her tone pleasant, scrubbed clean of any lingering resentment.

Daniel smiled the smile he gave when he was proud of himself.

"Good as new," he answered.

The games are in full force when Davy makes it back to where the other kids are. He sees that teams have already been chosen, sides clearly drawn. He missed his chance to play when he went to show TJ the rock. Stupid TJ and his stupid friends, thinking they're so cool—too cool for shiny rocks and little kids. Maybe he'll tell his parents about the plastic bag full of lumps, about how mean TJ was, and get TJ in trouble.

Davy stands outside of the group of kids, looking in as he debates whether to get on his bike and pedal home without telling TJ he's leaving. Let him worry. He imagines TJ searching the fields, calling his name, panic mounting. He imagines TJ having to tell their parents he lost him. A smile creeps onto Davy's face as he savors that scenario. It would serve his brother right.

He looks over to see a girl standing several feet away, also on the fringe of the action, smiling back at him. She gives him a little wave and begins walking toward him. Davy realizes she probably thinks his smile was meant for her. He gulps, recognition dawning as she draws closer.

She's the new girl in his class. He's heard the other girls making fun of her on the playground, pretending to be the Peanuts character who talks about her "naturally curly hair" as she pats her curls. To be fair, the girl's hair is quite curly. The other kids, while not exactly nice, aren't wrong. The mass of it bobs as she walks, coils springing from her head in all directions. He's never seen someone with hair as riotous as hers. He kind of likes it, though he'd never admit that out loud.

She comes to stand beside him, and he panics at the thought of speaking to her. As a rule, Davy doesn't talk to girls. Not if he can help it. TJ has told him it won't stay that way much longer, but he still firmly believes girls have cooties.

"You're Davy, right?" the girl asks.

Internally, Davy blanches. She knows his name? He nods, his voice no longer accessible to him.

She points to herself and says, "I'm Anissa." The action reminds him of the black-and-white Tarzan movies that come on Channel 18 on Saturday afternoons: *"Me, Tarzan. You, Jane."* He bites back a smile and nods again.

Behind her the games continue. They are playing red rover, two lines stretching across the field, a human chain. Davy is actually glad he was too late to join this game; the impact of the bodies always hurts his arms. He tries to recall the names of the arm bones. They learned all the major bones of the body in science class last year. Davy likes science. His dad says maybe he can major in it someday. Maybe he could even be a doctor. The problem with being a doctor, though, is he doesn't like the sight of blood.

Davy and the girl stand side by side quietly watching the game as Davy wonders how to get away from her. The night stretches out in front of him, a long inky ribbon of boredom waving like a banner. He can't just stand around watching other kids play all night. Yet he isn't sure he should leave without telling someone. But he doesn't dare go back to TJ and his friends.

The girl points at the game. "You got here too late too?"
She pulls a mournful face.

"Sorta," Davy says. He doesn't want to explain the whole
story to the girl with the bouncing curls. It's too embarrassing
to admit how much his brother doesn't want him around,
how his parents abandoned him to go to a stupid party, how
his only other choice this evening was to stay at home with a
babysitter and his little sister.

"Do you live around here?" the girl asks. She seems
determined to get him to talk.

He points to where the road in front of the farm forks off
in the general direction of his neighborhood.

"Over that way," he says. "I rode my bike." A moment of
silence passes before he realizes he should ask her if she lives
nearby. She might live in his neighborhood, he supposes, but
he doesn't think so. He knows pretty much everyone in his
neighborhood, including the dogs and some of the cats.

"You?" he asks.

She turns and points toward where he left his bike. "See
those houses, on the other side of the street?"

Davy nods. He's always wondered about the people who
live in those tiny homes; mostly he's wondered who would
ever want to. They're old, run-down houses with mud for
yards, missing shingles, and tiny front porches that slope into
the ground. His father called it "migrant housing." But Davy
doesn't know what a migrant is.

"I live in that middle one," she says.

"Oh." He works hard to keep any pity out of his voice, to
find something nice to say in response. "That's pretty close
to where I live," he adds. "You can't see it from here, but
mine's over there." He uses his finger to draw a line in the

sky from her house, as a bird would fly, to where his house is tucked away around the bend and out of sight.

"We just moved here," she explains, and he wonders if she's embarrassed about where she lives. He would be. "My mom got a new job. She says this house is temporary. That once she gets a few paychecks we'll get something better. We had to move here because she broke up with her boyfriend, Les. Les used to take care of us, but now, since they broke up, he doesn't anymore. So she has to make her own way."

She heaves a world-weary sigh. "It's hard to be a single mother and take care of two kids." She glances over at Davy with wide eyes. "I have an older sister." She points at the house again. "She's in there right now, waiting on some boy to call her. She was supposed to make popcorn and watch a movie with me, but noooo."

"So who invited you here?" he asks.

She presses her lips together and thinks about it, then laughs. "Well, no one."

Davy's eyes are saucers. "I don't think I could do that."

"Do what?"

"Just come over here without an invitation," he says.

She shrugs. "It was better than sitting at home waiting on my sister to stop waiting for the phone to ring." She nudges him with her elbow. "And hey, look, I already made a friend."

Embarrassed, he ducks his head, hoping she doesn't get the wrong idea and think he likes her or something. TJ told him it was easy for girls to get the wrong idea. TJ was talking about Larkin, of course, though he would never admit it. TJ and Larkin used to be friends, but he doesn't think that's true anymore.

TJ doesn't know Davy saw them kissing after Kristy's birthday party last week. He'd been headed outside to find out what Larkin thought about his juggling performance. And there they'd been, their bodies mashed up against each other, their mouths pressed together. It had been so gross that Davy had felt the birthday cake in his stomach go sour. He'd hurried away before they saw him watching.

"What's your name again?" Davy asks, because he has forgotten it already.

"Anissa," she says and does not scold him for forgetting, which he appreciates.

He nods once and says it aloud. "Anissa." Now he will remember. They stand silently and watch the games, the batch of kids spilling out across the field.

"What is this place anyway?" Anissa asks.

"It used to be a farm, but I don't think it is anymore," Davy says.

"How come?"

Davy shakes his head. "I think the farmer died. Or something." He stretches out his arms. "When we first moved here, all these fields were planted. There was stuff growing everywhere. Corn mostly, but other stuff too. Once, over there"—he points to his right, to the farthest field away, down closer to the farmer's house—"they grew cotton. I didn't even know you could grow cotton! I thought they made it in factories!" He drops his arms and shakes his head. "Now there's nothing."

Anissa shakes her head along with him. "It's like that John Cougar Mellencamp song, 'Blood on the Scarecrow.'" She raises her eyebrows. "Have you heard it?"

Davy isn't sure he has. The only music he's been listening to lately is his cassette tape of the *Back to the Future* soundtrack. But he nods like he has, then changes the subject.

"The old lady—the farmer's wife?—still lives there," he says. "I think." He points in the same direction where the cotton once grew. "Her house is way back there. Once, TJ—that's my older brother—and I rode our bikes all the way down the lane that goes right up to the house." He takes his finger and traces where the lane starts up by the main road, following the path down to where he can barely make out the roof of the big house in the distance. His throat feels tight at the memory, not because of what they did but because it was a time when TJ didn't mind doing things with him.

"TJ said we were trespassing, that we could get arrested."

Anissa widens her eyes at this and he nods, then grins.

"But we did it anyway."

Anissa's eyes light up. "Let's go see," she says. Together they stare out into the distance toward where the big old house sits, a grand house where danger could lurk. He shivers a little at the thought, but he can't look like a wimp in front of this girl, especially considering she's the one who suggested it.

"It's kinda far away," he tries to hedge. "And it's pretty dark. I mean, there's not much of a moon tonight. You know, to guide us."

Anissa squints up at the sky. "It's a crescent," she says, pointing at the sliver.

"Like I said, it's not much," he says again, hoping he's talked her out of it.

She puts her hand on her hip. "You'd rather stand around here doing nothing?"

"We could get arrested for trespassing." He doesn't feel as safe attempting something risky at night with this girl as he did with TJ in broad daylight. "It's against the law."

He looks toward the farmer's house, then fleetingly in the direction of where his brother and his friends are. Then he looks over at the other kids. Red rover has broken up and they seem to be chasing each other around with no rhyme or reason. If they stay, he and Anissa could get in on the next game.

Or they could get left out again.

"Come on," she beckons with her whole arm. "Live a little."

When she starts walking, Davy doesn't see that he has much choice but to follow.

CHAPTER 17

Thaddeus

After his parents left to go watch the search, Thaddeus plunked down on the couch in the family room and stared at his phone. He had lied about having a call scheduled but debated calling Nicole.

He could, he thought, act like he was just checking in to let her know he'd made it there safely, then maybe they'd continue the conversation, and in doing so start to sidestep the exposure he felt whenever he thought about her. They had to get past this. She would be in his meetings when he went to New York. She was the one he spoke to the most about his tour arrangements. He shook his head at himself. Why had he revealed so much to her?

The answer came from somewhere deep inside him: *Because you wanted her to know.*

But why? He pressed himself. Why had he wanted her to know? Before he could come upon an answer, the telephone on the end table next to him began to ring. Thaddeus eyed it skeptically, wondering if he should answer it or just let it go to the answering machine. He didn't live there anymore; no one expected him to answer.

He decided to let it go, then went back to staring at his phone as the ringing stopped, only to start again almost immediately. He glared at the phone until it stopped ringing a second time. He decided he was thirsty and rose from the couch to get something to drink from the kitchen. Before he could take a step, the phone rang for a third time.

Annoyed, he reached for the receiver and raised it to his ear with a gruff "Hello?"

"Thaddeus?" his sister, Kristyn, asked, clearly taken aback by his tone.

He cringed and apologized. "I thought it was the press calling." Which was not exactly a lie. It could've just as easily been an annoying reporter hoping to catch one of them off guard and get a scoop. "What's up?"

"I was calling to give Mom—or Dad since I guess he's there too—an update on our travel plans."

"Oh, you guys are coming?" Neither of his parents had mentioned Kristyn coming. He figured she'd gotten a pass because she had a husband and kids and lived all the way in California. Or if he wanted to be cynical about it, because she'd only been four and not responsible for Davy the night he'd gone missing. Both could've been true.

Kristyn sighed. "Well, we're trying to. My youngest has been sick, and Jeff's got a meeting he can't miss on Monday, so it's looking like it'll be Tuesday before we're able to get there." She sighed again. "To be honest, I haven't even purchased plane tickets yet because I don't know if I should." She paused, probably thinking of how much she should say and how to say it.

"This might blow over and you might not need to come," he supplied.

"Yeah," she said. Another long pause followed before she spoke again, her voice sounding more like that of the little girl he remembered than that of the young woman he barely knew. "But what if it doesn't blow over? What if this time's for real?"

Thaddeus said nothing for a moment, thinking about how glad he was to be meeting Phillip at the bar later, how good a cold beer would taste.

"Tell you what," he said. "Why don't you give it another day before you book the tickets?"

"Um, because the cost of the tickets goes up exponentially with every day I wait?" A teasing tone edged her voice, but he knew she was not teasing. His sister was a young stay-at-home mom. She and her husband were living off one income so she could be home with Thaddeus's niece and nephew. Thaddeus admired what they were doing. It was more than he had done.

"Ok," he said. "Why don't you let me buy the plane tickets?"

"Oh, Thaddeus," she said. "I can't let you do that."

"'Course you can," he replied. "It'll make me feel good. It's been far too long since I've done a good deed."

She laughed. "Well, I mean, you *are* a bestselling author. You probably have money to burn."

He chuckled. "Not necessarily. But I do have money to help my little sister. Besides, I've got to do something to live up to our perfect missing brother." He stopped as soon as the words left his mouth. He hadn't meant to say that aloud. "I'm sorry," he blurted. "That was an awful thing to say."

Kristyn was silent for a moment before she spoke again.

"I dunno. I think it was one of the most honest things you've ever said. It's not like I haven't felt the same from time to time. Davy was a hard act to follow. And I didn't know him like you did. I can't imagine how it felt to be in your shoes."

A part of him wanted to say more, to really talk to his sister about how it felt to be Davy's siblings. His sister was the only person who could possibly understand. Maybe, he thought, they'd get to really talk if she visited. All the more reason to buy those plane tickets and make it happen.

Thaddeus thought about how honest he'd been with Nicole and the regret he'd felt afterward, the exposure like an open wound. What would it be like to share parts of himself with another person and not feel vulnerable afterward? Maybe he could become someone who emoted instead of withdrew, someone who could dig deeper and live to tell about it. It was something to consider.

"Still," he said. "I shouldn't have said it."

Kristyn lowered her voice to a whisper. "I won't tell if you won't."

Thaddeus smiled in response. "I hope you do come. It'd be nice to see you guys."

"One thing you can say for Davy," she said. "He's always had a way of drawing us back together."

Thaddeus felt tears prick at his eyes as he brushed his fingers against his pants pocket.

"That he has," he said. "Just keep me posted about your plans. I meant that offer. Let that be one less thing you've got to think about."

"Thanks, Thaddeus," she said.

When they hung up, Thaddeus still had tears in his eyes but a smile on his face.

Three beers in he had started to forget why he was there, in a dive bar, in his hometown. He allowed himself to relax, to let Phillip introduce him when friends came by the table. He shook hands and hoped no one recognized him. This was the kind of place where men chatted about sports and women, not bestsellers or the latest headlines. He felt safe, insulated, lured into the kind of complacency that comes from alcohol and the company of an old friend.

Except when the old friend turned the conversation around to the one thing he was trying not to think about.

"So, do you think anything'll come of them finding the jacket?" Phillip lowered his voice as he spoke, although between the din of music and voices, he needn't have bothered. "I went by there today. You know, just to see. Your folks were there."

Phillip didn't ask why he hadn't been there and for that Thaddeus was glad. He simply nodded and looked away, scanning the scene at the bar, looking anywhere but at Phillip's intense, inquisitive face. Was Phillip with him because he wanted to see him or because he was nosy about Davy's case? Thaddeus ignored the nagging sense that it was the latter, focusing instead on the patrons gathered in the bar. Some of the faces looked vaguely familiar, others were complete strangers. He'd been gone a long time.

He caught the eye of the server, a young woman with a ponytail and several piercings, and held up his beer mug. She nodded and bustled over to the bar to fetch another. If only his relationships with all women were that simple: I need, you respond. No discussion, no feelings involved.

"Are you worried about what they're gonna find?" Phillip's voice was gentle, tentative. Thaddeus tried to give him the benefit of the doubt. Maybe he was just trying to be a sounding board, a friend who would be there for him. But Thaddeus didn't need anyone to be there for him. He needed to forget why he was there at all.

He gave Phillip an irritated glance. "I'm trying not to think about that tonight, Philly."

Phillip lifted his hands. "Ok, ok."

They sat in silence for a beat. Bob Seger played on the jukebox, singing about blaming things on the moon. There'd barely been a sliver in the sky the night Davy went missing, which was why it had been so dark.

"So you keeping up with baseball? The Cardinals looked all right in spring training." Phillip changed the subject by returning to an older, safer topic. Once upon a time baseball was the bond between them. They'd met as teammates in Little League, playing on fields just a short walk from where they now sat. So many weekends spent on those fields. They'd both been bound for greatness—everyone said so. Then his junior year Thaddeus blew out his knee in a slide into home plate. He got the run, though. Phillip had gone on and played baseball on scholarship at a small liberal arts college. But their friendship wasn't the same when baseball no longer served as a bond.

"I'd forgotten how much you loved St. Louis," Thaddeus said. "I was there yesterday." *Jeez, was that just yesterday?*

"I'm from there," Phillip said. "Originally." Sometimes Thaddeus forgot that about his old friend. Like so many people in Wynotte, Thaddeus included, Phillip had not started his life there, but had made it home nonetheless.

The server deposited his beer on the table, setting down one for Phillip as well. Phillip thanked her, then leaned toward Thaddeus. "Is it cool, traveling around? I bet it is."

Thaddeus shrugged. "It's a lot of airports and hotel rooms. I'm in and out of a city so fast, it's not like I see much."

Phillip leered, looking exactly like high school Phillip, albeit with thinning hair and a doughier face. "I bet there's lots of women at your events. Do they, like, throw themselves at you?"

Thaddeus paused for a moment but decided not to tell Phillip the truth. Instead he just said, "It's, uh, not really like that." He changed the subject. "Speaking of girls." He tipped his head to indicate a table of women across the room. "Is it my imagination, or do those girls look familiar?"

Phillip looked over, then smiled and waved. "Oh yeah, we know them. Or we did. Back in the day. That's Krista and Carrie and Amy. They're here a lot. They come for 'moms' night out,' which, as far as I can tell, means they leave their husbands home with the kids and come here to drink too much and flirt." He leaned forward in his chair and squinted. "There's another girl with them tonight. I can't tell who it is, but she kinda looks familiar too."

Thaddeus looked over as if he could help place the girl, as if he hadn't chosen long ago to forget them all, leaving high school—and this place—as far behind as he could. He sipped his beer as he took in her face, his heart beginning to pound at the same moment his brain produced her name. He set his beer down.

"It's Larkin," he said to Phillip.

Phillip's eyes widened. "No shit," he said and laughed. He clapped Thaddeus on the back. "It's your lucky day, man."

"Ha," Thaddeus said. "'Fraid not." Larkin had probably forgotten all about him. She was married now, after all. His mom had attended her wedding several years ago, then explained the experience to him in boring detail. He'd just begun working on the memoir and was staying in a cabin in Wyoming on the arts fellowship he'd won. He'd had limited cell service, but his mom had gotten through. Very late on the night she'd told him Larkin was married, he'd written about her. What he'd written that night about the girl next door had made it into the book with almost no changes.

He looked back over, as if to confirm it was indeed her sitting right there, in the same room as him. He wondered if she'd read the book, if she knew what he'd written about her, the girl next door. He felt heat rise in his cheeks at the thought of her reading his words. The readers from the bookstore the other night would've loved this moment.

"Dude," Phillip teased. "You're blushing." He stood and grabbed his beer. "Come on." He swaggered toward the girls' table without waiting for Thaddeus to say ok.

Thaddeus started to protest, but Phillip was too far away to hear over the music, and he wouldn't have listened even if he had heard. Thaddeus thought about staying put, but that would look weird and rude. So he rose with a sigh, grabbed his own beer as a paltry shield, and headed the same way Phillip had.

By the time he got to the table, Phillip had already struck up a conversation with the whole group. Thaddeus gave Larkin a closed lip smile as they each dipped their heads in mutual acknowledgment. He'd assumed she'd left this place behind just as he had. According to his mother, her husband was in the military. (*You should've seen their wedding, Thaddeus. So lovely. She was in this gorgeous gown, and he was in his dress uniform. So were all his groomsmen, all lined up beside him. I always did love a man in uniform.*) Apparently, so had Larkin. Not that he was jealous.

"Y'all remember T—" Phillip stopped himself from using Thaddeus's old name. "I mean, Thaddeus Malcor, right?" Phillip swept his hand out as if he were a nobleman introducing the gentry.

The ladies nodded enthusiastically, and he hoped they wouldn't bring up the news about Davy. He wished he hadn't gone out with Phillip, then quickly recalled why he had. The alternative was staying home with his parents, breathing in air thick with sadness, memories, and the tension that comes with divorced people forced to sit in the same house for hours on end, waiting for news that may never come. Rock, meet hard place.

"So no more TJ, huh? It's *Thaddeus*, now?" one of them asked. He couldn't decide if it was Krista or Carrie. Once upon a time he'd danced with these girls, drunkenly belted '80s rock lyrics, eaten countless slices of pizza at countless parties. Once upon a time they were part of his everyday life. Now he could barely place them.

"Yeah," he said. "*Thaddeus* just sounded more . . . professional, I guess." He gave them an aw-shucks look.

"Well then, welcome back, *Thaddeus*," she chided, her grin good-natured.

"Yes," Larkin chimed in. "Welcome back." Unlike her companions, whose fingers encircled the stems of their wine-glasses, Larkin didn't appear to be drinking. Only a glass of water sat in front of her.

"Thanks," he said and took a nervous pull from his beer. No one said anything for a moment, and he could see they were all deciding what was safe to say to him.

"I read your book," one of them ventured. "It was good."

"Thank you," he said stiffly, wishing he could bolt from the scene. The other girls nodded but didn't say they had read it, which he was grateful for. He didn't want to have a Q&A session in the middle of the bar.

"I've been meaning to read it," another one offered. "I just don't have the time; I've been so *busy*." She rested one hand on her bosom and made a dramatic face as the others affirmed that they, too, had very little time to read or do anything else they wanted to do because of their children.

"That's fine." Thaddeus chuckled. "It's not required reading."

"Well," the one who'd read it said, "I mean, it's not every day that someone you grew up with writes a bestselling book. I mean, I remember so much of what you wrote about." He watched as something dawned on her, crossing her face like a shadow.

"Wait a minute." She pointed from Larkin to Thaddeus. "Didn't you two grow up next door to each other?" She nudged the woman next to her. "This is all coming back to me now."

Thaddeus knew why, if she'd read the book, she was asking. He hoped against hope that Larkin had also been *so* busy, far too busy to read.

"We did," Larkin said, then reached for the glass of water sitting in front of her. A lone lemon slice bobbed on the surface. She took a drink. "But that was a long time ago." She set the water glass back down.

Carrie or Krista added excitedly, "I picked Larkin up tonight, and the press was already at your house. It was a zoo!" She dialed down her tone, looking at him with large, sympathetic eyes and saying, "I feel so bad for your family, dealing with all this again."

Thaddeus nodded curtly. "Yeah, well, it's weird to say we're used to it, but . . ." He paused, shrugged. "We're kind of used to it." He decided to use the moment to attempt an exit. "So, hey, it was good seeing you guys."

But instead of the women letting him go, one of them shouted, "No, wait! There's Lee Watkins! Y'all need to say hey to him. You remember him?" She waved her arm and hollered, "Lee, get your ass over here!"

Thaddeus looked over to see the man in question making his way over. His head was shaved, and Thaddeus could see several tattoos on his arms. Being that he probably had far fewer tattoos and a lot more hair in high school, he didn't look familiar at all.

"What's up?" Lee Watkins called out as he approached the table. "What is this? A reunion?"

The girl who had called him over said, "It is now!"

Lee Watkins held out his hand to Phillip. "Good to see you, man."

Phillip shook his hand, and Lee quickly turned his attention to Thaddeus. "And you are?"

Before he could answer, one of the girls—Amy?—called out, "You know TJ—I mean, Thaddeus." She hurried to correct herself. "Everyone knows Thaddeus," she added just as Lee reached for his hand.

It seemed as if, upon hearing his name, Lee Watkins's grip on Thaddeus's hand loosened for a fraction of a second. He recovered so quickly it left Thaddeus wondering if he'd imagined it.

"Of course, of course," Lee said. "The prodigal son returns." He let go of Thaddeus's hand and turned to scan the table of girls, pausing when he spotted Larkin.

"Don't believe I know you," he said, winking at her. Thaddeus suppressed a grin as Larkin's face registered her distaste at being winked at.

"This is Larkin. She used to be Thaddeus's next-door neighbor," the one Thaddeus was almost certain was Krista said. He'd had a brief crush on her in high school, but now he couldn't remember why.

Thaddeus decided to attempt an escape a second time. He lifted his now empty beer in a salute to them all. He was drinking too much too fast, but he couldn't help himself. There was such a thing, after all, as drowning your sorrows.

"Well, it was good seeing you guys," he said again, then added, "Take care." He walked away from their chorus of parting words, heading back to the table he and Phillip had occupied. The server stood waiting for them, new beers sweating on her upheld tray. Phillip was right behind him.

"It looked like y'all were wrapping up over there," she said. "So I figured I'd just meet you back here."

Phillip thanked her and lifted his beer from the tray, then stepped back so she could hold out the tray to Thaddeus. Thaddeus grabbed his own beer, looking up just in time to notice how Phillip unabashedly ogled her chest before she fled with the empty tray, cheeks aflame.

"I see you haven't changed a bit," Thaddeus said.

"Hey, I'm married, not dead. I can look, just so long as I don't touch," he said. "Am I right?"

Thaddeus shrugged and let it go. What business was Phillip's fidelity to him? He barely knew the guy anymore. After tonight he probably wouldn't see him again for another decade. With any luck he'd be out of there and back on tour in a day or so. He thought of his conversation with Kristyn and felt a little pang at the thought of not getting to see her and her little family.

They both sank back into their chairs with the kind of weariness that accompanies the awareness that the night would end soon. What a strange night it had been. He looked over his shoulder, making sure Larkin was really there, that he hadn't dreamed her. He caught her looking back at him and they both quickly looked away.

Phillip also looked in the direction of the table they'd just left as he took a long pull from his own beer.

"You have no clue who that guy is, do you?" he asked, probably an attempt to steer the subject away from his wandering eye.

"Who?" Thaddeus asked.

Phillip glanced over at the table again, then turned back to pick at the label of his beer. "Lee," he said. "Watkins?" He looked up at Thaddeus. "You don't remember him? From that night?"

Phillip didn't have to indicate which night. There was only one he could be speaking of. Why did they have to keep returning to it? Thaddeus felt his heart rate pick up as he looked over at the man who'd shaken his hand moments ago. He studied his profile as he animatedly continued talking to the girls.

"He was there?" he asked without looking at Phillip. There were a good many guys there that night. It was possible Lee Watkins had been one of them.

"He was drinking with us. He was older, and we thought he was cool," Phillip said.

Thaddeus felt the reel begin to play, the worn, warped memories from that night flashing in fragmented images inside his head: feet running over desiccated cornstalks, flashlight beams lighting on his friends' faces, spinning with his arms outstretched, laughing even though nothing was funny, disembodied children's voices emanating from the darkness as they called to each other, and later, his brother's name carried on the wind, shouted by adult voices.

He saw himself walking over to retrieve that rock Davy had tossed when they'd sent him away. Thaddeus had tried to inspect it, curious if Davy had indeed found a piece of fool's gold. But it was too dark to tell. Blame it on the moon, indeed. He'd put the rock in his pocket so he could give it to Davy the next time he saw him. He felt the weight of it still there, in his pocket all these years later, growing heavier with every hour he was back in this town.

"He's the one who dared you to shotgun that beer," Phillip said. "Remember?"

"That was him?" He resisted the urge to glance over one more time. Lee Watkins was more than just some random dude from high school. He had been there that night. And that made him significant.

"Yeah," Phillip said, his voice suddenly hoarse. "I know you said you don't want to talk about it, but . . . don't you think about it?" When Thaddeus didn't respond, he rushed to add, "I mean, of course you think about it. You wrote a whole book about it. But I read it, and—you didn't talk about that part. I mean, about why we were really there."

Thaddeus glared at Phillip. This wasn't the time or the place to dig into the truth about that night. While his memoir was truthful, he had left out some damning details. To Thaddeus, the obvious stuff was damning enough. He'd been with his brother but had failed to protect him. He couldn't underline that fact by providing the specific details of just how bad of a brother he'd been. It was his story, and he'd told it the way he wanted to, the only way he could bear to.

"I'm not doing this," he said. "I can't."

"You were fifteen years old," Phillip said, his voice softening. "People do dumb things as kids. And later in life, they wish they hadn't. It's part of growing up."

The roaring began, a wind tunnel inside Thaddeus's head. It meant he needed to get up, to walk, to flee. Instead he drained what was left in his beer bottle and slammed it back down.

"I was his older brother," he said.

"You might've been older, but you were a kid too. No matter what you got up to that night, it doesn't make it your fault," Phillip pressed.

The cyclone's intensity increased, the wind howled, and the twister spiraled faster and faster inside his head.

"Yeah? Well, then whose fault was it?" he asked, a question he'd turned around in his mind endlessly. Phillip opened his mouth to respond, but Thaddeus held up a hand to stop him and stood up.

"I'm sorry, I just can't talk about this. Not here, not now." He started to walk away, then turned back. "Is this why you brought me here? So you could push me about this? Force me to have some sort of cleansing moment?"

It was all coming back to him, the memories, the feelings, the guilt. The roaring inside him was fueled in part by rage at himself and in part by rage at Philly—for arranging that night at all. Phillip had been his best friend, but he'd also been his idol. The younger version of himself had wanted nothing more than to be like Phillip with his good looks, effortless coolness, and athletic ability. So he'd done whatever Phillip said he should, including drinking the beer Phillip's uncle bought them that night. He'd wanted to go so badly that he would've done anything. Including let his younger brother tag along just so he could be there.

He looked over at Lee Watkins, still chatting up the ladies, still smiling. At that moment Lee Watkins glanced in his direction. Their eyes met and Lee looked quickly away, his smile momentarily gone. Thaddeus looked from Lee to Phillip, who stared up at him with a frightened expression, as if he knew he'd gone too far.

All Thaddeus wanted was to get as far away from both of them as he could, away from what their youthful exploits had unwittingly set in motion that night. Phillip started to protest, to justify, to reason, but Thaddeus just turned and walked away.

He was at the outer edge of the parking lot, pacing in front of his dad's Camry when Larkin emerged from the bar. He'd been looking back and forth from the car to the bar, calculating just how many beers he'd had that evening and debating whether to risk driving, until she stepped through the door. Their eyes met and he took a stutter step backward, throwing off his balance as he listed slightly. She hurried toward him as if she could catch him if he fell, as if he wouldn't take her down with him.

"Everything ok?" Larkin asked when she reached him, concern lining her brow.

He chuckled, leaning on the Camry's bumper to aid his balance. "Uh, now that you mention it, no." It occurred to him that it was the first real thing they'd said to each other in eighteen years.

"I saw you leave and, well, I was hoping I could catch a ride home with you," she said. He looked at her, slowly comprehending what she was asking: the two of them, alone in a car together after all these years. Maybe she didn't hate him as much as he thought. "I'm miserable in there," she added, a pleading note in her voice. "I rode with those girls, and they seem intent on closing the place down."

He couldn't dwell on what she did or didn't mean by her request. The simple truth was, she had just answered his question of to drive or not to drive. He held out his keys.

"How about I provide the car, and you provide the driving?" He shook the keys a little, carrot before horse. Not that he saw her as the horse in this scenario. "I mean, I noticed you weren't drinking in there, and I can't say the same for myself, so . . ."

The desperate look left her face. "Deal," she said as she took the keys from his hand and walked over to the car. Neither spoke as they climbed in, the sound of their doors slamming in unison like an exclamation point.

In the close, quiet space of the car he could smell her perfume. She smelled different, yet the same. He watched as she put the key in the ignition and turned the engine, then shifted into Reverse. His stomach roiled as she backed up, then lurched forward a little too quickly. He gripped the door handle to steady himself.

"Sorry," she said without looking at him.

They drove mostly in silence. Thaddeus thought of and discarded at least twenty conversation starters before giving up and turning on the radio, scrolling through the stations without really listening to the music. He stole glances at her profile, taking in the strange sight of her there, up close. He didn't know her anymore, but he knew her just the same. She was strange yet familiar—new and old. A phrase crossed his mind: *all at the very same time.* No doubt they'd already run that video on the evening news that very evening.

Larkin had been standing right beside him when that video was recorded. Even though he'd been trying to be cool around her that night, he couldn't stop himself from laughing in response to the look of sheer joy on Davy's face after he successfully kept all four balls in the air. Larkin had laughed too. They'd all laughed, together.

She pulled into the driveway of his house and parked. The press had given up for the night. The yard was empty and the house was dark. At Larkin's house next door, a light was on in the den.

"Thanks," he said. "For driving. When you came outside, I was debating driving myself even though I knew I shouldn't. That's how bad I needed to get out of there."

"Well, I'm glad I could help." She turned off the car and took her hands off the steering wheel, resting them in her lap.

He went to open his door, then stopped and turned back to look at her, curious. "How come you weren't drinking tonight? Are you in AA or something?"

She smiled and shook her head. "No."

"Oh." He lowered his voice to a whisper. "Are you, like, religious now?"

She laughed and lowered her voice to match his. "I'm, like, pregnant now."

His mouth opened and his eyes went straight to her midsection, then quickly back to her face. "Oh, I, um, had no idea. I mean you don't . . . look . . ." Unable to say the last word, his voice trailed off. He hoped she couldn't see his cheeks reddening in the dark car.

"It's early still," she said.

Thaddeus glanced over at her house, then back, confused. Maybe she was going through a divorce. He recalled his mom saying something about Larkin earlier in the day, but he'd tuned her out. Now he regretted it. His mom would've given him the whole scoop and he wouldn't have had to ask Larkin dumb questions.

"Do you live with your mom now or something?" This, too, was said in a lowered, apologetic tone.

"Sort of, yes. Not permanently, though. My husband's deployed. He's in the Middle East. With me being pregnant and having Audrey—that's our daughter—to look after, and since my dad died, we just decided it would be better if I came here while he was over there. I can look after Mom and she can look after me." She said this last part like it was a good thing. He wondered if she meant it.

Speaking of looking after, his hand went to his pocket, just making sure the rock was where it was supposed to be. Larkin watched him but didn't ask what he was doing. He'd told Nicole about the rock that night. Even taken it out and showed it to her. Though she'd said all the right things, the memory still made his stomach churn.

"That's a lot," he hurried to say. "To handle." He paused. "And I'm sorry about your dad. I should've said that sooner."

She reached up and grabbed the steering wheel again as if she was going to drive away. "Life goes on." She shrugged. "Or whatever you're supposed to say."

He nodded solemnly. "You sound like a grown-up."

She laughed in spite of herself. "I guess that's what we are now."

He racked his brain for a way to keep her talking; he wasn't ready to get out of the car yet. "Speaking of grown-ups, it was surreal to see all those people tonight, huh?"

"Yeah, kind of like a reunion I didn't plan on going to."

"No kidding."

They both went quiet. He knew he should let her go inside her house, and he should go inside his own house. Before he could say as much, she spoke again.

"You looked like you left the bar angry." Then she quickly added, "Sorry. I'm being nosy." She moved her hand from the steering wheel to the driver's side door handle.

He reached over and put his hand on her shoulder, attempting to keep her from leaving the car.

"You aren't being nosy," he said. The light coming into the car was filtered through dew collecting on the windshield, making her face appear pockmarked. She looked at him, saying nothing as she waited for him to go on.

He opened his mouth, then closed it. He wanted to talk like they used to on those long nights that summer before Davy disappeared. After that, he'd walled himself off from her, ruining any chance at a future with her. It was too late to make that up to her, to him, to who they might have been had things not gone the way they did. He exhaled.

"It's been a long night. And I've had a lot to drink." He rolled his eyes at himself to make her smile.

"If you ever want to talk . . . I'm right next door."

Inside he felt a little burst of hope. Another opening, a long-closed door cracked open just the tiniest bit. Of course, she was married now and pregnant. So the crack would stay a crack. Still, it would be nice to have her there, close by, to talk to again.

"You might regret that offer," he said and smiled even as his heart began to ache a little. When he spoke again, he had to force the words past a lump that had swelled in his throat. "I could use a friend right now." He gestured toward his house, and all that it symbolized.

As if on cue, the downstairs lights flashed on and his mother stepped out on the porch, squinting to see who was sitting in the Camry.

"My mother's timing is impeccable, as always," he said.

Larkin smiled. He started to get out of the car, then stilled, remembering his manners.

"Thanks again. For the ride."

"Thanks for getting me out of there." She removed the keys from the ignition and dropped them in his hand. "And now you are the Keymaster," she intoned, doing her best Sigourney Weaver impression, the joke hearkening back to so many summer days in his family room watching a well-worn VHS copy of *Ghostbusters*.

Thaddeus smiled and stepped out of the car, then walked quickly toward his mother, who beckoned him inside, leaving Larkin to make her own way home.

PART 3

Sunday, April 30, 2006

CHAPTER 18

Anissa

The ringing phone jarred her from a fitful sleep. Her dreams had been filled with images of hungry cats and lost boys. Or perhaps it was lost cats and hungry boys. Anissa had no idea. The details of the dream departed as she opened her eyes. She sat up and reached for her phone, bleary-eyed, answering just before it rolled over to voicemail.

"Hello?" she croaked.

"It's Pete," the sheriff said.

"Yes?" she asked, her stomach knotting in advance of whatever he was going to say. Calls from her boss in the wee hours were never for good news.

"They found him," Pete said.

Neither of them said anything, each observing a moment of silence for a lost boy, now found. Pete's breathing seemed to slow. She waited for him to speak again, but he didn't. She wondered if he'd been there when they found Davy.

"Where was he?" she asked, though she could guess it wasn't very far from where the jacket was found. In her mind she was standing beside Seth, watching the search team, so close to where Davy had been all along, yet miles away from where she'd last seen him.

"Buried," the sheriff said. "In a wooded patch about forty yards from where the jacket was." He exhaled and she knew that as he did so, he removed his hat and wiped his brow before depositing the hat back on his head.

"It was pretty deep. Whoever buried him . . ." Another silence elapsed. "Whoever buried him"—his voice sounded pinched—"wasn't worried about taking their time or being caught in the act."

"Or had help?" she ventured.

He was quiet, probably thinking about that possibility, probably not for the first time. "Maybe. Who knows."

She shuddered at the thought of more than one perpetrator living and working in their town all these years. She wondered if she'd stood behind them in the grocery checkout line, given them the right of way in traffic, sat beside them in church.

"Also," he said. She cringed at the word. There was more. "Gordon Swift. We're gonna have to bring him in today. For more questioning. You're gonna need to communicate to the Malcors the whys and wherefores as they happen."

"Why?" she said on a breath. She thought of the handsome, gentle man maintaining his innocence in his driveway, longing to be left alone, seeing her as just another tormentor.

The sheriff sighed wearily. She wondered if he'd slept at all since that jacket was discovered.

"There was . . . an item . . . with the kid. We're running finger-prints, but we're pretty sure whose we're gonna find. There was . . . indication of where the item came from that's just about as reliable as fingerprints or DNA." He sighed again. The item was clearly an unwelcome complication.

"The thing I need you to keep in mind is that the last thing we need is for this new development to get misconstrued by the family or the press. Innocent until proven guilty and all that. Swift's lawyer will have a field day if we mismanage this."

"I'll do whatever you need," she promised, even as her heart pounded and her throat constricted. She slid out from under the warm covers and went to stand by her bedroom window, her eyes scanning the dark sky for a glimpse of the moon. She found it, the barest crescent of light, just like that night more than twenty years ago.

"For now, just get dressed, get some coffee in you, then go to the Malcor house and wait in your car outside. I'll be there as soon as I can, and we'll go in together."

She breathed a sigh of relief that he would be with her. She didn't know if she could face the Malcors alone. Especially Thaddeus. Since the moment he'd arrived at their house, he'd watched her, his wary eyes questioning why she was there. He looked at her like he knew she was withholding something. Or maybe that was just her own conscience. She owed the Malcors the truth—that she was there for more than just her job. She was there because, for the briefest moment, she'd loved Davy too.

"So *you're* going to tell them?" she asked, hoping that was the case. She didn't think she could be the one to tell the Malcors that Davy was dead.

"Yes," he said. "But I can't stay afterward, so I'm going to need you to." He yawned into the phone, then apologized for doing so. "There's going to be a press conference later today. Make sure they're prepped for that too. It'll be . . . hard for them, but if they can manage to be there, I think it would be good. It's gonna be a tough day, a lot for them to handle. They'll need someone." His voice caught and she got the distinct feeling that he would cry or scream or punch something as soon as they hung up. Or maybe he'd just go pick up his baby and hold him close.

She agreed to meet him at the Malcor home, replaced the phone in its cradle, and returned to the window, seeking the moon once more, as if it would tell her why. She stared up at the sickle in the sky, as thin as the sliver of hope the Malcor family had been holding on to.

"You were here," she said aloud in the emptiness of her room. "You were right here." She pressed her forehead into the cold glass as she said her own private goodbye to a boy who was really and truly gone.

She was about to turn away, to start getting ready for the long day ahead, when movement below caught her eye.

She looked down at the sidewalk and saw the cat there, sitting on its haunches, blinking up at her as if it expected something. The two stared at each other for a moment before she turned away from the window in search of something to feed the poor thing.

By the time she stepped out onto her front stoop holding a can of tuna, the cat was gone.

"Here, kitty kitty," she called softly. No response. She set the can down, barely feeling the chill of the night air as it blew through her.

October 12, 1985
8:17 p.m.

TJ finishes his second beer and belches loudly as he crushes the can. Beside him, Phillip crushes his can too. Together they toss them into a growing pile. TJ looks over at the large garbage bag, still bulging with can-shaped lumps, and feels something like relief. There is more beer to be had, more fun with his friends in this wooded hideaway near an abandoned field, while in the distance the children play their games.

TJ is not a child anymore. In the span of a few weeks, he's had his first kiss and gotten drunk for the first time. His mother is always telling him not to be in such a hurry to grow up, but sitting there with his buddies around him joking and cursing, he doesn't agree with her. He wants desperately to grow up—the faster, the better. He is more convinced than ever that good things await him on the other side of childhood. And he can't wait for all of it.

"Hey, Phillip, did your uncle really get this beer for you?" a kid named Mike asks.

Phillip narrows his eyes at Mike. "Yeah, why?" This close to Phillip, TJ can feel Phillip's body stiffen in response to the question.

"I mean, it's just cool is all."

"Well, just make sure you keep it to yourself. If this gets him in trouble with one of your asshole parents, I'll be the one to pay the price." Phillip smiles like he is joking, but TJ can tell he's not. Phillip's uncle is nice enough, but he has a temper. TJ has seen the evidence on his friend through the years, but he's never said anything, feeling like it would break some unspoken code between them. Phillip had to move in with his uncle after his parents died, and though he was a father figure, he was not a father in the normal sense of the word.

Mike pretends to zip his lips as some older guy beside him named Lee Watkins raises his beer can and says, "To Phillip's uncle. Coolest cat in town."

TJ and Phillip have no cans to raise in response, so Phillip crawls over to the bag, extracts two cans, and hands one to TJ. Together they pop the tops, listening to the satisfying sound of the carbonation releasing from its seal. It will be a sound, TJ thinks, he will always tie to this night, to this time with his best friend beside him, learning just a little more about what it means to grow up.

"To Phillip's uncle," TJ agrees, holding the fresh can aloft before he takes a long swig, adding an "ahhh" after he swallows like they do on the beer commercials on TV.

For a moment all the boys are quiet as they listen to the night sounds and breathe in the cooling night air. TJ looks up to find the barest suggestion of a moon in the sky, and for the briefest moment, he wonders where Davy is, what he is doing. He pats his pocket, making sure the rock he picked up after Davy ran off is still there. He will give it to the kid when he sees him, a peace offering meant to smooth over the rough edges created between them tonight. He even thinks about running over to check on him real quick, just so he can say he did if his parents ask. He is about to get to his feet when Lee Watkins speaks up again.

"Anyone ever shotgunned a beer?" Lee asks with a devilish grin. As TJ shakes his head no, all thoughts of Davy leave his mind.

CHAPTER 19

Tabitha

The sun had barely started coming up when there was a knock at the front door. She'd gone back to bed after Thaddeus arrived home in the middle of the night, but her sleep had been fitful, her dreams foreboding. For a moment her addled mind decided it was Thaddeus knocking on the door, and she hurried out of bed, pulling on her old velour robe as she rushed downstairs.

She tugged the door open to find not Thaddeus on the porch but two people, a man and a woman. It took her a moment to grasp that it was the sheriff and the girl who'd been assigned to them. It took her less than a moment to understand that they were there to deliver bad news. She turned away.

"Daniel!" she called, her body beginning to shake involuntarily. "Daniel!" she hollered again, louder, glad he was there, that he was near.

Daniel appeared at the top of the stairs, and then beside him, Thaddeus. She turned to face the sheriff and the girl. Anissa. Her name was Anissa. Anissa would not meet Tabitha's eyes, turning her gaze toward the sheriff instead. She looked to him because he was the source, Tabitha understood. He had come with the answer to a question none of them wanted to ask.

Daniel and Thaddeus came to stand behind her, flanking her like guards. She did not know if this was intentional but thought perhaps it was wise for them to be there, just behind her, in case she collapsed. In case she couldn't withstand what the sheriff was about to say.

But she did. She stood there as Pete Lancaster delivered the news that her son, after missing for twenty-one years, had been found. He'd been buried near the rusted building where they'd found his jacket. He was not somewhere else, having grown up as a completely different person, someone who had simply forgotten them as the years passed. He had not been abducted in order to replace someone else's son. He had not run away. He had not been trafficked. None of her imaginings that allowed him to still be alive had been true. Davy was dead.

The sheriff said other things, things she was sure were important, something about Gordon Swift, something about a press conference later that afternoon. But her mind stopped receiving information beyond the fact that Davy had been found. Her head filled with a white light, a rushing sound like wind through aspen trees, her errant thoughts the silver sound of clattering leaves. She asked to sit down and the girl, Anissa, took her arm, helped her to the couch.

Daniel and Thaddeus followed, lowering themselves to the spots on each side of her. She felt them there but could not see them. All she could see was Davy that last night. Davy whining, asking why she was leaving him with Thaddeus, why she couldn't just stay home.

"Sometimes moms get to have fun too," she'd said.

Je ne regrette rien. She repeated the words to herself again and again even as the sheriff left and Anissa walked him out.

Even as Thaddeus fled the room. Even as Daniel stayed by her side, saying her name like a question, his face a mixture of concern and grief. He said it louder and louder, but his voice could not drown out the voice inside her head. The one that insisted, over and over, that she regretted nothing.

FROM *EVERY MOMENT SINCE: A MEMOIR* BY THADDEUS MALCOR

PUBLISHED SEPTEMBER 20, 2005

The farmer's widow did sell the land. And who could blame her after what happened there? After it was sold, the property sat for a while, as if no one wanted to be the one to break ground, to knock down the farmhouse and the manager's cottage and the outbuildings, to mow down the grove of trees in back of the house. But eventually someone did. They built condos on the site.

Someone lives there now, in the exact spot where Davy was last seen. I can't imagine who would want to. But so many people have come along since then, strangers who aren't familiar with what happened or who don't want to know. The people who live there probably don't know the first thing about my brother, that his last happy moments on earth likely took place in the spot where they now scramble eggs or wash clothes or watch TV. They don't know that their lives are going on in the very place a little boy's life was cut short.

How can I say that, you ask? Put it out there like that, that my brother is dead? Well, if he wasn't, he would have come back to us by now. It is that simple. There is nothing that would keep him from us except death. I know that. My mother knows that. As do my father and my sister. Though we would never say it aloud, we have accepted Davy's death deep inside ourselves. It is not something we know in our brains; it is something we feel in our bones.

My brother was taken from the spot where a condominium now stands. Whoever took him killed him hours or days after he was taken. And now he is waiting for us to find him, waiting for us to bring him home.

CHAPTER 20

Thaddeus

The pastor showed up as he always did when something happened with Davy's case, even though the Malcor family had not attended church in years. Thaddeus said something brief but polite to the man, then sought shelter in the backyard.

He stood alone in the dewy grass and inhaled great gulps of the cool morning air, his mind a jumble of thoughts, his heart clenching with what he knew were the beginning pangs of grief. In a way, he had been grieving his brother for over two decades, but the true grief began when the sheriff and that skittish woman showed up at their door, bearing news bad enough to warrant pulling sleeping people from warm beds.

He concentrated on breathing in and out, in and out, doing his best to ignore the headache he'd woken with thanks to the countless beers he'd pounded the night before. Slowly, the night came back to him in flashes, ending with him sitting in the car beside Larkin after she'd driven them home. He remembered talking to her but couldn't remember everything they'd said. He didn't think he'd said too much; he didn't have that nagging feeling he'd had after his night with Nicole. At least there was that.

As much as he'd prefer to think about the night before—the last night, it would turn out, his family would ever carry the scrap of hope that Davy was alive—the words the sheriff said reasserted themselves.

Davy was dead. They'd found his body. Gordon Swift, the man they'd long suspected, was being brought in for more questioning because of evidence found with Davy's body. There would be a press conference. They were expected to be there. They wanted someone from the family to make a statement.

Without an ounce of hubris, he knew all eyes would be on him at that press conference because of his book, and he wished writing a memoir had never crossed his mind. He thought back to when he'd had the idea. He'd gone to a writer's conference, paid one thousand dollars to spend a weekend with other writers trying to be published. The workshop leader, a writer of some renown, had asked her students what haunted them. When they were alone and quiet, she'd asked, what thoughts came back to them?

The answer for him, of course, was plain. He'd planned to spend that weekend working on his novel about a man rebuilding his life after being cut from a Major League Baseball team. Instead he'd written about Davy. At the end of the weekend he'd read what he'd written aloud to their little group, and afterward the writer of some renown had encouraged him to *"see where it led."*

He looked around at the irony of where it had led him, which was right back to the place he'd hoped his writing would take him away from. What had ever made him think that putting himself at the center of his brother's story was a good idea? Because, he realized now, he'd held on to the false security that Davy would stay missing and never be found. He'd banked on Davy remaining a mystery forever with Thaddeus existing safely inside that mystery. He cradled his aching head in his hands and closed his eyes. In the blackness of his mind, Davy was there, as he always was.

"Will you throw the baseball with me, TJ? I need to practice before Little League starts."

"Wanna see me juggle? I can keep three balls in the air at once! Soon it'll be four!"

"I saw you with Larkin. You like her, don't you? Do you wanna kiss her? That's gross."

"Please let me go with you, TJ. I don't want to stay here with Kristy. She's a baby. I won't bother you and your friends, I promise. Mom said I could."

He squeezed his eyes tightly together, as if the act would banish Davy from his mind. But Davy persisted, just like he always did. Davy was gone but not gone, haunting him, forever his eleven-year-old kid brother, forever asking things of him he hadn't been willing to give and now, it was official, never would.

The sound of a child laughing interrupted him and he thought for a panicky moment that Davy was there. He opened his eyes, half expecting to see the ghost of his brother in front of him. But there was no one. Had he imagined the laughter? He scanned the yard, and a pink blur caught his eye. Then, running after it, a blue blur.

He blinked, and Larkin and a little girl who looked just like her came into focus as they approached.

"Hi," the little girl said. Larkin had told him her name last night, but he'd either forgotten it or not really paid attention in the first place. Truth be told, he wasn't super interested in the child Larkin had with another man.

"Hi," he said, hoping it wasn't obvious that he'd been having an existential moment just before they showed up.

Larkin rushed forward and took the little girl's hand. "Ok, Audrey, you've said hello. Now let's leave him alone." She attempted to pull the child away, but Audrey—that was her name—didn't budge.

"What's your name?" the little girl asked, a challenge in her voice like she was daring him to answer. She had wispy blonde hair that was escaping from a ponytail and bright blue eyes that, he could tell, missed nothing.

"Thaddeus," he said, smiling in what he hoped was a reassuring way. "And you're Audrey."

The girl nodded proudly. "Audrey Marie Simmons. My middle name is after my grandma." She turned and pointed at the house next door. "That's where my grandma lives." She turned back. "What's your middle name?"

"Oh, Audrey, for heaven's sakes, it's early and Thaddeus has probably just woken up," Larkin said. She threw Thaddeus an apologetic look. "I know I have." She pointed at her daughter. "Someone escaped while I was trying to make us some breakfast." She looked down at her attire helplessly. Both she and the kid were wearing pajamas.

"I want to know his middle name first," Audrey argued.

"I don't see why it matters," Larkin argued back, and Thaddeus had a good idea how their days went in the house next door, engaged in a battle of wills, waiting for the day they could go home. For a moment he pitied Larkin. It felt good to pity someone besides himself.

"I just want to know." Audrey crossed her arms and looked from her mother to Thaddeus.

Larkin's sigh in response sounded like half exhaustion, half surrender. She looked at him. "I'm afraid my mother has been putting a lot of emphasis on middle names because Audrey's middle name is her name, and apparently she never wants Audrey to forget it." She widened her eyes as if to say, *"Please just play along."*

He smiled. "My middle name is James," he told Audrey as Larkin mouthed, *"Thank you."* She seemed so grateful, so he kept talking. "When I was a little kid, everyone called me by my initials, TJ, for Thaddeus James. And my brother"—his voice caught at the mention of Davy, but he made himself finish—"my brother's name was David Joel. At first my parents thought they'd call us TJ and DJ. But that turned out to be way too confusing. So they ended up just calling him Davy."

Tears pricked his eyes and he swallowed hard against the knot in his throat. He looked over to find Larkin staring at him, a wary look on her face.

"I bet you didn't know that," he said to Larkin. For a moment it was like they were back in that dark car, just the two of them.

She shook her head and reached to pull her daughter closer, the mention of Davy probably reminding her that bad things can happen to innocents. When she met his eyes, her own were shining with unshed tears.

"Audrey," she said. "Why don't you run inside and see if Grandma is up yet."

"If she's not, can I wake her?" Audrey looked up at her mom, and he could feel the love that passed between the two, superseding the bickering.

"Sure," said Larkin. She gave Audrey a gentle push toward her house, and thankfully, this time the child didn't protest but scampered off, singing to herself as she ran.

"What happened?" Larkin asked, her voice barely audible.

He both loved and hated that she knew something significant had happened, something more than the jacket that had summoned him home. Maybe she'd seen the pastor arrive and put two and two together, or maybe it was the way he'd just spoken of Davy, but she didn't need to be told. He hadn't had to spell it out for her. She knew him. She always had.

"The sheriff was here," he told her, working to control his voice. "They found him." Her hand flew to her mouth and her eyes widened. The tears she'd been holding back fell freely.

She stepped forward, erasing the space between them as she reached for him in much the same way she had reached for her daughter, reflexively, protectively. He let her take him into her arms and sank into the comfort he hadn't known he was looking for when he ran from the room where he'd learned that his lost brother had finally been found.

October 12, 1985
8:30 p.m.

The white wine has grown warm in her hands, yet Tabby makes no effort to refresh it as she half listens to the small talk made by the women surrounding her and half surveys the clusters of people dotted around the Myerses' house. She's reached the stage in the night where her head hums pleasantly, her senses satisfactorily dulled by the wine so that everything matters and nothing matters at the same time. She feels free and unfettered yet bound to those she loves. And at that moment, she loves everyone—her friends, her neighbors, her children, her husband.

More than once she's caught Danny's eye, thrilling a little when he winks at her from across the room, a fantasy playing out in her mind of going home to find the kids tucked in their beds, fast asleep, then hurrying to their room. She will, she decides, perform a slow striptease for him once they get behind their own locked door. Normally she shucks off her clothes and dives under the covers so he can't see her post-childbirth body. But not tonight, she promises herself. Tonight she will be brave. She will stand naked before him. She will leave the lights on, even.

"Don't you think, Tabby?" Marie is asking. Tabby turns toward the sound of her name, caught in the midst of her little fantasy.

"Sorry, what?" she asks her best friend, the woman she'd been fortunate enough to move next door to. When she first arrived in Wynotte, Tabby had felt displaced, homesick, a simmering anger at Danny constantly burbling under her skin for moving her far from her home and family in Ohio. How had she ended up in the South, of all places, where people said "ma'am" and "y'all" with no sense of irony, where a vowel was stretched to two syllables without an ounce of shame?

She'd hated it, but then she'd met Marie, who'd made it bearable. In the years they've been next-door neighbors, this place has become home. She shudders at the thought of going back to Ohio, with its gray, cold winters, to her family of origin, who no longer understand her. Geography, Tabby knows now, matters. Geography can change everything.

"Please don't tell me you're fantasizing about going home with Danny after this," Marie says. "The last thing y'all need is another baby."

Tabby pretends to hit her friend. "Don't you dare wish that on me when I'm finally getting my life back. This is the first time I've been out of the house with makeup on in weeks."

Marie laughs. "Well, it shows. You two are like a coupla kids." She elbows Tabby. "Just look at Danny over there. He might be standing with Jim and those guys, but he can't keep his eyes off you." At once four pairs of eyes seek out Danny across the room. Caught ogling his own wife, he looks away, but not before they all break out in laughter.

"I'd be amazed if Jim has looked over here at me even once tonight," Marie says. Tabby starts to argue with her friend—Marie and Jim have what anyone would deem a good marriage, even if it isn't necessarily a sexually charged one.

Before she can speak, Belinda Watts cuts in. "I'd be amazed if Ted remembered I was here at all." Which results in more laughter.

As the others launch into complaining about their husbands, Marie whispers in Tabby's ear, "Face it, kid, you're lucky" and gives her shoulder a squeeze.

Tabby nods even as a lump forms in her throat. She recalls the scene before they left home: the boys fighting, Kristy covered in ketchup, her yelling at everyone. She'd forgotten, that's all. She'd forgotten how lucky she is.

From across the room Tabby waits to catch Danny's eye once more, then she gives him a wink, vowing to herself she won't forget again.

CHAPTER 21

Tabitha

She'd sent Anissa off with the sheriff, insisting they didn't need her there while they made phone calls and prepared for the press conference. She and Daniel promised they'd avoid the press as they ran the gauntlet to their car, that they'd meet her at the station later. Once the girl drove away, Tabitha went in search of Thaddeus, who'd fled the house when Pastor Rivera arrived. She hadn't blamed him, half wishing she could do the same thing. She scanned the front yard, then went to check the back and saw him there, though not alone.

She watched from the window as Thaddeus and Larkin stepped apart from what must have been a long embrace. She scolded herself for watching them like a voyeur, but she couldn't look away from the picture of them there, together. There was something about the way they'd held each other, less like an embrace and more like they were keeping each other upright. When they parted, the air around them shimmered with sadness and something else. Loss. And not just the loss of Davy.

Though there had been a brief spark when they were kids, she'd never really thought there were real feelings between them. She'd clearly missed it, like she'd missed so much about her remaining two children. It was obvious to her now, the truth glinting before her like the morning sun bouncing off Larkin's diamond wedding ring as she lifted her hand to wipe tears from her eyes. Tabitha felt suddenly, irrationally angry at Thaddeus, leaping to the conclusion that he'd been the one to blow it with Larkin back when he'd had a chance. She and Marie could've been grandmothers together.

She felt the tears begin to fall, uninvited and unwelcome, over a grandchild that would never be. She ran to her room to hide, closing the door behind her as she threw herself on the bed and sobbed into her pillow. Even as she cried, she knew she was grieving over the wrong loss. She could not cry for Davy—not yet—but she could grieve all the things she didn't get after he went missing. These tears were good, cleansing, normal. But she'd wanted to save them for later, till after the press conference, till everyone went home.

Now, she coached herself, was not the time to fall apart. She forced herself to stop thinking about fairy-tale grandchildren, to sit up, and to squeeze her eyes shut so no more tears could fall. A light knock sounded at the door just before Daniel peeked in.

"You ok?" he asked, his voice creaky and uncertain as he studied her there, sitting on the bed, her feet planted on the floor, but her face tear-streaked. She looked back at him and gave a weak nod.

She could've sworn he'd aged since they stood in the doorway listening to the sheriff. He'd always been youthful-looking; people often remarked that he didn't look his age. But somehow in the past hour he'd leapt past the age he hadn't seemed to be and into an old man he wasn't yet meant to be. Even the way he walked over and sank next to her on the bed seemed like the movement of an elderly person. Or maybe it was the weight of the news they'd received acting as its own kind of gravitational pull, a force too great for the human body to withstand internally without external change.

She wondered then what she looked like, though she didn't really care. She had cared the night Davy disappeared, before they went to the party. She'd taken her time selecting the right clothes, applying makeup. She had wanted to feel beautiful, to be more than someone's mother for one evening.

"All this time," she said aloud as she stared at the floor. "I told myself I knew how it was going to end. I told everyone not to get their hopes up. I cited statistics. I spoke of closure, of needing to know because it would help us move forward."

With hesitance Daniel rested his hand on her leg, much like he'd done at the movie theater on their first date. Would she have gone on a second date with him if she'd known that marrying him would lead to all this?

"I told myself I was ready for it to be over—that we just needed to know already, so we could . . . what? Live? We've been doing that. But I thought . . ." She couldn't finish her sentence.

"You thought that knowing would be better than not knowing. You thought answers would bring peace," Daniel finished for her, his voice cracking on the word *peace*. They turned toward each other.

"I thought I was ready," she said, the tears threatening. "I wasn't ready."

"How can you ever be ready for news like this?" He put his arm around her, pulling her toward him. At first she felt panic—they weren't supposed to be doing this. Divorced people didn't do this. But the rules no longer applied, she decided, so she let herself be held. Both of their bodies radiated heat, as if they were trying to burn off the pain that filled them. Together they breathed in and out, in and out.

The odds had been stacked against them from the moment Davy went missing. *"Most marriages don't survive,"* the experts said. And the experts had been right, even as she and Danny attempted to defy the odds. But there just hadn't been enough left of either of them to fight the inevitable drift that pulled them apart. They'd handled their grief so differently, so individually, that it had been too hard to come back together. Yet here, now, it felt natural to cling to each other, to cross the great divide, if only for a moment.

They let go at the same time, silently deciding in unison that it was time to get up, to set the grief and pain aside, and get on with the business of being the Malcor family, the public version. They had a press conference to prepare for, a memorial service to plan, friends and family to notify before they heard the news from the press. She would need to tell Marie soon, before Larkin did, if she hadn't already. And Kristyn.

Daniel squeezed her shoulder. "I'll call Kristyn."

She gave him the side-eye. "How did you know I was thinking about her?"

He gave her a little half smile. "I've known you for a very long time." He stood and walked out of their room, and she watched him go.

"Yes, you have," she said quietly. "Yes, you have."

CHAPTER 22

Anissa

Outside the station Monica Allagash was waiting, her normally eager, dogged expression replaced by a wan, stricken look. Anissa almost didn't recognize the reporter without her determination. She nearly walked right past her.

But then Monica called her name. Anissa turned reflexively, then regretted it when she realized who it was. *Not now.*

"Yes?" Anissa asked. She stood frozen in place, not making any effort to close the gap between them.

"I heard," Monica said. "About Davy."

"I'm sure you did," Anissa said, crossing her arms. "But I'm not going to give any statements now. There'll be a press conference later this afternoon." She turned to go.

"Wait!" Monica called. "I-I don't want a statement. That-that's not why I came."

Anissa turned back and raised her eyebrows as if to say she was listening.

Monica shifted her weight, then looked at the doors leading into the police station before looking back at Anissa.

"I was asleep when I got the call, and of course, after I heard the news about Davy, I couldn't go back to sleep. So I got out of bed and went to my computer. I started pulling up all the stock photos and videos we have of him. You know, the ones we've all seen."

She looked at Anissa, who nodded at her to go on.

"I started looking at them all, one after the other. And I was just . . . struck. It was like I was seeing him for the first time. Seeing him as something other than a story." She sighed. "So I started putting them all into a file, like a slideshow. Then I added this instrumental piece that I thought was really beautiful, to set the tone. I was thinking maybe we could run it at noon or tonight. Or both. You know, as a tribute to Davy?"

Anissa nodded again, still not sure why Monica was telling her this but unsure how to ask without sounding rude.

"That's a nice gesture," she said.

"But then I thought maybe it's something you guys would like to show before the press conference. Kind of like a—I don't know—moment of silence kind of thing? So everyone there realizes what I—" She broke off, blinking rapidly to stave off threatening tears. Anissa watched with a kind of fascination as she witnessed what she'd once thought impossible: Monica Allagash being an actual human being.

Monica composed herself and went on. "So everyone there realizes what I lost sight of a long time ago. That Davy was an actual person, a little boy with a sense of humor and things he loved and a family who loved him."

Anissa felt tears collecting behind her own eyes. She thought of that little boy, laughing and running and alive that night. When she spoke, her voice was thick in her throat.

"That's kind of you."

Monica looked down at the ground, then back up. She held out a flash drive. "Feel free to make it available to all the other outlets." She shrugged. "To anyone who wants it."

"I'm sure they will," Anissa said. She walked toward Monica and accepted the flash drive. "Thank you for doing that."

Monica grinned and winked. "Maybe don't tell anyone where it came from, though. Wouldn't want anyone thinking I'm losing my edge."

Anissa smiled back. "Your secret's safe with me."

CHAPTER 23

Gordon

He'd been working in the studio early that morning when Harvey called with the news about Davy and the evidence they'd found on him. Gordon listened to his attorney tell him about the putty knife in the boy's pocket. A long time ago Gordon had convinced himself that the boy had dropped it or lost it—that the putty knife wouldn't come back to haunt him.

He'd been wrong about that.

"They're asking you to come in voluntarily," Harvey said. "For questioning." The older man's sigh was world-weary. "The way I see it, you've gotta do it."

"Ok," Gordon said.

"I'll come get you," Harvey said. "And I'll be with you every step of the way."

"Uh-huh," Gordon agreed. After all this time, he knew the drill.

"So go get a shower and have something to eat. I'll be there in about an hour." Harvey paused. "Ok?"

"Yeah," Gordon said. Though he didn't think he could eat. He'd lost his appetite the minute he'd heard Harvey's voice on the phone.

He hung up with Harvey and stood still for a moment, thinking about that knife, about the mistake he'd made that night—all the mistakes he'd made. So much he would've done differently, had he known what was going to happen. But wasn't that what life was—a long, slow dissection of how things could've been different, if only?

He replayed the cop coming to his door early that next morning, asking if he'd seen a kid. His lie had been a reflex. And now they had proof that he'd lied.

He shook his head, dispelling what might've been as he accepted what was. He put his tools back in place and walked out of the studio, just in time to see a flash of feet running away.

He watched as the kid from next door slowed long enough to look over his shoulder in case Gordon was chasing him. The kid must've been spying on him while he worked. He thought about hollering something after him. But he couldn't find the words.

Gordon sat very still, pressing his palms onto the cold Formica tabletop in the interview room they'd left him in. Harvey had excused himself to make a call, so Gordon was alone for the first time in hours.

He concentrated on not moving or humming or doing anything else beyond very slowly and deliberately inhaling and exhaling. Above him and to his left he knew the camera's eye was trained on him, eager to pick up any movement, any utterance that could be used against him later. He'd watched *Dateline*; he'd seen what happened when a person let down their guard, the recordings later beamed into living rooms as people sat with bowls of ice cream or popcorn on their laps and watched someone else's downfall as their evening entertainment.

He did not want to end up on *Dateline*. He did not want to go to prison. And yet here he was, one step closer to that possibility. They'd found Davy. Davy, forever eleven years old, appeared in his mind, his beseeching brown eyes asking Gordon for help on that night that has gone on forever.

He looked around the small room and thought, *It is going on even now.*

The door opened and the woman who'd been at his house yesterday walked in, the one who had treated him kindly, who hadn't looked at him like he was a felon. He'd seen humanity in her eyes, and though she was on the side of the enemy, he felt he could trust her, that maybe she hadn't already decided he was guilty. He hoped he'd see the same thing now.

Their eyes met, and he decided to speak to her, even though Harvey had given him explicit instructions to keep his mouth shut.

"Three of the kids that were playing in the fields that night said they saw a car pull into the drive that led to the farmhouse. Did you know that?" Gordon felt the need to assure her he hadn't done what he was suspected of. He couldn't say why it mattered; it just did. He wanted her to believe him, to believe *in* him.

"I did know that," she said. Spots of color bloomed on her cheeks.

"So I just wonder why it's me sitting here and not whoever was in that car?" His words were weary, not combative. Their eyes met again and she opened her mouth to answer just as another man entered the room, the cop who'd told him he was free to go at any time. Though they both knew that wasn't exactly true. Gordon glanced at his watch, the same watch his parents had given him for his graduation from college the spring before Davy disappeared.

With the cop in the room, the woman's demeanor changed. She spoke as if their exchange had never happened.

"I just came in here to let you know that the Malcor family is coming in for a press conference. We are going to do our best to keep you separate from them, to make sure they don't encounter you. They would be, understandably, upset by that, and we're trying to spare their feelings as much as possible during this difficult time. Which means it's possible we will have to keep you sequestered back here." She swallowed and looked down. "It's a delicate situation."

The cop chimed in, hitching up the belt where his gun was holstered.

"It's for your protection as much as theirs. Grieving families can do unpredictable things." He raised his eyebrows as he looked at Gordon. "Wouldn't want one of them to shoot ya or something. A little vigilante justice." He smirked at the woman, who narrowed her eyes at him before sending Gordon an apologetic look.

But the cop, undeterred, crossed his arms, and continued, "So what she's saying is, we don't want you anywhere near that family. The last thing they need is to see the man who's responsible for what happened to their son."

Gordon lowered his eyes to the table and waited for Harvey to return, thinking all the while that the cop wasn't entirely wrong.

Davy and Anissa talk as they cross the expansive field. Anissa tells Davy about her older sister, Marissa, and Davy tells Anissa about his older brother, TJ. They lament over how mean their older siblings are, how unfair it is that they once played with them and loved them, but now it has all changed and they want nothing to do with them. They trade stories of sibling injustice, which leads to Davy's coming clean about tonight—how TJ made fun of his jacket, then ditched him to be with his friends over in the woods.

Davy waits to feel shame over being the one left out, the one not even his brother wants around, but confessing this to Anissa doesn't feel as bad as confessing it to someone else. Because Anissa understands. She's been left out too.

As they reach the big house where the old lady lives, Anissa reaches over and pats Davy's shoulder.

"I'm sorry he was so mean to you," she says, keeping her voice low. "And I think your jacket is cool. You should wear it every day. I would if I had one. I love *Back to the Future*."

Davy turns to look at her, surprised. "You do?"

She makes an exaggerated face. "It's only my *favorite* movie."

Davy raises his eyebrows. "It is?" he asks, his voice louder than he'd intended. He claps his hand over his mouth and glances around, then exhales with relief when no one comes running out of either the big house or the little one.

"We don't want to get caught trespassing," he whispers. "You don't want to get arrested, do you?"

Anissa shakes her head vigorously, making her curls bounce. She'll get in a lot of trouble if she gets arrested. Her mom might even cancel her birthday party.

They've come to a stop in front of the big house and stand in a shadowy patch so the widow won't see them if she happens to look out one of her windows. But that is unlikely because the house is completely dark. She's probably gone to bed, or maybe she's not even there. Maybe she moved into one of those homes where they put old people.

Davy stares up at the large, dark house and thinks of the creepy house in *Psycho* with the dead old lady sitting in the window. A shiver runs through him and Anissa looks over.

"Someone just walked over your grave," she says.

Davy's eyes go wide. "What?"

She laughs. "That's what my mom says whenever someone shivers like that for no reason."

Davy gives her the side-eye. "Well, it's creepy."

Anissa shrugs, her shoulders touching the coils of her hair. "Yeah, I guess it is." She looks over at him, her face plaintive. "Sorry."

He grins. "It's ok." They stand there a moment longer, looking up at the house.

"So what do we do now?" Anissa asks.

Davy looks backward at the field they crossed in the dark. He'd been frightened walking through the dark like that, but he hadn't dared admit it to Anissa. He doesn't want her thinking he's chicken. Davy wonders if all his jumbled feelings about her mean he likes Anissa the way boys like girls. He thinks maybe it's too soon to tell. He wishes he could ask TJ about it. He feels certain TJ would know.

"I guess we go back," he suggests.

"I mean, at some point we're gonna have to," Anissa deadpans.

"Well, yeah, but I was just hoping there'd be something . . . interesting here. Like someone we could spy on or something."

Anissa jabs him with her elbow and points to their right, turning his attention away from the big house to the smaller version beside it, a cottage not much different from the ones where Anissa lives. But this one has been kept up nicely. This one looks like a dollhouse version of the big house. A little yard separates the two houses with a stone walkway connecting them. Inside the smaller house, the lights are on, and Davy can hear noise coming from the open windows—a baseball game playing on TV.

Davy makes the "follow me" motion before creeping toward the house, staying low and moving stealthily like he's seen people do on TV when they do surveillance. Keeping out of sight, the pair hunkers down below the windows that look into the main living area where, Davy sees as he peers in, a man sits on a couch, furiously drawing on a large sketch pad.

The man isn't as old as his dad, but he isn't a teenager like TJ. He's somewhere between the two. Davy wonders why he's all the way out here on an abandoned farm living next door to a creepy old house. He doesn't look like the type of person who would choose such a situation. But to Davy adults do many things that don't make sense.

Through the window Davy surveys the layout of the place. Off the living area he can make out a galley kitchen to the left and to the right a hallway that likely leads to a bedroom or two and probably a bathroom. Davy turns his attention back to the room where the man is, his eyes tracing the sparse furnishings—couch, chair, lamp, small television on a little stand—then moving to the rest of the room, which is the most interesting part.

A long table is filled with paints, brushes, pencils, erasers, putty, and odd things that look like they came from the hardware store in town. There are even—and Davy all but presses his nose to the screen to confirm this—oddly shaped knives, flat and rounded, almost like the spatulas his mom uses to cook. Some are caked with a substance; some look brand-new. Davy wonders if they are sharp. He wonders if the man would grab one and use it if he caught them spying. Davy drops back to the ground where Anissa sits, waiting for his report.

"Anything good?" she whispers.

He shrugs and whispers back. "Not really. He's just drawing."

"Drawing?" she asks. "What's he drawing?"

That's a good question. Davy hadn't tried to see.

"I'll look," he says and gestures that he is moving to another window to get a better view. She nods and watches him go.

Pine needles prick his palms as he crawls away, but he doesn't mind. It's for a good cause. Davy likes doing surveillance. He thinks maybe when he grows up he'll be a professional spy, or a private investigator like *Magnum, P.I. Private Investigator* is what the *PI* stands for. TJ had to tell him that, which made him feel dumb. But he knows it now.

From another window Davy peers in, focusing on the drawings the man has cast onto the floor. He has drawn hands, lots of hands, a few normal-looking hands holding . . . grapes, maybe? But a few of the hands are old and gnarled, holding shriveled stems with no grapes at all. Davy thinks of the house next door, then of the *Psycho* house with the old lady dead in the window, her face—and probably her hands too—like a mummy's.

His eyes dart over to the big house and for just a moment he thinks he sees movement in the upstairs window. Is the old lady there, watching him? Could she come after them? Maybe she isn't an old lady at all. Maybe she's the old lady's ghost. The images—of the hands and the knives and the creepy house and the drawing man—swirl in his mind. He drops back to his hands and knees and crawls, fast, back to Anissa.

"Let's go," he says.

"What's wrong?" she asks, alarm filling her face.

"Nothing," he says, willing his voice to sound calm. "It's just him drawing hands."

"Hands?" she asks, forgetting to whisper this time. Inside, Davy hears the man's pen fall to the ground, then footsteps crossing the floor.

"Go!" he hollers and begins to run.

Behind him, he hears the screen door creak open, hears the man yell, "Hey, you kids!" But Davy doesn't hear the rest, the thunder of his feet and Anissa's drowning out whatever threat the man calls after them.

They run until they are sure the night has hidden them, then stop to catch their breath, listening carefully for any sound of the man chasing them, but it's hard to hear anything over their ragged panting. As their breathing slows, the only sounds they can hear are the critters in the woods singing their nighttime songs and, away in the distance, the children they left behind, still playing their games.

Without a word, they begin the long march back to where they came from, the darkness ahead of them a gauntlet to cross.

CHAPTER 24

Anissa

Seth followed her out of the interview room, chuckling to himself. "Did you see his face? He's scared shitless. And he should be. That son of a bitch is guilty as sin."

She stopped walking and turned on him. "You need to be careful. The sheriff'll have your hide if he finds out you were messing with him like that. He's already sued the department once and he's not afraid to do it again."

He gave her his innocent-little-boy face. "I didn't do nothing wrong."

She frowned at him. "You know I hate it when you use a double negative."

She turned and walked quickly away, ducking into the women's restroom to escape Seth. He'd had no business coming into that room with her, standing so close she could smell the onions on his breath from lunch, taking potshots at poor Gordon Swift, who looked scared and alone and—as much as it pained her to admit—guilty. She hated the thought that she'd just been in the same room with the man who might have killed Davy.

Still, she couldn't deny or explain that, while in the room with him just then, the main thing she'd wanted to do was hug him and tell him everything would be all right. She pictured two versions of him, the older man in that interview room and the younger one on the night Davy disappeared. That night his hands had been drawing hands. Now, his hands rested utterly still.

She studied her reflection in the bathroom mirror, finding dark circles under her eyes, her hair gone frizzy from sleeping on it and then rushing out of the house after she was roused from sleep by the sheriff's call. She hadn't been able to return home and prep for the press conference and hated that she was going to appear on TV looking exhausted and unkempt. When she'd imagined this moment, she'd imagined things so differently—appearing professional, attractive, and confident on camera. But Pete had insisted she make the opening remarks. She'd done this before, but never for a case with this level of interest or with this level of personal stakes.

She patted her curls, as if that would subdue them somehow. She sighed and turned from the mirror. No amount of staring at her reflection would change how she looked. It was time to do her job and not let vanity or insecurity get in the way. This was about Davy, not her. No one would be looking at her anyway; all eyes would be on the grieving family.

She needed to make sure the Malcors were settled in the makeshift green room they'd assembled on the fly, a place for the family to wait before being trotted out onto the stage under the hawkish eyes of the press and the public. How could they do this in the midst of such grief? Anissa felt she knew what Tabitha would say if she asked her: years of practice.

She peeked in the room to find them all in a line, first Daniel, then Tabitha, then Thaddeus, perched on a short row of folding chairs. Each of them held a Styrofoam cup of coffee and looked uncomfortable and uncertain. Looking, she thought, a lot like Gordon Swift had.

All these lives, touched by one night. *"Mine was too,"* she wanted to say to them. When Gordon Swift had spoken of the three children who'd said they saw a car that night, she wanted so badly to admit that she'd been one of those children. But to admit that now would likely end her career.

She wanted to tell the Malcor family that Davy was the reason she pursued this job. That night a female officer had interviewed her about what she'd seen in the fields, her presence so authoritative. That night something had stirred in her, a wanting. She wanted to be like that officer—tough and unafraid. Someone unlike Anissa's mother. Back then, Anissa had thought it was that simple: that a career choice could make her the kind of woman she longed to be. She hadn't known that confidence and strength did not emanate from one choice but many.

She couldn't think of that right now. She had to focus on the task at hand. And the task at hand was to make this next part of the process as painless as possible for a family already in so much pain. She plastered on a smile for the Malcors, tried her best to channel that officer from long ago, someone she never saw again, as if she was a mirage, a fantasy instead of a real person. She'd always wanted to ask someone in the department about her, but she didn't know her name, and when she scanned the staff boards of headshots from years back, no faces looked familiar. Sometimes Anissa wondered if she'd dreamed it all.

"You guys doing ok?" Anissa asked the Malcors.

They nodded in unison. Then Thaddeus sipped his coffee, Daniel looked down at his feet, and Tabitha attempted a reassuring smile. *I'm the one who's supposed to be reassuring you.* Tabitha's coffee cup was empty, and Anissa offered to fetch her more, but Tabitha declined.

"We'll be taking y'all out any minute," she said. "They're just dealing with some of the sound equipment first."

"Yes, please don't make us sit out there on display any longer than necessary," Thaddeus said into his coffee cup. "Not sure why we have to be out there at all." He gave her a look. "Ratings?"

"If you'd like," Anissa hurried to reply, "I can ask the sheriff to come discuss other options if you'd rather not be out there." She could feel Thaddeus baiting her, but she refused to engage. What was the saying? Hurt people hurt people.

Thaddeus shrugged. "All I know is, if you guys expect us to say something out there, I'm not making some sort of family statement." He pointed at Tabitha. "Mom can do it. She always has."

"Thaddeus, I actually think it'd be best for you to do it this time," Tabitha said. "You wrote that book; people will expect it to be you."

Thaddeus frowned. "One has nothing to do with the other," he said. If Anissa didn't know better, she would bet he'd had a few nips of something before they left the house.

Tabitha rose from her seat. "It's time for someone else to do it. I'm tired of doing it. I did it for years. I talked and talked and talked about hope, and now that hope is gone!" Her voice broke and she sat down, crossing her arms in front of her.

Daniel reached over and patted her shoulder, then gave his son a stern look. "That's fine," he said. "I'll do it."

Tabitha jerked her head toward him. "But you . . . You never wanted to . . . You said you couldn't."

Daniel gave Tabitha a weary half smile. "It was never about could or couldn't. It was about doing what needed to be done. It took me a long time to learn that." He winked at his ex-wife, the action so quick Anissa wondered if she'd imagined it. "Too long," he added.

"Well," Thaddeus said, the sneer still in his voice. "I guess that's settled." He tilted his cup up and drained the rest of the coffee, then crushed the Styrofoam until a hole appeared in the side and remnants of coffee dribbled onto his jeans. He grimaced and cursed.

"I'll go get some paper towels," Anissa said and hurried out of the room, grateful for an excuse to flee the tension.

As she was carrying the paper towels back to Thaddeus, Pete jogged over and grabbed her elbow, halting her.

"Look," he said in a low voice. "I thought about it, and I need you to warn the family that we've got Swift here for questioning. Reassure them that they're not going to have to see him. I don't want someone asking about it out there"—he hitched his thumb in the direction of the front of the station, where the conference would be held—"and them not aware."

She glanced out the front windows to see people scurrying around making last-minute adjustments as members of the press milled about waiting for the event to start. They'd been lucky the weather was nice enough to hold the press conference outside.

"I'll tell them," she said. She headed back to the room where the Malcors were waiting. Three sets of eyes looked at her when she returned. Thaddeus reached out to take the paper towels and mumbled a thank-you as he dabbed at the coffee spill.

While he worked at the stain, she addressed the room. "Sheriff Lancaster wanted me to let you all know—just as a courtesy—that we have Gordon Swift here on the premises. As we told you this morning, there was some evidence recovered that we need to question him about. So he was asked to come in. And he did. Voluntarily." She couldn't help but emphasize that last word.

Thaddeus stopped working at the stain and looked up at her, his fist mashing the paper towels into a ball as his eyes widened. "Why would you have him here at the same time as us?"

"This is an active investigation," she said, feeling a defensive edge creep into her voice. So much for being diplomatic. "Time is of the essence."

"You mean you were afraid he was going to run if he knew you'd found evidence that he did what we've known he did all along?"

"Thaddeus," Tabitha said in a warning tone.

"I'm not involved with that aspect of the case," Anissa said, standing her ground. Thaddeus unnerved her, but he also angered her with his entitlement, his expectancy. He'd spent his formative years being treated as a victim, and as far as she was concerned, it showed. "I'm not an investigator. My job is to communicate on behalf of the department."

"Yeah, well, you should *communicate* that the *department* mishandled my brother's case from the beginning."

Daniel spoke up. "Thaddeus, this isn't the time or place to be discussing this."

Thaddeus rose from his seat. "What are you talking about? Of course this is the time and place. If not for their Barney Fife approach, we wouldn't be sitting here twenty-one years later waiting to be paraded in front of strangers to talk about Davy." He looked from Anissa to his parents to the door, as if he was thinking about bolting. "Contrary to popular opinion, I don't actually like talking about my brother all the time."

"I'm sorry," Anissa said, desperation welling up inside her. She couldn't allow the wheels to come off just yet. She had to get them through this press conference, then she could make sure they got home and were hidden away from the press. Then they could fall apart in private. They could grieve as loudly, as angrily, as they deserved.

"I wasn't involved with Davy's case back then." She heard the lie just underneath her words. "So I don't know how it was or wasn't handled. All I know is that now, here, today, we are working to get you the justice you deserve."

Thaddeus gave a caustic laugh and threw the paper towels toward the wastebasket to Anissa's left. The towels landed in the trash can with a soft *thunk*, and she remembered he'd been a baseball player back when everything happened. He'd been pretty good, as she recalled.

She thought about him that night, off with his friends in another, darker part of the field. With nowhere else to go, Davy had walked over to where she was standing. They'd stood there for a time, silent, watching the other kids play. Then he'd smiled at her and she'd smiled back. That was how it had started.

The door to the little room opened.

"We're going to get started now," the sheriff said, and wordlessly they all filed to the door.

CHAPTER 25

Tabitha

Before the press conference they'd been warned that a tribute video—a montage of photos, one giving way to the other—would play on a large screen erected for the occasion. Tabitha didn't have to see the screen to know which photos would be used: Davy's last school picture. Davy in his baseball uniform. Davy holding a toy airplane pretending to make it fly. Davy with Thaddeus and Kristyn, all of them so little. Lastly, Davy at Kristyn's party, wearing his *Back to the Future* jacket and balancing an armful of colorful balls as he grinned proudly. He'd driven them all nuts as he practiced juggling obsessively in the weeks leading up to the party. The people watching didn't know that part. How could they? They were strangers.

The tribute finished, predictably, with the video from the night of Kristyn's party, a private family event that had become public fodder because of a tragedy. *No one*, Tabitha thought, *should've ever seen that video but us*. But, desperate to find their son, they'd given the press any and all images of him they had, especially the most recent ones, in hopes that the right one at the right time would bring Davy back. From where she stood tucked out of sight, Tabitha could hear her little boy talking a mile a minute on the video, the lines she'd heard so many times since. *"Did you see, Mom, did you see? I did it! I kept four balls in the air! All at the very same time!"*

Anissa had given them the choice to stay in the green room until it was over. But Thaddeus and Daniel said it was nothing they hadn't seen before, and she'd nodded mutely, agreeably. Waiting in the wings, Tabitha had tried to steel herself for the sound of his voice, yet it was impossible not to feel the assault. As the video ended, Anissa took the stage, giving Tabitha time for her heart to return to a normal rhythm, for her legs to feel capable of holding her up.

Tabitha watched as the wind pushed Anissa's curls out of place and she reached up in vain to tame them. She could tell Anissa was working hard to hide her nerves as she spoke into the microphone, welcoming everyone and introducing herself as Anissa Weaver, Public Information Officer for the Wynotte Police Department. She announced that there would be a memorial service for Davy on Wednesday at Wynotte Methodist Church and that the public was welcome to pay their respects. She reiterated to the members of the press what would and would not be addressed during the conference, in hopes that they would abide by the rules.

Then she introduced the Malcor family and waved them forward. As they started the short walk, she felt Daniel reach out and take her hand. He squeezed it, a reassurance. She squeezed back and held fast, steadying herself by leaning on him.

Thaddeus and Daniel stood until Tabitha was seated, then Thaddeus sank into the chair beside her, and Daniel moved toward the podium.

Tabitha could hear the nerves in his voice as Daniel thanked everyone for coming, thanked law enforcement, and thanked the community. Then he asked the press to give them time to process and grieve, promising that they'd make future statements when they were ready, but not before.

"After almost twenty-one years, you'd think this wouldn't be a shock. But it has been. It's been—" He broke off, turned his head to look back at Tabitha, who could barely see through the sheen of tears filling her eyes. She nodded once and he turned back. "I don't think there's anything harder," he finished. Daniel slumped into his seat beside Thaddeus and wrapped his arm around his remaining son's shoulder as he wiped his eyes with his fist.

"I said I wouldn't do that," he said to no one. Tabitha reached over to pat his knee, a signal that he'd done a good job, but also a gesture of gratitude for doing what she could not.

Then it was the sheriff's turn. He peered at the crowd, gripping the edges of the podium as if, given the chance, he could tear it in two. He explained to the crowd that, after an extensive search, Davy's body was discovered buried approximately forty yards away from where his jacket had been found by a property owner. He clarified that the official cause of death was as yet undetermined and that speculation would not be tolerated. Tabitha wondered how in the world he could enforce that.

The sheriff took some questions, most of which concerned the evidence possibly implicating Gordon Swift, as if the wily press could trick the sheriff into answering something Anissa had clearly stated they would not address. Then Pete Lancaster turned and expressed his condolences to the three of them, as if he hadn't already, privately. Fumbling for words to close out his part, he thanked all the law enforcement personnel and volunteers who worked night and day to search for Davy after the jacket was found.

"They went without food, without sleep, to find this child," he said. "They knew how important this search was and they committed to it as a team. Their thoroughness and tenacity made all the difference in finding Davy."

He let go of the podium and leaned back as if to better take in the crowd, his long arms dangling at his side. "We don't do these searches just for those who go missing. We do these searches for their families as well, to provide closure, or the closest we can come to it." Once again, he nodded at the three Malcors, his eyes searching their faces for validation, or maybe commendation. But all three stared blankly back at him, blinking in the bright spring sun.

FROM *EVERY MOMENT SINCE: A MEMOIR* BY THADDEUS MALCOR

PUBLISHED SEPTEMBER 20, 2005

I was never a hunter, never wanted to shoot a bird out of the sky midflight or fell a majestic buck. I never had a physical fight in school, choosing words as my weapons instead of my fists. When it came time to pick a sport, I didn't pick football because I didn't relish hitting or being hit. Baseball seemed the safer choice.

The rage that boiled up inside me whenever I saw a photo or heard the name of the suspect in my brother's abduction not only surprised me; it made me call into question what I'd believed about myself. To find this part of me existed—this angry, vengeful, dangerous part—was akin to learning I had horns, or a tail, or eyes in the back of my head. I was not who I fancied myself to be, and it scared me.

Because I knew this: given the opportunity, I could hurt the man I believe hurt Davy. It's quite possible I could take his life. And I don't know if I would even need a weapon. When I envisioned getting my hands on him, it was just that: my hands going around his neck, thin and exposed with its cords of tendons, its knobby bones, its tracks of veins. I imagined crushing it all, smashing his Adam's apple like an egg as he gasped and coughed and tried to plead. My eyes would watch as the light dimmed in his. My face would be the last thing he ever saw. I relished this fantasy throughout my younger years the way many young men relish fantasies about nurses or maids or teachers. My fantasy, I knew, was far worse than those, and needed to be kept hidden.

That knowledge didn't stop me from buying a hand grip strengthener, using it multiple times throughout the day as I played the fantasy out in my mind. I got as fixated as any addict, and somewhere along the way I knew I'd crossed over some line. I'd wandered into a mental terrain as pervasive and twisted as that of a person who would harm an eleven-year-old boy, my own mind consumed with hurting and killing.

The problem was, I wanted to stay there in that place in my mind. I liked my fantasy. I liked feeling the strength grow in my hands and imagining using that strength as I exacted my revenge. It fueled me, propelled me, and comforted me, as strange as that may sound. It was a buffer, a way to think about my brother without really thinking about him. For me, revenge replaced responsibility.

I wish I could tell you that eventually I abandoned the fantasy entirely. But that would not be the truth. I learned to suppress it, to bury it underneath other, more acceptable fantasies, like having a relationship, buying a house, getting a book deal. If sometimes that fantasy reentered my mental arena, I would let it stay just for a bit, like a guest you hadn't invited but felt obligated to entertain out of politeness. And then I would usher it out, only to realize that even after the fantasy was gone from my mind, my hands were still clenched, a reminder that I was always, still, ready to do what needed to be done should the time ever come.

CHAPTER 26

Thaddeus

Closure!" His mother spat the word once they were all inside the car. "I hate when people throw that word around. Like it means anything at all."

"He didn't know what else to say," his father said, ever the diplomat.

"To them this case may get closed, but for us there is no closure," Tabitha argued. She thought about it and added, "Not that *they* can give us at least."

Thaddeus couldn't resist. "So who can?" The question hung there like a cartoon speech bubble by his mouth with no reply from his mother. They all knew the answer: no one could. It was stupid and fairly heartless to goad her, but all day he'd felt cantankerous, itching for a challenge, a fight, anything to keep from feeling the grief and regret that simmered deep inside.

For the rest of the ride they were silent. His father didn't even turn on the '70s radio station that normally provided background noise. Thaddeus looked out the window and wondered how he would fill the rest of this first day that Davy officially did not exist in. He looked at his watch. It was only 3:00 p.m. There were hours to go before he could fade into the sweet oblivion of sleep.

As he'd sat on that platform, pinned under the hot gazes of curious citizens, he'd let his mind wander, carrying him away from that place and the reason he was there. He'd put his hand in his pocket and gripped the rock. It was silly to keep carrying it now.

He'd decided then and there that as soon as they got home, he'd go back to the place where Davy was last seen. He'd have his own little ceremonial transfer, returning to his brother what he'd thrown away that night. He'd leave it in the place Davy was last seen; he'd take a moment to pretend like that night had gone differently—that he'd made different decisions. He'd give himself that brief, fleeting reprieve, then he'd walk back home and face reality, his pocket empty for the first time in two decades.

When they pulled into the driveway, he got out of the car along with his parents and followed them inside. Instead of heading to the bathroom or his old bedroom or slumping in front of the TV, he mumbled that he was going for a walk and exited out the back door. Once outside, he looked left then right for any sign of the press but saw no one.

It was generally understood that the press would not broach the property line, staying at the edges of the front lawn, filming glimpses of the family wherever they could catch them. But they never knew when a cameraman would attempt to creep around and get some footage that no one else had. He knew now more than ever, with the developments in Davy's case, that this scenario was possible.

Satisfied that most of them would still be en route from the press conference, Thaddeus took off through the backyards of his neighbors, staying hidden until he felt it was safe to step out onto the road and follow it back to a place he had not been for years, except in his mind. And his nightmares.

The field where Davy disappeared was now a condominium development. Hallowed ground had been rendered into multi-family dwellings, bunched up together, ugly and impersonal, all evidence of the farm removed. He resented those condos, resented the men who developed them, resented the people who bought them with no regard or respect for what had happened there. The land should've been turned into a park, a baseball field, a school, anything that would honor Davy. But money, as it always did, had ruled out. The condos got built, the developers got their fortune, and a bunch of people got a home. Who was he to question it? But the closer he got to the site, the more he did.

When he reached the edge of the property, he closed his eyes and pictured the land the way it had been. He'd spent his childhood driving by the place and could still see the corn planted in the red dirt in perfect green rows across the massive fields, a narrow gravel drive splitting those fields in half, ending in front of the large white farmhouse, the cottage sitting just to its right. That, he recalled, was where Gordon Swift had been living. That was where Gordon had somehow encountered Davy that night.

And now, for the first time, instead of it just being a theory that Swift had abducted and somehow concealed his brother that night, they'd found actual evidence on Davy's body that linked the two. Thinking of Gordon made his heart pound, made his breathing shallow. He wanted to hurt the man, and had he seen him at the station, he had no doubt he would have. Though hurting Gordon would solve nothing, thinking about hurting Gordon was a consolation of sorts.

Thaddeus kept walking, picking his way through the condominium development around to the spot where Davy was last seen. He still knew where it was. For a while there had been a marker, a makeshift memorial of rocks and faded stuffed animals and tiny crosses. But the developers had removed it all when they leveled the ground for the construction, pushing the mementoes into a larger pile of debris, just more trash to be burned. The press, for all their interest in the case, hadn't covered that story. His mother had cried herself to sleep that night and Thaddeus, home from college by then, had turned up the volume on the television to drown out the noise.

He arrived at the spot and noted the number of the condo standing in that location, willing it to be something of significance—the date Davy was born or the date he disappeared, something. Instead the numbers meant nothing. They were just random numbers on a random street.

He'd put off coming here for so long, not wanting to see this cookie-cutter residence tainting what was, to him, a historical landmark. And yet, upon leaving the press conference announcing his brother's confirmed death, it was the only place he could think of to go.

He lowered himself to sit on a stranger's front stoop, resting his back against the door. A skinny Siamese cat crawled out of the bushes and mewed at him, a plaintive wail that echoed the way he felt inside. He extended his hand to the cat and called out a half-hearted "Here, kitty."

He was surprised when the cat actually responded, trotting over like it had been waiting for him. It rubbed itself up against his knees and allowed him to scratch its ears. The cat flopped down beside him on the stoop, and together they sat for longer than he'd intended, the cat purring and Thaddeus thinking through the events of the day, trying to hold the weight of them.

He willed himself to remember everything since the moment the sheriff woke them. There was the news delivered, Larkin and her daughter and the long hug in the yard, the tense wait in the room at the station before the press conference, he and his parents listening to each other breathe as they waited for it to begin. There was the press conference itself, the woman assigned to babysit them giving the opening remarks, his father's brief, nervous statement on behalf of the family (that had been a surprise; he'd counted on his mother to give in and do it), the sheriff taking the podium, the press snapping photos of him and also of the three of them as they worked to keep their faces impassive while on display. Then there was the ride home and his mother's talk of closure. He should've said it aloud, that she was right: closure was impossible. Davy's disappearance was forever an open loop. Thaddeus pulled the rock from his pocket and wondered if he could let it go, just leave it behind, on some stranger's stoop.

Suddenly the door he was resting against opened, sending him sprawling backward into the entryway of someone's home. Only, as he blinked and looked up in confusion, he didn't see a stranger's face looking back at him. He saw a familiar one, recognizing the curls first as their designated babysitter bent over and peered into his face.

Anissa, he thought, recalling her name as he wondered why and how she'd managed to be there at that moment. His first thought was that she took her job too seriously. His second one was that she had followed him there. But that didn't explain how she had gotten *inside* the house.

"Thaddeus?" Anissa asked, her voice sounding as confused as he felt. "What are you doing here?" She was holding a can of tuna and a little of the juice had sloshed out when he fell into the house. It dripped down her hands, the air filling with the smell of fish.

"What am *I* doing here? I should be asking *you* that. Are you following me?" He heaved himself off the floor and looked back at her as he rose to a standing position.

Her eyebrows nearly met in the middle as she squinted at him. "What are you talking about?" She held out her hands, gesturing to the air around her. "I didn't follow you. This is my house. I live here."

He looked around, taking in the surroundings as he worked on grasping what was happening. He noted the floral sofa, the peach-colored walls, a large framed photo of a seascape, a coffee table book about Georgia O'Keeffe displayed on a little table in the entryway. It was definitely a female's residence. In fact, he could see no trace of a male, as if it had been specifically, intentionally, purged.

He closed his eyes as he let it sink in that this was indeed her house. But how? He'd always wondered who lived in this particular condo, in this one special spot. He'd thought of knocking on the door, introducing himself, and asking if the residents knew what had taken place there. Not to freak them out, just to inform them of the importance of the place where they lived. And she, of all people, was the person who would've answered the door. This couldn't be a coincidence . . . could it?

"Thaddeus," she prompted. "What are you doing here?" Without waiting for him to answer, she added, "Were you waiting for me?"

His reply was defensive. "I wasn't waiting for you. I was—" How to explain what he'd been doing? He shoved the rock back in his pocket. He wouldn't be leaving it here, not now.

The smell of tuna had intensified as they stood there, and it was starting to make him feel nauseated. Anissa was still holding the can. He looked away from her, at the doorway he'd fallen into, wishing he could just walk right through it and disappear. Instead he looked back at her and calmly asked the question on his mind.

"How is it that you live in the last place my brother was ever seen?"

The darkness has grown thicker since they spied on the man in the little house. Walking back seems to take twice as long. Davy keeps his eyes forward, concentrating on getting to the road that runs in front of the farm, where Anissa's house sits.

The darkness is disorienting. To their left, he knows, is the gravel drive that leads down to the big house and the little house beside it. If he gets confused, he can always veer that way and find the road, then walk along it, even if cutting across the field is a faster way to get back to where the other kids are.

Davy regrets leaving the group, regrets coming to the fields with TJ at all. He should have stayed with Larkin and Kristy. He could have juggled for Larkin. She always clapped when he kept all four balls in the air.

"So do you think you could?" Anissa asks for what is obviously not the first time, her raised voice jarring him from his panicky thoughts. "I mean," she adds quickly, "you don't have to, obviously." She gives a little laugh. "I mean, I only just met you, so . . ."

Davy hears sadness.

"Sorry," he says quickly, trying to stave off whatever hurt he's caused. "I was just thinking about how we need to get back. My brother's probably looking for me by now." Davy wishes that were true but knows it likely is not.

"Oh yeah. We should," she agrees. She begins walking faster.

"No," he calls out and she stops. His eyes have adjusted to the dark enough to see her face, but her curls are lost in the blackness. "What were you asking me?" It suddenly seems important for him to know. "I'm sorry I wasn't paying attention."

She glances backward at where they'd come from, then turns her gaze toward the direction they are headed. Davy wonders if she wants to get home as badly as he does. Somehow, he doesn't think so.

"It doesn't matter," she says and starts to walk again. He reaches out to stop her, catching only the edge of her T-shirt. The fabric slips through his fingers, but the tug is enough to stop her.

"What?" he asks again. "I'm listening this time." There in the black field, they blink at each other as an understanding, a connection, forms between them. Though they are too young to name it, they aren't too young to feel it. He nods at her, assuring her.

Anissa sighs, then speaks. "My birthday is next week. And I was wondering if, maybe, if your parents said it was ok, maybe you could come to my party? It's at McDonald's." She grimaces. "Lame, huh?"

Davy shakes his head. "I don't think it's lame. I love McDonald's."

Half of her mouth turns up. "You aren't just saying that?"

"Can I have a Big Mac if I come?"

"You can have anything you want!" she says, and Davy watches as the other half of her mouth joins to make a whole smile.

"Then I'll be there," he says. He isn't sure this is true. He has no idea if his mom and dad will say yes, if they have other plans like going to one of TJ's lame baseball games, or if his parents will feel like driving him when the time comes. But he senses that, for now, the best thing he can say is yes. They'll figure out the rest later.

"Now let's get back to civilization," he says.

"I'll race ya," she says, then takes off running before he can even agree to the race.

"Hey, no fair!" he calls after her. But she is already gone.

It is a while before Anissa realizes she can no longer hear Davy behind her, huffing and puffing as he tries in vain to catch her. She was the fastest girl in her class back in Illinois. It's too soon to tell if she will be the fastest girl here.

She looks back but doesn't see her new friend, then stops short, panting as she scans the darkness. She feels a prickling sensation on the back of her neck and swats at it as if it's a mosquito or a fly.

"Davy?" she calls, hesitant, into the night. She waits, but there is no response. She turns in a slow circle, her eyes roving for a glimpse of movement, light, something that means she isn't alone in this field.

She hears an engine sound and turns hopefully toward the noise, watching as a car pulls into the gravel lane that leads down to the big house. She assumes it's someone there to visit the man in the smaller house, a girlfriend perhaps, or a friend coming to watch the baseball game with him. The car drives slowly, in no hurry to reach its destination.

Anissa squats as it passes, hoping whoever's driving doesn't see her. She watches the dust dance in the fading taillights. In the quiet of the field, she waits for the sound of the car parking as it reaches the man's house, the sound of a crisis avoided.

Instead she hears the car turn around at the end of the lane, its headlights swinging back in her direction. Her heart leaps into her throat as the car approaches. She cannot tell if it is blue or black, but she can see that it's small, one of those hatchback kinds. They are probably lost, she tells herself, just turning around. Nothing to worry about. They will get back out to the main road and go back where they came from.

The car stops before it reaches her, pulls up parallel to the field, stops far enough from where she's hidden that she can barely make out what's happening. Still, she watches, squinting against the blackness, her eyes adjusting to the light the headlights provide.

A large figure gets out of the driver's side and steps into the cornfield, looks right, then left.

Anissa flattens herself against the ground to avoid detection. This person is a stranger. She knows about stranger danger.

The figure calls out, a male voice trying to summon someone. But from the distance, over the noise of the car's idling engine, she cannot make out what he says. She stays where she is, taking silent, shallow breaths, wishing she could press herself closer to the ground as the person goes back to the car and the door slams.

But the car doesn't drive away.

She wishes there was corn in the field, something that would conceal her better. But the darkness is her only ally.

When the car finally drives away, Anissa exhales in relief. She wants to call for Davy, but her voice is stuck in her throat. She whispers his name, knowing he won't hear her. She gets to her feet and turns around in the field again but sees no one. She wonders if any of the kids are still up by the road.

With no other options, she trudges forward, making her way back to where the night began, hoping she will find her new friend Davy there waiting for her. He will brag that he beat her. She promises herself she won't argue with him, even if it means she has to let him win.

Sometimes losing is worth it.

CHAPTER 27

Anissa

Pete sent her home as soon as the press conference was over. *"I'm gonna go by the Malcor house and make sure they're squared away,"* he'd said. *"I'll call you if they need anything urgent, but I bet they'd like some time alone, and I think you could use a break. So go home and get something to eat, freshen up, take a nap, feed your pets, whatever you need to do. Later we'll reconvene, see what needs doing."*

He'd waved vaguely in the direction of the room where Gordon Swift was being questioned. *"He'll be in there for a while, and they don't need us hanging around while they do their jobs."* He gave that little half smile of his and added, *"They get pissy if they feel like I'm looking over their shoulders anyway."* Then he pretended to sniff under his armpits. *"Besides, I need a shower."* He'd patted her shoulder, nodded, and walked away.

She, too, needed a shower. And food. Maybe a nap if there was time. And she could feed the stray cat and pretend for a moment that she did have something, if not someone, waiting for her at home. She drove straight there, making sure to park and enter through the back of her condo just in case any nosy neighbors had been watching the press conference and had questions for her. It had happened before. And over a case much less high profile than this one.

She ate a peanut-butter-and-jelly sandwich standing at the sink, then opened a can of tuna to leave on the front stoop for the cat. She hoped the cat would see it and come eat. Maybe it would let her scratch its ears. What she really wanted was a hug from a human, but she wasn't going to get that. Brief contact with a stray cat was as much as she could hope for at present.

She tugged at the door, noticing it felt heavier than usual. It gave way and a man fell backward into the open doorway, sprawling at her feet, landing like a turtle turned on its back, his arms and legs briefly clawing for purchase. When he stopped moving and looked up at her, their recognition was simultaneous and disbelieving. For a moment she hoped they would both crack up laughing at the absurdity of the scene, but then she saw a look pass over his face that was the opposite of laughter.

"Thaddeus?" she asked, trying to remain calm, not to let his imposing, angry presence get to her. "What are you doing here?"

He had jostled her when he fell and tuna juice was snaking down her hand, then her forearm. She looked around for a place to set the can. Only her little entry table was nearby, and she didn't want to mess up her art book with tuna juice. So she continued to stand there, absurdly holding a can of tuna, the strong odor wafting between them.

She knew why he was there, and why he didn't understand why she was. When he asked her how it was that she lived in the very spot where his brother had disappeared, she decided to play dumb. Deny, deny, deny. She'd worked in law enforcement long enough to know that, when cornered, it was as good a tactic as any.

"What do you mean?" She answered his question with a question, forcing herself to look surprised.

Thaddeus ran a hand through his hair in frustration. "Davy went missing from a field in 1985."

"Right," she said, keeping her voice even and calm. "I know that."

He shook his head. He thought she was slow on the draw. Of course she knew where Davy disappeared from. Anyone on this case would know that, regardless of whether they'd been present on the night in question.

She wanted to tell him the truth, but what would he think if she did? And what if she told the truth and he told the sheriff? It wasn't like she'd hidden it—her address was in her personnel file, after all—but it wasn't as if she'd been completely transparent either. If she told Thaddeus Malcor the truth, he could go to the sheriff and spell it out for him in no uncertain terms. Then she might lose her job, the only thing she had left.

No. She had to pretend not to know that her condo stood on the very spot where Davy was last seen. But of course she knew that. She'd been the last one to see him. He'd been standing right about where her dining room table sat now. She'd asked for this plot of land within the complex, even waited months for them to get to this phase of development. She couldn't ever say why exactly, except that if someone was going to live in this location, she felt it should be someone who could appreciate the boy who was last seen here. She felt it should be her.

"That field was right here." He pointed at the floor of the condo. "The land was sold a few years later and eventually these condos were built. But because I was there that night, I know exactly where he was before he went missing."

She inhaled as if incredulous. "You actually saw him here?" This was low and borderline cruel because she knew his answer already. This was the inconvenient part of the story, the part he'd left out of his book.

He didn't directly lie about it. Like her, he just left it out. Some might call this a lie of omission, but she wasn't in a position to point fingers. He could have his omissions and she could have hers, and they could both do what they had to do to live with what happened that night.

He huffed. "No. He was with his friends, and I was nearby with mine. But I know where he was when he was last seen." He gave her a hard look. "And it was right here."

"Even though you weren't with him," she said, knowing this exposed his great shame and that, if necessary, she could use it against him to save her job. She hoped he would never realize that she'd been there too, just a kid herself.

"No," Thaddeus said. "I wasn't with him." He huffed again. "I should've been, but I wasn't." In his hand his phone rang, but he shoved it in his pocket instead of answering it. "I guess I'll always wonder what would have been different if I had."

"I'm sure that's hard," she said. "The wondering." She wanted to tell him that she, too, wondered over the what-ifs. If she hadn't insisted they check out the old farmhouse . . . If she hadn't challenged Davy to that race . . . If they hadn't felt the flutterings of a first crush that night.

The weekend after he disappeared, she'd spent her entire birthday party glancing at the door of the McDonald's. By then she'd invented a fantasy of Davy walking in and everyone cheering. In her fantasy he confessed to her that it was because of her party that he'd found his way back, that it was all for her. Even now her ridiculous heart could still soar at the thought.

"I'm sorry," she said to Thaddeus, but the consolation was for them both.

In his pocket his phone rang again and he grimaced. He went to retrieve it and said, "I better see who this is."

She nodded and he ambled off, raising the phone to his ear. She closed the door between them, pressing her back against it as she waited for her heart to slow down, her breathing to return to normal. When she was sure Thaddeus was gone, she opened her door and finally left the tuna for the cat, who was as usual nowhere to be found.

CHAPTER 28

Thaddeus

His editor's call was just the excuse he needed to leave Anissa's condo. He'd seen the welcome relief on her face in response. Neither of them knew how to extricate themselves from the odd situation they'd found themselves in, but both were desperate to do so. He knew he'd see her soon enough, back at the house anxiously hovering over his parents, eyeing the front window as if the members of the press might at any moment take up pitchforks and rush the house.

"Thaddeus, are you there?" Felicia, his editor, asked in her distinct New England accent.

"Yeah, I'm here. Sorry. I was just out . . . for a walk." He gave her the simplest explanation possible. "We just got back from the press conference," he added, playing on her sympathy just in case she was mad at him.

"Yeah, kiddo. I saw. That's why I'm calling. That must've been rough."

He laughed in spite of himself. "Now, Felicia, didn't you always tell me to reach for *le mot juste*? *Rough* doesn't do the situation justice."

He heard her smile through the phone. "Touché. Then I will say it must've been awful. Horrible. Excruciating."

"The worst," he agreed.

"Well, for what it's worth—and please don't think me tacky for saying this—we're already seeing an uptick in sales. We couldn't pay for this kind of press. You're everywhere."

He forced himself to look at the bright side, to find the silver lining, to do all the things the motivational types tell you to do in times of hardship.

"Well, that's good," he managed.

"If some good can come from this, all the better." She paused. "Right?"

"Yes," he said. "All the better." He could see the entrance to his neighborhood just ahead, the sign still the same as the day they'd moved in: white brick adorned with carved iron oak leaves that used to be green but were now oxidized, flanking the words *Vista Woods*. He used to think his home was a place where nothing bad could ever happen. He'd believed that until he was fifteen years old.

"I don't do this emotional stuff all that well, so please forgive me if I come across as insensitive. I don't mean to be. I want you to know how sorry I was to hear about your brother. I don't want to diminish what I know you and your family are going through. Contrary to what some may believe, I *do* have a heart. And mine is breaking for you right now," Felicia said.

Thaddeus stopped walking before he reached the entrance.

"Thanks," he said. Threatening tears made his eyeballs ache, but he would not break down and cry while on the phone with his editor. Thankfully, she quickly moved the discussion back to business.

"I've got to run to a meeting here in a minute, so before I do, I just wanted to say that, when you're up to it, we should talk about the next book. There'll be a real demand for a follow-up, what with the new, um, developments. So—and again, *please* don't think I'm tacky—just maybe jot down some notes about things that happen, how you're feeling, anything that could be usable later."

He resumed his walk, passing through the neighborhood entrance and down the main street.

"It's not tacky," he said, even though that wasn't really true. Now was not a good time to be talking about another book. Once upon a time all he'd wanted was what he had at that moment: an editor who wanted another book from him.

Trouble was, he wasn't sure he wanted to write another book about Davy. He didn't know if he wanted to write the "part two" of this story, the part he was living even as his feet carried him home from the spot where his brother had disappeared. He knew one thing, though. If he did write another book, he couldn't hold back again. He'd have to go deeper than he had before. He'd have to share himself, even the ugly parts—especially the ugly parts. To do anything less was to cheat Davy, to hustle him in a way he didn't deserve. He wanted to be the guy who could tell the full truth, but he wasn't sure.

"Well, dear heart," Felicia said. "I do need to run. But before I go, I saved the best for last. With all this press you're getting, I decided to send in reinforcements. I don't want you to have to deal with reporters, but it wouldn't be a bad idea for someone to speak on your behalf. She will, of course, confer with you before saying anything."

Thaddeus's head spun with the implication of what she was saying. "She?" he asked, his voice cracking like a teenager's.

"Nicole. I've sent her down there." She sounded confused. "I asked her to call you. Didn't she?"

"She might have," he admitted. "I've not been on my phone much today."

"Well, that's understandable," Felicia tutted. She shrieked and Thaddeus jumped. "Shit, shit, shit!" she yelled into the phone. "I really do have to go now. Talk soon. Kiss kiss." And then she was gone.

By then he had reached his house, keeping out of sight by going through the neighbors' backyards again. He blinked at his own backyard, seeing it as it used to be. There was where the tetherball pole stood. There was where Kristy used to swing, tipping her toes into the air as she screamed, *"Higher! Higher!"* at whichever brother she'd conned into pushing her. There was the clothesline where his mother used to hang their sheets, letting them snap dry in the breeze, the fabric carrying the fresh smell of line-dried laundry into their dreams.

All those things were gone now.

He heard a familiar voice call his name and suppressed a grimace as he turned to spot his mother standing on the edge of the patio, barefoot, her toes at the line where the grass met the concrete.

"Thaddeus," she said in a scolding tone. "Where have you been? I've been looking all over for you!"

He shook his head and walked over to her. Movement in the yard next door caught his eye, and he saw Larkin standing in her yard by the picnic table. For a moment it was as if no time had passed. She was still there and he was still being scolded by his mom. He lifted a hand in greeting as he neared his mother. She had changed out of the clothes she'd worn to the press conference.

"What'd you need?" he asked.

"I *needed* to know where you disappeared to," she retorted, hugging herself a little tighter with crossed arms.

"I didn't disappear," he said, sounding like a petulant teenager. He added an "I'm fine" as a half-hearted reassurance. He didn't know why he couldn't do what a normal son would—reach out and hug her, offer real words of comfort. Things had never been normal between them after that night. Though she'd never said it out loud, he knew she blamed him.

"Well, you should at least let us know if you're going somewhere."

He started to protest that he had told them, but she held up her hand to silence him. "I know, I know. You don't have to inform me of your whereabouts. I get that. But right now, while you're here, could you please just let me know where you go?" She smiled at him and he softened. In some ways he missed his mother as much as he missed Davy.

"Sure," he said.

She reached out and patted him stiffly on the shoulder. "Ok, well, some people brought food. If you're hungry."

"The tragedy brigade in action," he said, and they both smiled sadly at each other, at the fact that people bringing them food had been part of their lives for far too long. But now, he hoped, it would be over. Davy had been, finally, found.

His stomach rumbled at the mention of food, and he started to follow his mother into the house. Larkin called his name, halting his steps.

"Hey, Mom," he said, demonstratively pointing in the direction of Larkin's house. "I'm going next door."

"Smart-ass," she said and headed inside, leaving him to rotate on his heels in the direction of where Larkin waited.

For a moment they stood, silent and awkward, by the picnic table. Looking everywhere but at her, Thaddeus scanned the surface of the table for evidence that he'd been there long ago, but he couldn't find his initials carved in the wood.

"Believe it or not, this isn't the original table," Larkin said.

"Really?" Thaddeus responded, incredulous. "It looks just like it."

"Apparently the other one got hit by lightning," she said and gave a little laugh.

Thaddeus laughed too, shaking his head. "You'd think at some point our parents would've been like, 'Peace out, this place is cursed.'"

"You would think," she agreed. He watched her mull it over. "But your parents—or your mom, at least—wouldn't leave and, well, I guess my folks felt like someone had to stay with her." She shrugged and Thaddeus winced.

"I watched today," she said. "That must've been awful."

He thrust his hands into his pockets and nodded. "It was pretty hard." He dragged the toe of his shoe across the grass, turning the blades over to the paler underside, leaving a streak through the green.

"Are you ok?" she asked.

He started to nod, but then stopped and cocked his head, making full eye contact for the first time since he'd walked over.

"What do you think?" he asked, the words somewhere between a jest and a jeer, as he tried to be the Thaddeus she remembered, the one who teased and taunted, always staying aloof, especially after that night.

"I think you're probably miserable," she answered.

He lobbed a question back at her. "And you, happy?"

Just as he said it, a wasp flew in between them, buzzing around her head. She tried to swat it away, but it dodged her hand and went back for another run at her face. This time, before it could reach her, Thaddeus pawed it to the ground and stepped on it. He smashed his foot into the earth more than necessary, taking delight in destroying the threat.

"My hero," she joked, placing her hand on his arm, her touch electric. He thought again of being in the dark car with her, but then remembered that in that dark car she had told him she was pregnant. He stepped back, just enough for her hand to fall away.

"I'm hardly a hero," he said, carefully drawing a boundary line with his words, even as he tried to forget her touch. "I mean, your husband is off doing something that's actually heroic. Fighting for his country." He raised his eyes to the sky. "I travel around the country telling the same old story to strangers."

Larkin hopped up to perch on the edge of the picnic table and gave him a look. "You wrote a bestselling book, Thaddeus. That's huge. You're famous."

"I'm not famous."

She jutted her chin in the direction of his front yard, where, no doubt, the press was lining up to get ready for the evening broadcast.

"When they go live in a little bit, they'll talk about Davy, yes. But they'll talk about you too. About the book, about what you shared. That takes bravery of its own, to share your story with the world like that."

He felt the compliment more than he heard it but shrugged it away, focusing instead on the possibility that she had read the book, that she knew she was the girl next door. But he didn't dare ask her.

"That's just it," he hurried to say. "It's not because I was brave. My book sold because people are nosy. They saw us in the news; they wanted the inside scoop; they bought the book." He looked back over his shoulder at his house, sitting there just the same as it always had, before and after Davy.

"They wanted to know what it would be like to be us without actually having to be us," he continued. "Because who would want that? Who would want to be us? No one should have to be us." He turned back to her. Their eyes met and held for a moment, his brown boring into her blue. He could feel the emotion building, a storm bearing down on his soul. He needed to get out of there before she witnessed its landfall.

"Don't you see?" he asked, his breath coming in little gasps. "I didn't want you to have to live with all of this."

He heard her intake of breath and knew that she understood.

"Wait," she said. "So you're saying that's why you . . . that's why we . . . never . . . I thought you just weren't interested anymore." Her eyes were wild, darting all over the place as she tried to grasp what he'd just admitted. Perhaps he shouldn't have blurted it out, but it was too late now.

"I was trying to save you," he said. "From me. From us." He took a deep breath. "I was trying to set you free." He turned and fled, once again leaving her with no choice but to watch him go.

TJ wakes to the sharp sting of pine needles digging into his cheek. Spitting and cursing, he struggles to sit up. Once upright, he blinks as he tries to bring things into focus, reorienting himself as to where he is and how he got here.

He is in the field with his buddies. They tried beer for the first time. He had several, growing more used to the taste with each one. Then Lee Watkins convinced them to shotgun one. That's the last thing he remembers. He looks over at the trash bag that held all the beer. There are no more can-shaped lumps underneath the plastic.

He scans the field, sees another still form on the ground near him and crawls toward it with hope, calling, "Philly— hey, Philly. Wake up." He leans over the form and shakes it gently, then backs away. Phillip is likely to come up swinging if awakened. But when the form turns and he gets a look at the face, he sees that it's just a guy named Greg from school. They had Spanish together last year.

"Sorry, man," TJ says. "I thought you were Phillip."

Greg slumps back over. "Nah, man. He left."

"Left?" TJ asks, confused. Wouldn't Phillip have told him he was leaving? And why would Phillip leave? It doesn't make sense. With a gathering fear TJ wonders if Phillip is angry at him for getting so drunk that he passed out. He feels panic welling inside. He needs to find Phillip. Phillip is his best friend. Phillip arranged this whole thing, included him.

"What time is it?" Greg asks, rubbing his eyes. Greg must've shotgunned beer too.

What time *is* it? A new panic fills him as he thinks of Davy for the first time since waking up. Davy, who is somewhere out in that vast dark field. He looks at his watch, remembering how he'd promised his mother that he'd keep track of the time, how he'd waved this same watch under her nose to prove his point. Relief fills him when he sees it is only a quarter to ten. His parents won't even think of leaving the party till eleven at the earliest. He still has time to collect Davy and get them both home safely. When he goes to stand up, his head pounds, his stomach lurches in protest.

TJ decides he will never drink again. It was fun—and cool—to try it, but it wasn't worth it. Beer makes people do stupid things, and TJ doesn't need any help in that department. He calls out the time to Greg, who groans loudly in response, then he trudges off toward where the kids had been playing earlier, expecting that Davy will be with them.

Footsteps, heavy and plodding, run up from behind, and he looks over to see Lee Watkins closing in. The dude is tall. TJ has to look up to see his face. He wonders if maybe Lee was held back a couple of grades. He wonders who this guy even is. He doesn't remember seeing him before tonight.

"Where ya goin?" Lee asks, sounding genuinely disappointed that TJ is leaving.

"I gotta find my brother and get home. If my parents get back and we're not there, there'll be hell to pay." He gives a "you know how it is" laugh. But Lee doesn't laugh along.

"I was gonna see if you wanted to come to my house," Lee says, pointing in the direction of the road that runs in front of the farm. "It's not far from here."

TJ makes a disappointed face for Lee's sake. "Man, any other time I'd love to, but like I said, I gotta find my little brother. He's"—TJ waves vaguely at the field—"out there somewhere. Or he'd better be."

Lee studies the darkness as if he can see through it. "I could help you find him, if you want."

TJ looks at him, surprised. "I mean, sure, if you want."

"We could split up? Look in different places," Lee suggests as they walk.

TJ sees no kids around, hears no sounds of laughter or thundering feet like before.

"Ok," he says. "I'll go over where he left his bike when we got here. It's up there near the road."

He doesn't wait for Lee to tell him where he's going. He breaks off toward the road, feeling the gravity of the situation. With every step he takes, he can feel the fuzziness in his head being replaced by the clarity of the urgency. He guesses this is what people mean when they talk about "sobering up." But he doesn't need coffee like in the movies. Davy's absence has provided all the coherence he needs.

His feet pound in time with his head as he picks up his pace, running toward where Davy left his bike. He prays it will be gone, that Davy gave up on him and headed home hours ago. He'll give him a hard time for doing it, but deep down he'll be proud of the kid for taking care of himself. TJ keeps his eyes peeled for the bike.

"Davy!" he calls into the expanse of the field. "Davy!" he tries again. He keeps calling as he runs, his voice growing more ragged as he gets closer to the junction between the road and the field.

He feels his heart sink as he spots the bike right where Davy left it, the little bit of moon in the sky glinting off the metal as if it intended to lead him right to it.

Davy runs back to the man's house, his heart pounding after seeing a large shape walking in the field. He doesn't know who it was—it could've been one of TJ's friends heading home, but he is afraid out here, alone in the dark. It was one thing when he had Anissa by his side, but he has lost her. So he goes back to where they started, hoping she has too.

As he draws nearer to the house, he does not see her. "Anissa?" he whispers into the dark stillness. There is no reply. He tries again, then again. But Anissa is not there. He looks over his shoulder, back at the vast darkness of the field, and wonders if he can ask the man for help. Perhaps he has a flashlight he can borrow.

At the man's screen door, he casts about for what to say to the stranger who still sits drawing, then tearing away the drawings and tossing them to the floor. The pile of discarded hands has grown. Davy observes him, feeling safe in the warm glow of light with the sound of the baseball announcers calling plays on the television. He understands that the man, too, feels safe there, doing what he is doing.

Suddenly Davy hears the sounds of a car approaching and turns to see headlights sweeping across the little house, across him, standing there in the doorway. He tries to dodge the lights, pressing himself against the house as if it can shield him, but it is too late. Whoever is driving the car has likely spotted him there, lurking outside the man's house.

Heart pounding, he waits for the sound of the car parking, the driver's side door opening, footsteps coming toward him. Pressed flat against the house, he opens his mouth to call out to the man inside. The word *help* sits on his tongue.

But the car does not stop, it executes a perfect three-point turn in the space in front of the two houses, then drives away just as suddenly as it appeared. Davy watches the taillights and exhales a long sigh of relief, unflattening himself from the man's house.

Then he hears the protesting sound of the screen door being yanked open and looks up to see the man standing there, holding open the door. Davy knows bugs will get into his house that way. He starts to tell him that, but the man speaks before he can.

"What the hell?" he asks, glaring at Davy.

Davy starts to apologize for being at the man's door, to explain why he is there. But his words come out in an indistinguishable jumble.

The man shakes his head. "Are you the kid who was spying on me earlier?"

Davy wants to lie, but he can't. He nods miserably and looks down, studying the tops of his sneakers. They are white Nikes with a red swoosh, just like Marty McFly's. They've gotten dirty tonight as he ran through the field. He will have to clean them tomorrow.

"Beat it, kid," the man says and goes to shut the door.

Davy extends his arm to stop the door from closing. He will be brave like Marty, fearless.

"Do you have a flashlight I can borrow?" He points back toward the field. "I've got to cross the field by myself, and it's so dark tonight. If I just had a flashlight, I think it would be better. I was with my friend, but she ran ahead of me and I lost her, and now—"

"I don't have a flashlight," the man says, sounding tired. Davy wonders what time it is. He thinks about his warm bed. He thinks about his parents coming to kiss him good night when they get home, how his mom will smell like wine and perfume and his dad will smell like the stinky cigars he always says he doesn't smoke.

"You sure?" Davy asks, because that is what Marty McFly would do.

"Look, it's late; you better get home." The man rubs his hand through his hair. There is ink on his fingers. "I'm sorry I can't help you."

Davy stops listening. He peers past the man into his house, at the table he'd seen when he was spying. Davy thinks about the funny-looking knives he saw, like sharp spatulas. If he can't have a flashlight, he thinks, maybe he can have a weapon. He'll be like a soldier, crossing enemy lines with his trusty knife for protection. He'll fight his way home.

"Can I have one of those?" He points in the direction of the table.

The man sighs and looks over his shoulder at the table. "One of what?"

"Those knives you've got over there," Davy says. "I just need one." This, he feels, is reasonable. "And I can bring it back tomorrow," he adds. "I don't live far. I'll ride my bike here and bring it back. I promise." Davy holds up his hand, making the Scout's honor sign though he's never been a Scout. After TJ quit, his parents lost interest in the whole enterprise. But this man does not know that.

"Please?" he adds, because sometimes that works on his mom.

The man shakes his head but then turns and walks toward the table. He peruses the selection before plucking one—the smallest one, from the looks of it—and walking back to Davy. He hands it over.

"It's a putty knife," the man tells him. "But it's sharper than it looks. So be careful."

Davy brandishes it as he bites back a smile. He has a weapon. Everything will be ok.

"Thanks," he says on a breath. He tucks the knife into his pocket, feeling better already.

"Now beat it kid. I gotta get some sleep," the man says. Without waiting for Davy's response, he closes the screen door, then the wood door behind it too.

As he turns to make his way back across the field, Davy hears the lock click, noting how the darkness grows even darker when the man turns out his lights.

Davy stands in the drive for a moment and debates following the lane back up to the main road, but then he thinks of the car he saw. What if the person is pulled over down the lane, waiting for a kid like him to come walking along? No, better to cross the field and do his best to move quick and stay out of sight. He pats the knife in his pocket. He'll be ok.

He goes along at a good clip, his pace picking up a little more with each shadow along the outer edges of his vision, each strange noise coming from the woods. He wishes he'd run into one of the other kids. He starts to wonder if he is the only one left, if they've all gone home. He does not think Anissa would do that, but he supposes her mom could've come home and demanded she go inside her little falling-down house.

Up ahead, he spies someone else walking in the darkness. The figure is too large to be Anissa, so he does not call out. He slips his hand in his pocket, touches the handle of the putty knife, even as he begins to tail the person, keeping his distance and doing his best to move quietly.

At the very least, he is not alone anymore. The figure stops and so does Davy, staying very still, barely even breathing as he waits to see what will happen next. The person clicks on a flashlight, bringing the relief that only a light in the darkness can.

The figure swings the light one way, then another, then turns in a new direction, cutting sideways across the field instead of back toward the road. Davy guesses this must be a shortcut. With the aid of the light, Davy sees the person's face and recognizes it. He smiles with relief but says nothing to reveal he is there as he continues to follow the figure in a direction he hopes will lead him home.

CHAPTER 29

Tabitha

As soon as she could, Tabitha retreated into Davy's bedroom, the place she'd wanted to go since hearing the sheriff's news that morning. She'd wanted to be alone with him, or as close to him as she was able to be.

They'd kept his room intact. At first because they'd truly believed he'd be coming back, and how would it look if they'd turned his room into a guest bedroom? If he'd come home to find they'd removed all his personal effects just because he'd been gone too long? And then it became, at what point *did* you give up? When did you pronounce that he was never coming back? It wasn't like they needed a guest room anyway.

Over the years his room had become something of a shrine, not just to Davy but to her activism regarding missing children. There were clippings of interviews and photographs of various politicians and minor celebrities who'd shown up to this hearing, to that fundraiser. There were the photos of her at the North Carolina capitol and at the U.S. Capitol in Washington. There were the missing posters of Davy, the various age progressions of him lined up at age fifteen, age eighteen, age twenty-one, and age twenty-five. They'd spent their own money for some of those, but to Tabitha it was no different from commissioning a portrait. She'd rationalized that it was just reallocating all the money she hadn't spent for school pictures through the years, pictures of her son as he might've been instead of as he was.

But now they knew he'd never been any of those ages. The theory was that he'd been killed within hours of the abduction. She reached up to tear those photos from the wall, intending to shred them with her bare hands. But as her hand got close to Davy's face, she softened and, instead, reached out to caress his cheek, remembering as she did how baby soft his skin had been, even at eleven.

Small for his age, he'd still been a long way from adolescence when he'd been taken, his round face and unshed baby fat making him look much younger than he really was. She stood there stroking the photo and thought of being the first person to greet him when he'd entered the world.

When Thaddeus was born, the doctor held him aloft as he'd screamed his indignation at being evicted from his cozy, warm refuge into the glaring white lights and coldness of the delivery room. But with Davy everything had been different. Because they'd been new in town, they'd had no help when she went into labor early, so Daniel had stayed home with Thaddeus and waited for her mother to arrive from Ohio, hoping her labor would last long enough that he'd make it in time. But Daniel had missed his son's birth, a disappointment she knew he carried with him to this day. Just another time, he'd said to her late one night toward the end of their marriage, he hadn't been there for Davy.

But Tabitha hadn't minded being alone for Davy's birth. In fact, she treasured the time. She'd expected another angry, red-faced tiny human. But beyond a few initial sputtering coughs, Davy hadn't made a sound. Because she thought all babies cried at birth, she'd panicked, asking the doctor and nurses if he was ok. As they put him, bundled and warm and utterly content, in her arms, they'd assured her he was just fine. And so it was that she'd been the only one in the family there to welcome Davy. It had been, in its own way, the perfect reception.

Her initial meeting with Thaddeus had been an investigation of the other person with a sense of *"Who are you?"* complete with all the wariness and uncertainty that comes with any introduction. But with Davy, mother and son had relaxed into each other, each seeming to say, *"Oh, I know you."* She couldn't recall any noise as that transpired; it was as if the world had fallen away. It was one of the most holy moments of her life.

As she stood in Davy's room she imagined that, in heaven, God and the angels had paused to watch the scene of his birth. That God had said to the angels, *"This one's special. He won't be there for long."* She lowered herself to Davy's bed, pulled his pillow to her face, and grieved a loss she finally had to accept. Though she had returned to this room many times, her son never would.

A presence in the room awoke her. Disoriented, she struggled to sit up, frightened by the large form looming over her, confused about where she was. But before she could get a word out, she felt a blanket falling over her.

"Shh," the figure said. "It's just me." Daniel. She blinked him into focus. "You fell asleep. You looked cold." She wasn't surprised she'd fallen asleep. She'd been exhausted from the moment the sheriff woke her. She'd lumbered through the day like a zombie, all sensation but no feeling.

She looked down to see that it was Davy's airplane bed-spread Daniel had covered her with. She was in Davy's room. She remembered curling up on his bed and sobbing herself to sleep. The bedsprings protested as Daniel lowered himself on the edge of the little twin-size bed.

"I'm going to go home," he said. "Unless you need me to stay."

Sorrow bloomed in her chest, spreading its tendrils down into her stomach and out into her shoulders. She had to admit, she'd liked having them all there, enduring this together like the family they'd once been. Of course she'd known it would end, but she wasn't ready.

"No, it's ok," she said, her voice still thick with sleep. "There's really no need for you to be here anymore." In a factual sense, this was true. And the emotional sense no longer applied.

"Thank you," she said. "For speaking today. I just didn't have it in me."

He looked down. "I should've done that a long time ago. I shouldn't have made you do all the talking for us. It wasn't fair to you."

She leaned back on her elbows. "I didn't mind, back then. It made me feel like I was doing something." She thought about all of Daniel's searches, of the late-night phone calls with the psychic, of him hanging on her every word. He'd wanted to feel like he was doing something too. If only they could have done something together. Maybe if they had, he wouldn't be returning to his own place now, leaving her alone in the house they once shared.

"You sure you don't need me to stay?" Daniel pressed. She wondered if perhaps he wanted her to ask him to stay. *Don't be ridiculous*, she scolded herself. He had a life of his own to get back to, someone waiting for him. With a pang she wondered if he would bring the girlfriend to the funeral. *Probably*, she decided. *And that's to be expected*, she told herself.

"Go," she said. "I'm fine."

Daniel gave a little laugh. "Now, we both know that isn't true."

She smiled. "Ok. As fine as I can be. How's that?"

His smile disappeared and he leaned forward, crooking one arm around her as, for the briefest moment, he pulled her to him and planted a kiss on top of her head.

"You always were," he said into her hair. He pulled back and she saw tenderness in his eyes. "Go back to sleep," he said. She watched him rise from the bed and walk toward the door. As it clicked shut, she closed her eyes and did exactly what Daniel ordered.

The doorbell rang, startling her out of sleep for the second time. Confused, she looked around to see that it wasn't the middle of the night as she had supposed. Instead, night was just beginning to fall, the darkness gathering at the edges to begin its slow creep inward, pushing the light back.

She guessed she'd been asleep an hour, tops. She waited for the sounds of someone else in the house going to the door, the protesting sound of it being tugged open. But no sounds came. The doorbell rang a second time and Tabitha, with an angry sigh, got up to see who was there. Maybe Anissa was back. Maybe some stupid reporter was daring to come to the door. Maybe it was just another casserole delivery.

She hurried to the door and pulled it open to reveal . . . no one. The reporters turned at the sound of the door opening, their faces eager at the hope of something happening. She stood there blinking at them as they blinked back. One of them snapped a photo she hoped they wouldn't use. She hadn't looked in a mirror, but she knew she looked frightful. Seeing her, one of them, a woman, broke away from her conversation and began striding toward her, purposeful.

She almost closed the door in the woman's face. But something—perhaps intuition, perhaps mere curiosity—made her hold the door open to see what she would say.

"Hi," the woman said. She was pretty with the fresh face and bright eyes of a young person that life had not yet beaten down. Tabitha knew she'd had the same look at one point in her life.

"I'm sorry to disturb you," the woman continued. "I was just asking them"—she glanced over her shoulder at the members of the press—"if they knew if you guys were home. I tried calling first but got no answer."

Calling? Tabitha was confused. Why would a reporter expect to call and get an answer? They'd made it plain that they would make statements only through the police.

She peered inside the house, over Tabitha's shoulder, then looked back at her expectantly. "So is Thaddeus here?"

"Thaddeus?" Tabitha asked.

The woman wrinkled her brow. "Didn't he tell you I was coming?"

"No," Tabitha said and hoped she sounded kind even as irritation at Thaddeus sparked inside her. "He must've forgotten."

She gave the girl a second once-over and restrained herself from rolling her eyes. It was just like Thaddeus to have some woman show up, now, in the middle of everything, without asking if it would be an inconvenience. Kristyn was arriving tomorrow with her children and husband in tow. There was, she thought with a pang, a funeral to plan. She could not add a strange houseguest.

The woman's face turned a shade darker underneath the porch light. "I'm so sorry. You must be so confused, me just showing up here like this, at a time like this." She extended her hand and Tabitha shook it.

"I'm Nicole, Thaddeus's publicist. His editor asked me to come here, just to help navigate everything, assist with the press and . . . whatever needs to be done. She said she was going to inform him that I'd be coming." A pained expression crossed her face. "Gosh, I hope she did." She chewed her lip. "I'm not sure he's going to be happy, me surprising him like this."

Tabitha suspected there was more to this story. The thought of Nicole being an unpleasant surprise for Thaddeus caused her to open the door wider. "Please, come in," she said with a smile. She thought it was perhaps the first time she'd smiled that day and was grateful to the girl for providing a moment—however fleeting—of levity, even if it was at her firstborn's expense. She loved her son, but she also recognized that he could benefit from the occasional dose of humility, and she was happy to be complicit in this one.

She directed the woman to have a seat so she could go fetch Thaddeus. As she turned toward his room, she glanced over her shoulder at the woman perched on her couch, looking stricken. She had identified herself as his publicist, but Tabitha had a feeling she was more than that to Thaddeus, or could be.

She entered Thaddeus's room without knocking and, as expected, found him curled up on his bed, fast asleep, oblivious, looking like a living, breathing age progression of the boy he'd been when he lived in this room—just elongated, widened, darkened. He slept on top of the covers, as if he'd not expected to fall asleep or stay that way. As if sleep had come for him against his will.

She lowered herself onto the side of his bed, a queen-size they'd bought him when he'd outgrown his twin. The bedspread was the same one he'd had in high school, a blue-and-white seersucker she'd chosen. She'd put up a wallpaper border with sailboats and hung a painting of the ocean on the wall. She'd been proud of her decorating efforts, surprising him when he returned from baseball camp the summer before Davy disappeared. Instead of thanking her for her efforts, he'd grumbled about it. He wanted a less-coordinated bedroom, something nondescript, a place he could hang posters of nearly naked girls and rock stars. But she'd told him to get over it. And, she guessed, somewhere along the way, he had. Because, like Davy's, the room had never changed.

She placed her hand on his arm, and he opened his eyes, startled. "Jeez, Mom, you scared me." He rolled over, giving her his back. "I'm trying to sleep," he grumbled.

She poked him in the bicep with her finger, admittedly a bit too hard. "You can't go back to sleep," she said. "You have a guest."

He turned back to face her, his thick, dark eyebrows connecting just over the bridge of his nose. "Guest? Who?"

"She says she's your publicist. That your editor told you she was coming." She tried to keep an accusing tone out of her voice, refrained from saying, *Some warning might've been nice.*

He groaned and buried his head in his pillow but continued talking, his voice muffled but audible.

"My editor mentioned it this afternoon, but she was in a hurry and gave me no details. I figured I'd find out more tomorrow." He emitted something best described as a growl. Tabitha stood and took a few steps backward.

He turned and looked at her. "She's here? Now?"

She nodded. "Do you want me to tell her to leave?"

He covered his face with his hands. "No." The word came out like a plaintive moan. He sat up. "Will you tell her I'll be there in a minute?"

"Sure," Tabitha said. She left the room and went back to find Nicole intently pressing buttons on a BlackBerry that matched Thaddeus's. She wondered if the publisher handed those out to everyone. "Sorry that took a bit. He was sleeping."

Nicole stopped typing and dropped the device into her lap like she'd been caught doing something wrong. "Oh gosh, you didn't wake him, did you?"

"Well, yes. I told him he had a visitor."

Nicole looked nervous. "I could've just come back if he was sleeping," she said. The same pained expression from before crossed her face. "I should've just waited to come tomorrow." She leaned forward. "Was he mad?"

Tabitha gave her what she hoped was an encouraging smile even as she thought of Thaddeus's deep growl. "Of course not. Just surprised, is all. Would you like some water? I can get you some water," she offered, anxious for an excuse not to be in the room when Thaddeus entered. "Or tea. I could get us some tea?" She would take her time fixing the tea; she would snip mint from the spot by the back door where she grew it to add to the tea. By the time she came back, Thaddeus and Nicole would be past their awkward greeting.

"Yes, sure," Nicole said weakly, no longer the confident young woman who had rung her doorbell. "That would be nice. Thank you."

Tabitha nodded and walked through the kitchen and out the back door to the spot where the mint grew. She squatted to pluck some, wondering how long it had been since she did this, since she took the time to make something nice, to care about the added details like she once had.

Ignored, the mint patch had held on without her assistance. She was grateful it was still there despite her neglect. So many things left untended, too many things left to slip away. The words she wrote each week played in her mind: *je ne regrette rien*. Nothing could be more untrue. She laughed at herself as, clutching the mint, she went back inside to tend to their uninvited guest.

CHAPTER 30

Thaddeus

It was late when he walked Nicole out to her car, the front yard now empty except for a few stray soda cans and wrappers left behind by careless members of the media. They were supposed to clean up after themselves, but some chose to ignore the rules. He stopped to pick one up, then decided against it. He could clean up tomorrow or tell Anissa to insist that the press clean up after themselves.

He felt a new wave of exhaustion wash over him, the effects of the day weighing on him. This morning he'd woken up to the news about his brother. Tonight he'd go to bed for the first time and not let himself wonder if Davy was, by some miracle, alive out there somewhere. Was it worse to have false hope, or no hope at all? He guessed he'd find out.

He felt the rock still in his pocket. He knew now he could not leave it at what had turned out to be Anissa's place. So what could he do with it? He didn't want to leave it on Davy's eventual grave for fear some random person would find it and take it as some sort of macabre souvenir. But if he didn't do that, he didn't know what he would do with the thing.

Beside him, Nicole was fussing with the keys to her rental car. He reached out to help her, their hands brushing as he did. She pulled away as if she'd been shocked, then apologized.

"I'm just jumpy tonight," she said. "I feel really uncomfortable, being here now with all your family's facing."

He shrugged. "Don't worry about it. You being here doesn't make it any worse."

There was a beat before she spoke, her words tentative. "Does it make it any better?"

He gave her a small, sad smile and the answer he knew she needed to hear. "Yeah," he said. "It does." Though residual embarrassment over the last time they'd been together fought for dominance, he ignored it, reaching for her and pulling her in for a hug.

"I want us to talk about . . . the other stuff. I do." He glanced over his shoulder at the house, then back at her. "But first I need to get through the next couple of days."

"Of course," she hurried to say. She smiled. "The 'other stuff,' as you so eloquently put it, can wait."

He rolled his eyes. "I've got quite a way with words, huh?"

She nodded, then leaned over and kissed him, her lips barely making contact with his before she pulled away.

"Maybe you should write a book," she said, and he smiled in spite of himself, the heaviness leaving him for just a moment. She put her hand on his arm. "I'm here to help you, not to make your life more complicated."

"I can complicate my life without help," he quipped, and she winked at him, then got into her rental car and drove away.

He stood there for a few minutes after she was gone, breathing in the night air, looking up at the stars. A police cruiser came by doing its rounds and slowed when it saw him there. He lifted his hand to the cop, assuring him that things were fine.

Anissa hears someone else calling Davy's name. As she gets closer to the road, she spies Davy's brother and some other kids gathered near where Davy left his bike. Anissa hopes it hasn't been stolen. As she approaches, she sees that it's still there.

But Davy isn't.

Dread fills her heart like black smoke. Her sister, Marissa, is standing next to Davy's brother and some older boys Anissa doesn't know. Probably the boys who were with Davy's brother tonight. The ones who'd teased Davy and sent him away.

Marissa runs toward Anissa, catches her in her arms, and presses her to her chest.

"Anissa! I was worried sick!" Marissa says. She looks so concerned, Anissa almost believes her. But the act, Anissa thinks, is for the boys' benefit. Marissa is playing a role—dutiful, loving sister—while also drawing attention to herself. Marissa loves the attention of boys. Boy crazy, her mother calls it.

Davy's brother runs up to Anissa. "Is my brother with you?" he asks, his breath coming out in short, anguished huffs. He looks frantic and panicked and sick. Anissa wishes Davy could see him right now. It serves him right to have to worry after how he treated Davy.

Davy, where are you? You're missing it.

Anissa shakes her head. "He was. We were racing across the field." She points back in the direction she has come. "But then I looked back, and he . . . wasn't there. I went over to the driveway over there." She points again, this time in the direction of the drive. "But he wasn't there either. I did see a car, though."

A couple of the boys speak up. "We saw that car!"

TJ wheels around. "You saw a car? What kind? When?" Anissa and the boys all talk at once. The car was blue, it was black, it was small, it was medium-size. It was an hour ago. It was a half hour ago. None of the stories match.

"Do you think Davy got in the car with someone? Like maybe he knew the person and they gave him a ride?" TJ asks.

Anissa doesn't know how to answer that. Anything, she supposes, could've happened. Maybe Davy had gotten into that car. She didn't see it happen, but it was so dark and she was scared, hunkered down as she attempted to hide. Maybe she is wrong about what she saw.

Already she is starting to doubt, wondering if she can rely on her memories of tonight. She wonders if she should mention the man in the little house but thinks better of it, since she and Davy had been trespassing. She thinks about Davy's warnings. She doesn't want the police to arrest her. She decides she will leave out the part about spying on the man. She hopes the man will leave it out, too, if anyone asks him.

TJ paces around, pressing his hands to his face. He keeps talking into his hands. "Oh shit, oh shit. This is bad. This is really bad."

Anissa wants to yell at him and say, *"This is all your fault! You left him!"* But she knows it is also her fault. She left Davy too. She hadn't meant to, but she had.

Marissa offers to go call the police from their house across the street. TJ looks to Anissa, his eyes asking if she thinks it has come to that. Anissa can tell he wants her to say, *"No, don't be silly. He'll turn up."* But she can't say that.

Davy is so lost that none of them can find him, too far away to hear them all screaming his name.

She nods, then watches as Marissa runs across the road and disappears inside their house. There is nothing left to do except wait for the police to come.

CHAPTER 31

Gordon

Harvey drove him home from the station, both men silent. Harvey played country music while Gordon tried to block it out. He was not a fan of the twangy voices, the songs about lost love, the simplistic portrayal of life in the South. His life in the South had been far from simple.

He rested his head against the glass and watched the free world go by. He wondered how much longer he would be allowed to remain in it. Especially now that they had found that putty knife.

He could hardly claim it wasn't his. He'd written his initials on it, an old habit from art school. Harvey had gotten the police to admit there was no reason to believe it had been used in any kind of crime. But the mere fact of its existence and the connection to Gordon only further cemented the cops' original theory as to what happened to Davy Malcor: The kid had been playing on the same property Gordon lived on. Gordon had pedophile tendencies he'd repressed. But that night, he'd seen Davy and, unable to repress them any longer, he'd grabbed the boy, assaulted him, killed him, then hid him somewhere until he could dump the body. If he'd

never seen the boy, the investigators wanted to know this
time, then how did the kid end up with Gordon's putty knife
in his pocket?

Gordon couldn't answer. So he'd sat, mute and reticent,
for seven hours, as they took runs at him, separately and together, as they called in reinforcements, as they made threats
against him and his family, his livelihood, his reputation.
It seemed as though they'd forgotten he'd been through all
of this before. He'd endured in the past; he would endure
again. Or maybe he wouldn't this time. The knife, he had
to admit, was powerful evidence. The knife made him look
guilty.

And he was guilty, just not of being the one to kill Davy.
Gordon was starting to realize it didn't matter; they could still
take his freedom. With the right jury and a public demand for
justice in any form, they could make a case for locking him
up forever. A knot of emotion collected in his throat, then
swelled, but he did his best to swallow it. He would not let
Harvey see him cry.

Harvey parked the car and turned to him. "Want me to
walk you in?" he asked, looking at Gordon's house to assess
any threats that might be lurking. Gordon shook his head.

He rested his hands on the dashboard, imagined handcuffs
around his wrists, wondered if he could get used to the funny
walk he'd have to do with his feet shackled at the ankles.

He thought of a courtroom, his sickly parents in attendance
day after day, their faces hot with shame at hearing what the
prosecutors would claim he did. If it went that far, he would,
he decided, go ahead and plead guilty. He would spare his
folks one last indignity.

"You can't give up now, Gordon," Harvey said. But even he sounded out of steam.

"They've got my knife in the kid's pocket. It's got my DNA on it. Hell, I even signed the thing for them. They've always wanted me for this, and this is just more proof. No jury is going to find me innocent once they lay it all out the way they will. You know that." He gave Harvey a long look. "And so do I."

They were silent as each thought about what he'd said. It was as if they'd been in this car together for decades and had finally reached the end of the road. After a moment, Harvey spoke.

"Get some sleep. Things always look brighter in the morning."

That sounded like something Gordon's mother would say, and he forced himself to nod in agreement. He knew things would not look brighter in the morning. Only a dark, sleepless night lay ahead of him, spent alone. He would be more tired in the morning than he was now. And that was all. But he said good night to his attorney, thanked him for trying, got out of the car, and walked toward his house.

Harvey waited until Gordon was safely inside before he put his car in Reverse to head to his own house, his own sleepless night.

He had poured himself a whiskey, neat, and turned on the computer to try to distract himself when he heard a hesitant knock at the door. He rolled his eyes toward the ceiling as he pictured Monica Allagash's face, her eager, prying eyes boring into him. He wondered if she would have the cameraman with her at this time of night. He had to hand it to her: she didn't give up easily.

He got up, tiptoed to the door, and looked through the peephole to confirm his suspicions. But it was not Monica's face he saw on the other side. It was the young woman who had come into the interrogation room, the police spokesperson who was afraid he'd sue the department again. She had nothing to worry about. This time they had valid reasons for bringing him in, for questioning him. He could concede that. He opened the door and held it with his hip.

"Mr. Swift?" she asked. She touched her chest, her hand resting just above her breasts. "I'm Anissa Weaver, with the police department? We saw each other today at the station."

"I remember," he said.

He was still holding his whiskey, so he took a sip. He held it up to her. "Want one?" He knew it was a ridiculous thing to ask, but the night was already absurd. There was something freeing about knowing the end was near. After all this time, he could stop resisting his fate.

She gave him a polite, closed-lip smile. "No, no," she demurred. "I just came by to check on you. Sheriff Lancaster wanted me to make sure you got home without incident."

He felt the alcohol hit his bloodstream like a lubricant, emboldening him. "I'm happy to report there was no lynch mob waiting for me. And no member of the Malcor family hiding in the shadows, loaded for bear. It's just me"—he held up the drink, took another big gulp—"drinking alone. Unless, of course, that's an offense you want to take me in for."

"Oh no, not at all. After the day you've had, I can certainly understand."

He looked down at his drink, which was already nearly gone with only a few sips. He planned to pour another just as soon as he got rid of his visitor. Then he would distract himself with work. He needed to decide what he wanted his last sculpture to be. Maybe they had art studios in prison, but he doubted they'd let him have the kinds of materials he was used to using—sharp things, dangerous things. Things little boys could put in their pockets.

He smiled and dipped his chin. "Well," he said, "thanks for stopping by." He stepped out of the way so that, without his hip propping it open, the door would swing shut and their encounter would be over.

Instead the woman reached out and prevented the door from closing. Their eyes met across the threshold, and he could tell from her expression that this move had required courage. Was she going to confront him? Grill him further? Hit him? His stomach clenched as they blinked at each other.

"I was there," she blurted. "In the field that night. With the other kids." She looked around as if someone might be listening, then lowered her voice. "I just wanted to tell you that. I wanted to tell you today, but . . . obviously, I couldn't."

He stood speechless as his mind offered up, then discarded, several reactions to her admission. He wondered if the sheriff knew this, and, if so, why he didn't think it a conflict of interest to assign her to this of all cases. But Wynotte was a small town, and small-town politics—or lack thereof—were to be expected. Perhaps her father was someone important, or perhaps as long as she did a decent job, Pete Lancaster just didn't care. But these things didn't seem appropriate to say, so he said nothing. The two of them stood there as insects circled the lamp above their heads.

Finally, he asked, "Do you want to come in?" She nodded with a look of relief and followed him inside the house.

Wordlessly, he walked to the kitchen and refilled his glass, then took an old jelly jar from his cupboard and poured her some whiskey as well. He handed it to her, and they took a syn-chronized sip, both looking everywhere except at each other.

She took a second sip before speaking. "Our house was one of those across the street from the farm."

"Used to be migrant housing," he said, thinking of the row of four shanty houses in various stages of disrepair, leveled long ago.

She nodded and looked into her glass, but not before he saw the shame on her face. The tiny shotgun shacks that once housed the farm workers were no longer used as such by 1985, but the widow had restored them to some degree and con-tinued to rent them to people who needed a place to live and couldn't afford better. Residents rotated in and out with some regularity. He'd barely paid them any mind when he'd lived there. Those people, he had to admit, hadn't concerned him. Not much had, back then. He'd been tunnel-visioned, intent on starting the life he was sure awaited him out there in a bright, exciting future.

"My mom said we wouldn't be there long. But we were there till they sold the land and we had to get out." She stared hard at her glass. He gestured for her to sit, and she sank into the nearest chair by the table. He did the same.

She turned her glass around and around in her hands. "I saw the car that night like you mentioned today," she said to the glass. "I was one of the kids you were talking about. We all gave different descriptions, but I know there was someone else there, someone they never found, or even tried to find."

She set her glass down and reached across the table to rest her hand on his. He jumped, a reflex. It had been a long time since he'd been touched in a kind way. He felt her soft skin and forced his eyes to meet hers. She took her hand away. He reached for the whiskey bottle and poured another round in both of their glasses without even asking if she wanted more. They each took a long pull, then grimaced in unison as the alcohol burned its way down.

"What I'm saying," she said, then shook her head and started again. "What I'm trying to tell you is, I know—I've always known—that you were in your house when that car pulled in."

She took a deep breath, like someone about to go underwater, then she plunged ahead. She told him how she'd met Davy that night, how they'd crossed the field together, how they'd spied on Gordon as he drew. She watched him warily as she spoke, clearly not sure about the wisdom of spilling her secret. And yet she seemed compelled to tell someone. He felt a warmth grow in his chest as he listened to her. She hadn't asked him to keep her secret, hadn't made him swear never to tell, but he never would. It was as if they'd entered an unspoken agreement, a bond springing up where once there'd been only secrets.

She talked until she came to the end, at least of her story—the moment she lost Davy in the field. "One minute he was with me, and then he was just . . ."

"Gone," Gordon finished. He gripped his glass so tightly that he feared it would shatter in his hand. After a day of hearing what a guilty son of a bitch he was, how other inmates reserved special punishments for pedophiles in prison, how his life was over, her words were a balm.

Someone believed him.

He set down his glass. For a moment they were both silent. He listened to the hum of his refrigerator, the second hand on his wall clock ticking away the seconds as he recalled his selfishness, his lack of grace toward Davy Malcor, the shame surrounding that night he'd never wanted anyone to know about. But was that shame any worse than the shame he'd carried all these years?

There was the shame of what really happened, but there was also the shame of what people thought had happened. To shed one, he understood, he'd have to admit the other.

But not now, not here. He swiped at a tear that slipped from his eye. "Thank you," he said. "For telling me."

He heard the scrape of her chair as she dragged it closer to him, felt her hand rest on his knee. He sat frozen for a moment, then lifted his own hand and placed it atop hers as together they cried, each grieving a boy who graced their lives for mere moments, then disappeared forever, leaving them to question what they could've done differently, how they could've changed the outcome.

After some time he lifted his hand and without a word she rose from her chair, looking embarrassed and avoiding his eyes.

"I should go," she said. He nodded and stood as well. She was so close to him that he could smell the whiskey on her breath when she exhaled. He found himself wanting to reach out and smooth her unruly curls, even though that was impossible. He would sculpt her, he decided; she would be his last piece. He would assemble each loop of her hair carefully, with intention, an homage to the person who believed him when no one else did.

"Did you really come here tonight because Pete Lancaster asked you to?"

She gave him a rueful smile and shook her head.

"I came here, at the risk of losing my job, to tell you the truth. It seemed important after today. I don't want you to give up just because of what they found. I don't think—I never have—that you had anything to do with what happened to Davy."

He covered his face, trying to hide his reaction to her words. He felt her arms go around him, a hug so brief he would later wonder if it had happened at all. When he took his hands away from his face to look at her, she was gone.

PART 4

Monday–Tuesday,
May 1–2, 2006

CHAPTER 32

Thaddeus

Most days when he woke up he had to work to remember what had transpired the previous day, taking a mental inventory upon opening his eyes, deciding whether he'd left things in good or bad condition before giving in to sleep, all while pushing back against the foreboding feeling he carried. This day was no exception as he lay still in his childhood bedroom, recalling where he was, and why.

He peered at the clock radio that had sat on his bedside table since high school and was pleased to see he'd managed to sleep half the day away. Then two disturbing recollections came in rapid succession: One, Davy was dead. And two, Nicole was here. But not at his house. At least not that.

He heaved himself out of bed with a sinking feeling as he went in search of coffee, hoping he wouldn't find Anissa in his kitchen. He wondered when she would stop coming to the house and guessed it wouldn't be until after the funeral. With the discovery of not just Davy's body but also the new evidence implicating Gordon Swift, public curiosity would remain at a peak for a while.

He didn't find Anissa in the kitchen, but he did find his mother. She was loitering there, pretending she wasn't ready to pounce before he'd even had his first jolt of caffeine. This meant she had an unfair advantage, but at least she'd kept the coffee hot for him. He retrieved a cup from the little mug tree she'd had for as long as he could remember and filled it.

"Your publicist called this morning," she said as he was lifting the first sip to his mouth. "Nicole, was it?"

He caught the suspicious tone in her voice, and it occurred to him that the years she'd spent guarding and observing and caring for him had given her a pervading awareness of what simmered under his skin, even the things he worked to tamp down, to keep hidden.

He nodded. "She probably tried my cell, but I was still asleep," he said, making sure to sound nonchalant. Nothing good could come from his mother picking up on whatever was happening with him and Nicole.

"I'll call her back." He looked around the room, grateful there was no sign of Anissa, the memory of sprawling in her foyer a little too recent.

"Where's Anissa?" he asked, changing the subject. "Shouldn't she be here by now?" He wondered if his mother knew that Anissa lived in the spot where Davy was last seen. Anissa had acted like it was a coincidence, but he wasn't sure he bought the act. The world was a strange place, but he wasn't sure it was that strange. He sucked down more coffee, willing it to enter his bloodstream, to fuel him to get through another day.

"She was needed at the station," his mother said. "I hope it's because they're finally gonna arrest that SOB." She pointed at the newspaper that lay unfolded on the kitchen table. The headline read, "Davy Malcor Discovery Yields Incriminating Evidence." Under the headline were two photos, side by side:

Davy's last school picture and Gordon Swift's bio photo, lifted from his artist website.

Thaddeus felt his free hand involuntarily clench into a fist, an old habit. He understood in the most basic way the need to exact justice, to take an eye for an eye, a life for a life, something that was less of a conscious decision than a conclusion reached in his soul. Perhaps he'd write his next memoir from prison as he did time for justifiable homicide. He'd have to give phone interviews instead of in-person readings when the book came out.

He looked away from the front page, out the window above the kitchen sink, needing to see anything but the image of Davy, forever linked to a man Thaddeus hated. Was there a stronger word for hate? He thought of synonyms: *despised, reviled, loathed, abhorred*. He needed *le mot juste*. Yet none of these came close.

He looked into his empty cup. He'd sucked down the coffee like a shot. He reached for the coffeepot for a refill and saw Larkin through the window back at the picnic table. He remembered kissing her there all those years ago. And for once, instead of pushing away that particular memory as he should, he let himself have it. It was healthier to think about that than harming Gordon Swift.

He lifted his coffee cup toward the window.

"I'm going to talk to Larkin."

"You've been spending time with her," his mother said.

He stopped his trek to the back door and made a face at her, meant to indicate that he thought she was crazy. "No, I haven't."

She shrugged like it was no big deal. "More time than you did when you lived here. As I recall, you basically pretended she didn't exist once you two were in high school."

He felt a shimmer of anger flash through him. Not because what she said was untrue but because she had noticed it.

"We just didn't have much in common, Mom," he said, as if that explained why after October 12, 1985, he'd pretended he'd never kissed Larkin, ending their burgeoning relationship after deliberation and with intent. As if it had been a simple thing to forget, to never wonder what might've been.

"But now we do have something in common." He took a sip of his coffee.

"Oh, and what's that?" his mother asked.

"We're both stuck back here with our mothers." He carried his coffee outside, chuckling to himself over the look on his mother's face.

Larkin, bent over a book, didn't hear him approach and startled when he said hello.

She put her hands over the book and scolded him. "Thaddeus, you scared me!"

Thaddeus looked down to see what she was covering up, then recognized the typeface they'd used for his book, as familiar to him now as his own handwriting. He pointed at the book.

"What are you doing?"

She kept her hands in place, as if she could keep him from seeing the words on the pages, as if he hadn't written every one of them.

"My mom had a copy of your book. So I thought I'd read it."

He shuffled his feet. "I kinda figured you already had."

She rolled her eyes. "You mean because everyone else in the world has?"

He gave her a look. "My own mother hasn't."

"Well, in her defense, she lived it, so . . ."

He shrugged. "I guess. But then, so did you."

Their eyes met and a moment passed. He saw her consider, then decide where to take the moment.

"Not really," she said, an edge to her voice. "You decided to save me from it. Remember?"

"Look, I'm sorry for what I said."

"Why?" she asked. "Didn't you mean it?" She closed the book without marking her place.

"I mean, I guess. Yes. I meant it. I just . . . didn't know I was going to say it until it came out. Then I was so mortified that I'd said it, I ran away."

She pointed at the closed book. "That admission's not in here, though. At least, not that I can find."

He smirked at her. "So you're trying to see if I wrote about you?"

"No," she said, a defensive tone creeping into her voice. "I just needed to see if I'm the last to know."

He squinted at her. "Know what?"

"The truth about what happened to us, the reason things just . . . stopped. I mean, we were only fifteen years old, and it was probably never going to be anything, but I think about it sometimes. You know, what might've been. I always thought it was something I did—or didn't do. I spent a lot of my life telling myself it didn't matter, but the truth is . . . The truth is, I never understood and . . . Well, I guess I've always wondered. And it never entered my mind that you . . ."

"That I what?" Thaddeus asked, placing his coffee cup on the picnic table. The coffee had gone cold anyway.

She looked down as she spoke. "That when you started avoiding me, you thought you were saving me."

"I did," he said, his voice low, almost a whisper. "I wouldn't wish our lives on someone I hated. So why would I wish it on someone I lo—"

She jumped up, finger in the air. "Don't you dare finish that sentence. Don't you dare." She started to walk away from the table, but then turned back and picked up the book, hugging it to her chest.

"The thing I don't understand is why I never got a vote. Why didn't you let me decide?"

He pressed his lips into a hard line and studied her for a moment. "Because you're a kind and loyal person. You're one of the best people I've ever met, to this day. I knew what you'd choose. And I couldn't let you do that."

This time, she walked away from him, and he had no choice but to let her go.

FROM *EVERY MOMENT SINCE: A MEMOIR* BY THADDEUS MALCOR

PUBLISHED SEPTEMBER 20, 2005

The first time I ever wrote about my brother was in a freshman English class in college. I'd always been considered a jock, and though I had deep thoughts, I had never expressed them on paper. I held a general disdain for all things academic, and right or wrong, I felt that writing fell under that category. It was a thing teachers made you do and, therefore, surely not enjoyable.

The assignment was the standard "Tell us about yourself" introductory essay. I remember it was very late at night when I sat down to write it. The essay was due the next day and I had procrastinated, as usual. I was a little drunk from a party as I sat in front of the paper, my pen poised, just hovering there for the longest time. I did not know then that Ernest Hemingway had long ago advised writers to "Write drunk, edit sober," or maybe I would've seen my inebriation as an asset.

Finally, I wrote, "My name is Thaddeus James Malcor and I'm from a small town outside of Charlotte, North Carolina, called Wynotte. My parents are named Tabitha and Daniel. My father is the vice president of sales for a chemical company (that shall remain nameless) and my mother is a homemaker. (She prefers that term to *housewife.* She says she is not married to the house.) I have one sister named Kristyn and I used to have a brother."

I remember I froze, staring at what I'd written, the black letters spelling out what I'd never actually said aloud: *I used to have a brother.* I'd never written or spoken about Davy in past tense before. It looked so final, like my hand was able to admit something the rest of me couldn't: that Davy was never coming back.

I used to have a brother, but I didn't anymore.

I remember finishing the essay in a rush of words and feelings. I wrote about what happened that night, the whole story, tears and snot pouring down my face. When I was finished, I read what I'd written, then I tore the whole thing up and threw it away, burying the bits in the wastebasket under empty beer cans. I didn't want anyone to see it. I felt something like shame, like I'd put into print what was never to be uttered or even thought. I felt I had betrayed the brother I used to have.

Sometime in the wee hours, as the sun was coming up, I wrote another essay. That one was very short, and it wasn't about my family at all. It was about my knee injury and why I couldn't play baseball anymore. It was about a minor tragedy, far less shocking, something that happens to people all the time. The teacher gave me a B.

As the party has progressed, so have the partygoers, moving from indoors to out, gathering on the Myerses' large deck, lit tiki torches blazing against the darkness. Tabby can feel fall in the air, finally. She thinks of Davy wearing the jacket she made him, of TJ's anger at him for wearing it these past few weeks. And yet, she doesn't have to worry about him being cold.

She looks at the slim Timex on her arm. It's almost 11:00 p.m. The boys will be home by now, hopefully exhausted from their games, tucked safely into bed. She shivers a little.

"You cold?" Marie, beside her, asks.

Tabby shrugs. "Not too bad."

"We'll leave soon," Marie says. She yanks a thumb in the direction of the menfolk, sitting in a ring of chairs and puffing on cigars. "As soon as those bozos are done." Marie pinches her nose and makes a face as Tabby laughs and nods her agreement.

Danny will carry the cigar smell into their bed with him later; he will try to kiss her, and she will push him away, pretending he smells too bad. Then she will pull him back.

Inside the Myerses' house, the phone rings. Tabby turns her head toward the noise, her eyes locating the phone on the wall just inside the doorway that leads from the deck to the kitchen. The phone is yellow, the color of the sun, of those smiley faces on T-shirts, of caution lights, the cord outrageously long so the Myerses' teenage daughter can stretch it outside onto the deck and talk to her boyfriend in private.

June Myers had told them a story about this earlier in the night, about a time last winter when an icy rain was falling and the lovesick girl put on her ski jacket, knit cap, gloves, and a hood so she could still sit outside and talk. *"Young love,"* they'd scoffed to each other, as if they didn't remember exactly what it felt like.

Tabby watches now as June Myers hurries over to answer the phone, a worried look on her face. It is too late for anyone to be calling for a conversation. Tabby scans the faces on the deck and wonders who the call is for. She hopes it isn't anything bad, nothing more than a child who won't go to sleep for the babysitter, an unexpected fever cropping up, a scary noise heard outside.

Clutching the phone to her chest, June comes to the doorway and surveys the crowd, her eyes landing on Tabby, then quickly scanning away. Tabby feels herself exhale a breath.

But then June's gaze travels over to the men, and she calls out Danny's name. She has to say it twice before he hears her, before he registers the phone in June's hand and the look of alarm on her face. He holds his cigar aloft as he blinks at June, then seeks out Tabby.

Their eyes meet at the same time that June says, "It's the police on the phone. They can't find Davy."

CHAPTER 33

Tabitha

The first thing she did when she got home from the church was pull out a piece of paper and begin her regret list for the week. It wasn't even close to Friday, but with the funeral tomorrow and Kristyn and her family due anytime, Tabitha decided to get a jump on things. She would start the list with the way she'd broken down and cried in front of the pastor while planning the memorial service, her makeup staining his white dress shirt as he comforted her. He'd looked down at the shirt and said, *"Occupational hazard,"* and they'd both laughed. But still, she'd vowed to save her tears for when she was alone.

She wrote:

1. Cried in front of Pastor Rivera. Stained his shirt with my mascara.

What next? She was poised over the paper, pondering regret number two, when she heard someone tap at the back door. She put down the pen and went to peek through the gauzy curtains covering the window and saw the outline of a familiar face. She pulled open the door and greeted Larkin, knowing Larkin had not come to see her. She watched as Larkin's eyes swept the kitchen, then all but stood on her tiptoes to see beyond it.

"I'm sorry," Larkin said. "For interrupting you."

"You're not interrupting me," Tabitha said. "But if you're looking for Thaddeus, he isn't here." She looked around and shrugged. "I think he went on one of his walks."

"Oh, well, I was just going to tell him something," Larkin said. "We had a sort of . . . disagreement earlier, and I"—she waved her hand—"Well, it's stupid."

"He was important to you," Tabitha said, surprised at the words as they came out of her mouth. "I mean, back when you were kids." She raised her eyebrows in question.

Larkin ducked her head and gave the smallest of nods.

"I didn't see it back then, but I see it now," Tabitha said. "I didn't see a lot of things." She gestured behind her, where her regret list lay. "You know what I was doing before you showed up?"

Larkin shook her head, her expression curious.

"I was writing a regret list. It's something I do every week. I usually write it on Fridays, but I decided to get an early start on this week's list since we've got so much going on."

Larkin nodded as if this made sense when it couldn't possibly. Saying it aloud, Tabitha heard how foolish it all sounded. Still, she felt the need to explain it to Larkin, or at least to try to.

"I started it the Friday after Davy disappeared. It had been such a terrible week, and I kept thinking of all the regrets I had. I needed somewhere to put them, something to *do* with them, so I wrote them all down. Then I read over the list a few times and threw it away. The next Friday I did it again, and I just kept it up. For twenty-one years, I've kept it up."

Tabitha glanced over at the list, waiting to be filled. There were always regrets; there always would be. It was impossible to get through life without them.

"The thing about that list—and the thing I would tell you—is some of the regrets are of things that happened to me, things I can't help or change. But there are some I could've prevented. Through different choices, or words, or actions, I could've avoided them completely." She raised her eyebrows.

"Thaddeus being here—the two of you being sort of thrown back together like this—must be conflicting. And that's fine— it's normal to have jumbled emotions about the past. Just don't let it mess up what you've got now—that man I saw on the computer screen the other day, that little girl." She pointed at Larkin. "This new baby on the way."

Tabitha watched as Larkin's eyes filled with tears, and she reached out to embrace the young woman.

"It's all so precious." Tabitha spoke low, her lips close to the girl's ear. "You can't appreciate now just how precious it is."

And that was the biggest regret of all. That was what each week's list was saying again and again. *I missed it. I missed it. I missed it.* She hadn't appreciated how rare and fleeting it would all be, that the simplest moments were actually remarkable. She'd looked right past them, her eyes always scanning the horizon for something else. She'd had it all, and then it was all gone. She would regret those oversights for the rest of her life, no matter how many times she wrote that she regretted nothing.

She let go of Larkin and stepped back to look at her.

"So," Larkin said, wiping her eyes. "I guess don't tell him I came by."

"I think that's best." Larkin mustered a smile. "See you at the memorial tomorrow?"

"Of course," Larkin said. "Of course, we'll be there."

Just like you always have been. Tabitha watched as Larkin turned to make her way back to the house next door, then she closed the door and went back to the regret list. Instead of writing, she seized the paper, closing her fist around it, the crumpling sound loud in the quiet house. She held the ball of paper in her hand and studied it for just a moment, then walked over and tossed it into the trash. She stood over the bin and knew that she would never again write a regret list. The one she'd written last Friday had been her last.

She tried to recall that last list, what had been on it, but she could not. And she guessed that was the point: *Je ne regrette rien. I regret nothing.* Though, if that were true, wouldn't she have stopped the practice long ago?

The truth was, she regretted everything, all the time, beginning with the moment she allowed Thaddeus and Davy to go play night games. For the second time that day, the tears came, unrelenting and unavoidable. She turned to the counter—the same counter where she'd assembled peanut-butter-and-jelly sandwiches and written checks and yelled commands—as sobs wracked her body. At least she was alone this time.

And then she wasn't. Arms went around her, pulled her in. For a moment she thought it was Daniel. Then she heard a voice that was not Daniel's, but close.

She looked up to find her son's face. But not the son she lost. No, this was the one she had left, the one who, God help him, had regrets of his own, regrets she'd left him to wrestle with alone.

"I'm sorry," she cried. "I'm so sorry."

He stepped back and looked at her quizzically. "Mom, what are you sorry for?"

"I left you with him. That night. And when you came back without him, I blamed you. I made you responsible. But it was only because I couldn't accept my own responsibility."

He had stepped away from her, yet his hands still gripped her arms, just above the elbows. They were a man's hands, but she still saw them as the hands of a boy, a boy who'd had to grow up overnight, a boy who had been cheated out of so much because his brother disappeared.

"It wasn't your fault, honey." Her words were less of a statement and more of a plea: *Please believe it. Please move forward with your life.*

He pulled her back to him, crushing her against his chest as he hugged her. He spoke into her hair, and she remembered when it was the reverse, when it was her speaking into his hair, baby curls damp from sleep as she softly sang a lullaby.

"Mom, you don't understand. I sent him away." Thaddeus began to sob, and she wanted to soothe him as she once could.

But she couldn't promise that it was just a bad dream, that the sun would rise in the morning and chase away the darkness. That was what made her the angriest—that she'd been robbed of something most mothers have: the assurance that there was no bogeyman. Her children grew up knowing that was a lie.

"He wanted to be with me and my friends, but I sent him away," Thaddeus moaned. Still sobbing, he crumpled and she bent with him, sinking to the floor together.

"Shh," she said. "Shh." There, cradling him as best she could, she let herself recall the party they'd gone to that night and the phone call that ended it. On the way home from the party, she'd practiced what she'd say to Thaddeus about being more responsible after they located Davy. She'd brooded the whole ride home, not absorbing the severity of the situation, refusing to think it could be anything other than a misunderstanding that would quickly be resolved.

She hugged Thaddeus tighter, as if the sheer strength of her grip could communicate the force of her love for him. She'd gotten so much wrong. This, she thought, this was her regret. Though the words had never made it onto a single sheet of paper in all these years, this was what she regretted most—the mother she hadn't been to Thaddeus after they lost Davy.

And then Daniel was there, crouching unsteadily on the floor with them, his arms encircling them both, gathering them like chicks under his wings. They remained, the three of them, like that for a while.

Until another voice, familiar but out of place, joined them.

"Mom? Dad?" Kristyn called as she wandered through the house to find her father, mother, and older brother in a damp heap on the kitchen floor. With a nervous laugh she asked, "What are you guys doing?"

The three looked up to see the baby of the family standing there, all grown up and a mother herself. Behind her, her two children and husband stood clumped together and cast uncertain glances at her, at them. What had they walked into?

What indeed. Tabitha couldn't help but think of how they must look. And soon Kristyn's children, Tabitha's grandchildren, began to giggle. Soon everyone else, with a kind of relief, laughed too.

FROM *EVERY MOMENT SINCE: A MEMOIR* BY THADDEUS MALCOR

PUBLISHED SEPTEMBER 20, 2005

I distinctly recall one thing from that night, after it was clear that Davy was gone and not just lost or hiding. I'm not sure why it sticks out so prevalently in my mind, except it was a moment of sheer calm, an oasis in the midst of a night consumed by terror. I have tried to write about it so many times, but the words to explain what I felt, what I saw, elude me and I fail. Since this is a book composed of words, I will try to wrangle them into submission, so that perhaps you can understand if not what the moment meant to me, then at least what it involved.

I had returned home after going back to the field with the cops to retrace my steps, to answer questions, to look in vain for Davy. I was dirty and hungry and bone-tired, yet wired at the same time, my mind racing, my nerve endings frayed and sparking. I could smell the nervous energy in the air around me, my body radiating a mixture of sweat and adrenaline. I wanted to fall in bed and forget, but I knew that wouldn't happen.

So I went looking for someone to talk to. I went looking for the girl next door.

All the lights were on at her house. I went to the door and saw her father on the phone, her mother making coffee and sandwiches for the cops. They looked older than I remembered and I wondered if that was my imagination or if they had, in fact, physically aged that night. I knocked on the door, which was silly. I could've walked right in, but I felt like doing so would be an intrusion.

They both looked over and saw me, hope alighting on their faces. Her mother raced to open the door for me; her father hung up the phone.

"Is there news?" They spoke at the same time.

I felt bad disappointing them as I shook my head no. "I was looking for—"

"She's at your house," her mother answered, cutting me off. Her face had gone from hopeful to dashed in a moment. "She stayed with Kristy so your parents could help the police."

"Oh," I said. "Ok." I turned to go, but her mother stopped me.

She held out a sandwich. "Are you hungry?"

I was. "No," I said. "I couldn't eat right now." I felt that saying anything else would be disrespectful to my brother. Her mother nodded like I'd given the right answer, and I went back to my own house.

I entered my home like a visitor. The TV was still on. These were the days when the TV signed off at a certain time each night, but that hadn't happened yet. A rerun of *Bonanza* was on, but the sound was turned down so I couldn't hear what Little Joe was saying. *Bonanza*, I remember thinking, was a show about brothers. I shut off the TV.

The girl next door was not on the couch where I expected her to be. I called her name softly but got no reply. I walked to the kitchen, but she was not there either. Her mother said she'd stayed with Kristy, so I went to Kristy's room.

The door was cracked, but I pushed it open to find the two of them crammed together in Kristy's little bed, both huddled under her Holly Hobbie quilt. She had wrapped her arms around my sister and pulled her close. They were both fast asleep, the only sound in the room the rhythm of their breathing.

Just then a helicopter with its tractor beam of a spotlight made a pass over our house, looking for Davy in the one place I was sure he was not. The light filled the room, and I feared it would wake them. But they slept on, undisturbed, as I stood and watched them, timing my own breathing to sync with theirs, feeling my heart slow for perhaps the first time since I'd discovered Davy was missing.

I breathed with the two of them in that little room, bathed briefly in that brilliant light, and I felt . . . restored. Even now with the wisdom of age and ample time to reflect, I can't explain why or how being there with her in that room, in that moment, brought a peace I couldn't find elsewhere. It's a peace I've searched for ever since.

See? I have failed to conjure the right words again. Maybe I don't have the words, or maybe I just don't want to use them. Except to say, that peace was her. It was her, it was her, it was her.

PART 5

Wednesday, May 3, 2006

CHAPTER 34

Tabitha

The three of them rode to the funeral together, just as they had ridden to the press conference together. Daniel drove with Tabitha in the passenger seat and Thaddeus in the back seat, parents and child.

They'd been instructed to arrive early and park in back. Anissa would be there to escort them into and out of the church. Kristyn and her family opted to arrive later, driving from their hotel, hoping to shield the children from the reality of what was happening as much as possible.

Sometimes Tabitha worried for her grandchildren, growing up with an enigma for an uncle, understanding from birth that something terrible had happened in the family they'd been born into. Though she missed them, she was grateful they were in California, far away from this place. Maybe, she thought as Daniel eased into the designated parking space, when this was all over, she'd go to California too.

Daniel put the car in Park but did not cut the engine. They looked at each other, exhaling in unison. Daniel looked from Tabitha to Thaddeus like a coach to his players.

"We can do this," he said.

Tabitha heard the doubt in his voice. He went to remove the key from the ignition, but she reached out to stop him.

"Not yet," she said.

Both Thaddeus and Daniel looked at her quizzically. She didn't want to admit she wasn't ready yet—might never be ready.

"I don't see Anissa. Maybe we should wait for her?"

Thaddeus peered out his own window. "I don't see any press. I think we're safe."

Tabitha shrugged. "But what's the hurry?"

Daniel put his hand back in his lap, left the car running, the radio playing low. She could barely make out the voices of Crosby, Stills, and Nash singing about wasting time along the way.

The three of them sat silently. She couldn't have said what the two men in the car were thinking, but she thought of the many Sundays she'd spent inside the building in front of them. Being back yesterday had been the first time in a long time that she'd darkened the doorway.

The warning chime that indicated a door opening interrupted her thoughts and she looked back to see Thaddeus with one leg out of the car.

"I can't just sit here twiddling my thumbs," he said. "I'm gonna go on in." She let him go without protest. They would each do this day however they could. The point was to get through it.

She and Daniel looked at each other, then away. She couldn't remember the last time she'd been alone in a car with him. She'd been surprised when he suggested last night that they ride together, assuming he'd drive directly to the church from his own place, probably with his girlfriend.

"You didn't have to drive me," she said. "I could've driven myself."

"I wanted to," he said. "We should do this as a family."

Were they a family anymore? She supposed in some fractured, dysfunctional way they were. At least, when it mattered. And today, it mattered. "Well, that was nice of you," she said. Then added, because she wanted to be prepared, "Is your girlfriend meeting you here?"

Daniel shook his head. "That was part of why I went back to my place the other night. I had to—I wanted to . . . end it with her." He swallowed. "Being with you these past few days, it just . . . it wasn't right to stay with her when I've still got all these feelings for you."

He looked over at her, raised his eyebrows as if he'd asked a question when he hadn't, not really. Still, she nodded an assent. What they'd shared, what they'd lost, what they'd endured—so many feelings were unresolved. Was it possible to resolve them? In spite of the heaviness of the day, Tabitha felt her heart lighten a little. She didn't know what it meant, and she didn't need to know. Not now. Now it was enough that he was there. She couldn't help but wonder if somehow what was happening was what Davy wanted.

He pointed toward the church. "I think that's our cue."

Tabitha turned to see Anissa beckoning them in. She looked back at him, a sense of growing panic at the thought of what lay ahead for them both. This was goodbye, real and official. This was the end of something that had shaped their lives for too long.

"It's ok," he reassured her. "We'll do this together."

"Ok," she said. "Ok." She remained in the car as he got out, came around to her side, opened her door, and held out his hand for her to grip.

CHAPTER 35

Gordon

He, of course, had no intention of going to Davy Malcor's funeral. Him showing up would be disrespectful to the family, even if he'd like to pay his respects. Anissa had stopped by to check on him before she went to the church, pretending again that it was part of her job, but he knew she was lying. In this case he didn't mind being lied to. He'd wanted to see her again too.

"You nervous?" he asked her, though he knew the answer. Anxiety flickered across her face. The truth about the night of Davy's disappearance weighed on her as much as it weighed on him. He wanted to hug her and tell her it would be all right, but he wasn't sure she'd want that. The night in his kitchen had been, he told himself, a one-off, a step out of time.

At her car door she turned to him. "You could come, you know." He began shaking his head before she finished speaking.

"That's not a good idea," he said. "It'd only lead to trouble."

"Not if you went in after it started, sat in the back, and got out before it was over."

"I'll pay my respects here, in my own way," he said.

"And what way is that?" she asked, a teasing note to her voice.

"Through my work," he said. He pointed at the studio, where he would hole himself up and think of Davy as he sculpted the little girl who was the last one ever to see him, a girl Gordon suspected Davy would've grown up and loved, had he gotten the chance. His hand moved to touch her hair, but he quickly thrust it in his pocket before he could make a fool of himself.

"You could come over," he said. "After. You could tell me about it and then it'd be like I was there."

She smiled. "I might need some more of your whiskey by then."

He smiled back. "I'll have it waiting."

He watched her leave until her car disappeared around the bend, and he wished she didn't have to face that funeral alone. Someone should be with her. But it was the last place he could show his face, no matter how much he wanted to be there for her, and for Davy, the three of them linked to that night and each other forever.

He turned around, walked back inside, through the house, and out the back to his studio. He opened the door and felt the light pour in. He breathed deeply, telling himself this was enough: this place, this work, this life. He'd stopped expecting more a long time ago. He thought about Anissa's visit and wondered if maybe, possibly, there could be more after this day.

A noise behind him made him turn on his heels, forgetting the whiff of possibility that had just skimmed past him like the tip of an angel's wing barely brushing his face—there, then gone.

The boy from the other night stood a few feet away, pushing his glasses up the bridge of his nose, his eyes blinking nervously.

"You said to come back another time," he said. "And I could see your studio. My mom said I could." The boy rocked back on his heels as he waited for Gordon's answer.

It was the expression on his face that brought it back to Gordon—the cautious, hopeful look, the eagerness to be admitted. This time Gordon would not say no. Sure, it wasn't a great idea for someone suspected of what he was suspected of to have a child of a similar age on his premises. But his goose was as good as cooked, as far as he was concerned. What was the harm in welcoming a boy who was only asking for access? He could do this one right thing.

He could not recall the boy's name because only one name was on his mind: Davy. *Goodbye, Davy*, Gordon thought. *I sent you away, yet you stayed with me.* Today, he was having his own kind of memorial for Davy Malcor. Now he'd have an assistant for the task.

"What was your name again?" he asked.

"Stuart," Stuart said.

"Well, Stuart, you couldn't have come at a better time."

Stuart's eyes widened. "Really?"

"Yes, I've got something very important to do today, and you can be my helper. I mean, if you don't have anything else going on," he said, feeling a warmth spread within his chest as he watched a smile fill the boy's face.

"No!" Stuart said. "I don't!"

Gordon beckoned him into the studio. "Well then, let's get in here and figure it out together."

CHAPTER 36

Thaddeus

Ignoring Anissa's edict about entering through the back of the church, Thaddeus went around to the front, intending to walk the perimeter of the grounds until the service started. He couldn't just sit in a pew and wait in silence for the event to begin any more than he could sit closed up in that car with his parents. *Tomorrow*, he thought. Tomorrow this would be over and he could leave.

He was surprised to find people gathered in front already, milling around in clutches of twos and threes, talking in low, somber tones. He spotted Phillip talking with Lee Watkins, the guy from the bar, the one who'd also been there that night. Was it weird that he had showed up? Thaddeus supposed not. The guy must've felt a connection, having been there, the echoes of that one night rippling across decades, touching people he'd forgotten all about.

He strode over to the pair and laid his hand on Phillip's shoulder. Phillip startled, turning around with a surprised expression.

"Thaddeus!" he exclaimed. "I thought you'd be inside already."

Thaddeus glanced back at the church, thinking of the last time they were ever there as a family. The children's choir had sung and, watching them, his mother had begun to cry. She'd stood up and walked out in the middle of the song, all eyes on her. Though he understood what set her off—he himself had been staring at the spot where Davy would've been standing on the risers—Thaddeus had squirmed with embarrassment. He'd never wanted to show his face in that church again. Then, like a miracle, the next week they hadn't gone, nor any week after that. Church, like normalcy and his parents' marriage, had disappeared after Davy did.

"Eh," he said, turning his eyes away from the building, "I'll go in in a minute." He looked at Phillip, who, in the moment he'd turned and looked at the church, had somehow made Lee disappear.

"You didn't have to get rid of him on my account," Thaddeus said.

"I didn't," Phillip said and shrugged. "He left on his own. I think you make him uncomfortable." Thaddeus started to ask why that would be, but Phillip spoke again before he could.

"Are we good? I mean, after the other night?" His features were pinched with concern. Before Thaddeus could reassure him that yes, they were fine, Phillip continued, "I'm really sorry. I was out of line. I've thought a lot about how it must feel to be in your shoes, how upsetting it must be to have it all come back up like this. I shouldn't have pressed you so much. I just wanted you to know—"

"Phillip, man, don't worry about it. It's fine. I caught a ride with Larkin, and we had a nice talk, and it all worked out. I've been so busy with everything since then I haven't given it a second thought."

"Ok, good," Phillip said, looking relieved. Thaddeus studied his old friend. The dude had softened as he'd aged. Maybe becoming a dad changed him; he was definitely different from the cocky, defiant athlete Thaddeus had once followed around.

"I just don't want you to feel guilty anymore. You know, for what happened. It wasn't your fault. I just hope you know that. I hope—"

"Philly." Thaddeus clapped his old friend on the back. "Let it go."

Phillip looked away. When he looked back he was smiling, but it was a forced smile. They were both ashamed, Thaddeus understood. Both guilty for setting the stage from which Davy was abducted. They could fake-smile forever, but it would never make that fact less true.

A memory came back to him and for once he didn't push it out of his mind. He just let it play. Because wasn't that what this day was for, remembering? He saw his younger self crossing the field alone, doing his best to sober up as he began to search for his brother. He'd touched his pocket as he walked, making sure the rock was still there. He'd give it to Davy, he'd decided. He'd apologize. He'd try to be a better brother.

Now, all these years later, Thaddeus patted his pocket to make sure the rock was still there. He had to stop carrying it.

"I could go in with you," Phillip said. Thaddeus thought of how Phillip wasn't with him that night as he looked for his brother, how he'd faced the bad part all alone. It would be good, he decided, not to be alone for this.

"You could sit with us too," Thaddeus said. "My sister and her husband are going to sit in the back in case their kids get fussy. So there's room. If you want." Phillip swallowed, nodded, and together they walked toward the church.

As the memorial started, Davy stared out from a huge screen on the stage, looking out at them all with those soulful brown eyes, eyes much older than the face they went with. They'd opened the service with a soloist singing a slowed-down rendition of the song "The Power of Love" by Huey Lewis and the News, the *Back to the Future* theme song that had been Davy's favorite when he died. During the song, a montage of photos of Davy replaced the portrait on the large screen. Some of the pictures Thaddeus had seen hundreds of times thanks to the media, but some were more personal, more candid, all evoking so many memories.

When it got too hard to look at his brother, Thaddeus turned away, looking to Phillip instead. Their eyes met and Thaddeus thought he saw tears in Phillip's eyes. Embarrassed for them both, he turned away, looking to his mother on his other side. She was failing to blink back her tears. He reached out and took her hand, squeezed it. She squeezed back and gave him a sad, brave smile.

He felt someone reach for his other hand and looked to see that it was Phillip. *Ok, this is weird.* He willed himself not to show his discomfort. He'd reached out for his mom's hand, so Phillip had reached out for his. His old friend was clearly swept up in the moment, and as Thaddeus had written in his own book, there was no one right way to express grief. It was out of character for the Phillip he used to know, but maybe this was the new Phillip, one more in touch with his emotions.

Then Thaddeus felt Phillip's grip on his hand tighten. A small sob rose from somewhere deep inside his old friend, and

Phillip uselessly tried to hold it inside until it seemed to explode from his mouth.

Tabitha looked at them both, concern replacing her smile. On her other side, his father also looked over, equally concerned. Thaddeus gave them a don't-look-at-me-it's-him look and tried to act normal.

All hope of normalcy was lost when Phillip began to sob openly and loudly, his eyes locked on the images of Davy on the screen as he tried to say something between sobs.

His words were nearly unintelligible. Only Thaddeus, who was closest, could make out what Phillip was saying. Or what it sounded like he was saying. To Thaddeus, it sounded like he was saying, "Forgive me." But that couldn't be right. Davy had nothing to forgive Phillip for except calling him "McFly."

Phillip's grip clenched tighter, to the point that he was actually hurting Thaddeus. When Thaddeus tried to pull away, Phillip would not let go.

Phillip makes his way across the field, tired and filled with
regret. Tonight was stupid. Though he'd been everyone's hero
for supplying the beer, in the end his friends had gotten
drunk and acted like idiots, caring more about the beer than
the person who got it for them. Phillip himself had stopped
drinking the minute things got out of hand.

He was glad when it was time to go, his promise to meet
his uncle for a ride home a good excuse to slip away.

He pauses to check his watch, switches on his flashlight to
see the time. If he hurries, he won't be late and set his uncle
off on one of his tirades. Phillip swings the flashlight left,
then right, getting his bearings in the dark, unfamiliar field.

He wishes his uncle hadn't picked such an obscure place
to meet, but that's his uncle, always ducking and covering,
staying under the radar since he is usually driving under the
influence. He avoids the main roads, where the cops are most
likely to be. Phillip has learned to drive on the back roads,
counting the days till he can get his license and the freedom it
will bring.

He finds the path that will take him through the woods
and spit him out into a neighborhood under construction.
It is a neighborhood his uncle is working on, so he knows it
well. Phillip does not know why his uncle allowed this night,
made it possible, even. He thinks he wanted Phillip to fall in

love with alcohol the way he has. But so far Phillip has not
seen the point.

He steps out into the cul-de-sac to see his uncle's car
waiting, the tailpipe emitting exhaust and the dim sound of
a radio playing within. He walks to the car to find his uncle
slumped against the wheel, eyes closed, mouth open. Phillip
opens the driver's side door and the dome light overhead
comes on. He nudges his uncle, but he doesn't respond.

"Uncle Joe," he says, "I'm here. Let's go."

Behind him he thinks he hears footsteps, but when he
turns, no one is there. It is creepy out here with the few
framed houses, just bones of a home against the night sky.
The only light at all is the light in the car—there are no
streetlights up yet and not much of a moon in the sky.

Phillip turns back to his uncle and nudges him again,
insistent. "Uncle Joe," he says, louder this time. "Wake up."

His uncle wakes up swinging, which is normal, but Phillip
is caught off guard. The bigger man's arm—muscular from
years of physical labor—catches Phillip in the shoulder and
shoves him so hard that he wobbles for a moment, nearly
sprawling on the pavement, but recovers, anger welling
up inside him. He takes steps back to his uncle, who is
looking around wild-eyed, confused, and disoriented. He has
forgotten where he is and why he is there. Phillip sees the
beer cans on the floorboard of the passenger side of the car.
He counts to four and then stops counting.

"I'm driving," he says to his uncle.

"The hell you say," his uncle slurs, turning to grip the wheel
like a drowning man clinging to a life raft. "This is my damn
car and I'm driving it." He gives Phillip the side-eye. "You

get your own car and a driver's license, you can drive all you want."

Undeterred, Phillip pleads with his uncle. "If we get stopped, you'll get arrested. You know if you end up with another DWI, they'll take your license."

"I ain't gonna get stopped," his uncle says. He hitches his thumb in the direction of the passenger seat. "So get in if you want a ride home." He huffs. "I wouldn't even be out here if it weren't for me having to wait on your ass."

For a moment Phillip doesn't move, weighing his options. Though many of his friends live nearby, Phillip doesn't. Walking home would take at least an hour, and he is tired, and he just wants this night to end. He tries once more to reason with an unreasonable man.

"Please let me drive, Uncle Joe."

In answer his uncle looks away from him, his gaze on the windshield as he revs the engine and says, "You comin' or not?"

With a defeated sigh Phillip walks around the car. He thinks he sees movement in his peripheral vision, but when he looks over, nothing is there. He gets into the passenger seat and slams the door harder than necessary. He kicks at the beer cans on the floorboard just to make them clatter.

Before they drive away, his uncle looks over at Phillip. "Don't I get a thank-you for tonight?" he asks. "Sure would be nice if you showed me some gratitude once in a while."

Phillip locks eyes with his uncle and makes himself speak.

"Thank you," he says, forcing the words from his lips.

If he could take this all back, he would. If he could be anywhere else, he would. He'd hoped for something to come out of tonight, but now he cannot name what that something was. Not popularity—he is popular enough. Not more friends. He has friends. Respect, maybe? Or was it just a way to let the other guys know that someone cares about him, will do nice things for him like their families do for them?

"Can we just go?" he asks.

His uncle lets out a mean growl-like laugh. "Well, by all means, Your Highness. I'll be happy to take your ungrateful ass home right now."

With his eyes still locked on Phillip, his uncle presses hard on the gas, shooting the car forward at the same moment Phillip turns his head to see that someone is in front of the car.

A boy, standing there for reasons he will never understand.

A boy, waving his arms, saying something they cannot hear.

A boy, who is there, then gone.

Phillip can feel the skin on his hands blistering under the wooden shaft of the shovel. He stops and pauses long enough to look up at the night sky. They've been digging for hours, and time is not on their side. Once the sun starts its climb, someone is sure to see what they're doing and they will be caught. Arrested. Taken to jail.

What they are doing is wrong, but Phillip has no choice but to go along. It is his fault it happened, after all, a point his uncle has driven home. If not for him, they never would have been out there, and the accident wouldn't have happened.

As he spears the earth with the blade of his shovel, Phillip's mind whirls with the images of what happened. He sees the two of them standing over Davy's still form, his uncle looking everywhere but at Davy. They hear, off in the distance, the sound of voices calling Davy's name. His uncle panics in response, coming up with a plan that Phillip isn't sure is right. But all the other options lead to them getting caught. In the end Phillip goes along with his uncle, who is, for better or worse, the one in charge of him.

Phillip tries to swallow, but his mouth is too dry, parched from exertion and thirst and fear. His muscles ache, his hands burn, and whatever moisture is left in his body takes the form of tears that collect in his eyes, stinging as he thinks of TJ sending Davy away, of them all laughing at him. He thinks of how the Malcors will be looking for him but will never find him, buried all the way out here. It doesn't seem fair that they might never know what happened to their son, their brother.

"You're movin' too slow. Better speed it along," his uncle says. He points at the large hole they're working on. "Keep it up," he adds, pulling a pack of cigarettes out of his shirt pocket. "I'll be right back."

Phillip watches as his uncle walks over to his car, gets in, and drives away. He is going to smoke his cigarettes and get more beer. He has sobered up in the hours since the accident, but he won't stay that way for long. He never does.

When his uncle is for sure out of sight, Phillip rests the shovel against a nearby tree and looks over at Davy, lying there so still and quiet beside the hole. Tentatively, he takes one step toward the boy, looks back over his shoulder just to make sure his uncle is really gone, then takes another step, moving quickly, resolved in what he has to do. He stoops down beside the kid, pausing just long enough to whisper.

"I didn't mean for this to happen." He begins to cry as he tells Davy how sorry he is.

Through his tears, before he can think better of it, he reaches down and begins to remove Davy's jacket—the special one his mom made for him. Phillip had teased Davy about the jacket, but in truth, Phillip would've proudly worn a Marty McFly jacket every day of his life if it meant he had a mother who'd make him one.

All Phillip has is his drunk uncle, and after tonight he risks losing even that. If his uncle is arrested, he will have no one. Phillip's tears blur his vision. He blinks them away so he can see what he's doing.

He removes the jacket swiftly, trying not to think about what he's doing as he does it. He folds the jacket in half, then runs over to an outbuilding not too far away. He looks around in the dark for a place to stow the jacket, thinking—hoping—as he does that someone will find it, that someone will remember that it is Davy's, and that they will look for him here.

He cannot make up to TJ or his family what he has done tonight, but he can do this for them. He finds a large piece of corrugated tin roofing, lifts it, drops the jacket under it, then drops the roofing back over top of it. It's a risky move, but Phillip doubts his uncle will notice the jacket is gone or remember what the kid was wearing in the first place. He hasn't looked directly at Davy since the accident.

Weary but determined to dig as fast as he can so they can get out of there, Phillip grabs the shovel and goes back to the gravesite. As he digs, he thinks that maybe he should pray, but he doesn't know what to say to God. The only funeral he's ever been to was his parents', but he was too little to remember that. He's never been to church. Other than school, the baseball field, and TJ's house, he's never really been anywhere. Plus, he doesn't know if someone responsible for a death is even allowed to pray.

Instead he says aloud, "I'm sorry, forgive me. I'm sorry, forgive me," hoping as he does that whoever is supposed to hear it will. He says it again and again, dutifully digging until he hears his uncle's car returning.

When his uncle gets out of the car, he is carrying a six-pack of beer. He pulls one off and extends the can to Phillip, so cold it drips with condensation. Phillip's mouth waters as his uncle holds it out to him. There is nothing he can do but take it from his hand.

CHAPTER 37

Anissa

At first what was happening was isolated among the four people it was happening to—the three Malcors and Phillip Laney, who appeared to be having some sort of breakdown. It took a few minutes for Anissa to register the disturbance as something beyond a normal display of grief.

The awareness quickly traveled past her to everyone in the church—outward from the front pew, into and across the aisle, and backward, into the rows behind them. People began elbowing and clutching each other, murmuring as they tried to process what was happening.

For a moment, Anissa stood frozen in place a few feet away, unsure if this was a threat and what to do about it if it was. To pull the family out of the situation was to stop their son's funeral before it had really gotten started. She watched as the seconds ticked by and Phillip Laney became increasingly agitated.

She caught Pete Lancaster's eye and he dipped his chin, indicating that they both should move toward the situation. In one smooth movement, as if they'd planned it, she moved toward Tabitha Malcor and he moved toward Phillip Laney. Neither protested as they were led out of the front pew. Anissa led the three Malcors through the choir entrance at the front of the church, and Pete hustled Phillip out the back.

Once they were safely behind the closed doors of the choir room, the three Malcors all began talking at once.

"What's going on?" Tabitha asked at the same time that Thaddeus blurted out, "What the hell was that?" A sheepish expression filled his face as he glanced around at his surroundings. "Sorry for the language," he said. He looked at Anissa. "But seriously, I don't know what that was about."

Daniel spoke up. "I think I do." Tabitha and Thaddeus looked back at him with matching confused expressions.

"If he didn't kill Davy himself, he had something to do with it," Daniel explained.

Thaddeus was already shaking his head before Daniel could finish his sentence. "Dad, he was with me that night. He—"

"He was with you the *whole* time?" Daniel asked.

Thaddeus's head drooped. "Well, no, not the whole time. But he was just a kid. Like me. Like Davy. Why would a kid harm another kid? *How* could a kid kill another kid?"

Daniel shrugged, his face impassive. "Maybe it was an accident. Maybe he was too afraid to tell what happened. Maybe he's carried that guilt since that night and that's what we saw today. He couldn't carry it anymore."

Anissa thought of her own guilt, also carried since that night. She thought of Gordon's tears in his kitchen. She looked at the three people she stood with and knew they, too, knew what it was to carry guilt about a night that refused to be in the past.

Tabitha spoke up. "He was there." She looked at Daniel and he nodded, then she looked at Thaddeus to explain. "He came to the search site the other day. He came over and talked to us. He said—"

She looked at Daniel again. "Danny, do you remember what he said?" Daniel shook his head. Tabitha hung hers. "I don't really either."

Anissa spoke up and they all turned in her direction as if they'd forgotten she was there.

"You're right," she said. "He was there. I saw him talking to you guys. I nearly went over to check on you, to make sure he wasn't hassling you. But you looked fine."

"We were fine," Tabitha said. "He didn't feel like a threat." She looked at the other three faces in the room with her. "I always thought if I encountered the person who hurt Davy, the hairs on the back of my neck would stand up, or . . . something. That I'd know somehow. He was in my house countless times after . . ." She shook her head. "It just doesn't make sense."

Remembering her position, Anissa spoke up. "I'm sure the sheriff will get to the bottom of it. I'm sure he's already headed to the station to question Phillip Laney, and I know he'll fill you in just as soon as he can." She rested her hand on Tabitha's shoulder.

"Answers are coming," she said, hoping she sounded reassuring, in charge, capable. That was all she ever wanted to be. "Now," she continued, "should we go back out and finish the service?" She was already walking to get the door for them before they could answer the question. She was grateful when they all came along.

After the service, she saw the Malcors back to their car and secured promises from them that they would go straight home and not discuss with anyone what had happened until they knew more. She watched until their car left the parking lot, then went back into the sanctuary to collect her things. The church was empty, but Davy's image remained on the screen. She looked away from him, scanning the panel of stained glass windows on the far wall instead, her gaze stopping at the Tree of Life.

There'd been a stint when her mother was dating a church deacon and Anissa had been dragged to Sunday school each week. She remembered bits and pieces from that short time—object lessons that still rattled around in her brain. Looking at the tree, she recalled that Adam and Eve were banished from the garden of Eden before they could eat from that tree. Because they had eaten from the Tree of Knowledge of Good and Evil, they were no longer perfect. If they'd eaten from the Tree of Life, too, they'd have lived forever in their imperfect state.

People often thought God punished Adam and Eve by sending them away from the garden, but in truth he was only making sure they'd still have a shot at redemption. Everyone, she thought, deserved that shot—even her, she decided. She thought of Thaddeus's defense of Phillip.

"He was just a kid," he'd said. As was she.

She looked back at Davy, there, on the large screen, looming over them all just as he always had.

"I'm sorry," she said to him. Then she added, "I'll always love you best of all."

She stood for her own moment of silence before turning away, a smile blooming on her face as she walked out of the church, her mind on where she was headed and the news she had to share.

When Gordon didn't answer his door, she remembered what he'd said about honoring Davy through his work. She wondered what piece of art he would make to honor Davy and hoped he would let her see it.

She went around the house toward where Gordon's studio was, stopping short when she saw Gordon standing in the yard beside a little boy, overseeing as the kid sprayed a hose. She recalled the kid who ran off that first morning she'd stopped by and wondered if it was the same kid. *They could almost be father and son*, she thought. She called Gordon's name, but he couldn't hear her over the sound of the water, so she walked closer.

The kid turned and saw her first, the water spraying in her direction as she sidestepped out of the way.

"Whoa there, partner," Gordon said to the kid. "Gotta keep your aim on the target." He looked at Anissa and she thought she saw the slightest blush creeping onto his cheeks as he greeted her. She could feel her own cheeks warming too. She went to stand beside Gordon and watched as the kid moved the hose back and forth over an assortment of what looked like a pile of scrap metal.

After a moment, she asked, "What are you guys doing?"

"Well, this is Stuart," Gordon said. "He's my next-door neighbor." Gordon looked at Stuart, who nodded. "And he's helping me with my rust garden."

"Rust garden?" she asked.

"I use a lot of metal in my sculptures," Gordon explained. "But I don't want it to look shiny and new. I like it to be aged, weathered, a little battered-looking. The imperfection adds texture, character, personality—whatever you want to call it—to a piece. But it can take a long time to get to that state, so I help the rusting process along by wetting the metal." He walked over to the spigot and turned off the water. "In its own way, rust makes things more beautiful."

Their eyes met. "I have news," she said.

Though she didn't know the full story, she knew suspicion had been cast in a new direction. For the first time eyes would be looking in that direction instead of Gordon's. And if things went the way she thought they would, she felt sure he'd be exonerated once and for all, possibly before the day was through.

"Hey, Stuart," Gordon said to the kid. "I need to talk to this nice lady about some grown-up stuff. You should probably head on home."

Stuart didn't try to hide his disappointment. "But I wanted to help you make the lady's curls."

Anissa's hand went to her own hair as she and Gordon exchanged a look.

"We can do that another time. Right now I've got a guest I need to talk to," Gordon said.

"Ok," Stuart said, though it was clear he didn't really think it was ok. The boy started to walk away, then stopped and looked back at them. Anissa could hear the water dripping off the metal items, making a chorus of plinking sounds. It was almost like music. "But I can come back, right? I can come back later?" Stuart asked, hopeful.

"Anytime," Gordon said. "You're welcome here anytime you want."

As the kid disappeared into the woods, Anissa felt Gordon's hand reach for hers. Neither looked at the other as they grasped hands. But they quickly let go when they heard the sound of a car pulling into Gordon's driveway.

CHAPTER 38

Thaddeus

They sat alone in the house, sequestered and silent, until the sheriff showed up. Pete Lancaster's knock was different this time—the urgency and the power he usually presented with were gone.

When his father went to answer the door, it opened to reveal a hatless sheriff, his bare head bent almost penitently. He looked up at Daniel, then past him at Thaddeus and Tabitha, who had come to stand behind him. Kristyn had taken the children back to their hotel to wait. They were going to let them swim in the indoor pool and pretend like everything was normal.

"May I come in?" Pete asked. In answer his father opened the door wider and they all made space for him to enter.

"Have a seat," his mother said, but Pete shook his head.

"What I have to say won't take long. There's more details to delve into, some facts I need to verify, but I feel like what I just heard is the God's honest truth." He looked directly at Thaddeus, making eye contact. "Your friend is in a lot of pain. A lifetime's worth."

Thaddeus nodded because he didn't know what else to do.

"So it was him?" Tabitha asked. There wasn't a trace of anger in her voice, just sadness.

Pete nodded. "Like I said, there's more to the story than I can get into right now, but yes, he does have guilty knowledge and some culpability in what happened." His gaze swept across the three of them. "But it's complicated. And it's not going to be easy to prosecute. Suffice it to say that the real bad guy in all of this is already dead."

Thaddeus thought of Phillip when he'd called him in St. Louis. He'd called, Thaddeus thought, because he'd known this was it. He thought of how Phillip had kept bringing up that night. Thaddeus had silenced him every time. He'd been, Thaddeus guessed, trying to confess, to finally—after all this time—unburden himself. But Thaddeus hadn't let him.

"His uncle had something to do with it, didn't he?" he asked.

The sheriff dipped his head just once. "I promise you folks will have the whole story just as soon as we put all the pieces together." He clapped his hands together and the loud sound startled them all.

"We're real close to closing this case." Pete looked out the front window at the beautiful day outside, at the reporters gathering again, hungry for news. "And this will all be over, once and for all. In the meantime I'm gonna go out there and run those vultures off. You folks deserve some peace."

In unison Thaddeus, his mother, and his father all nodded their agreement.

As soon as the last of the reporters were gone and the coast was clear, Thaddeus asked to borrow the car for the second time. He was thankful when his father simply dropped the keys in his hand and didn't ask why he needed to leave or where he was going. Thaddeus wasn't sure he could've explained it if he'd been asked to.

As he drove the familiar roads, he thought about that night, about what he'd thought it had been versus what it had turned out to be. He thought about Phillip as a kid and Phillip in the church that morning, his guilt and grief bursting out of him because it couldn't stay locked inside any longer.

He thought about how he'd searched for his brother, his own guilt and grief mounting with each step he took. At first he'd thought Davy was messing with him, hiding on purpose to get him back. A girl had been there and said she was with Davy until they got separated in the field. He'd thought she was in on it, helping Davy with his ruse. He hadn't yet grasped how desperate the situation was.

He eased the car onto the shoulder and shifted into Park, his breathing erratic, his heart rate elevated as he went back in time in his mind, allowing the images instead of pushing them away like usual. The little girl who was with Davy was the last one to see him. She kept insisting she saw a car pull into the drive that led to the farmhouse that night. Her sister had been the one to call the cops. Both she and her sister had wild curly hair.

But then the little girl had been swallowed up in the drama of the search, her name never shared because she was a minor. She'd been questioned, his family had been told, but her story wasn't of much use. She and the other kids had been deemed "unreliable witnesses."

He'd never really thought about her after that, assuming she'd grown up and gone on with her life. He'd never seen her again.

Until she walked into their house a few days ago to act as their Public Information Officer.

"Anissa," he whispered. She'd never said a word, not even when he'd been flat on his back in her foyer, trying to understand why she lived there, in the place where he'd gone to fulfill his long-ago promise.

He felt for the piece of fool's gold. Pyrite was its real name. He'd researched it at length, intending to include it in his memoir, until he realized that if he included the rock he'd carried since that night, he'd have to tell why Davy had tossed it at his feet and stormed away. He'd have to reveal just how bad of a brother he'd been. So he'd left it out entirely. He'd never been able to share what he'd learned about pyrite—just how close to gold it was, how it was used as a fire starter in ancient times, how the Thai people believed it to be a sacred stone, used to ward off evil.

Thaddeus couldn't help but think that, had Davy held on to the stone instead of tossing it away, the night wouldn't have unfolded the way it did and he, Thaddeus, would not be driving his father's car in his hometown on his way to forgive a man he'd hated for decades for no reason at all.

He looked both ways, put the car in Drive, and eased back onto the empty road.

When he arrived at Gordon's house and found Anissa there in the yard, Thaddeus didn't even question her presence. He just looked from her to him and back again. They all stood silently for a moment before he realized he should explain his visit. But how?

First, he looked to Anissa. He wanted to say, *"I know who you are, and I know you've been keeping secrets."* But what good would that do? Anissa lived in the exact spot where Davy disappeared. She'd devoted her life's work to helping victims. It made a sad kind of sense. That night had not just impacted her; it had shaped her, and she had used it for good. He'd always wanted whoever lived in that spot to appreciate what had happened there. And they did. She did.

"Is there news?" she asked, the naked hope shining on her face as she spoke. Beside her, Gordon stiffened as if bracing himself.

"You didn't do it," Thaddeus said to Gordon, thinking about his memoir as he spoke, of the things he'd written about this man. He hadn't named him, but he'd said enough that anyone could've surmised who he was referring to. He'd been wrong.

Maybe he should write another book, a better book, a book that told the whole truth this time—even the parts that made him look bad. He owed it to his readers. He owed it to Gordon Swift, and Anissa, and his family, and the girl next door. He owed it to himself.

"I know that now," he continued. "And I wanted to say I'm sorry. For all the terrible thoughts I've had about you. For how much I've ha—" He broke off as a knot of shame and regret clogged his throat. "I've hated you," he forced himself to continue. "When you did nothing wrong."

Gordon stood stock-still as he absorbed the words. He didn't even blink. Anissa watched him warily, a look of fear replacing the hopeful look she'd just worn.

Gordon seemed to be waiting for the "but" to come out of Thaddeus's mouth, for the other shoe to drop. Thaddeus had always thought of himself and his family as The Victims. But there had been so many that night.

He reached inside his pocket and held up the rock. Once shiny, it was now dull and worn with hardly a trace of the gold surface that had once caught a little boy's eyes.

"I wanted to give you this," Thaddeus said.

Gordon nodded and extended his hand to take the object Thaddeus was offering. Thaddeus took one last look at the piece of fool's gold—knowing what a fool he'd been about so many things—and put it in the other man's hand.

"I've carried this rock for a long time. I don't want to carry it anymore. So I tried to think of someone who might be willing to take it off my hands, someone who would understand how I feel, who could decide what to do with it from here." Thaddeus watched as Gordon turned the rock over in his hands, inspecting it.

"It used to be shiny," he added. "If you didn't know it, you'd have thought it was real gold."

Gordon turned the rock in his hands, examining it. "I bet I could use this in a sculpture. I've got one I just started working on." Gordon looked over at Anissa. "Today, in fact." Anissa smiled at him and Thaddeus wanted to—but didn't—ask what was going on between them.

"I could incorporate it in a way that, I think, you'd find meaningful." Gordon looked over at a dripping pile of scrap metal, then back at the rock he now held. "I like things that are worn," he said, but not really to Thaddeus. Not really to anyone at all.

Thaddeus got out of the car and stood for a moment, collecting himself. While he was gone, people had come over. Cars were parked along the street and in both his and Larkin's driveways. He'd had to park down the street and walk back to the house he'd grown up in.

As he got closer, he could hear noise coming from the direction of the backyard. He could smell a . . . grill? They were barbecuing? It sounded and smelled like a party. Not what he'd expected to come home to.

He stood there, puzzled, until someone called his name. He looked over at Larkin's house to see her coming toward him. He'd seen her arrive at the funeral, but they'd been escorted out so quickly afterward that he'd not gotten the chance to speak to her. Though he'd wanted to speak to her, he still didn't know what to say.

"Hi," he said when she got to him.

"Hi yourself," she said, her voice hesitant. He could tell she was holding herself back from him. He didn't blame her.

"I think I'm going to leave tomorrow," he said. As he said it, he knew it was true.

He saw a momentary flash of disappointment cross her face—there, then gone. "Then I guess I'll say goodbye," she said.

He exhaled, ran a hand through his hair. "Yeah, I guess so."

She shifted her weight from one foot to the other, then looked down at the ground before looking back up again. "But first, can I just say something?"

"Sure?" Though he'd meant it as a statement, his answer came out sounding like a question.

"I think—" she started, then stopped, waving her hand as if to wave the words away.

"What?" he asked, his heart beating faster.

"Not my place," she said.

"No, say it. I want you to," he urged.

She grimaced but continued. "I think you haven't let yourself have things like a home and a family because Davy never got them. I think it was your way of paying some sort of penance." She studied his face as if she was checking that it was safe to go on.

"I just hope that now—now that you know what happened—you can start allowing yourself those things. You're allowed to grow up and move on. And I hope you will." She pretended to punch him in the arm. "And stop saving people from you. I'm betting there's someone out there who doesn't want to be saved."

She hadn't wanted to be saved, and that was a mistake he could never take back. They looked at each other, the what-if hanging like a fog between them. But like a fog, it burned off quickly, replaced by a little voice calling out, "Mommy! I've been looking for you!"

Larkin turned and waved Audrey over to where they stood.

"We should let you get inside," Larkin said. "I know everyone wants to see you, to make sure you're ok."

"I will be, you know," he said. "Ok." His hand went to his pocket before he could remember the rock was gone.

"I have no doubt," Larkin said.

He wanted to reach out and pull her to him, to hold her for a moment before he let her go, once and for all. But he'd given that up when he was fifteen years old. In another universe, if Davy hadn't disappeared, they might have ended up together. But they didn't live in that universe. They lived in this one.

The three of them walked toward the Malcor house. The sky was blue and the birds were singing and the smell of good food wafted on the breeze. It was spring, and everything felt new.

As they got close, the front door opened and Nicole stepped out. Thaddeus remembered Larkin stepping out of that same door just before he and Davy left that night, Kristy beside her, asking to look for fireflies, not believing they were gone for good.

Nicole saw the trio and stopped short, her eyes straying to Larkin and Audrey. He introduced them.

"Larkin, Audrey, this is Nicole. She's my publicist, here to help with the publicity around the case." He looked over at Nicole and added, "And for emotional support." Nicole bit back a smile. As soon as they were alone, he'd tell her he was going to book a flight for tomorrow. He'd ask her to accompany him. And then they'd see what happened.

"And this"—he turned to Larkin—"is Larkin." He gestured toward her house. "She lives next door."

"Oh, so you're the girl next door?" Nicole asked, a teasing tone to her voice.

"Yes," Larkin said. She and Thaddeus exchanged a look, an acknowledgment, a goodbye in a glance. "That's me."

At first when he hears the knocking, Gordon assumes it's the widow at his door, there to ask him to help her with something. The old bird is an early bird, accustomed to farming life, in the habit of going to bed when it gets dark and rising as soon as the sun peeks above the horizon. It is not uncommon for her to show up at what to him is an ungodly hour, dressed and alert, surprised he isn't also. If she's feeling chatty, she will extol the virtues of being early to bed, early to rise. But her sermons fall on deaf ears. Gordon is still a young man, still prone to all-nighters like in college. He's not quite ready for full-blown adulthood. He has decided to ease into it.

As Gordon nears the door, he can see that the figure looming in the window isn't the diminutive widow. It is the shape of a big, broad man. Gordon looks down at his watch as if to verify that it is indeed too early for any usual call. He thinks of the helicopter he'd heard flying overhead during the night and wonders if there was some emergency he slept through. He peeks through the muslin curtains and is met with a pair of hooded eyes squinting back at him in the bright morning sun.

"Mr. Swift?" the mouth below the eyes asks. "Might I speak to you a minute?"

The sight of an officer at his door so early in the morning is unsettling. Though he has done nothing wrong, the police

presence makes him feel as though he has. Still, he nods and
tugs the door open.

"Yes?" he asks.

The officer points at the widow's house. "Sorry to disturb
you so early, sir," he says. "But I was just chatting with the nice
lady who lives over there, and she said you might be able to
help me."

Gordon nods in a way he hopes makes him look like a
good guy. Because he is a good guy. Other than some minor
traffic violations, he's never intentionally broken a law.

"Whatever I can do to help," he says and means it.

The officer makes a pained expression. "We're looking
for a kid, actually," he says through his teeth. "A little boy.
Seems there was a group of them here last night, getting up
to some mischief, I guess. Did you happen to see any of 'em,
maybe?"

The kid, Gordon thinks. The kid who showed up at his door
alone. The kid who was afraid. The kid, Gordon remembers
with a creeping sense of shame, he sent away. But no one
knows about that but him, and the kid. Gordon does not need
to wonder if he's the kid who is missing. The awareness of
this fact is just there all of a sudden, sitting in his gut like the
paving stones that lead to his door, flat and oblong and heavy.
Still, he decides it's best to keep quiet about the kid being
there, lest he rouse suspicion.

"Um, yeah," he says. "I heard them running around. I guess
they were playing games or something." He gestures toward
the upper fields, near the main road, far away from where he
and the officer stand now.

He should've called the cops himself last night, put a stop
to all the shenanigans from the get-go. Then they would've

come and run those kids off, and the kid never would've come near this house, never would have gone missing, maybe.

"Didn't see any of them down here near your place then?" the cop asks, and his nostrils flare as if he's sniffing out a lie.

"No," Gordon says. He gestures vaguely at the room behind him and the officer stands on his tiptoes to see over Gordon's shoulder into the place he calls home. For a second he thinks of inviting his guest in, proving he has nothing to hide. But the pile of discarded hands he drew last night is still there on the floor. The hand drawings are a bit macabre. They could be misconstrued. He will clean that up as soon as the cop leaves. If for some reason they decide to come back to search, the hands will be gone.

"I had the ballgame on the television," Gordon says. "So I didn't really hear anything once I turned that on."

The cop nods, taking him at his word. And why shouldn't he? Gordon is telling the truth. Or mostly telling the truth. The cop pulls out a card with his name and the station's phone number on it. He places it in Gordon's hand as he says, "Well, if you think of anything, just let us know. We'll be looking." The cop gives a long sigh. "As long as it takes to find him, I guess."

"I'm sure you will," Gordon rushes to say. "Find him, I mean."

"Yeah, the little tyke probably got himself lost and fell asleep in the woods. He'll wake up and make his way home soon enough, I imagine." He rolls his eyes. "We had a helicopter fly around, did our best to search in the dark, but it wasn't easy. His mama and daddy are all spun up about it, as you can imagine."

Gordon nods even though he is not a father, so he can't imagine. Gordon is not sure he ever wants to be a father. His mother says he'll change his mind as soon as he meets the right girl.

"Well, I better keep canvassing. Lots of ground to cover," the officer says. He bends the brim of his hat, a departing gesture. "You have a nice day."

Gordon wishes him the same, then watches him amble over to his patrol car, not appearing to be in any real hurry. Gordon watches as the car backs up in an arc, then proceeds forward, kicking up dust and rocks as it accelerates down the drive. He watches until the police car disappears from sight, the nagging weight at the center of his body the only indication that his life has just changed forever.

CHAPTER 39

Tabitha

No one had planned for a reception at their house after the service. But with everything that had happened, there'd been an unspoken, collective compulsion to gather. It seemed no one wanted to be alone after the scene with Phillip at the church. After the sheriff shooed the reporters away, she'd called Marie and asked her to come over, then Daniel had called a few people. The word had spread.

People from the community had showed up. They brought food, and Tabitha and Daniel pulled out the food that was already there. Others fired up the grill and threw on various cuts of meat they brought from their refrigerators. They dragged in coolers filled with every drink imaginable from punch to Pepsi, wine to whiskey. In the midst of their grief, they sought shelter in each other.

Someone put a glass of red wine in Tabitha's hand and she took it gratefully, downing a big gulp just as one of her grandchildren whizzed past her. She sidestepped and saved the wine. Whoever she was talking to—the faces had become a blur by that point—praised her agility and foresight. She was taking a silly little bow, the wine making her lightheaded and punchy, when another child came barreling through the den.

This time she wasn't so agile. Her grandson made impact and the wine splashed all over the green dress she'd worn to the service. Davy had loved green; she had worn it for him. She stood there, a dark stain on the front of her dress, red wine seeping uncomfortably into her bra as everyone stared, silent.

She wanted to make a joke, to say something witty and care-free. She did not want them feeling sorrier for her than they already did. But she could feel the tears pricking, so she set down the now empty wineglass and fled upstairs to her room.

Behind her closed bedroom door, she stripped out of the stained, stinking dress, stomping on it for good measure as it puddled to the floor. Then she kicked it too. She took off her bra, then slipped into the nightgown she had shed that morn-ing, still hung over the footboard of her bed. She longed to climb back into that bed and pull the covers over her head.

Instead she went into the bathroom to run her bra under cold water. And that was how Daniel found her, clad in a night-gown, rinsing red wine from a bra, her tears mingling with the cast-off water in the basin. He came up behind her and shut off the tap, pulled the bra from her hands as he turned her toward him, which made her cry harder.

"I miss him," she wailed into his chest.

"Yes," Daniel said. "So do I." Then, quieter, he added, "I miss you too."

For a moment neither of them said anything. They just held on to each other.

Finally, she said, "I think I'd like to go."

"Go?" Daniel asked.

"Away from here. Somewhere else. Now that he's been found, I think it's safe to leave."

Daniel smiled into her hair. "What did you have in mind?"

"Kristyn's been saying she'd love for me to come to California."

She could feel Daniel's heart beating. "I could go with you." It was a loaded statement with so many implications. But today was not the day to examine them. "We'd be near our grand-kids," he added.

She laughed in spite of herself. "You mean the ones that knocked my glass of wine on me?"

"The very same," Daniel said.

There was a knock on their door, and they stepped away from each other as if caught.

"You guys ok?" Thaddeus asked. He was back from whatever mystery errand he'd gone on.

"Yes," Tabitha and Daniel said in unison, and how familiar this felt, how ordinary. Them together in this bedroom while one of their children stood on the other side of the door.

"We'll be out in a minute," Daniel said. They listened as Thaddeus's footsteps faded away.

"I guess we better get back out there. Face the hordes," Tabitha said.

Daniel pointed to the bathroom. "You go change and I'll wait for you. Then we'll go back out together."

Silently, resolutely, she changed her clothes and they left the room to find that the party had moved outside. Their grand-daughter was singing a song and a small crowd had gathered to watch her. The child had motions that went along with the song, hamming it up as Kristyn held a camera to record it all. Around them, children shrieked and ran, and people ate and drank, and voices chatted and laughed. It almost felt like a party.

Tabitha and Daniel stood side by side as the melee swirled around them. She took a step closer to him, needing the near-ness of the one person who'd experienced it all. She and Daniel were lovers and strangers, whole and broken, weak and strong, jaded and optimistic. The trick, she was beginning to understand, was to let the jumble of emotions exist inside her without working to understand or validate them. She didn't have to sort out her feelings. Not yet, and maybe not ever. She could just let them be. There, in her heart, all together.

All at the very same time.

AUTHOR'S NOTE

When I was a preteen, I watched two movies that, unbeknownst to me at the time, made a huge impact on my life: *Without a Trace*, starring Judd Hirsch and Kate Nelligan, and *Adam* (about the disappearance of Adam Walsh), starring JoBeth Williams and Daniel J. Travanti. I think the concept of these films—of a parent separated from a child and the *not knowing*—must've really stuck with me because, well, I wrote this novel all these years later.

Two things stand out to me from those movies that I think you see reflected here, in these pages: First, the storyline in *Without a Trace* follows a young man who worked for Kate Nelligan and is accused of having something to do with her son's disappearance, and it ruins his life, at least for a time. And second, in *Adam*, the scenes where JoBeth Williams repeats, "He must be so afraid," and when Daniel J. Travanti tears a hotel bed apart upon learning of his son's death. I did not have to rewatch or look up either of those movies to confirm these things. They have stayed with me through the years and were, I guess, formative.

Joan Didion wrote, "I write entirely to find out what I'm thinking, what I'm looking at, what I see and what it means. What I want and what I fear." I suppose that's what this book was for me—an exercise in all of that. To the families who have lost a child in a similar way, I sincerely hope I represented you well. And my deepest apologies if I didn't.

ACKNOWLEDGMENTS

All books are hard in their own way, but this one was the hardest thus far. This one took me to lengths I didn't think I'd ever go to for one story. Many times I almost gave up. Along the way, there were people who kept me from doing so. This is the place I get to thank them all. (Get ready for some clichés and repetition because it's hard to find new and inventive ways to say "thank you" and "I love you!")

First and foremost, Kimberly Brock, a stellar writer and an even better friend, without whom you wouldn't be reading this book. Kim, your bold moves on a summer afternoon changed everything, and I will always be grateful.

Along those lines, Amanda Bostic and the team at Harper Muse, thank you for saying yes to this story, for understanding what I intended within these pages. Special thanks to my editor, Laura Wheeler, for loving this story and gently nudging it to where it needed to be. And to Jodi Hughes, who knows how to strike the perfect balance between asking for changes and handing out compliments. And thank you to the entire team at Harper Muse, especially Savannah Breedlove, Becky Monds, Caitlin Halstead, Nekasha Pratt, Kerri Potts, Margaret Kercher, Jere Warren, Patrick Aprea, Natalie Underwood, Colleen Lacey, and Taylor Ward.

A huge thanks to my agent, Ariele Fredman, who said yes to representing me as I stood at an empty gate in the Detroit airport trying, and failing, to appear professional and composed. Thank you for championing this story.

To Blake Leyers—you were the first person to believe in this book and the first person ever (that I know of) to get a tattoo inspired by something I wrote. Thank you for helping me find *le mot juste*.

To Jodi Warshaw—it was such a delight to get to work with you on this book as I'd worked with you on my others. You knew my writing, and you believed in me, which made you the perfect person to spur me on. I'm so glad you were a part of this book.

To John and Jennifer Tuckwiller—I didn't know you all that well when you provided a reason for Larkin to be next door. I'll never forget going on a long walk in the midst of a pandemic as you filled me in on what it was like to face John's deployment with small children in the exact same time period I was setting this book. It was just the impetus I needed to keep going forward with this idea. Thanks to both of you for your sacrifice then and for your friendship now—you guys are more than friends; you've become family!

To my cousin Nancy, thank you for letting me borrow your name, my own small tribute to your dad, Major General Dennis Malcor.

To Emily Allison, thank you for giving me access to your studio and for answering my questions about your amazing sculptures. You gave such good insight into the artist's life, taught me what a rust garden is, and the putty knife made for a great plot point!

To my friends who faithfully ask about the book and my writing, and who provide lots of laughter and joy in my life: Lisa and Mike Shea, Micah and Maria Swett, Rick and Rachel Olsen, Laurel Sauls, Kelman Dow, April Duncan, Kimberly

Young, Karen Baker, and the SBGG—Pam Johnson, Kelly Andrews, and Kelly Clemmons. I don't know what I'd do without you all!

To Mac and Jenna and the staff at Grapevine—you two have been consistent encouragers and friends throughout this process, even when you didn't know you were doing so. Thank you for providing an oasis on my desert days.

To the ladies in my Bible study on Mondays—you never stopped praying for this book, and I am so grateful.

To my local indie booksellers, Dawn Miller and Candace Blackwell of Pelican Books—you guys were enthusiastic and steadfast cheerleaders during this process and always inspired me to keep on keeping on. And to all the booksellers out there, thank you for inspiring readers and writers alike by what you faithfully show up and do every day.

To Suzanne Cisneros and Jeff Dugas for making Dread River Writers a thing—you two welcomed us and made us feel so at home we never wanted to leave! Thank you for supporting the arts by hosting a gaggle of chatty writers in your beautiful space.

To my writer friends who listened to me whine and complain for, lo, so many years, and then cheered for me when it all worked out (as, like I tell my kids, it always does): Liz Fenton, Catherine McKenzie, Emily Carpenter, Laura Benedict, J. T. Ellison, Mary Kay Andrews, Patti Callahan Henry, Meg Walker, T. I. Lowe, Kim Wright, Joy Callaway, Erika Marks, Joy Jordan Lake, Anne Bogel, Claire Gibson, Tori Whitaker, Traci Keel, Lauren Denton, Lanier Isom, Gin Phillips, Lindsey Brackett, and Abby Belbeck.

Lisa Patton, you walked with me every step of the way, and I don't know what I would've done without you in more ways than one. While some of this process I would trade in a skinny minute, I wouldn't trade the chance for our friendship to grow stronger as we went through this together. Thank you for being there, my friend.

Ariel Lawhon, you've been there for this particular book, and you've been there for the ones before it. Two things stand out to me this time: First, you gave me editing advice that Thaddeus should have something that only the reader sees that shows his vulnerability, his humanity. I was like, "Yeah, thanks for this ambiguous advice. Real helpful." That night I dreamed Davy threw a rock, and there was my answer. And second, at a time when I was going to quit, you said something to the effect of "You can't give up on Davy," which was a low blow, but supereffective. So, as always, thank you. I love you muchly.

To my mom, Sandy Brown—thank you for being my mom and my cheerleader. You faithfully listened to me week after week as I struggled with this book, and your belief in me is unwavering. Your laugh, your smile, your voice, and your spirit keep me going. I love you, Mom.

My husband, Curt Whalen: you have both my undying gratitude and my never-ending apologies for all you sacrificed and endured during the writing of this book. You sat with me while I cried; you took me out when I wanted to hide under the covers; you did whatever it took to keep me going. I often doubted, but I don't think you ever did. I am so grateful to do this life with you. Always, MB.

Our kids: Jack, Ashleigh, Matt, Bekah, Brad, and Annaliese, above anything I ever write or anything I ever achieve, being your mom will always be the best thing I've ever done. There is never a time when we are all together that I don't marvel at the true miracles each of you are. I love you guys!

And finally, "Lord my God, you have done many things—your wondrous works and your plans for us; none can compare with you. If I were to report and speak of them, they are more than can be told" (Psalm 40:5 csb).

1. When the story opens, Thaddeus is on a tour for his bestselling memoir about Davy's disappearance. He says that the theme of his memoir is that he has moved past the tragedy. In what ways does Thaddeus show that he actually hasn't moved on?

2. When we first meet Tabitha, she's writing her weekly regret list, which she started after Davy disappeared. Do you have a daily, weekly, or monthly ritual that has lasted years? When did you start it and why, and how did you maintain the habit? Is there a ritual that you want to start but haven't yet?

3. Gordon lived in a cabin on the property where Davy vanished, and most members of the community think he's responsible for Davy's disappearance. Still, he decided to stay in Wynotte to help his parents, despite facing constant suspicion and gossip. Would you have stayed in Wynotte, or would you have left? Why?

4. Anissa is the Public Information Officer for the Wynotte Police Department and tasked with guiding the Malcors through the latest break in Davy's case, but very few people know that she was the last person to see Davy alive. Would you have kept the same secret? Why or why not?

5. Thaddeus and Larkin were growing closer when Davy vanished. What do you think would have happened

to their relationship if Thaddeus hadn't pushed Larkin away?

6. We see flashbacks of Tabitha and Daniel getting ready for and attending a party the night that Davy disappears. Can you relate to Tabitha wanting a break from being just Mom for a night, despite the events that unfolded while she was out?

7. The morning after Davy vanished, Gordon lies to a police officer about Davy coming to his house, even though he did give Davy a putty knife. Why do you think Gordon chose to lie? How do you think Gordon's life would have been different if he had told the truth?

8. Before Davy's funeral, Anissa pays a visit to Gordon. Why do you think she confessed to him about her presence the night Davy disappeared? Would you have done the same thing?

9. Thaddeus and Davy's younger sister, Kristy, is only four years old when Davy vanishes. How do you think Davy's disappearance has affected her even though her memories of him aren't as strong?

10. We find out who was involved in Davy's disappearance near the end of the book. Did you correctly suspect who played a role? If so, what were some clues that led to your suspicion?

ABOUT THE AUTHOR

Kristee Mays Photography

MARYBETH MAYHEW WHALEN is the author of *Every Moment Since* and nine previous novels. Marybeth received a BA degree in English with a concentration in Writing and Editing from North Carolina State University a long time ago and has been writing ever since. She is the cofounder of The Book Tide, an online community of readers where "a rising tide raises all books." Marybeth and her husband, Curt, are the parents of six children, with only one left at home. A native of Charlotte, North Carolina, Marybeth now calls Sunset Beach, North Carolina home.

Visit her online at: https://linktr.ee/Marybethwhalen

LOOKING FOR MORE GREAT READS? LOOK NO FURTHER!

HARPER MUSE

*Illuminating minds
and captivating hearts
through story.*

Visit us online to learn more:
harpermuse.com

Or scan the below code and sign up to receive
email updates on new releases, giveaways,
book deals, and more:

@harpermusebooks

From the Publisher

GREAT BOOKS

ARE EVEN BETTER WHEN THEY'RE SHARED!

Help other readers find this one:

- Post a review at your favorite online bookseller

- Post a picture on a social media account and share why you enjoyed it

- Send a note to a friend who would also love it—or better yet, give them a copy

Thanks for reading!